Together they baited the elegant officers of the British Hudson's Bay Company, sharing a common vision of American statehood.

It was not strange that they should want the same woman, Kitty Gatewood, who left the luxury of a South Carolina manor in search of her girlhood sweetheart.

This was the great adventure and, typically, Kitty met it with trunks full of finery. Before the startled eyes of Oregon men—too long without women—she put her neat little figure on a common grain scale and bought additional passage to Puget Sound—at thirty cents a pound.

Despite herself Kitty thrilled to the raw strength of The River and The Mountain . . . to the arrogant passion of Curt Fletcher. But it was the gentle mountain man, Sunset Lee, who gave her comfort over the terrors of the trail, and at the desperate journey's end.

You will thrill to the drama of their lives —a new testament to the faith and hope that led men and women to seek fulfillment at the end of the Oregon Trail.

"We will
To each

BY
MILDRED MASTERSON McNEILLY

EACH BRIGHT RIVER

A NOVEL
OF THE OREGON COUNTRY

NEW YORK
WILLIAM MORROW AND COMPANY
1950

DEDICATION

To three generations of Masterson men who helped to open and to build, or are building, the West—

JAMES MASTERSON—1833–1913
Of the Oregon Country, Oregon Territory, Washington Territory and Washington State

HARRY C. MASTERSON—1868–
Of Dakota, Wyoming and Washington Territories and Washington State

B. L. MASTERSON—1896–
Of Washington State

★

Foreword

IT would take more than one volume to recount the deeds, or even to mention the names, of all those who played a part in the struggle for the Oregon Country. The names of only a few appear here: Dr. McLoughlin and Peter Ogden; the British officers; Joseph Lane and Isaac Stevens; Sheriff Joe Meek; Peter Burnett, James Marshall, Michael Simmons, George Bush, Captain Irving, Smith and Sylvester, the Denny Party and Dexter Horton. They, like the Indians, Delaware Tom, Yellow Serpent, Five Crows, Tomahas and Tiloukaikt, appear in this story in the roles which they actually played, and which, in each case is a matter of historical record. Each of these true characters bears his own name.

The fictional characters, Kitty and Jessie Pearl, Fletcher and Sunset, Philip Davis, Lisa and Bull Le Seuer, Charlefour and Polly Careless, Dr. Manning, Read and Evans, Captains Craig and Kemp, Mr. Sims, the Sparks, the Hansens, the Trainors, the Mc-Nairs, the Lintons and Deaf Wilson, John Homet, Dundee and Correll, Foster and Williams, and the Indian Dick Tom, are all purely imaginary and are in no instance drawn from life. If any of them bears a resemblance to any actual person it is by coincidence alone; or perhaps because the courageous, dream-driven Westerners had some traits in common; because they were, as the British put it, a "special breed."

MILDRED MASTERSON McNEILLY

ACKNOWLEDGMENTS

For their aid in securing material for the historical background of EACH BRIGHT RIVER, I am particularly indebted to:

HELEN LOVETT, of the McLoughlin House, Oregon City

MRS. GERTRUDE BRUMBAUGH, Oregon City Public Library

WALTER W. R. MAY, Editor and Publisher, Oregon City *Enterprise*

DUNCAN EMRICH, Chief, Folklore Section, the Library of Congress

CHAPIN D. FOSTER, Secretary-Director, Washington State Historical Society

ELISE WOLFE, Oregon Historical Society

ALTA F. WEST, Librarian, Washington State Historical Society Library

HARRY C. MASTERSON, Kittitas County, Washington

The late DR. WILLIAM McCLURE, Yakima, Washington

WILLIAM D. WELSH, Crown Zellerbach Corporation, San Francisco, for permission to use material contained in his booklet "A Brief History of Oregon City and West Linn."

PRISCILLA KNUTH, Research Associate, Oregon Historical Society

EACH
BRIGHT
RIVER

1

KITTY GATEWOOD WAS CROWDED most uncomfortably in the bow of the boat between a trunk and two traveling cases, and the round rear of Dr. Thomas Manning was wedged almost against her knees. The light rain and an occasional shower of spray from the wind-swept river drenched her from her elegant and very becoming bonnet to the pointed toes of her small kid slippers. But the shivers that occasionally ran through her slim young body were not from the cold. She set her teeth against them, reluctantly recognizing them as a first sign of panic.

The boat was the yawl from the American bark *Sea Bird*, Captain Nathaniel Craig from New York, now at anchor in the Columbia River outside the Willamette bar. Two hours ago Craig had put Kitty into the small boat and had solicitously tucked an oilcloth about her shoulders. Actually the covering had only deflected the water from her upper to her lower extremities, for the hem of her fine dress was sodden and her ankles were numb.

For an instant Kitty wished fervently she was back aboard the *Sea Bird* in the snug cabin in which she had spent the last six months; and then, sternly, she reminded herself that she must expect these minor and temporary discomforts. After all, it was not every girl in 1845 who dared to leave a country seat in South Carolina to round the Horn, traveling alone—except for Jessie Pearl, of course—all the way to the Oregon Country to be married.

But it was odd that she should be so nervous now that the dangers of that incredibly long ocean voyage were over. If she could find the cause, she reasoned sensibly, perhaps she could stop this uncomfortable inward quaking. For six months she had been looking forward to this day and now that it was here she was almost terrified. Certainly it was not fear of seeing Philip again, nor fear of marriage, for all her life she had planned one day to become the wife of Philip Davis; and she was too enlightened to believe in premonitions. She reminded herself that a Gatewood was always poised. Gatewood women were feminine, charming, appreciative of the gallant help of gentlemen, which was their rightful due. But they were not helpless flutter-wheels, and if ever they were for a brief moment uncertain they allowed no one to know it. Kitty swallowed to release the tightness in her throat.

Finally, probing deeply, she remembered just when she had first felt this uneasiness, this foretaste of fright. Four mornings ago she had been resting on the deck of the *Sea Bird* when the ship had abruptly changed its course from north to east and she became conscious of a dull, distant roar. Captain Craig had paused beside her and had spoken with unaccustomed excitement.

"We're here, ma'am! It's The River—the Columbia, the Great River Of The West. We're opposite the mouth and we'll go in now, slowly. If tide and wind and luck are with us we'll be over the bar by nightfall. It'll be pull Dick, pull Devil! We'll be in Oregon then, Miss—or we'll be in hell!"

Kitty had strained her eyes to see, but there was nothing, nothing but the ocean. The Captain's steel-gray eyes were shining. Kitty's head came only to the Captain's shoulder and she had looked up at him, wonderingly.

"We're still nine miles off shore, Miss Gatewood, but if you lowered a bucket now you'd bring up fresh water."

Kitty had stood entranced, listening, trying to grasp the fact that the Columbia, which rolled through the heart of fabulous Oregon, had such great strength that its roar and its fresh waters could invade the sea this far. That was when she had first felt the prick of apprehension. The look on the Captain's face, that of a man who loved to pit his strength and seamanship in fierce battle, and who was happily anticipating such a contest now, increased her disquiet. Craig spoke of the Columbia, the Great River, as though it were alive, possessing a personality all of its own; an old antagonist whom he was anxious to meet again. There was a fight ahead. Kitty waited, determined to watch, yet afraid.

Dr. Manning, the medical missionary, had advised her to go below and Jessie Pearl had begged her hysterically, but Kitty had ignored them. The swells had increased; the ship rolled, pitched, shivered, decks awash, and still Kitty stood, clinging to a mast amidships, while the vessel plunged, complained, rose, poised, plunged again. At last she saw land on either side of the foaming field that was the river mouth, and her heart pounded to the droning of the leadsman who, lashed to his post, disappeared now and again in the foam and spray, then reappeared to sing out, even, powerful, clear, "Thirteen—nine—six—four—two" as the *Sea Bird*, guided by his soundings, inched her way across that grave-yard of ships known as the Columbia River bar.

She had heard Craig's shout of triumph as at last they reached good water. There were few shipmasters who could time their arrival at the river mouth with the tides and on the first try plunge boldly into those smashing seas and safely enter that treacherous pass between Cape Disappointment on the north and the long, low ridge of Point Adams on the south. At dusk they had come to anchor in a sheltered cove near to shore. The River's flow was interrupted here by a myriad of islands and both islands and main-land were forested thickly to the water's edge, so dense that in the twilight the trees were all one green-black mass. Kitty had gone to her bed, chilled, exultant and utterly exhausted. The rich, wel-come, half-forgotten smell of green things and rich, oozing earth filtered into her cabin. The ship had rocked gently, creaking against its anchor chains, lulling her into deep sleep.

But in the night she had awakened, her heart pounding pain-fully. The ship, which she had thought at last so safe, so sheltered, was being rocked as it had sometimes been in violent seas; and yet there was no storm, no wailing wind. Kitty had gripped her blankets pulling her fine sheets with the ornate Gatewood mono-gram up tight under her chin. She could feel the deep tug and pull upon the straining, complaining ship, and, fully awake, she had realized what it was. The tide was going out of The River like a millrace; added to the tremendous current of The River itself, the immense, sucking force carried all before it. For a long while Kitty had sat shivering, feeling with every nerve the elemen-tal sweep of the waters. She knew that the *Sea Bird* was protected by the encircling, forested shore, avoiding the full force of that mighty current. But still she could feel it, pulsing like a giant heart, four, five, nine miles wide, angrily driving the salt water back ten miles to sea.

That was it. . . . From the moment the ship had left its natural element, the dark blue sea, and beat her way deep into Oregon in the fresh, pale green water of The River—even in a land of a thousand rivers the mighty Columbia, The River of Many Names, was still The River—this overpowering excitement and feel of danger and fascination had possessed her.

◈ 2 ◈

THE twice-daily help of the ocean tides in their eternal war with The River had helped the *Sea Bird* fight her way the ninety miles against the current, past numerous wooded or rocky islands, through channels now narrow, now comfortably wide, to the mouth of the tributary, the Willamette. It had taken the ship four days to make that distance into Oregon, and Kitty spent every waking moment on deck.

"That's Pillar Rock," Dr. Manning had said of a great stone spire, a quarter-mile from shore, towering forty feet above The River. "The Indians believe that once a chief tried to imitate a god and wade across The River and for his presumption was turned into a rock. . . . There's the mouth of the Cowlitz River, Miss Gatewood. It flows from the north and is glacier-fed. On the north shore is Mt. Coffin, an Indian sepulcher. . . . Look eastward. On a clear day you can see five peaks of the Cascade Range —from far north clear to California. They guard The River."

Finally, off the Willamette bar, near sprawling Wapatoo Island, the triumphant, ocean-battered *Sea Bird* had folded her sails like giant wings, and Kitty's six months' journey by bark was over. The remaining thirteen miles to Oregon City, southward, up the Willamette, would be made by small boat.

Craig had launched the ship's yawl to enter the Willamette at today's sunrise. Kitty had stood at the rail in the first faint morning light, her face turned eagerly toward the east and the great, looming, jagged silhouettes of the Cascade mountains, much higher, much more magnificent than she had ever imagined, which slashed the horizon from north to south. She had become used to the limitless sea; but she had been unprepared, as was every newcomer to Oregon, to see land as rugged and as vast, the great snow peaks and lesser peaks, stretching on into infinity.

Rosy light had preceded the sun over the mountain range and Kitty had watched breathlessly as the great red-gold globe itself had appeared and all the world had jumped into quick, glowing, colorful life. Towering peaks become proud and massive jeweled coronets, with shades of ruby and saffron and dazzling white above the green and blue and purple shadows of the forested lower slopes; The River itself had been stained a shivering blood-red and birds had appeared, dipping and skimming about the ship. Every leaf of every shrub on The River's banks was edged by dew with shining silver, and the overpowering, unexpected splendor of it left Kitty breathless and awed.

There had been that one brief glimpse, a swift unveiling of the majesty of the mountains, a short demonstration of the power of Nature to paint at will colors of unearthly beauty on The River and the land it drained, and then gray muddy dumplings of clouds had moved in front of the sun. After a while, in leisurely fashion, not like the swift sudden downpours of her South Carolina, the rain had begun. It came softly and steadily, intensifying the smell of green and growing things, setting the birds to scolding in clear, shrill ripples of notes. Never had Kitty breathed air as stinging fresh, laden with the smell of black loam and dripping evergreens and the tingling, spicy odors of ferns and herbs buried deep in the forest, reached only by the tiny, infinite fingers of the rain.

Now Kitty gripped her gloved hands tightly beneath the oil-cloth. The hands were small, the fingers slightly pointed, the palms square, pampered hands, trained to grace. The gloves were damp. She would discard them in Oregon City. She had never worn a pair of soiled or worn gloves in all her life. She forced herself to relax. Her neck ached and she knew that strain brought unbecoming lines even to an eighteen-year-old face. The first impact of this amazing country was indeed a shock, but one could adjust oneself to it by careful attention to familiar routine, she told herself firmly.

After all, she had nothing to worry about. Very soon they would be in Oregon City. She would first see to the care of her belongings, she planned, practically. She had five trunks and in-numerable smaller pieces, though she had brought only the barest necessities for her voyage and her short stay in Oregon. Captain Craig had sent them all with her on the small boat's first trip, though it had meant leaving the belongings of other passengers piled on the wet deck of the *Sea Bird*. She had thanked him with a dimple and a demure flutter of her long, golden, dark-tipped eyelashes, and it was then that he had brusquely wrapped the oilcloth about her. . . . Yes, all of her possessions were here, including Jessie Pearl. Jessie's bacon-colored face was blank and she sat awkwardly and miserably in the stern of the boat, all angles, all knees and shins.

Kitty studied the Negro girl. She had known Jessie all her life, for both had been born at Wildcliffe. But this morning Jessie seemed strange and alien. *Nonsense*, Kitty whispered to herself. *She's pouting 'cause I scolded when she couldn't find my storm boots or because I made her stop giggling with that colored seaman. I'm just imagining all sorts of things. It's the strangeness— and knowing that soon I'll see Philip again.*

The Willamette was a quiet, businesslike river, with many gentle curves, a welcome contrast to the turbulent Columbia. The six oars of the small boat moved with clock-like regularity and the faces of the oarsmen seemed never to alter expression. They talked only briefly, out of the sides of their mouths. Kitty's glance rested on each one in turn. Dr. Manning had told her that many sailors deserted their ships in the Oregon Country. That was why the *Sea Bird* had taken a dozen Hawaiian sailors aboard when they touched at the Sandwich Islands. It was the Oregon Fever, the lure of the land, Dr. Manning had said, and Kitty wondered if these oarsmen had been selected because they were forever faithfully wed to the sea. The seaman, Lige Read, looked at her sharply, and Kitty smiled automatically. His oar faltered noticeably and an answering, very bold grin spread over his beefy face and then his powerful arms resumed their motion again, but he did not take his eyes from Kitty. To her annoyance Kitty could feel her face flushing. She looked away, irritated at the man's impudence. She was quite used to being stared at, but there was a look in the man's hard eyes which she did not like. The other sailors had caught the momentary hesitation of Read's oar and they looked at him inquiringly and followed his glance to Kitty. They ducked their heads then, grinning.

Never mind, she told herself, *it won't be much longer. Once I have found Philip everything will be all right.* For encouragement she clutched her reticule and felt the rustling paper within it,

Philip's letters, the last written from Oregon City a year ago. How amazed he would be to see her, how wildly delighted! She would lift the magnificent Gatewood wedding gown from the trunk which now crowded her, and they would be married in a picturesque little church. They would return to Wildcliffe, perhaps aboard the familiar *Sea Bird*. What a great adventure it would be to discuss when they were safely home! No other girl in South Carolina could match it, Kitty thought smugly. She twisted Philip's ring on her finger beneath her glove. Back at Wildcliffe, the voyage, the hazardous entry into The River, the Indians and their ghostly legends, the sunrise over the Cascades, the trip up the Willamette in the rain—all this would seem like a distant dream.

That was why she need not be afraid. She need not be terrified at the immensity of this wild and beautiful country. She was here only to visit it and regard it politely, not to grapple with it. She must remember that and keep herself detached from it, not frightened by it, not fascinated by it. How odd that seamen should leave their ships in The River and disappear into the awful isolation of Oregon! Oregon did not even have a flag. Oregon was occupied jointly by Great Britain and the United States; it was not actually possessed or protected or governed by either nation, though Philip had written that the settlers themselves, at Champoeg, had chosen the flag of the United States over that of Britain, by a margin of one vote. Officially, however, it was simply the Oregon Country, the raw and ungoverned Far West, a great area of free land stretching from the Alaska of the Russians on the north to the California of the Spanish on the south, and from the Rocky mountains to the Pacific Ocean. Uncontrollably, Kitty shivered again, but she sat up straighter to give the impression that she was completely self-possessed. It would be most unseemly to reveal that inside her were these little flutterings of fear.

She had never understood the Oregon Fever which lapped like a tide against all the states in the past few years, washed even into her own South Carolina and contaminated some of the best families there. The papers mentioned it often; politicians were forever arguing the Oregon Question, and Kitty's father, Robert Gatewood, had declared that Southern senators never would permit the nation to fight for Oregon unless slavery were permitted there. He was unalterably opposed to the annexation by conquest, purchase or treaty of free territory eventually to become free states, and he thought it scandalous if Southerners who planned to settle in Oregon were prohibited by federal law from taking their "property" with them. Kitty heard phrases like Manifest Destiny and Expansionism and "Fifty-four Forty or Fight," and she knew that all along the Missouri frontier in the spring thousands of people were yoking up oxen, preparing to head west for Oregon.... Philip had not had the Oregon Fever, that strange compulsion to go west for free land. He had simply thought it best to leave Wildcliffe for a while—the unfortunate aftermath of duelling. He had drifted to the Missouri and allowed himself to be caught up in the excitement of the departing immigrants. Once in Oregon City, the end of the Trail, he had written a disgusted account of that two-thousand mile journey from Independence, Missouri. How much nicer, Kitty thought idly, if one wished to come to Oregon, to come comfortably aboard the *Sea Bird!* But then she supposed that there were people—though she couldn't think of any she knew, right off—who did not have the six hundred dollars which Craig charged to bring each passenger around the Horn, and so they must come by wagon over the immigrant trail.... To Kitty, six hundred dollars meant three gowns, imported for her from France, or the price of a single, untrained house servant for Wildcliffe. She allowed her thoughts to drift back, now, to Wildcliffe, to her father, to the last time she had seen Philip.

◇ 3 ◇

THE estate of Wildcliffe had belonged to the Gatewoods since the time of the Lords Proprietors, and subsequent generations had developed it into a perfect setting for Kitty's father, Robert. Robert had extravagant tastes; he loved possessions and he appreciated plenty and quality and beauty in all things—in foods and wines and horses and women. Wildcliffe gave him the means to afford them and the leisure to enjoy them. But he was not a stupid man; he selected for his wife, not one of his gay companions, but a true patrician, Margaret Keith.

Margaret, many people said, was a saint. A spiritual, cameo-perfect woman, she was Robert's most exquisite and cherished possession, and his exact opposite. She graced Wildcliffe magnificently, but Robert made no pretense of living up to her standards. The Gatewoods were a stubborn breed, not easily changed. It was equally unthinkable that Margaret would compromise her principles, no matter how deeply she loved the handsome and charming man who was her husband.

And she did love him. Kitty, from early childhood, knew that there was deep love as well as sharp conflict between her parents. She saw her lovely mother's intense and silent suffering brought on by Robert's excesses, and it affected her deeply. Margaret never criticized Robert to Kitty; but quietly and very thoroughly she instilled into her the belief that upon women fell the burden of maintaining the conventions and the decencies, that it was their cross to endure the weaknesses and appetites of men, and that their salvation and peace came only in strictly maintaining their own high standards of behavior against all temptations and persuasions—and those persuasions could be great, indeed, from someone you loved. . . . Kitty had no reason to doubt her mother; she worshipped her, and even Robert declared that Margaret was perfection.

There had been much speculation among their friends about the little daughter who was christened Catherine, but immediately became "Kitty" to the adoring slaves who attended her. She would become another Margaret, many said, for she had inherited her mother's white-gold hair and luminous skin and perfect, small-boned body, and Robert never interfered with Margaret's strict training. But Kitty had the Gatewood eyes—the rebellious, expressive brown eyes, and she had Robert's restless blood. It appeared, suddenly, when, at fifteen, she blossomed forth into a most disturbing combination, with Margaret's astonishing beauty and decorum, Robert's sensuous grace and warm, magnetic charm.

It was quite natural that Philip Davis should fall in love with her. A great many men did, but Philip had the advantage of propinquity. He was the orphaned younger son of a distant relative and Robert, through choice, and Margaret, through duty, took him to Wildcliffe. Philip was carefully trained by Robert to succeed him as master of the estate, and between him and Robert there was a close companionship and complete understanding. When the engagement of Philip and Kitty was announced, it was considered a happy arrangement all around.

Kitty had been secretly fascinated by Philip's rash escapades and it was not surprising that she should consider herself in love with him. He was much more exciting than more worthy and proper swains. He was much like her gay father, reckless, excitement-loving. When he had found it wise to leave Wildcliffe, it was quite like him to go off to the Oregon Country. Philip had always been an extremist.

And then, suddenly, Margaret died. No one knew she had been ill, for Margaret never complained. Robert, shocked and stricken by remorse, castigating himself for not realizing she was ill, for all the things he had not done for her while she lived, wild with grief, began to drink more heavily. With Margaret went his strength and with her death came the full realization of what she had meant to him. His heart failed him and he had no desire to recover. He talked to Kitty of Margaret's virtues, urged her to be to Philip what Margaret had been to him. She must see that Philip returned to the stability and beauty of Wildcliffe. . . . He had no fears for Kitty; she, like Margaret, would follow the right path. But his concern was for Philip. He explained that a single girl's property rights were sometimes questioned, and, in any event, control of her property passed to her husband on her marriage. Therefore, to save Philip embarrassment, to make him a man of independent wealth, to bring him home to a respected place in the community, he was willing the estate directly to Philip. Robert felt he had guarded Philip's and Kitty's future, taken nothing from his daughter but given something to Philip; he believed he had put his house in order before he died.

Kitty had answered Philip's letters from Oregon faithfully but she had no assurance that he had received her replies. His messages had grown increasingly bitter and uncertain, as though he believed she had turned from him altogether. He had always needed constant reassurance and applause. His letters worried her more than she would admit.

She had been sitting in the library at Wildcliffe, after her father's death, when she had made her decision to go to Oregon. She had glanced about at the group of kindly people, Judge Stuart, her legal adviser, old friends, and she realized that now, despite their help, she must make her own decisions. She need not wait passively wondering if or when her message would reach Philip by the irregular Oregon mails; indeed, it suddenly seemed to her that she could not. Her own future, as well as Philip's, was at stake. With no warning she made her startling announcement. She would act as her own envoy. She would go to Oregon—to Philip.

Remembering the sensation her words had caused, Kitty smiled. There had been scandalized protests and pleas. There had been tears and prayers and dire warnings, but no one could shake the decision of Robert's daughter. Some said it was her father's blood in her that was sending her off on this wild adventure; it was just the sort of rash thing that Robert would do. There were others who said it was only the courage and strict training of Margaret that drove the dutiful girl to make such a sacrifice; to hide her grief, to dare the rigors of such a journey; to double the Horn to find Philip, to bring him back as master of Wildcliffe as her father had wished.

In a way, both opinions were right. Kitty herself knew only that she must go to Oregon. She had to try her wings. And—she must find Philip.

In the end, Judge Stuart had arranged for her passage on the *Sea Bird*.

◆ 4 ◆

Dr. Manning saw the oarsman grin at Kitty. He knew Read as a rough and brawny fellow whose wenching and drinking and fighting had set a new record even in the lusty Sandwich Island ports. Thomas' plate-shaped face, pink with cold and wet with rain, lost its accustomed good-nature. He tucked his heavy chin down in his short neck and frowned, becoming suddenly a pugnacious bulldog, far removed from the jovial, graying minister and doctor. Deliberately he turned to face Kitty, to determine if she was inviting the sailor's attention. Slowly the disapproval faded from his face.

She never failed to meet his eyes squarely, a trait he liked; and each time it was a new shock to him. It was startling to see eyes so dark and velvet-brown in that lovely face; for her abundant hair, so demurely pinned and netted, was the palest gold that Thomas had ever seen, just short of white, and yet it gleamed and rippled with such life it seemed more vivid than the brightest red. Sun and wind and ocean spray had tinged her flawless skin a shade darker than her hair and it was flushed with cold and health and excitement. Her short straight nose, that of a mischievous and very appealing little girl, belied the dignity of her manner. But her lips, though very young, very rosy and soft, were not childish and there was nothing weak about her pretty chin. She was so small and sweet and young, Thomas thought, with a quick rush of tenderness—and so proud and stubborn and spoiled.

When she laughed her eyes sparkled and she laughed at Thomas now, putting her head back, letting the rain reach her face, loving it, breathing deep and long of the wet, scent-laden air. The paler skin beneath her chin seemed to gleam. The brim of her bonnet was edged with tiny droplets of moisture like chip diamonds. Everything about the girl seemed to shine.

"Don't you love it, Dr. Manning? Doesn't the air smell wonderful?" Kitty kept her tone carefully light.

Thomas nodded his big head slowly and rain dropped sadly from the broad brim of his black hat to his heavy shoulders. In fairness he must admit that she behaved at all times with the utmost decorum; the marks of a thoroughbred were unmistakable. But, he admitted honestly, he could not blame the sailor for staring at her. It would have been a strange man who would not. In all his long life, he concluded, he had never before seen a girl as radiantly, warmly desirable.

Studying her, Thomas' brows lowered again. The missionaries had been well instructed how to deal with the harlots likely to follow in the wake of the wagon trains. But what was the church to do about a young and voluptuous gentlewoman who came alone to a raw frontier town like Oregon City? Worse than that, with feeling running high in Oregon over the slavery issue, what would happen when Kitty went ashore with a black servant at her heels?

This morning Thomas had tried to persuade Craig not to put Kitty and Jessie ashore, but Craig had cut him off shortly.

"She paid me twelve hundred good American dollars to deliver her and the Negro to Oregon City," Craig had said curtly. "I haul goods and passengers, Doctor. I don't meddle in politics."

"Oregon City is an incorporated town now, Captain Craig, and the Oregon Provisional Government—" Thomas had begun stubbornly.

"What's that? An organization of settlers with no nation behind it! No one knows who the Oregon Country belongs to, yet.

And it may take a war to decide it. Until that's settled there is no recognized government in Oregon. She's only a visitor, anyway. She's no settler."

"Nevertheless," Thomas had persisted, "the Provisional Government is opposed to slavery and has banned Negroes. There's a penalty against blacks coming into Oregon, slave or free. Twenty to thirty-nine lashes on the bare back."

"Hah!" Craig had snorted. "Show me the man who would lash that Negress! He'd have to deal with Kitty first. Anyway, you Oregon people will have more important things on your mind. The United States may be fighting two wars at once—with Mexico over California, with Britain over Oregon. Soon, too. There's already one British war sloop in the Columbia, the *Modeste*, with twenty guns, lying off Fort Vancouver, and maybe another in Puget Sound."

But Thomas, watching Kitty now, was apprehensive. He knew what he would find in Oregon City. He knew the year's cycle all too well. Each fall the immigrants arrrived, exhausted, half-starving from the gruelling journey over the Oregon Trail. All of this year's immigration would likely have reached Oregon City now, and the town would be jammed with the sick and hungry. Some would have filtered out into the valleys to stake their land claims, each his square mile, but there would be the work of clearing, building, planting before the next harvest, another full year before this year's weary immigrants were self-supporting. Shortages of food and shelter would be acute and there would be another shortage which would further endanger Kitty—the shortage of women.

The safest place for her while she awaited marriage to her young man would be one of the mission schools, Thomas decided, or the British Fort Vancouver. The luxury and gaiety of the Hudson's Bay Company post on the north bank of the Columbia, six miles up the river from where the *Sea Bird* lay, would be more to Kitty's liking, and the venerable factor, Dr. McLoughlin, was famed for his hospitality. But *was* there such a thing as a safe place in Oregon? With the fleets of Great Britain and the United States in the Pacific, and a British warship already in The River, could it mean that actual hostilities would break out at last? Greater powers than individual men thought so. Had not Thomas' own mission to the Sandwich Islands to purchase emergency supplies for the Americans in Oregon been a failure because Russia had already cornered all the stores available there? No, it would not do to have the American girl housed in the British fort.

Thomas sighed deeply. Kitty's elegance alone would be in shocking and cruel contrast to that of the poverty-stricken women of Oregon. Craig might better have landed a cargo of muskets for the British or of liquor for the Indians, than to have brought Kitty and Jessie Pearl to troubled Oregon at this time, Thomas thought, in irritation.

Kitty had been watching Thomas with amusement. Now he was thoughtful, benign, now he glowered. She grinned at him, her eyes twinkling.

"You are so serious, Dr. Manning!"

Thomas started. He knew that to lecture her would be useless. He realized that he could influence this lovely, willful girl only if he could keep her friendship.

The boat swayed a little, rounding a point, came close to the thickly wooded bank. To the west, between the Willamette and the sea, loomed the Coast Range, and to the east, hidden behind the forest wall and the pewter sky above, towered the Cascades, ever present barrier to sap the last ounce of endurance of the immigrants from the East. Thomas could feel the overpowering presence of the majestic mountains even when he could not see them. He wondered if Kitty could not feel them, too. He searched her face shrewdly. Perhaps, after all, she was not so calm as she appeared. Her soft lips seemed almost tremulous. Thomas, with rare perception, searched for safe words that would reassure her, and would not reveal he had guessed her inner disquiet.

"I was thinking," he said gently, "that Jonathan Swift must have been inspired. Or perhaps it was just coincidence. Do you know that in longitude and latitude this is actually the land of Brobdingnag? To Swift, of course, the Columbia was only a legend, a river that 'rose in the shining mountains, flowed westward into the sunset ocean;' but Swift actually placed his Brobdingnag, where everything was so enormous, near the mouth of the Columbia."

"Is that really true?" Gratitude to the pleasant old doctor flooded over her. Her trembling lessened. It was comforting to know that the doctor, whose round face had seemed to be twisted with concern over the weightiest of problems, had simply been recalling the delightful parable of Gulliver.

A canoe was skimming down river at breath-taking speed. Kitty was astonished to see that the two buckskin-clad passengers were white men. Their stares raked her deeply as they swept by and then they turned squarely around to look at her again. One wore a fur cap, the tail of the animal hanging down at the back like a skimpy chignon.

The rain slackened and finally stopped. A raft, carrying two boys, round-eyed and grinning, met them, and they poled frantically to lessen their speed as they recognized the jolly-boat. A wider, longer craft than the canoe, so lightly laden it seemed to ride the water like a paper shell and with both ends high and pointed, followed. Above it flew the triangular pennon of the Hudson's Bay Fur Company. Kitty caught a glimpse of the rampant beaver and the bold letters H.B.C. upon the blue field of the banderol. The men beneath it wore capotes of the same Hudson's Bay blue, and they waved as they passed, their curious eyes on Kitty.

Kitty became aware of a faint, even drumming sound, above the noise of the river. Thomas, his ear catching it too, spoke again, reassuringly.

"That's Willamette Falls," he said, "do you hear it? The Indians call them The Beat Of the Heart." He pointed to a stream, tumbling into the Willamette. "Abernethy Creek. Oregon City is just beyond."

Kitty sat forward eagerly to see. At last, up the river, she could glimpse the falls, magnificent rushing, plunging tower of white. Suddenly the eastern bank of the river widened out to a broad, rock-strewn flat, against which a multitude of canoes and rafts and other craft were beached. Behind the flat rose an abrupt, high bluff, topped by smooth-barked madrona trees. Nestled between the bluff and the river, walled in by the forests, close to the falls of the Willamette lay Oregon City, the teeming little unofficial capital of all the Oregon Country, the only incorporated city west of the Rockies; the far frontier town toward which Kitty had sailed for half a year—the end of the overland Oregon Trail.

2 CURT FLETCHER, LIKE ALL OF ORE-
gon City, had known for three days of the approach of the *Sea Bird*. The word had come
from Astoria, near the Columbia's mouth, by
canoe up river, by moccasin telegraph, finally
by an Indian on a fleet cayuse, across the
Tualatin Plains and the Willamette to Oregon City. Oregon City knew the vessel's iden-
tity; the people had been quick to determine whether she were a
trader or a man-of-war, and under which flag she sailed.

But Curt was not on the river bank to welcome the yawl from
the *Sea Bird*. He had more important work to do—to inspect and
repair his own bateau, beached at the foot of Eighth Street near
the horse-ferry landing. He was pleased enough that the *Sea Bird*
had come, for the ship would bring goods to stock the almost
bare shelves of the stores of Abernethy and Couch, and in the
ledgers of both establishments there were numerous orders in
favor of Curt.

It was going to be a fine day, too, after the early morning rain.
Curt stretched his arms wide. He was a tall man of powerful
build, lean and hard-muscled, with the deeply bronzed skin and
clear eyes of those who live out of doors, the grace and balance
and endurance of a *voyageur*. In any group Fletcher was outstanding, not only for his size and his great strength, the stubborn,
ruthless set of his chin, the hard, straight handsome mouth, but
for his cool assurance—that of a man who knows what he wants
and expects to get it, by force, if necessary. There were many
legends in the Oregon Country about Fletcher. Most of them
were true.

He examined the sky carefully through narrowed, weather-wise eyes and was pleased to see that the small patch of blue was spreading. A man grew used to these fall rains in Oregon; they washed the air and swelled the rivers and made Oregon wheat run seventy-two pounds to the bushel and crop failures unknown. But you appreciated clear days, and Charlefour, his French-Canadian bowman, might be more inclined to lend a hand with boat repairs if he were dry and comfortable for a change.

Curt ran his hand down the elaborately carved prow of his bateau. He was very fond of this small craft. It was a peculiar shape, very high and broad, propelled with oars and steered with paddles. It was thirty feet long and of light draft, so strong it could carry a very large load, so light it was easy to convey around portages, and more steady and roomy than the Indian canoes. It had carried Curt hundreds of river miles; and it had proved its strength and endurance when, loaded with exhausted immigrants, it had made many a dash down the fierce Columbia River gorge from The Dalles—that terrifying fifty-mile stretch of angry waters that alone joined the terminus of the Oregon Trail with the valley of the Willamette. It would carry him and his partner, Sunset Lee, and Charlefour northward next trip, up the Cowlitz River.

Planning that trip brought him pleasure. It was good to think of wintering on his own land claim with a partner like Sunset. A dependable man of strength and gaiety, Sunset, who'd earned his nickname, spoken with affection by every Oregon settler, because of his knowledge of the West. They would travel fast up the Cowlitz to the Landing; Dick Tom, the Indian, would have horses for them there, and they'd go on overland to Puget Sound, to Newmarket, the new and only American settlement north of The River.

The Puget Sound country had everything a man could want, Curt thought, pulling the oars one by one from the bateau and inspecting them. Timber, right down to tidewater; the Sound itself a great inland sea, big enough to shelter all the navies in the world. Lush land. Water power, there on the Deschutes River at the falls the Indians called Tumwater. And beauty—Curt raised his eyes again, wondering if it would clear sufficiently for Mount Hood, the sentinel of Oregon City, to be visible today. Once you grew used to the mountains you watched for them always, and you had a secret hunger for them. Sometimes they were hidden for days and then they emerged in glory like all the renewed hope and unlimited power in the world. At Newmarket Curt and Sunset lived in the shadow of another great peak in the Cascade Range, the mightiest of all—Mount Rainier, to the British; Mount Takhoma, the Fountain-Breast of Milk-White Waters, to the Indians.

Curt took a long satisfied breath. On a day like this a man was glad he'd cast his lot in Oregon. He snorted, thinking of the propaganda the British had spread throughout the world in an effort to keep Oregon for themselves; that Oregon was a worthless country, rocky, barren, not worth fighting for. Trouble was—some gullible Congressmen believed them. But three thousand settlers had laughed at the British and had come over the Oregon Trail this year, and plenty of them had "54-40 or Fight" painted defiantly on their wagon covers. They would not be easy to dislodge.

Curt began to whistle through his teeth the bars of *Pretty Betty Martin*. . . . Already people were beginning to gather on the bank, to welcome the yawl from the *Sea Bird*. Many stopped to pass the time of day. Sidney Moss of the Main Street House and H. M. Knighton of the City Hotel; settlers from Salem and Champoeg and French Prairie; Medorum Crawford, who moved goods around the falls with his ox team for settlers above the portage; John Ricord, and Peter Burnett, the prairie lawyer. Many strangers also spoke, for even newcomers knew Fletcher. He reflected that a year ago he would have known them all, what year they came and what wagon company they belonged to. It was gratifying that the population of Oregon City—of all the Oregon Country, for that matter—had doubled with this year's immigration.

But this year's immigration was over now. The relief party had made contact with the Barlow group, which had refused to wait for bateaux at The Dalles and with thirty wagons attempted to find a pass around the base of Mount Hood. And the Lost Company, that tragic, ill-advised band of two hundred families which had turned away from the Trail at Fort Boise and attempted to find a mythical cut-off to the Willamette through the mountains of southern Oregon had at last been located. The survivors were on their way to Oregon City. Sunset was bringing them.

"Howdy, Fletcher."

"Howdy, Williams. Howdy, Foster."

The two settlers were dressed alike, in buckskin. Each carried a rifle and each wore a bullet pouch and powder horn beneath his right arm. There was several inches' difference in their heights, and ten years' difference in their ages; one spoke with a flat Middle-western accent and the other was unmistakably a New Englander. But, like seasoned soldiers, they bore upon them the same stamp.

"Not readyin' to go to The Dalles again?"

"No. Anyone who isn't off The Trail by now won't get here."

"Reckon so. Goin' to Newmarket?"

"Yes. Soon as Sunset comes."

Foster shifted his rifle and leaned against the bateau, ready for talk. "I hear the Lost Company had a mighty bad time. Lucky for them Sunset went out after them. No better mountain man than Sunset. Has plenty of sand and fights clean."

"I reckon there'll be a road through the mountains next year," Williams observed. "That Barlow party is comin' through with a pack train. Killed eleven horses, gettin' to them, so I hear. They left their wagons, but swear to go back and get 'em, come spring, and cut a road. No need to ferry folks down from The Dalles once they get a road through. Wagons'll roll right on to Oregon City."

Curt pulled a pipe from his pocket and tamped it. "Good thing to have a road. Good for immigrants—and you can move an Army over it," he said. He glanced around at the rapidly growing crowd. "Lots of redcoats here."

The settlers, cool and unhurried, followed his glance. Their eyes were as steady and sharp as though they sighted down their rifle barrels.

"Yeah. Couple of British navy officers, name of Park and Peel, up the Willamette lately, talking to settlers. Tryin' to figure if we'd fight—come a war." The men exchanged amused glances.

"Two fellows name of Warre and Vavasour of the Royal Engineers were at The Dalles," Curt remarked, "counting the number of immigrants."

"They had plenty of 'em to count," Foster observed with satisfaction.

"Ought to be some news on the *Sea Bird*," Williams said.

Curt laughed without mirth. "There'll be papers. Quoting Congress."

Foster struck a pose and deepened his voice. "I would not give a pinch of snuff for the whole territory of Oregon!" he quoted, trying to imitate a Southern accent. "Damn that South Carolina senator all to hell," he added in his natural tone.

"Ah, Foster, Senator McDuffie can't help it if he was just born ignorant," Williams said tolerantly. "Anyway, he's no worse'n Daniel Webster. But Polk got hisself elected on '54-40 or Fight.' Either he'll get a settlement with Britain or he'll send the Army and Navy out here." He paused thoughtfully. "That is, maybe he will. If Oregon is lost to England it'll be only because of slavery. Why in hell do senators have to keep playin' that string?"

"The government better get Oregon to 54-40, Fletcher, or you and Sunset'll have to fight the British north of The River by your own selves," Foster joked, "and that's the land they swear they'll hold, too. Fort Nisqually ain't far from Newmarket, is it? Guess you'll be kinda busy, fightin' against a whole British post. I allus figured the reason you and Sunset settled north of The River was because the British were so dead set on keeping you out of there. Show Fletcher a locked door, I allus said, and he's bound to smash through it. Tell Sunset he can't climb a mountain or ford a river, and danged if that ain't a sure way to get him to do it."

Curt did not smile. "I like that country," he said. "I staked a claim there. I aim to hold it."

William shifted his rifle. "Well, we fought the British at the border and we fought 'em at New Orleans, and we fought Indians all the way to the Missouri. I reckon we can fight them again— them *and* the Indians *and* the Mexicans, too, if we have to."

"We'll sure be plumb surrounded," Foster said cheerfully, "and don't forget the *Modeste*. She's got twenty guns and five hundred men on her."

"Maybe a man-of-war will take the *Modeste* out of The River," Williams said hopefully.

Curt's forehead was creased. "It's going to be bad, if it comes to war," he said softly. "Damned if I can see Dr. McLoughlin turning guns on settlers. He laid out Oregon City. He wants to live here when he retires. He's sent Company boats up to meet Sunset and the Lost Company. It'll go hard on him if he's ordered to fight us. Some other Canadians and Frenchmen feel the same way. It'll be neighbor against neighbor—civil war. It may even be a religious war, for some say the Black Gowns won't help the Protestant missionaries. It will be one hell of a fight— with the Indians helping the British."

"McLoughlin's been mighty helpful to settlers," the men agreed. "He's a man wouldn't let nobody starve, if he could help it, no matter what country he belongs to. But he sure tried to keep us all south of The River; and you notice he'll sell settlers a work horse, maybe—but none for breeding. He's Canadian, and he's Hudson's Bay."

"They pay the sailors on the *Modeste* in silver dollars, out of a whole barrel of silver, so I heard," Foster contributed, after a while. "And there's no shortage of rum aboard, either. Keepin' their boys happy so they won't desert."

Curt raised his eyebrows. "Hm-m. Think I'll visit Fort Vancouver before I go north."

The settlers regarded Curt enviously.

"Reckon the government will change the law against liquor in Oregon City soon now. More settlers than mission folks now. Man wants his drink legal," Williams said hopefully.

"Plenty of changes comin'," Foster agreed. "Price of town lots is goin' up. Wheat's already a dollar and a half a bushel. I hear Pettygrove has laid out a townsite down at the mouth of the Willamette. They named it already. Him and Lawyer Lovejoy flipped a coin. Lovejoy wanted to call it Boston, but Pettygrove's a Maine man. Pettygrove won so they named it Portland. He figures it'll be near as big as Oregon City, some day. Ships can come that far easy and with a shingle-camp and a store, might build up real fast, at that."

"Hope the *Sea Bird* brings some good tobacco. I'm damned tired of smokin' kinnikinnick."

"Quite a crowd, ain't it? Most of 'em hopin' for mail."

Foster and Williams drifted away. The voices rose to a hum as excitement increased. The British were there to gather what information they could and to look over the people who came on the *Sea Bird*, but so far they had made every effort to keep relations with the Americans friendly. It was a pleasant enough game, eyeing one another, sparring politely with words.

◆ 2 ◆

CURT ran an appraising glance over the women in the group on the bank. A number of attractive girls had come in this season's wagon trains and many were well aware of Curt's presence here this morning. God, he thought, what they have been through! All of them showed the ravages of the journey. It was triumph enough for a man to have covered those two thousand miles of plains and mountains, of barren desert and roaring torrents; yet often it was the slimmest and smallest of these courageous women who stood the journey best. They meant homes and permanence and it was their coming which had disturbed the British this year. Yes, Oregon needed women—women like Clara Linton.

Curt noticed her now in the gathering crowd, her cloak not hiding her advanced pregnancy, her young face bright beneath the old bonnet. Jeff must be feeling better then, Curt thought, for Clara's mobile face was not gay when her husband had taken a turn for the worse. The Lintons were from Illinois and had come in '44. Curt remembered when he had first seen them. A lone wagon, a straggler, had arrived at The Dalles late at night. Clara held the reins and her husband lay in the wagon bed, fighting for breath. Clara's face was blistered crimson, her dust-inflamed eyes swollen almost shut. Curt had thought then that neither the Lintons nor their outfit would add much to Oregon.

But now they had a cabin in Oregon City and Jeff was able to work a little and perhaps soon he could pay back the money Curt had loaned him on his tools. And Clara was going to have a child. It was surprising, Curt thought, how many of those in the wagon trains came to Oregon in search of health and how many of the ailing actually survived the trip.

The faces of the immigrants were thin and burned by sun and wind, drawn with a fatigue that went too deep to be erased by a few nights' sleep. Their costumes were brave attempts to make themselves presentable with what little they had. Here and there Curt saw a woman in a dress which had originally been designed for evening wear, the only gown left to its owner at the end of the Trail, and some were barefoot. Occasionally a woman wore a good pair of shoes and a dress neatly made of a canvas wagon-cover.

But the group was not drab. Among them were Indians in bright blankets and head scarves and there were French Canadians, too, for none of them would have missed any occasion for gaiety. The dress of the *voyageurs* was never dull in color, and Curt's teeth flashed in a rare grin as he saw Charlefour approaching. He could hardly have missed him, even among his gaily garbed compatriots, for Charlefour was dressed in his vivid best. The sun warmed him outwardly and Charlefour, from his gait, apparently was well warmed inwardly, too. He swayed as he walked, and his cap, as tall as a drum major's, swayed with him. The cap was heavily embroidered with beads forming rosettes, trailed by long silken vines of green. His trousers were of fine buckskin, fringed and beaded at the cuffs and down the sides and adorned with garters of gaudy knots of ribbon. His coat, once of Hudson's Bay blue, was almost completely covered by ornate designs of beadwork and embroidery in all the colors of the rainbow. Charlefour was a huge man, with powerful shoulders overdeveloped by his years at oars and paddles; his features were large, too, his mouth a big slash across his broad brown face. In one of the fights in his lusty past he had lost an eye, and he covered the socket on state occasions such as this with a bright red handkerchief. A front tooth had been knocked out, but Charlefour's loose, wet grin was friendly rather than fierce. He reeled toward Curt, trying hard to maintain dignity, with little success.

"You'll be of no help today, you muttonhead," Curt greeted him, disgustedly. "Where'd you get it? Indian liquor?"

Charlefour shook his great head, grinning happily. "It's real Blue Ruin," he announced triumphantly. He brought his great head close to Curt's and his heavy breath pounded into Curt's face. "Lisa is looking for you," he confided, and at once he broke into loud and boisterous song.

"*Malbrouck*," Charlefour bellowed, "*has gone a-fighting—*"

Curt grabbed his arm and shoved him behind the bateau.

"Charlie, Joe Meek'll have you in jail. One more drink before we leave and I'll lock you up myself." Curt made a threatening gesture with his fist beneath Charlefour's nose. "Stay out of trouble till we get north of The River, Charlie; you want to get home to Polly Careless, don't you?"

Charlefour smiled happily. "Oh-h, yes, now Curt. I sure do want to see Polly Careless," he agreed. He clasped his hamlike hands and rolled his one eye skyward as he extravagantly recounted the charms of his Indian wife. "Polly Careless is a ver' fine woman, Curt. She can cook, she can sew, she can clean fish, she can love—and I been gone from her for so-o long—"

Curt looked up the street toward the center of the town. Two ox-carts were moving toward the river, down the rutted, unpaved street. Behind them, and then overtaking them, raced a white horse, a small but beautiful Indian pony, and on it was Lisa.

You knew when Lisa was coming even before you could see her for there were bells around the saddle skirt on her horse, and tiny bells or jangling bracelets on her wrists. No Indian girl wore more beads than Lisa, the half-Indian daughter of the Frenchman Le Seuer. The bells and the jangles of the bracelets preceded her, and sometimes her shout or her laughter as well. Lisa rode like the wind, she danced like a demon, and she laughed or she swore or she screamed with equal abandon. Her pony tore down the street and down the river bank now, and came to a stop at the water's edge, in a shower of gravel as the small hoofs ploughed into the earth. The little bells on the saddle tinkled and Lisa's laugh rang out as she leaned down and ran her long, thin fingers over Curt's hard cheek.

"Curt, you have not shaved! Everyone else dresses fine to greet the boat—and you, you so beautiful, you do not give a damn! You look like a brigand. What the people think, eh?"

Curt flung her hand aside roughly. He hated that possessiveness of Lisa; he would not tolerate possessiveness in any woman. The smile faded from the girl's face and it grew sullen. Her black eyes narrowed calculatingly. She drew back her brown hand, ready to strike him. He made no move to halt her but she met his ocean-gray eyes and finally her hand dropped. Lisa had good reason to fear the deep-buried streak of violence in Fletcher. Abruptly she wheeled her horse, dashing back to the rear of the crowd. Curt turned to his boat, his face expressionless, not bothering to watch her leap from the saddle, her skirts a cascade of gypsy-colored flounces and ruffles, the bells tinkling. Charlefour pursed his big lips and tried to focus his one eye on the damaged bateau.

"There's a weak place here, Charlie," Curt said, pointing, ignoring Lisa's interruption. "I'm going to Vancouver tomorrow. Sunset should come in the next day or two. We'll be ready to move shortly after. This is Tuesday. We'll leave Sunday."

There was a sudden shout from the crowd on the beach as the ship's yawl rounded the curve. What a heavy and awkward boat, he thought; he had pulled the oars on many a ship's boat like that and he hated them all. The last one he had rowed was on The River.

Yes, he had been at the oars of a jolly-boat from the *Mary Lane*. When he had landed on The River's bank, on Oregon land, he had shoved the boat out into the current again, and he had watched the powerful, impersonal River carry it downstream. He was glad to see it go, for that boat was carrying a dead man to the western sea. The man was John Flint, the sadistic first mate of the *Mary Lane*, and he was dead from a neat bullet hole in the head. Curt had promised Flint he'd kill him, even when he was in chains and Flint, laughing, had stood over him with a cat-o'-nine-tails. He'd deal out the same swift justice to any man who attempted to enslave him. It had taken four years of the beauty and freedom and work in Oregon to ease, but never to erase, the burning bitterness that hated bondage and nightmarish voyage had built within him.

Perhaps some of those oarsmen in the boat from the *Sea Bird* felt the same way. And Oregon needed men. Curt looked at the approaching boat with more interest. If any of them had been shanghaied as he had been and wished to desert, he could tell them the best places to hide out until the *Sea Bird* was safely out of The River.

◆ 3 ◆

LISA had come to stand beside him again as he knew she would. He could hear her bracelets as she moved, he could feel her warmth and he could smell the peculiar, not unpleasant odor that clung to her. It was a warm and earthy, smoky smell, for her clothing had hung in smoke-filled tents and cabins, and her glistening black hair, loose on her shoulders, smelled of the fir boughs on which she slept. But he did not look at her. There had been a time when he wanted Lisa near him—but not for long. She was beautiful and she was wanton and she was wild. She was of the ungoverned old days, gone forever now, when the Hudson's Bay Company fur brigades, mounted on their high-stepping, gaily-decorated horses, had swept southward in the autumn, down through the Oregon Country, into the warmer land of the Spanish, to hunt and trap and trade in California the winter through. Those hunters, Frenchmen and Indians, had taken their women with them, and made of it one great holiday with music and laughter and dancing at every camp, with wild races and hot savage battles; and then they had pounded northward again in a still more colorful and splendid cavalcade, their beads and embroideries sparkling anew with the silver bells of the Spanish on their saddle skirts and bridle reins, and heavier silver on the dark lean wrists and the pretty ears of their women. . . . Yes, Lisa belonged to the old wild days, when Curt had first come to The River, before American women came in the covered wagon trains, before hundreds of settlers invaded the hunting grounds and ended the gleaming, colorful, autumnal trek of the Hudson's Bay mounted brigade. Lisa was of the woods and of the night; in a city, Lisa was of the world of solitary men, of back streets—not for the clear light of the early morning, here with the respectable townspeople, the clean-scrubbed white girls, members of the Church and the Debating Society and the Multnomah Circulating Library.

Her presence irritated Curt and at the same time, conscious of the disapproving glances turned her way, he stubbornly refused to dismiss her. She was a savage and she belonged to the dark recesses of his past, and he had no intention of permitting her to interfere with his future. But no one else was going to tell him when to give her up. He let her stay beside him, but he ignored her.

There were six men at the oars of the jolly-boat, and in the bow, close by Dr. Manning, there was a girl, a slight girl, sitting very straight. In the stern was that rarity in Oregon—a Negro woman. Curt left the bateau and joined the group of men on the bank where the boat would land.

"A Negro," someone said, "the only one in Oregon City!"

"She can't stay. We can't have blacks here!"

"Who'd dare bring a Negro to Oregon? Some damned slave-owner! Don't they know our law?"

"I guess the States don't recognize our Provisional Government —yet. We'll show them!"

The rumblings grew louder, angrier, as the crowd waited. The boat scraped gravel, the seamen shipped their oars and leaped out to pull the boat high. Curt's interest had shifted from the men.

Dr. Manning clambered ashore and was immediately surrounded by churchmen. Jessie stood stiffly, her eyes wide with fright. Kitty dropped the oilcloth from about her shoulders.

Read was waiting, his hand outstretched, and she had no choice but to accept his aid. She gathered up her skirts and stepped daintily to shore.

She glanced swiftly about her and knew at once that Philip was not there. She raised her chin proudly, hiding her disappointment.

"Thank you," she said briefly, drawing her hand from Read's too-tight grasp. "Jessie Pearl, pile all the trunks and cases here and cover them with the oilcloth. When I know where we are to stay I'll send for them. You'll watch them while I find us a place."

She spoke swiftly, quite self-possessed, ignoring the stares. At the first sound of her slurred, velvety voice, Curt knew that she was a Southerner, and he knew, too, that Jessie Pearl was her slave. The Negro girl began to pile her mistress' belongings as she was directed, silently, not looking to right or left. Kitty turned and for a minute her eyes met Curt's squarely and their glances locked. She allowed her careless glance to touch his black hair, to travel over his strong face and unshaven chin; to take in his powerful shoulders, his slim hips in their buckskin trousers. She saw the ornamented belt, supporting two revolvers and a knife, and the worn place on the right side of his black shirt where his powder horn and bullet pouch usually rested. Her glance touched his boots and then left him, dismissing him completely, as though she found nothing in the survey of his lean length, his rugged face, to interest or to impress her in the least. At his right shoulder she saw a grinning Charlefour, a jovial-looking cutthroat, she thought, and at Curt's left stood Lisa, the look in her black eyes scorching Kitty, her full, moist lips curled in an insolent sneer.

Dr. Manning spoke to Curt and then he drew Kitty into the protective circle of his associates. Curt heard the introductions; Miss Gatewood, of South Carolina, Dr. Manning said. Curt's tongue found his cheek. The doctor's gentle old voice went on, pouring oil on the waters, explaining that Miss Gatewood and Jessie Pearl were only visitors to Oregon; they were not settlers, but guests, and the Negro would be removed from Oregon within the time allowed by law.

"There's not a spare bed in Oregon City, Dr. Manning," someone said bluntly. "There's eight women to a room at Main Street House and the City Hotel is just as crowded."

Kitty looked at the speaker and suddenly the hostile protests stopped. Curt, watching Kitty's profile, saw her beautiful cheek dimple and her lashes, thick as brushes, lower helplessly. There was a little silence.

Over Curt's shoulder Charlefour was muttering soft, flattering profanities as he stared at Kitty, and Curt began to grin as he watched her victory. There was no doubt that suitable accommodations would be found for the beautiful Miss Gatewood and her slave, even in overcrowded Oregon City. There were more potent weapons, Curt thought, than heavy sidearms.

Jessie Pearl was struggling with a trunk and Curt reached out, quite naturally, to help her. He lifted it easily to place it beside the growing pile of Kitty's possessions. Kitty turned quickly, her full skirts whirling about her, and put a possessive little hand upon the trunk. It was the one which contained her wedding gown.

"Jessie Pearl," she said imperiously, looking straight at the Negro girl, ignoring Curt beside her, "you will care for this trunk. No one else is to touch it. No one—you hear me?"

Jessie bowed her head but Curt did not. His eyebrows went up.

"Why, you little—" he muttered, in swift anger, and caught himself. He stared down at her, tiny and trim and lovely and defiant. You damned, pampered, beautiful little prig, he went on, silently. You'll need a helping hand in Oregon now and then, my girl, and if you stay here long you won't be too proud to take it, either. . . . Kitty had caught his low exclamation and her indignant glance slid up to him. Curt's anger died at once and amusement took its place. He bowed silently, with great gallantry, but his eyes were mocking. It was the practiced drawing-room bow of a gallant, not the sort of gesture one might expect on a river bank in Oregon, from an unshaven giant in buckskin. It was very disconcerting, perhaps even insulting. Kitty wasn't sure. She folded her lips against the quick apology and explanation she had meant to give; her chin went higher and she permitted Dr. Manning to escort her toward Main Street.

Curt noticed that Kitty did not lift her skirts from the mud and damp, nor did she look where she placed her feet. She seemed to take for granted that the path would be smooth for her, and she ignored with fine carelessness the expensive damage to the beautiful gown and to her small slippers. She did not look back to see that Jessie Pearl carried out her orders. A slave had never disobeyed her yet, and apparently it did not occur to her that one ever would. Obediently, silently, Jessie pulled the oilcloth over Kitty's trunks.

The girl's final look at him from those amazing dark eyes had been a cold scald, Curt thought, meant to give him all the discomfort of being frozen and burned at the same time. He ran his hand thoughtfully over his bristly chin and his eyes were shining. She had spirit as well as beauty, he thought; a flash-fire temper beautifully controlled. . . . Curt was not used to open defiance, particularly from a woman.

"You think she is a missionary lady, maybe?" Charlefour breathed reverently. "My God, that hair like moonlight, and—" Charlefour's hands made expressive gestures outlining other of Kitty's charms.

Curt shook his head slowly. "No," he said thoughtfully, "no, Charlie, damned if I can imagine her holding up lurid pictures of a fiery hell to convert the Indians."

Lisa looked at him sharply. She had never seen that look on his face before, nor heard that tone in his voice. She turned and spat fiercely in the direction Kitty had taken.

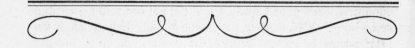

CLARA LINTON HAD THREE THINGS she wanted to do, all at the same time. She stood on the river bank, eager and somehow light, despite the awkwardness of her enlarged body. She wanted to run down the bank and speak to Curt about Jeff's tools, though it would anger Jeff, if he knew. . . . She wanted to run after Dr. Manning, and she could hardly take her eyes from the canvas pouch that the seaman was taking from the jolly-boat.

Clara, like every other woman there, knew that the bag contained mail from home and her hunger for letters made her almost ill. The women crowded forward as though propelled by an irresistible force, toward that bag that was their link with the States.

Of course there might be no letters in that bag for her. Sometimes it happened that way, for sailings to Oregon were irregular, unscheduled, and there was no government mail service. But until the pouch was opened no one knew for sure that the messages they longed for were not there.

But Clara had caught snatches of Dr. Manning's conversation. Miss Gatewood must have a place to live during her stay. She was obviously a person of great wealth. Why, the dress she wore probably cost more than all of Clara's clothes put together! And the trunks and boxes piled on the shore were neat and expensive. The one which Fletcher had lifted so easily was beautifully carved like a bride's chest. It was likely that Miss Gatewood would be able to pay—perhaps even in coin!—for accommodations for herself and her servant.

If she hurried, she could catch up with Dr. Manning. Clara caught her lower lip in her strong, square white teeth, her blue eyes thoughtful. We need money so desperately now; this is the opportunity I've prayed for. I'll rent the cottage to her—and Jeff and I—well, we've slept in the wagon before. If only we had a little money to see us through the winter. Or orders on the stores. . . .

Clara gave Curt and the leather pouch one last lingering glance and then she straightened. Her back ached a good deal now—why shouldn't it, she thought, laughingly, with the precious burden her body carried!

I've waited for mail six months, she told herself, stoically. I guess I can wait another hour. If there are letters for us they will still be there, an hour from now, at Abernethy's. But she felt silly tears rising in her throat, as she faced the little delay. She had hungered for those letters so long! She sniffed, disgusted at her own weakness.

Resolutely she hurried after Dr. Manning. . . .

◈ 2 ◈

KITTY sat before the fire in the Linton cabin, while Jessie Pearl knelt and rubbed her mistress' small white feet with a warm towel.

"Miss Kitty," Jessie Pearl said suddenly, desperately.

"What is it?"

"Miss Kitty, Ben, the sailor on the *Sea Bird*, he say it's against the law for a colored person to come to Oregon. He say the sheriff was to arrest any colored person and give 'em forty lashes ever' day till they left."

"Nonsense! Don't you worry, Jessie Pearl. No one's going to harm you. That law doesn't mean a thing. Dr. Manning told me no one ever had whipped a Negro here. You mustn't be afraid, Jessie. Do you think I'd let anyone lash you, ever?"

The Negro shook her head emphatically and relaxed slightly. Very gently she put on Kitty's clean stockings, buckled her slippers.

"You are to stay right here, in this cottage with me. It's tiny, but it's warm and nice. There's a little lean-to there, the kitchen, I suppose." Kitty wrinkled her small nose toward the dusky room at the rear. She giggled, a very young giggle. "Jessie, this is almost like a doll's house."

Together they looked about the small, single room. A bed occupied one corner, and it was beautifully made, of hand-turned maple. There was a small rocker beside the fireplace, a table and benches against one wall, and the rugs on the puncheon floor were of braided rags, gay and spotlessly clean.

"What's that, Jessie Pearl?" Kitty pointed toward a bench in a corner. Some simple tools lay upon it. Beneath it was another piece of furniture, nearly completed. Jessie picked it up and smiled.

"It's a cradle, Miss Kitty. A baby's cradle."

Kitty took it from her, turning it in her hands. "It's beautiful! Look at the workmanship!" She put it down carefully. "Put my sheets and blankets on the bed, Jessie, and hang up my dresses. Mrs. Linton said that at Abernethy's store there was a register of immigrants. I'm going to look for Mr. Philip's name, and maybe I can find right away where he is. Then, Jessie—" Kitty did a pirouette twice around the tiny room. "Then—a wedding!"

"Miss Kitty—you aren't goin' on the street alone?" Jessie Pearl's face closed again.

"Why, of course! This isn't Charleston, Jessie. Main Street is only a few blocks long. I couldn't get lost if I wanted to. And it's middle of the afternoon and I'm on business. It's perfectly proper."

"I never thought to see you in a place like this, Miss Kitty— after Wildcliffe." Jessie shook her head solemnly, but she was cheered immeasurably, Kitty knew. Kitty laughed and waltzed gaily to the mantelpiece on which stood a tiny mirror.

"Find me clean gloves. And a rain parasol, just in case." She peeked in the mirror and straightened her bonnet and tucked a tendril of hair carefully beneath its net. "I declare, if I didn't know we were going to be here just a short time, I might be worried, too. It's a wild place, Indians and rain and rivers and mountains, and all! But since we don't have to stay we needn't—" The servant handed her gloves and umbrella slowly. "Now what's the matter?"

"I don't rightly think you should go out alone, Miss Kitty."

"Jessie Pearl, we've come halfway around the world. And now you do not want me to walk down a little old street in broad daylight alone. Don't tell me you have visions again. For mercy sakes—why shouldn't I go?"

"I have a feelin'," Jessie said stubbornly. She shot a quick look at Kitty and saw that she was unimpressed. "This is a wild place, Miss Kitty," she finally said, reluctantly, "men all wearin' knives and guns, open-like. . . . After you left the boat today there was fightin'. Awful fightin'."

"Who was fighting? What about?"

"That sailor Mr. Read. He's bad. He say something and that young man hit him."

"Said what? And what young man? And what has that to do with me?"

Jessie rolled her eyes meaningly at Kitty.

"Mr. Read say somethin' about you, Miss Kitty. And the young man who bowed to you—he hit him."

Kitty stood motionless, her gloved hands clasped primly before her. "Tell me at once," she commanded. "What did Mr. Read say?"

Jessie swallowed. "Well," she blurted, "he say it was funny if'n they couldn't find a place for you to sleep in Oregon City. He say he—he say he'd share a bed with you—any time."

"Jessie!"

"And then the man hit him."

"Oh!"

"They fought hard." Jessie Pearl waited, savoring Kitty's suspense. "Mr. Read kicked and gouged and the other man knocked him down." Jessie warmed to her subject and demonstrated with gestures. "Mr. Read got up again and the other man got his arm around his neck and pounded him and choked him. Finally Mr. Read didn't get up no more."

"Oh," Kitty said again, weakly. She sat down in the little rocker. How perfectly dreadful, she thought; she had been in Oregon City less than ten minutes when two ruffians were fighting because of her—and fighting in full sight and sound of half the people of the town. That awful Read! But—that young man, to make her further conspicuous by fighting with him, a rough-and-tumble fight, no proper duel. Yet, perhaps she should be grateful. She didn't know. Nothing in her careful training at dame school or the Female Seminary had taught her the proper way to deal with a situation like this. Everything in Oregon was so strange! People were so odd in their colorful dress, with faces of every nationality and voices with strange accents. Not in her most

disturbed dreams had she expected such an assemblage as that
on the river bank. That young man was indeed a puzzle. She
had meant to apologize to him for being so abrupt when he had
helped Jessie with the trunk. It was just that she had a sudden
little start of fear when she had seen that trunk, containing her
wedding gown and her strong box, in strange hands. But she had
not meant to be rude. He had stopped her apology, however,
by his quick, mocking bow. She had never been so angry at anyone in her life. And then further to complicate things, he must
fight with Read.

"Was—was anything else said, Jessie Pearl?"

"That girl, the one with the black hair and all the beads, she
was whoopin' and swearin' and yellin' somethin' awful."

That girl. Savage and beautiful and, yes, evil. She had been
standing very close to the young man, as though she belonged
with him. Kitty's back stiffened.

"And that was all?"

"The young man say to Mr. Read he'd have to learn they didn't
talk that way about ladies in Oregon. He say he beat him up
again, didn't he learn his lesson."

"Well," Kitty said, "well." She stood, straightened her skirts.
Jessie reached slowly for her own cloak. She was terrified to appear on the streets of Oregon City, but she was loyal. Kitty
smiled at her and for a minute there was between the two perfect
understanding. "Thank you, Jessie," Kitty said quietly, "but
there's no need for you to go. I won't be gone long."

◈ 3 ◈

SHE let herself out of the cottage. Nearby was the Methodist
Church and she looked at it longingly. Perhaps she and Philip
would be married there. . . . Beyond it, in front of a building on
which was painted "Horse Billiards," a group of men lounged.
Kitty took a firm grip on her parasol, and, looking neither to the
right nor left, she passed them. Their conversation had halted at
her approach, did not continue until she was out of hearing.
There were many people on the plank sidewalk that bordered
Main Street. Two middle-aged women glanced at Kitty with interest and seemed about to speak, but Kitty passed on. She saw

Pettygrove's store and Couch's, and then the brick building which had been pointed out to her as Abernethy's. She passed a stable and feed store, and her nostrils flared at the barn odor; a sign on the wall beside the open door proclaimed that horses were bought and sold there, and all kinds of Oregon currency would be received in payment—"truck or turnover or orders on the stores."

Beyond the Main Street House was a small stockade and above it flew the Hudson's Bay Company flag. There was also the Hudson's Bay Company store, Ermatinger's, as Clara Linton had told her. Abernethy's was the former mission store for "Christians" and Ermatinger's was known as the store for "heathens," but both whites and Indians traded wherever they could now that stocks were so low. Couch's, Clara had said, was supplied by Cushing and Company of Newburyport, and Pettygrove had brought a full shipload of goods himself early in the season but now was moving some of it to the new townsite at Portland.

Horses lined the hitching rail in front of Abernethy's. A small white pony bearing a silver-decorated saddle snorted as though to draw her attention. He was a beautiful little animal and Kitty put out her hand and the pony nuzzled it with his velvet lip. She patted him, delighted with his beauty and his friendliness. Behind her a woman coughed, and Kitty turned to see several pairs of eyes upon her. She turned quickly into the store.

The room was crowded. A clerk or two leaned on counters or packing cases, leisurely talking to visitors. The coming of the *Sea Bird* was apparently occasion for holiday. At one end of the room was a signboard, and hand-printed notices were posted there. Kitty moved away from the doorway and waited to attract the attention of a clerk. It was then she noticed that the big, black-haired young man who had so disturbed her was near the signboard and the girl was on his arm. He was posting a notice of some sort and as he turned, Kitty stole a look at him. His forehead was scratched; even across the room she could see the new, raw, red marks; one eye was swollen. The girl was laughing up at him but as Kitty watched the man flung the girl away and said something to her from between clenched teeth. The girl caught herself and leaned for an instant against a heavy crate, her hands behind her, her body thrust out, sinuous, angry; her skin was almost a terra cotta color and it darkened now with fury and humiliation. But only for a moment; then she tossed her head and the bangles at her ears tinkled and she was gone, flying across the store, across the walk to the white pony. The horse reared and Kitty heard the cruel crack of a whip and the girl and horse disappeared.

The man did not seem to notice. Kitty turned her back on him at once and a clerk limped toward her.

"I understand you have a register here, for immigrants," she said. "I am trying to find Philip Davis, of South Carolina. He came two years ago."

Obligingly the clerk directed her toward the ledger. He was a middle-aged man with sandy hair and as he turned the book she noticed that one of his hands was twisted and misshapen. "It's not complete, I'm afraid, ma'am. All the newcomers this year haven't signed yet. But it's a kind of guide so folks can find their friends and kin. Folks move around some, till they decide on a claim. Davis, you say?"

Together they looked through the book. There were so many different kinds of handwriting, Kitty thought, just as all the people here were so varied. Spidery, careful, trained writing, neat, precise, school-teacherish letters, awkward, laborious, large scrawls, child-like printing. There were hundreds of names and the home addresses covered every state in the Union. Now and then she came on the words *South Carolina* and she hesitated, wished she might find those folks from her home state. Illinois, Kentucky, Iowa, Missouri, Ohio; all the Eastern cities, Newburyport, Salem, Boston, New York, were well represented. Virginia, Vermont, Pennsylvania, Maine. . . . Opposite their home states were the locations of their new homes in Oregon—French Prairie, Salem, Portland, Linn City, Newmarket on Puget Sound, Whitman's mission at Waillatpu, The Dalles. Their occupations were listed, too: weaver, wagonmaker, cooper, gunsmith, farmer, ship-carpenter, millwright, lawyer, minister, blacksmith, tailoress. . . .

Some Oregon addresses had been changed. The Homer family had left Oregon City for Astoria; Homer was a fisherman by trade. James Wilson Marshall, a carpenter from New Jersey, had crossed out his Oregon address and substituted "Sutter's Fort, California."

Hurriedly, Kitty scanned the pages, and at last she found it— Philip's handwriting.

"This is the one," Kitty said breathlessly. "See—Philip Davis—he was at Fort Vancouver, and now—what is that place?"

"Nisqually, ma'am? That's the British fort on Puget Sound, north of The River." The clerk settled back to talk. "It's a Hudson's Bay post, ma'am, like Fort Vancouver, and Colville in the Okanogan, and Walla Walla and Fort Hall—only, of course, Vancouver is headquarters. If you want to get a message to him there, likely you'd better see Dr. McLoughlin at Fort Vancouver. The supply ships run from there into Puget Sound. Might be you could send a message with them. Or, of course, you could send somebody over the trail."

"Is it far—by the trail?"

The clerk considered. "Depends on what you call far, ma'am. You go up the Cowlitz to the Landing, that's from four to ten days, depending on the weather and who you're traveling with. Then overland to Newmarket—that's sixty miles more. A party of settlers went in that way this year, the Simmons party, maybe you've heard of them? They cut a road from the Cowlitz to the Sound. Took them fifteen days. Newmarket's the first American settlement north of The River and it's nearby to Nisqually. A messenger could make it in, say, ten days, two weeks, maybe, if you could get a messenger. Hard going this time of year. Cold and mud. Maybe snow."

"You are very kind." Kitty's lashes brushed her cheeks and her lips almost trembled. Two weeks to reach Philip—a month before he could join her here, even if she could get a reliable messenger! The clerk leaned across the book and patted her shoulder comfortingly with his twisted hand. Kitty steeled herself not to recoil.

"There now, Miss Gatewood," he said. She had not told him her name. "I'm sure there's some way—sa-ay!" He started across the room toward the signboard. Obediently, Kitty followed. "I thought so!" He pointed to a bulletin that had recently been posted. It was neatly lettered in a strong hand.

"*Going to Newmarket, leaving Sunday, rain or no rain, mud or no mud, Indians or no Indians,*" the notice read. "*Haul anything that can be carried by bateau, pack horse or kitchen mule—but not without pay. Freight charges, thirty cents a pound. Curt Fletcher.*"

"There's your chance, Miss Gatewood. Fletcher'll take your message. Newmarket's nearby to Nisqually, like I said."

"Who is this Mr. Fletcher?" A tiny warning bell was ringing in Kitty's consciousness.

"You mean you never heard of Fletcher?" The clerk was incredulous. "Curt's a hard-boiled, easy-shootin' son-of-a-gun," he said, with great admiration, "and he's as well known as any man in Oregon, I reckon. He's—well, ma'am, he's not a man to step off a sidewalk for nobody, includin' the British! It would take a spell to tell you the things Curt's done. He come in '41, by ship, just in time to help build the first ship in Oregon—the *Star of Oregon*. Helped some other fellows sail her to Yerba Buena in California, sold her and drove back cattle and horses—plumb ruined the Hudson's Bay Company cattle monopoly in this country. He was one of the Wolf Council, and helped start the Oregon Provisional Government and the Oregon Rangers. Some say he'll be Governor some day, when Oregon becomes a state, or Senator—if he ain't shot or scalped first. . . . When Fletcher says he's going—" he looked back at the notice—"*rain or no rain, mud or no mud, Indians or no Indians*—then by Harry, he's goin', ma'am."

"I see. Could he be the young man who was just here? Tall, and dark?"

"That's him. Big, handsome fellow. Never in a hurry except in a fight. Can carry heavier packs on a portage than any man I ever did see, but Sunset Lee—that's his partner—might last longer on the trail. Sunset's not as heavy-set as Curt, more wiry, just as tall. Curt—well, he's a hard-hitting fighter; had a fight this very day down by the river—"

The clerk stopped and he blushed, remembering the details of that fight. Kitty's level eyes regarded him calmly. Not for the world would she permit him to know that she had heard of that battle or its cause. The clerk cleared his throat, coughed politely.

"If you'd like to write out a message to Davis I'll see if Fletcher will take it," he said, finally.

"No, thank you," she said, decidedly, "I prefer to try the Hudson's Bay Company. How may I reach Dr. McLoughlin?"

The clerk looked at her with disappointment and his voice was less cordial as he replied. "There's a little sloop the Company keeps on the Willamette. It goes to the fort every few days. They keep a stockade here, with supplies. They'd take you to the fort. Might even take pay for it. . . . You could go to Ermatinger at the Hudson's Bay Company store, or to the stockade itself and find out about the sloop. Or I could send someone."

"I'll go myself." Kitty smiled at the clerk and held out her hand and he thawed visibly. "I thank you kindly." The clerk took her fingers and bowed. "Mr.—Mr.—?"

"John Homet's the name, ma'am, at your service."

"Mr. Homet. You—you didn't happen to know Mr. Davis, did you?"

He shook his head. "No, ma'am. But likely he wasn't in Oregon City long. . . . The British fort is quite gay, you might say, and luxurious, compared to what we settlers have, but some day we'll have everything you could want, here in Oregon City. For them is of a mind to stay and work for it," he finished meaningly.

Kitty left the store. Why shouldn't Philip prefer the British fort, if it were hospitable and comfortable, she wondered, indignantly. Philip had no notion of staying in Oregon, no more than she. His letters had certainly revealed his dislike of the hardships and discomforts of the settlers. She looked forward to meeting Dr. McLoughlin, for whom everyone, American or British, seemed to have high regard. She would much prefer to appeal to him than to Fletcher.

It was odd, however, how Fletcher's path and hers had crossed, she thought, from the moment she set foot on Oregon soil. She went up Main Street, toward the stockade. Well, she told herself, he was obviously a rowdy who welcomed an excuse for a brawl, and on the frontier they made heroes of men like that.

Her heart-shaped face was troubled as she entered Ermatinger's store, but her step was lighter an hour later when she started back to the Linton cottage. She did not mind so much passing the knot of men now gathered in front of the stable and feed store, and the other group before the billiard parlor. The Hudson's Bay Company men had declared they were very happy to take her to Fort Vancouver tomorrow, to see Dr. McLoughlin. The sloop would not return till the following day. They were quick to offer her the hospitality of the fort for the night. More than that—they knew Philip and spoke of him highly; a gentleman, they said. The British had found him very agreeable and he had gone to Nisqually on a Company ship, at the invitation of the factor, Dr Tolmie. He had been of help to the officers of the British warship, the *America,* now at anchor in Puget Sound.

For mercy sakes, she thought stepping along swiftly and triumphantly, in the gathering dusk. *The settlers here seem so critical of me, and the British so polished and pleasant.* The British store was much better stocked than Abernethy's also, and the Company men were well dressed in their colorful uniforms and looked well-fed and content. The American settlers were so poverty-stricken, she thought; and with the great forts of Vancouver and Nisqually—with warships and powerful guns, how great was the strength of the British in Oregon!

If there is a war, Kitty thought, as she opened the door of the Linton cottage, what earthly chance will the poor Americans have?

◆ 4 ◆

JEFF LINTON stood beside the work bench in his cabin, his hands gripping the edge. He held on till his coughing spell was past and he waited for the flood of blackness to pass over him and ebb; when his world was clear again he turned his thin, white face slowly to his wife.

"Why did you do it, Clara?"

Clara knelt beside the fire. Very carefully she removed the reflector, behind which a pan of bread was baking.

"The bread doesn't need tending. Clara, why did you do it?"

"Why, Jeff," Clara tried to keep her voice light, "it seemed such a good chance! Think of it—three dollars a night! Jeff, if she stays only a few nights we'll have money enough—"

"That's my job. To provide money, or orders on the stores."

"Sh-h. Jessie Pearl will hear you." Clara motioned toward the small storeroom at the rear of the cabin, which Kitty had thought was the kitchen. Here amid the Linton's meager supplies Jessie was trying to arrange the pallet that would be her bed.

Jeff bit his lips and turned back to the bench. He picked up a chisel, put it down again. His hands were shaking too badly to hold it. Behind him stood the beautiful bedstead he had fashioned. On it now lay not Clara's intricate patchwork quilt, which she so treasured, but a great soft puff of down and satin. Pure linen sheets, heavily embroidered, were folded over it chastely, and pillows, light as air, nestled in a froth of snowy ruffles at the head. On the wall beside it hung layers of gowns such as Jeff had never seen, gowns and furs suitable to the drawing rooms of the great cities of the East, incongruous in their elaborate richness and delicacy here in the cabin Jeff had built for Clara.

At the foot of the bed stood Kitty's trunks, and one was opened to reveal a tray full of jars and bottles. They were of milk-white glass, daintily decorated with plump pink cupids clothed only in wisps of blue ribbon and festooned with rosebuds.

"It doesn't matter, Jeff," Clara said swiftly, in a low tone. "We'll have our meals here, same as always."

"And you'll cook for her, too."

"For twenty-five cents a meal, Jeff. It's no trouble, two more. Jessie will help. It seems downright inhospitable to be charging her, but she'd have paid at the hotel, if there'd been a place for her. Jeff, it's fun, really. You'll think so, too, when you see her. She's so little and beautiful—and it is a pleasure to see her pretty things."

Clara turned her innocent young face, flushed from the fire, up to her husband. With a sudden, quick movement Jeff was on his knees beside her, his arms around her, holding her tight. Her face was warm against his cheek and her arms went around him, too, perfectly content.

"Clara," Jeff said unevenly, "some day you'll have those things, too. I'll get them for you."

Clara kissed him and drew back, laughing up into his serious, shaken face.

"Jeff Linton," she said practically, easing herself into a more comfortable position, "what would I do with things like that?" She pointed to the flood of velvet at the foot of the bed, the small white satin slippers beside it. "Or that?" She indicated a gown hanging on the rough log wall, a gown of mauve satin, low-cut and full-skirted and heavily trimmed with lace. "Would I wear it to Abernethy's store, to stand in line with squaws for black strap molasses?" She threw back her head and laughed and Jeff, despite himself, smiled slightly. She was very lovely, he thought, her beautiful, wide mouth smiling, the soft, straight brown hair framing her face.

"And where are we to sleep tonight?"

"In the wagon bed. It's all fixed. Wasn't it fortunate she brought her own bed-coverings? We have that many more for us. We'll pretend we're camping out, Jeff. It's fun, when you don't have to."

"You're in no condition to be sleeping in a wagon bed, Clara."

Jeff's face was grim again. She smoothed the lines with her strong, square fingers. "I'm strong as an ox," she declared, and scrambled awkwardly to her feet. "It's you I'm worried about, Jeff."

Jeff stood and backed away from her and leaned against the bed. His hand touched the soft velvet of Kitty's gown and the perfume from her possessions came up to him, tantalizing, sweet, thin against the rich homey odor of baking bread. His hand gripped the velvet spasmodically, crushing it. It was true that Clara was stronger than he, but he wished fervently she would not remind him of it. Resentment, unreasonable and overpowering, boiled up within him. If only she were not quite so competent and uncomplaining, if only she could bring herself to lean upon him a little. He was improving. The asthma that had made an invalid of him back East was gradually giving way to the fresh air of Oregon. Inside him he was not weak. Inside him were all the desires to work and to build, to care for Clara and their child, to accomplish great things for them here in the West, all the dreams that come to an intelligent man with health and strength. It was true that except for Clara he would never have lived to reach Oregon. But he wished he could forget it. He wished she could forget it. A man's pride was hard hit when he had to lean on his wife.

His lips were shaking and he folded them tight. He raised the handful of velvet, looked at it, unseeing at first, and then he began to notice the delicacy of it. Slowly he loosened his fingers, let the soft folds fall back to the bed. He picked up the tiny slipper and held it gently in his sensitive hands. It was so light, so small, so fragile! He put it down carefully and his eyes, soft now, and indulgent, turned toward Kitty's creams and lotions, her brushes, her clothing, the foaming ruffles of her pillows. Again the perfume came to his nostrils, persistent and delicate against the practical, yeasty odor of the bread. The door opened.

Kitty, who already had taken possession of his home so completely, stepped across the threshold, her great eyes shining, her ridiculous little parasol closed and held primly before her. She smiled at Clara and then she turned to Jeff, her hand outstretched. She did not look at him as at an invalid. She smiled up at him, trustingly and sweetly, a smile that from any other woman would have been merely polite, but from Kitty was warmly personal and appealing and vaguely flattering. Her rich, drawling voice caressed Jeff like delicate slow fingers.

"You must be Mr. Linton. I can't thank you enough for allowing me to have your cottage. I don't know what I'd ever have done if it weren't for you."

Jeff took her parasol and her gloves and he returned her smile. For an instant he forgot Clara, staring at the exquisite and helpless little creature beside him, and then the rattle of the reflector as Clara moved it from the hearth called him back. Quickly he was beside her, taking from her the heavy pan.

"I'll lift it, Clara," he said, with authority.

Clara hesitated and then she yielded. Her eyes, wide, puzzled, went from Jeff to Kitty and understanding swept over her in a great, warm wave.

"Why," she said to herself, wonderingly, amazed that she could have been so blind, "she's done in one minute what I haven't been able to do in months . . . she's given him back his self-respect." It came to Clara suddenly that the deepest injury that Jeff's illness had inflicted was to his pride. "He hates being ill, hates it because I am physically stronger. He doesn't know how badly I need him—I haven't let him see. Oh, Jeff, Jeff!"

Tenderness misted her eyes as she watched her husband's thin hands, steadier now, move the heavy pan of bread and then reach for logs to replenish the fire. "He shouldn't do that," she thought, "he'll start to cough again." But she made no move to stop him. She smiled in gratitude at Kitty, who, untying her bonnet, did not see.

◊ 5 ◊

THE skirl of the bagpipes was strong stimulant, firing her blood. To Kitty, standing just inside the great double doors, the music seemed to come from the pipes in sharp-edged, metallic ribbons, that curled into the corners of the huge room, struck the walls and bounced back, till the shining crystal, the heavy, gleaming silver, even the bone-hard smoothness of the Staffordshire china seemed to catch it and send it out again in tiny echoes. The light from hundreds of tall candles, multiplied a dozen times in twelve-foot mirrors, and the Bohemian glass lustres on the mantelpieces glittered so brilliantly that they, too, seemed instruments of sound, sending out tinkling little chips of light. The music was like the plaids the pipers wore, Kitty thought, clear and bright and geometric in pattern, a clear call to arms, a plain declaration of intent, bold and challenging and without a single waver of tremolo.

The music, the glitter, the small army of uniformed servants bearing heavily laden trays, readying the tables for the five hundred guests of Dr. McLoughlin, excited Kitty, and the familiar, delightful thrill that came to her before a great party flushed her cheeks. She had not realized how hungry she was for fun; now her foot tapped with eagerness and impatience, her eyes sparkled, and she opened her fan with a quick, practiced little flip. The wide skirts of the mauve satin dress barely swayed as she moved forward; her smooth white shoulders gleamed and her hair seemed candle-light itself.

Dr. McLoughlin was coming to greet her, offering his arm with true courtliness. The natives called him the White-Headed Eagle, and Kitty, watching him approach, erect and towering, his great snowy mane of hair reaching the black broadcloth of his collar, thought he was well named. He had a strong, handsome, unforgettable face and deep-set, intense eyes. There was no doubt that this was Dr. McLoughlin's domain and that he was in command here.

He drew Kitty toward a group before one of the great fireplaces.

"About your letter," he said, "after you have eaten, child, you must go to my study and write your message. I'll see that it reaches Fort Nisqually. Address it in care of Dr. Tolmie, the factor there."

How very kind he is, Kitty thought; with great problems on his mind, yet he has not forgotten my request. . . . He had granted her an audience almost immediately on her arrival at the fort. He had directed that she be provided with comfortable quarters and she had been taken on a tour of the post. She was granted also the great honor of being one of the few women to be invited to the festivities at the banquet hall. Usually women took their meals apart from the men of the fort, her guide had confided, but tonight the factor was entertaining most distinguished guests and he had stated with great gallantry that the presence of the beautiful American girl would add to their pleasure.

"But I fear there will be some delay," the doctor went on. "I had expected to dispatch a vessel to Nisqually immediately, but it will be two weeks, perhaps longer, before a ship goes to Puget Sound. I hope you will not be greatly inconvenienced. . . . Miss Catherine Gatewood of South Carolina, Lieutenant William Peel, Third Son of Sir Robert, Prime Minister of England; Captain Parke of the Royal Marines; Captain Henry James Warre of the 54th; Lieutenant Vavasour of the Royal Engineers—"

Automatically Kitty curtsied, murmured the correct responses. The gold lace about the cuffs of the scarlet jackets of the English officers brushed her hand as they bowed before her, their eyes admiring. Kitty was glad now for her years of schooling in the social graces. She did not have to think, to make appropriate replies to their compliments. She could hear only Dr. McLoughlin's disturbing words—that there would be a delay before her message could be on its way to Philip.

Within her was a great urgency to reach Philip quickly. It seemed to her that there were many conflicting currents surging through Oregon, and she must fight them, to prevent them from separating her from Philip for all time. There was a feeling of approaching danger, and even in the strong stockade of Fort Vancouver she felt uneasy.

Her tour of the post had been an enlightening experience. The great fort stood a half-mile north of The River, on a bench of land two miles deep. A picket wall twenty feet high surrounded the parallelogram of the fort itself and behind the stockade were fifty comfortable log houses. The shops, for carpenters, blacksmiths, wheelwrights, coopers and tinners, the warehouses, bachelors' quarters, reading rooms, the well-stocked library, the gardens, four acres in extent, the huge granaries outside the palisades, would have done credit to a royal establishment. Within the inner square, and at one end, stood McLoughlin's own house, a two-story log structure painted white, with a white piazza. Twisted old grapevines, bare now, entwined the porch and before the horseshoe-shaped steps sat two old cannon on sea carriages. A little square building like a butter-tub, was pointed out to Kitty as the prison; within a bastion at the northwest corner were mounted twelve-pound guns, and wicked eighteen-pounders stood near a small Catholic chapel in the center of the enclosure.

Around the fort were nine square miles of farm land, walled by thick forests. There were thousands of milk cows, sheep, brood mares; the orchards on the north side and the fields on the east, west and south were well-tended and extensive and the garden plots awaited the spring seeding. The warehouses, almost innumerable and of great size, seemed ready to burst at the seams with produce from the farms and grist and saw mills farther up The River. Comfort and plenty were evident everywhere about the fort and the village southwest of it, nearer The River.

The village itself was a haphazard cluster of homes and stables and public buildings, a schoolhouse and a Catholic church, a hospital and store sheds, for the company servants and their families, and at The River wharf, the *Modeste* lay, her guns unveiled. A great many Indians, stolid and slow-moving in their bright blankets, *voyageurs*, bustling clerks and bookkeepers, stiff, uniformed guards, and numerous half-breed children crowded both the fort and the village.

From many of the cottages came violin music and from the fort there was an occasional roll of drums and finally, at evening, McLoughlin's own pipers, outdoing themselves to honor the factor's guests.

"Captain Baillie, commander of Her Majesty's war-sloop, *Modeste*," Dr. McLoughlin was saying, "and an honored friend, your countryman—"

Kitty's hand slipped from Captain Baillie's to another's, a stronger hand and brown. She saw a cap of black hair, newly trimmed and carefully smoothed, bent low before her. There was something familiar in that bow, and Kitty came back to the present with a shock. The black broadcloth collar, the very broad shoulders—the man straightened and met Kitty's eyes.

"Curt Fletcher," Dr. McLoughlin continued.

Kitty doubted that she had heard aright. This could not possibly be the same man whom she had first seen on the river bank at Oregon City. This man, smooth-shaven, well-groomed, was extraordinarily handsome in a hard, bold way, and he was taking advantage of this opportunity to regard her at close range. Kitty's glance went from his unsmiling lips to his appraising eyes. There was no doubt at all that one of them was ringed with a faint welt and there was a deep new scratch across his brown forehead. Kitty started and quickly covered her lips with her fan and curtsied low, her skirts brushing the floor.

He was a very self-assured person, she thought, but she was on sure ground now. He might have had the advantage when she arrived a stranger on the banks of the Willamette. But in a ballroom, surrounded by numerous admirers, she was quite at home. She turned to an Englishman beside her and bestowed upon him her most dazzling smile. The man was a middle-aged civilian, resplendent in his narrow-waisted, swallow-tailed coat with tight sleeves which unhappily revealed the thinness of his arms. His face was thin, too, and almost chinless, and he wore glasses with gold bows and a puffed and ruffled shirtfront above a waistcoat of salmon-colored satin. He was not an attractive man with whom to flirt, but he was nearest to her. She was very aware of Curt's presence at her elbow and she caught from him a faint odor of leather, of fine tobacco, and, undoubtedly, a whiff of Jamaica rum.

"Miss Gatewood," the Englishman said, and bowed, at great risk to the tight jacket and iron-stiff ruffles, "I'd no hope that at this far outpost I would have the great good fortune to meet—"

Words failed him and he straightened again, breathless, and stared.

"To meet as perfect a—a—rose—" he stumbled on, overwhelmed.

"I disagree, Mr. Sims." Curt's voice cut across the Englishman's smoothly.

"Mr. Fletcher," Sims protested.

"She is not at all like a rose."

Kitty refused to look at him. She closed her fan slowly, waiting. How insulting could the man be? His voice was slow, as though he considered the matter very thoughtfully, but sarcasm lay beneath.

"She is—much more like a flower we have here in Oregon. It is rare and we find it seldom, but very, very beautiful. We call it a phantom orchid. It is of palest lavender and very lovely—but also a very hardy flower. It grows in the wildest, deepest wood, where no rose would ever flourish. None of your English roses would thrive where Oregon's phantom orchid does."

"Ah," Mr. Sims forced a smile, "perhaps you are right."

Kitty stood very still. "Of course I am right," Curt agreed blandly. "You British have no imagination. No imagination at all."

Kitty opened her fan with a snap.

"My dear sir—"

To Kitty's intense relief Dr. McLoughlin interrupted. His eyes were twinkling.

"I think he has you there, Sims," McLoughlin said. "None of us can deny that the Americans have great imagination. And Fletcher, perhaps, more than most."

The music came to an abrupt stop, the puffed cheeks of the pipers deflated and the big doors were opened. Hudson's Bay Company men poured into the great room and Dr. McLoughlin offered his arm to Kitty and seated her with ceremony. On her right was Lieutenant Peel and directly opposite, so that she met his eyes each time she raised her own, was Curt.

Over the room rose a steady, comfortable hum of conversation. The servants were deft, the food extraordinarily fine. The bread had been made with pure cream; canvasback duck, choice cuts of venison, baked salmon, followed one another to Kitty's plate. Fruit and fine wines were brought and the men were on their feet, proposing toasts. It was Fletcher's turn and when he stood he seemed to dwarf the others.

He's going to say something startling and insulting, Kitty thought. But instead he raised his glass and spoke with good humor.

"To every honest man, his rights; to every rogue, his halter," he said. At the door there was some commotion and a smiling servant hurried to McLoughlin. Curt threw up his head, listening, his glass poised halfway to his lips. A grin broke across his face.

"Excuse me, ladies—gentlemen—" he said swiftly and he was gone.

Dr. McLoughlin was on his feet. "An American, one whom you should all meet, has arrived," he explained. "I would like to invite him to join us."

Lieutenant Peel nodded. "By all means," he said. A murmur went around the table. From the doorway came Curt's loud, delighted shout, and a more distant, answering whoop. As McLoughlin's tall figure filled the doorway, Kitty heard a new voice, the accent different from any she had ever heard before. It had a kind of deep music all of its own, with laughter running through it.

"Dr. McLoughlin! I'm interruptin' your meal, sir. I ask pardon."

"Sunset—you're welcome, welcome! Come join us. And a hot rum to start."

"Well, I'm savage as a meat-ax, and that's no time for arguin'. Not after a long diet of fish pemmican. Curt, you're lookin' mighty wolfish!"

McLoughlin stepped back and Kitty had her first glimpse of Sunset Lee. He was a laughing, blond young giant in a blue flannel shirt and buckskin trousers. From his belt hung a knife and whetstone and he carried his rifle. Curt and Sunset exchanged a few low words and then they moved together toward the table. They made an impressive team, hard-muscled and rawhide-tough. Sunset walked like a panther, light and graceful, his moccasined feet making no sound. His face was smooth-shaven, his sun-colored hair curled long on his collar. His skin was reddened as well as browned and there were fine lines around his blue eyes and deeper lines from his nose to his mouth. He was greyhound-thin, the skin drawn tightly over his cheekbones, and his lips were cracked and swollen.

"Miss Catherine Gatewood," Dr. McLoughlin began the introductions.

Sunset stopped before her. He seemed in no way embarrassed to be in the presence of the distinguished guests, and he was completely, surprisingly at ease before Kitty. He took his time now, looking her over, his face mirroring his honest delight, and he grinned at her boyishly, with such complete natural friendliness and admiration that she could not keep from smiling back at him. He held her small hand gently for an instant and then he sighed deeply.

"I, Dad!" he said, softly, "it's worth runnin' the Cascades in the dark in a leaky canoe to see her. Miss Gatewood—what part of heaven did you come from?"

Kitty laughed. "I'm from South Carolina, Mr. Lee. By ship, the *Sea Bird*."

"South Carolina," Sunset repeated respectfully. He shook his head, as though he could not believe she was real. He had the kindest eyes she had ever seen. she thought, and the merriest.

And she had expected Sunset would be a grizzled, profane, to-
bacco-chewing mountain man, fit partner for the grinning one-
eyed pirate, Charlefour, and the frontiersman Fletcher she had
first seen in Oregon City! Sunset had a clean look about him,
decent and sincere, she decided, and she liked him at once. Curt,
on the other hand, antagonized her instantly and repeatedly, and
yet between the two men was a puzzling resemblance.

Surprisingly the Americans were not overshadowed by the elaborately dressed British. The flannel shirt and buckskin trousers
Sunset wore so naturally were as proud a uniform for him and his
calling as were the red coats and gold lace of the conventional
British. Kitty looked from Sunset to Curt and respect for her
brash young countrymen began to stir slowly within her. Why,
they are gallant, she thought, and brave. They know this fort
well, and the rich stores within it, and they are neither awed nor
intimidated. Fletcher must have brought his bateau to the dock
right under the bow of the majestic *Modeste*. Sunset carried his
rifle proudly, straight past the cannon at the entrance to the fort.
They were meeting the British here without deference or apology,
with courtesy and self-respect, on an equal footing. That, Kitty
thought, was exactly as it should be. It was a new thought to her
and it pleased her greatly.

She had never been interested in politics before. She had sat
at many dinner tables, alert to turn the conversation from contro-
versial subjects to those more suited to good digestion. But now,
at Dr. McLoughlin's table, a contradictory luxury on the frontier,
her interest in the talk was intense and she drank it in, catching,
with a woman's sharp intuition, the undercurrents and hidden
meanings. She glanced at McLoughlin. She guessed correctly
that the shrewd old patriarch had his own good reasons for bringing Curt and Sunset and the British officers together over his fine
food and wines.

Only a few hours ago, looking about the British fort, Kitty had
been completely convinced that in any contest the British, with
their much greater resources, would be easy victors. The attitude
of the English visitors echoed this sentiment. They were interested in Sunset now, politely, but their confidence in their own
superiority was not even lightly hidden. Irritation at their smug
complacency began to burn within Kitty.

A mug of steaming rum was placed before Sunset by a smiling

waiter, whom Sunset greeted by name as cordially as he had Dr. McLoughlin; Sunset inhaled the perfume of the drink slowly and deeply. About the table the guests smiled indulgently at his frank pleasure. He lifted it, nodded to his host and fellow guests and drank with the great satisfaction of a weary, thirsty man.

"I, Dad! Dr. McLoughlin, that was what I needed." He caught the eye of Lieutenant Peel. "Lieutenant Peel," he said thoughtfully. The name of the Prime Minister of England was not popular among Oregon settlers. "You came by ship, of course?"

"The *America*," the officer answered. "Captain John Gordon, brother of the Earl of Aberdeen, is commander. A fifty-gun ship-of-war."

"In The River?" Sunset asked abruptly. His eyes narrowed.

"No. The *America* is in Puget Sound. Near Bainbridge Island."

"Hm-m." Sunset lifted his mug again and sipped his drink. He held the container in both hands and looked across it at the British officers. He regarded Warre and Vavasour thoughtfully.

"Didn't I see you at The Dalles, early this fall?"

Warre nodded. "You did, sir. Lieutenant Vavasour and I crossed the continent by Red River and Fort Colville. We did a little surveying."

Sunset's eyes turned toward Curt and Curt nodded ever so slightly. McLoughlin was watching them sharply, Kitty noticed, his eyes going from the Americans to the English officers.

"Captain Gordon is not favorably impressed with Puget Sound, Curt," the doctor remarked.

Lieutenant Peel toyed with his glass. "Captain Gordon is fond of angling," he explained, smiling, "but the salmon will not rise to his fly. He declares a country where the fish are not lively enough for his sport is worthless."

The men laughed. "Perhaps the salmon are not the only fish in Oregon that will refuse to rise to the fly of British anglers," Curt suggested smoothly, "but I assure you, sir, the Puget Sound salmon, and the Columbia River salmon, too, are among the world's gamest fish."

Well! Kitty looked down at her plate. She did not think it would be polite to her English hosts to let them see the pleasure in her eyes.

"I understand you men have taken out land claims on Puget Sound," Mr. Sims said. after a little silence. Curt nodded.

"Very ill-advised," Mr. Sims announced rudely.

Sunset considered him thoughtfully. "Why?" he asked innocently. "Ain't fenced in, is it?"

Kitty suppressed a chuckle. The British exchanged glances of exasperation. The Americans were hopeless, their eyes agreed. Sims settled the cuffs of his peacock dress and sought for simple phrases that the stupid Americans could understand.

"The River is the natural dividing line, if Oregon is to be divided between our country and yours."

Curt shook his head. He, too, was pleasant, but there was steel in his voice. "We don't think so," he said. "Our claims to all of Oregon—to 54-40—are sound. Captain Robert Gray discovered The River and named it for his ship, the *Columbia*. He was a Yankee. By right of discovery we have a right to The River and the lands it drains."

"Gray penetrated The River only a few miles—if at all!" Sims declared. "Lieutenant Broughton explored The River for a hundred miles—"

"He crossed the bar with the help of charts that Gray obligingly loaned to Vancouver."

Kitty saw the flash of anger on the British faces, felt the tension increasing. Her soft Southern voice eased delicately into the conversation. All eyes turned to her and the hot tempers cooled slightly.·

"This country is so immense," she observed reasonably, "it looks like there'd be room enough for all. Surely all the land to the south of The River hasn't been settled. Mr. Fletcher—could you find no place to suit you there?"

"Ah, a diplomat," Lieutenant Peel smiled.

"A sensible question," Sims approved.

"And one that Dr. McLoughlin himself put to me many times," Curt said, and the factor bowed his great white head. "Miss Gatewood, it's an interesting story. More than one circumstance sent Sunset and me north of The River, though the doctor tried his best to dissuade us. You see, a year ago a wagon train of folks who called themselves the Independent Oregon Colony, arrived from Missouri. They intended to settle in the Rogue River valley. One of them was Michael Simmons, a miller from Kentucky. Another was George Bush, originally a Pennsylvanian. While they were crossing the plains they had many hardships, and Bush was of the greatest service to Simmons and the rest. He's as kind and unselfish and uncomplaining a man as one could ever hope to meet."

Sunset nodded in agreement. He was watching Curt warily.

"But when the company got to Oregon—about eighty wagons, weren't there, Sunset?—they found the Oregon Provisional Government would not permit Bush to settle south of The River. So Simmons and some of his friends came to this side of The River and they explored to the north and chose the site of Newmarket on Puget Sound, where Bush and his family could live in peace. Friends stick together in Oregon, Miss Gatewood, and they don't forget past favors."

"I declare! If Mr. Bush is so fine a man why wasn't he allowed to stay south of The River? Is he a criminal?"

Curt lifted his wine glass to his lips before he replied.

"George Bush is no criminal, Miss Gatewood. At least we do not believe him one. He's a Negro. Free-born—but a Negro."

Kitty gasped and her face flushed hotly. Curt's words were a direct thrust at her and he had mercilessly pushed his point home.

"Mr. Fletcher, did you not assist in passing the—er—Oregon regulation barring Negroes?" Sims inquired.

"No. I strongly favored passage of the law against slavery of any kind. I do not think, however, that Oregon can solve the problem of the Negroes by barring their doors to them. It's shortsighted, in my opinion, and a law to lash a Negro and expel him from the country because his skin is black is little better than slavery. I believed Simmons and the group with him had right on their side; I wanted to live among that kind of people, who believe in giving a man an even break."

"And your so-called Provisional Government does not extend north of The River? Then—even the settlers recognize Britain's claims!"

"This year's legislation *has* extended the Provisional Government's jurisdiction over the Vancouver District—the land to the north and the west of The River, to 54-40. We recognize the claims of no other nation to any portion of the Oregon Country. Michael Simmons is a delegate to the legislature from Newmarket. I doubt that they will disturb George Bush.

"Then," Curt continued, "when we looked over Puget Sound, we decided that was as choice a location as anything the valleys south of The River had to offer. The land is rich, as the Hudson's Bay Company has proven with its Cowlitz and Nisqually farms. In fact, it has more advantages, for our purposes, than any site to the south of The River. We like the idea of being on tidewater, on a harbor close to Oriental ports. And some day—"

"Some day I suppose you believe you will build a railroad right over the Rocky Mountains!"

A ripple of relieved laughter went around the table. Sunset and Curt grinned at each other.

"You are sure right," Sunset said calmly. "A railroad from the headwaters of the Mississippi to Puget Sound—somewhere near the forty-seventh parallel, I'd say. Down the Columbia and up the Cowlitz, likely—or maybe there's a pass to be found through the Cascade Range further north. When I have time," he said pleasantly, "I aim to look for that pass. The Indians tell me there's one called Yakima, or Snoqualmie—but the snows are heavy."

"By the Lord, I believe he means it!" Sims exclaimed.

McLoughlin laughed. "God forgive me," he chuckled, "but they do mean it. These Yankees—the first thing you know they will yoke up their oxen, drive down to the mouth of the Columbia and come out at Japan. When I tell my men to stop, they stop. When you tell these Yankees to stop they keep right on going. . . . You were indeed hungry, Sunset."

Sunset nodded, his mouth full. He swallowed and laughed. "It's been long since I ate like this, Doctor. I got used to hard fare. We traveled light and didn't stop often to hunt." His face sobered. "What I really stopped by for was to tell you the first of the Lost Company are on their way down The River. They'll be here sometime tonight—in a couple of hours, I'd say. I came by canoe and was about four hours ahead. We're mighty beholden to you, sir, for the food and boats. I, Dad, when we got to The Dalles, was that a pretty sight! Food waiting and the boats, and all the way down The River the camps you had ordered, with fires to welcome and warm us. You are savin' many a life, Dr. McLoughlin, and the people of Oregon won't forget."

Kitty saw the English officers exchange meaning looks and several stared at McLoughlin with condemnation. Let the Americans die, those looks said. Don't help them into Oregon—let the mountains and The River claim them; there will be that many less for our guns to destroy. But McLoughlin raised his head and met their gaze unabashed.

"Was the suffering great, Sunset?"

"Very great, sir. . . . It was worst for the children. There's been many a prayer said for you these past days, Dr. McLoughlin. There were twenty deaths before we reached The Dalles and more died there. There will be still more. The thirst was the worst torture. The oxen gave out first—feet ruined on the rocks, no grass, only alkali water. Then the cattle, crazy for water, stampeded and they couldn't gather them again. A hundred men hunted for seven days and couldn't find water. Finally thirty wagons drove two days and two nights and they reached a tributary only about thirty-five miles from The Dalles. The banks are straight up and down there, and they could see and hear the water and couldn't reach it, and they near went crazy. Finally they lowered a man—Tommy Dundee—on ropes two hundred feet to reach water. Dundee is a gun-totin', glory-singin' Irishman with more sand—I think he kept the whole company together.

"That's where we found them. We rigged up a rope ferry— took us two weeks to get them all across, and brought them that survived into The Dalles. It was bad, mighty bad, stoppin' for buryin's all the time. Some couldn't walk, some could barely crawl. But they kept movin'. The women didn't cry—until they got to The River and saw the boats. Then they busted into tears. It gave them hope again. They could see the end of it, at last.

"They'd been scared bad by the Indians, too. Them blasted savages left arrows in the cattle so we had to kill 'em and leave most of the meat. Indians' idea of a joke—see men kill their own stock."

The table had been very silent as Sunset spoke. Kitty leaned forward, horror and pity on her lovely face. She had never seen the face of stark tragedy before, and now that Sunset had revealed it simply and almost casually, she felt cold and weak.

"Yellow Serpent?" Curt asked.

"Yellow Serpent—and the rest of 'em. Old Lookin' Glass of the Nez Perces. Five Crows, of the Cayuses. Delaware Tom, and some chiefs of the Pend d'Oreilles and Shoshones and Spokanes— the whole lot of 'em. Yellow Serpent is trying to raise two thousand warriors among all the tribes. He's figurin' to ride into California and take Sutter's fort. He says his son, Elijah, was murdered there last year. He wants to know if the whites in Oregon will try to stop him from avengin' his son. He figures to cut us off from California, I think. This year's immigration has got him worried—too many whites came, and they don't like the looks of the *Modeste* in The River. Lookin' Glass is blood-hungry. He'd just come back from a buffalo hunt and a raid on the Blackfeet and he had fresh scalps at his belt. They're confused because the Protestant missionaries tell 'em the Catholics are wrong, and because the Catholics talk against the Protestants. And they're listenin' to Delaware Tom."

"Who's Delaware Tom?" Warre asked.

"He's a renegade Indian—and mean enough to steal acorns from a blind hog." Sunset grinned suddenly and motioned toward Curt with his fork. "Friend of Curt's," he added, wickedly.

Curt laughed. "No friend of mine. He's a Delaware Indian, Tom Hill. Well-educated. Went to Dartmouth."

"What!"

"Yes," Curt said. "I met him—informally—when I was driving cattle from California to Oregon a few years ago. Tom stole some of them."

"And Curt went out one night and stole 'em back again," Sunset explained cheerfully. "Tom's been hankerin' for his scalp ever since. Shouldn't wonder he'd get five tribes on the warpath, just to get a chance at Curt's scalp."

"Tom's been living with the Spokanes," Curt went on, unperturbed. "He's urging them to keep the whites out. He saw what happened in the lands of the Delawares, and he has a convincing argument. He's an interesting man to talk to. Speaks fine English."

"The Oregon Country is no area for settlement," an Englishman stated flatly. "For trading posts, such as this, heavily armed, yes. But not for settlement. That is where you Americans are making your big mistake. If you persist in moving west there will be Indian atrocities such as you have never seen before. Your government can't protect settlers, not this far from the States. I fail to understand how American men can endanger the lives of their women and children by bringing them into this wilderness. And apparently your government isn't interested. You've not a single fort—not even a blockhouse."

Curt leaned back in his chair, his face dark, and he chose his words carefully.

"Our fur traders did not have government subsidies, Mister, like the Hudson's Bay Company has enjoyed. That is because we are a democracy and we give special privileges to none, equal privileges to all. Had Astor had government aid, his forts would likely rival yours. But ours is a system of private enterprise—not government aid and protection for one group of stockholders in one favored company. Of the two systems, we prefer ours; the majority of the people of Oregon—some not yet American citizens—have chosen it, by vote. Nor has our government forgotten us."

Kitty saw Dr. McLoughlin make a barely perceptible movement toward a servant. Almost instantly the Highlanders were in their places, the bagpipes at their lips. Suddenly the raucous music of the pipes burst through the room and the conversation was conveniently ended.

McLoughlin rose from the table and the others followed suit.

"I thank you kindly for the meal, Doctor," Sunset said. "It's been full long."

"I know," McLoughlin answered. To Kitty, standing beside him, it seemed his voice held infinite weariness, infinite kindness. "I'll go to make ready for our guests, now. They'll be here shortly?"

"Yes, sir. All who are still alive ..."

Kitty looked up into the doctor's face, lined by the weight of his responsibilities, weathered by his twenty-odd years in Oregon, saddened at the conflict between his sense of duty to his fellowmen and the political demands of his position. He's trying to prevent war, she thought; he's doing all he can to bring about understanding between the British and Americans—who should always be at peace with one another. And he's trying to help prevent suffering among the immigrants, though the British disapprove so strongly. What a wonderful man he is!

But already there were two British warships ready to fight for Oregon—two ships, with seventy powerful guns; and more guns in the forts, behind these immense, well-supplied stockades. Kitty had not imagined the tension in Oregon; the threat of war with England was all about and over them, and that other awful giant, the Indian menace, lay at their backs, ready to strike. The

faces of the British officers were closed and remote now as Mc-
Loughlin excused himself and went to give orders for the reception of the immigrants.

Kitty bade her goodnights. Curt's handsome face was stony,
but as he turned to her again his glance grew more personal. He
took her hand and it seemed to become one with his, and aware-
ness of his touch and his strength brought pink to Kitty's cheeks.
He had indeed condemned her openly, as though to teach her she
must not question Fletcher. He had been quite ruthless, pro-
pounding his anti-slavery, anti-British doctrines. *I could never be
friends with this man,* she thought. She turned to Sunset with
relief. Despite the ordeal he had been through, the tragedies he
had witnessed, he seemed to carry no burden. He said "I, Dad!"
again, admiringly, shaking his head, still amazed at her loveliness.
He was certainly without nerves, she thought, but he was not
heartless, as Fletcher seemed to be. At home, no lady would have
been subjected to the horrors of such a recital, she reflected; but
here, in her presence, Sunset had told his story, and she felt proud
that he had not excluded her. He seemed to take it for granted
that she would have the desire to hear it, the intelligence to understand it, the courage to face it. It was a strange sort of compli-
ment, but it gave Kitty great pleasure. It was very good to be
accepted on an equal footing with men, as though a woman were
as intelligent and courageous, in her way, as they.

Sunset had seemed to take hardship and suffering for granted
and it had not affected his appetite. But when he was closer to
her she saw that his eyes were deeply ringed with shadows and
the marks around his mouth were too deep for a man as young as
he.

Kitty went to the doctor's study and seated herself at his desk.
A clerk laid out a paper and quill for her and disappeared. The
door did not latch behind him.

◆ 6 ◆

"FORT VANCOUVER," she wrote, and then, "Dear Philip—"

She stopped. She had difficulty now in recalling Philip. He was
slight, graceful, easy-going, narrow-faced, but when she tried to

remember his features she saw instead the faces of Curt and Sunset. There was a stubborn metal in these restless Oregon men, reflected in their faces and their words to the British tonight. They had not conceded a single point.

Over the desk hung a great map of the Oregon Country. Kitty raised her eyes to it, studied the sweep of the Columbia River. The Warre expedition had come to Oregon by way of that river and she followed their route with her eyes, across Canada, down the fourteen-hundred mile length of the twisting River. She found Fort Nisqually on Puget Sound, and near it the American settlement of Newmarket. How odd that settlement, the only American one in that disputed territory north of The River, should have begun because of a Negro! It was strange that the stain of slavery and prejudice stretched even into this farthermost corner of the continent and caused disputes, and queer how it kept rising to haunt her, as though she were some way responsible for the institution of slavery. She sniffed indignantly. It had been a Yankee slave-trader who'd brought the first Negroes to the South, and many a Southerner had cursed him since. She would tell that to Curt Fletcher!

Her glance dropped to the Willamette, past Oregon City, Salem, Champoeg, all the brave new American settlements that had sprung up in the rich valley in the past few years. And up the Columbia, The Dalles, beyond that, Walla Walla, and Dr. Whitman's mission, and stretching tortuously southeastward the world's longest highway of free men, the Oregon Trail.

Kitty tapped the quill idly against the paper. Actually the elegant British officers were aristocratic spies, come to determine if The River and the lands it drained were worth a war, to measure the strength of the Americans and to find routes over which an Army could be moved. Kitty shivered, thinking of the violence and suffering of that nearing conflict and the awful plans and preparations that even now were being made.

Her glance shifted to the papers on Dr. McLoughlin's desk. A stack of sketches lay there and the top one was a detailed drawing of Oregon City. It was titled "American Village" and was signed "Captain Henry James Warre." She studied it, picking out the places she knew, the church, the Linton cottage, Main Street House.

But after all, Oregon was nothing to her. She was a visitor, merely. Forcibly she brought her thoughts back to the paper before her.

"Dear Philip—"

Why should Philip be at the British fort in luxury and comfort rather than among his own people? But of course he had come only on adventure, to observe, not to take part in empire-building. Her thoughts irritatingly jumped back to Sunset and Curt, the combined strength of them. They complemented one another. They had skillfully tossed the conversation back and forth, working as a team, each supporting the other without question, holding their own against the artful British.

But I need not become involved with the problems of all these people who mean nothing, absolutely nothing to me, she reminded herself sharply. She made experimental little scratches on the paper. Wildcliffe seemed to be retreating from her, becoming dim and far away, and the only reality was the exciting here and now. It seemed to her that tentacles were reaching out from Oregon, to take her in a powerful embrace. In sudden decision she tossed the pen away from her. *I can't risk delay. I can't write him. I must go to him myself, as quickly as possible—and I WILL go, no matter what the cost! I must be with him. I must beg him to take me away from here before—before—*

There were voices outside the door and she half-listened; then, as the words took on meaning, she froze in her chair.

"Well, are you convinced now that McLoughlin is right?"

"No! The American talk is all bravado—like the Patriot War of Canada—some noise and a great deal of smoke. We have as much right to the Columbia as to the Thames or the Humber. The Prime Minister has stated it. We'll make a small meal of these Americans, and I'm in favor of hitting them harder than we would anyone else."

"No, no!"

"Compare our strength. The British fleet—sixteen ships—over four hundred guns, ready and waiting! We've surveyed the route to bring troops overland and down The River. The United States is no threat to England. Why, a war with America could be productive only of good. The States are totally unprepared for war, and we have never been better fitted. The only rival we have to fear on the Pacific Coast is Russia. We can take California from

Mexico. Then it is merely a step to embrace all of Oregon. We need not compromise, even for the territory north of The River. We can have it all!"

"I disagree. I do not think it will be that easy. I'd as soon meet a grizzly on the trail as one of these settlers. Fletcher, for instance. That man is a killer. Or Lee. As much at home in the wilderness as—"

"And they with no gun larger than a rifle? How can these whittling Americans make a proper army? Unaccustomed to discipline, chafing against any restraint—border ruffians!"

"My dear sir, you heard Lee's story of the Lost Company tonight. What did he say—'gun-totin', glory-singin'?' You should also have talked to the settlers up the Willamette, as I have done these past weeks. They are fighters, I tell you, and they will never surrender. There are intangibles to consider, sometimes more important than ordnance. There is no fiercer opponent than a man fighting for his home. And they know this country! There would be snipers behind every tree—what good would our big guns do us then? It would be like fighting shadows in the forest. They are also expert marksmen, and they know how to live off the land. I think McLoughlin is right and I shall support his views. We must urge settlement by compromise. I tell you these Americans will keep coming and nothing will stop them. Even if McLoughlin had not aided them—they would have kept coming. More would have died, there would have been more suffering, but he could not have stopped them by withholding his aid. As soon try to dam the flow of the Columbia itself! You must not underestimate these people. I tell you, they are a special breed of men."

"Stubborn, yes. But untrained, uncouth. Deerskin and calico— and Indians for college mates! The girl, however, now she's an example of the culture of the South. And what a beauty! And how out of place on the frontier."

"To that I agree. She's exquisite. . . . There is some excitement outside. It must be the immigrants have come, the Lost Company."

The voices died away. Kitty picked up the paper before her and slowly tore it into pieces and dropped them into the open fire. She let herself out of the study and hurried to her room and grabbed up a cloak. She was outside then, the air sharp and cold and damp on her face, and she was past the guard, out of the stockade, following the bobbing torchlights down the dirt road toward the dock on The River.

She was breathless and her heart pounded painfully by the time she reached The River. The pier was crowded with men and several ox-drawn carts. The flickering torchlights cast heavy shadows and made a path of silver on the pulsing water. Overhead a thin moon and scattered stars slashed the blue vault of the sky. Lanterns aboard the *Modeste* silhouetted the British ship and the sailors lining the rail. At the end of the pier towered McLoughlin, his white hair gleaming, his heavy black cape blowing in the wind. He was shouting directions and gesturing with a cane and the gold head of it caught the light like a tiny star.

The first of a cluster of small boats had scraped the pier and shadowy figures were climbing from it. The crowd parted and four men, carrying a litter, neared Kitty.

"Easy, boys."

The stretcher-bearers stopped at Fletcher's deep voice and Kitty watched him bend over the litter. He pulled the blanket from the mound upon it, revealing a face, gray and shrunken and very small, a child's face, framed by soft, curling hair. Torchlight fell upon it and the thin eyelids flickered sensitively. Another hand, more like a claw than a woman's hand, came out very slowly, touched the child's hair, and Kitty's horrified eyes left the little face and went to the woman behind the litter.

"She's still alive," the woman said, "by God's mercy." Her face was as still as the child's own. Her features seemed carved of stone and her straight hair was scraped back tight against her skull. Her eyes were enormous and sunken, and there was no light in them. But there was infinite tenderness in the rough, knotted, fleshless fingers that touched the child.

Curt motioned them on. Another woman followed and staggered, righted herself and shook her head as a British officer reached out a hand to help her.

"No, thank'ee sir," she said tartly, and Kitty was surprised to see that the woman was no older than herself. "I can walk."

There were two more litters. A woman lay upon one, a man upon another. Even in the fresh, sharp night air the stench from their bandages made Kitty's nostrils flare. Bone-faced men lifted their scant possessions from the boats, held out their hands to their wives, and together the couples marched up the path toward the stockade. The second boat discharged its passengers; a third and a fourth. The line of immigrants stretched long, moved slowly. Kitty, watching the procession, The River at their backs, the torchlights marking their way, thought, *that is the way they have come, all the long miles of the Oregon Trail, not charging, shouting, with banners flying, but marching stubbornly, on and on and on, and nothing can stop them. Nothing.*

A young man was climbing from the last boat and the torches, held high, lighted his face. He looked up at the thin, slow line of immigrants, threading its way up to the Fort, and then he turned to the *Modeste*. For a long moment he regarded the British guns and the watching British sailors, well-fed and warmly clothed against the cold and wet. His jaw thrust out and his hoarse Irish voice cut through the small sounds of The River, the lowered voices, the shuffle of feet.

"Hallelujah, Brother!" he yelled. "Sing—you Americans—dang you—sing!"

A girl opposite Kitty turned with a sudden upsurge of energy and a smile lighted her gray face. Her voice rose, pure and lovely—"What'll it be, Tommy Dundee? Rock of Ages—"

"No," Tommy called back, his eyes still on the British fighting men. "Yankee Doodle!"

"Yankee Doodle went to town—"

The girl and Dundee started the song, and it spread, up the line, and the ragged boots marked its rhythm. The rhythm seemed to swell as more voices joined in, grew louder. The two-wheeled carts on which the litters were placed began creakingly to move, the wheels turning raspingly on the gravel. Chains rattled, ox-whips cracked with a sharp staccato, and the eternal song of The River softened all the sounds and knit them together in a stirring orchestration of defiance and courage and movement—of an unbeaten people on the march. It seemed to Kitty that the repetitive drumbeat entered her very blood, pacing her own heartbeats. It was the compelling music of the unvanquished, the home-hungry, adventure-seeking people of the Oregon Trail.

A little sparrow of a girl, painfully thin, her small legs pathetic little sticks, clung stoically to her mother's hand. She was panting, and the words of the song came from her lips in short gusts; she stumbled and Kitty saw Curt stoop and gather her up. The child stiffened at first in fierce independence and then relaxed suddenly, with a grateful sigh, against the broad curve of his shoulder and chest. A small boy, his proud little towhead bright in the torch-light, marched, singing lustily, beside Tommy Dundee, and he clung stubbornly to a rifle longer than himself.

That procession, destitute, blistered, ravaged by disease, but un-dismayed, passed her, and Dr. McLoughlin followed. Kitty turned then to make her way back to the stockade. She was trembling violently and tears streamed down her face and her knees would hardly hold her; yet her feet, automatically, sought fumblingly to follow in the same steady, brave tempo of the Oregon pioneers. She stumbled in the wagon tracks and caught herself.

She felt a hand beneath her elbow, steadying her, and she looked up to meet Sunset's understanding eyes. He smiled at her, but said nothing.

The Englishman had been right, she thought. No one could have said it better. The Oregon settlers were indeed a special breed.

◆ 7 ◆

"A DOZEN hickory shirts, fifty cotton handkerchiefs, white cotton drilling—Curt, won't Dr. Tolmie let you have goods from Nis-qually?"

Curt drew a leather thong tightly about an oilcloth-wrapped bundle. He shook his head. "I doubt it, the way things are going. I'd like to take some flour—it will be spring before Sim-mons gets his mill running, and the folks at Newmarket are get-ting mighty tired of boiled wheat. But there will be some hard portages, now the rains are starting, and we'll have to cut down our loads. Need some tobacco though, and tea."

John Homet checked off another item on the list he held.

"Candle molds?"

"For Martha Sparks. Got any?"

"Some came on the *Sea Bird*. I'll get them. Where's Sunset?"

"Vancouver. Had some business with McLoughlin."

"What's this next item—slates?"

"For the Sparks children. Reason and Wealthy."

Homet laughed and shook his head. "Never will I forget those young ones," he chuckled. "Reason clutching that rooster, and Wealthy with her pullet. Did they get those chickens to Newmarket?"

"They certainly did."

"Smart youngsters, those Sparks kids. Different than some."

"Yes. Got the slates?"

Homet nodded. "Frow, adz—" The clerk began hunting through his merchandise to fill the order.

Curt was glad not to have to talk longer. Preparing for this trip was not as pleasurable as he had anticipated. He was having trouble keeping his mind on it. He was thinking of Kitty, remembering that flawless face, those blazing brown eyes, the proud lift of her chin. Curt had made inquiries about Davis; the general opinion of the settlers was that Davis was a lazy and unstable fellow, apt to buckle in a crisis.

"Mr. Fletcher."

There was only one voice like that in Oregon City, blurred and soft and rounded. Curt turned and slowly pulled off his hat.

"Good afternoon, Miss Gatewood."

The russet bonnet she wore was tied with ribbons of deep gold and it seemed to Curt that the girl was all gold, hair, glowing skin, and with flecks of gold in the dark eyes that lifted to him and then lowered. The lashes on her cheeks and the fine lines of her brows were touched with gilt. She held a little reticule in both white-gloved hands, and there were gold threads in it, too, which shone against the rich russet of her cloak.

"Mr. Fletcher, you are leaving Sunday for Newmarket on Puget Sound?"

"Yes." Her fingers clutched the reticule tightly. *She wants me to take a message to Davis,* Curt thought. He did not help her to frame the request. Her eyes met his directly.

"I want to go with you," she said simply.

"What!" Curt stared at her in disbelief. "Why, that's impossible. It's no trip for a lady—"

The pretty lips set stubbornly in an expression Curt was beginning to know well. "I understand that a number of ladies have made the trip to Newmarket." Kitty named them to press her point—"Mrs. Simmons, Mrs. Kindred, Mrs. McAllister, and later Mrs. Sparks and Mrs. Trainor and—and—" Her memory failed her. "And others since then," she finished.

"That's true. But they were hardy women, ma'am. It's a rough trip, especially this time of year. We'll take no wagons—only bateaux as far as the Landing, then a pack train. The women of Newmarket had already crossed the plains. They were used to hardships."

Kitty's chin went higher. "I am in perfect health, Mr. Fletcher, and I have great endurance. I wish to go to Newmarket, as quickly as possible. It is imperative. Your party is leaving Sunday and I must join it."

Curt shook his head. "No," he said flatly, "we'll be traveling fast and we'll have no time to stop to help a girl. You've no idea what it's like. You couldn't keep up. We've no time to lose. We've been gone more than a month. We left our cabin only partly finished. Charlefour's wife, Polly Careless, was to oversee the completion of it, with Indian labor. I don't know whether we've even got a roof on it. We have work to do this winter— lots of it. Every day counts."

"Polly—*who?*"

How like a woman to switch the subject from a clear line of reasoning to an unimportant tangent! "Polly Careless. She got her name the way a lot of other Indians do in Oregon. Flea Jack. Lousy Liz. Big Drunk. Not refined, but that's the way things are in Oregon. It's a raw country. Someone gives them a nickname that fits and it sticks. Polly's a good Indian." Curt was being as forceful as he could be with those steady brown eyes fixed upon him. "You see, Miss Gatewood—you just couldn't take it. It's ridiculous to think of it. You'd have enough in twenty-four hours, or less, and then you'd be trying to hire someone to bring you back."

Homet had come to Curt's elbow and his eyes were bulging. The settlers, Foster and Williams, had entered and now they moved forward slowly, listening with interest. Beneath the wide skirt of her gown Kitty's small foot began to tap.

"Look, Miss Gatewood," Curt said finally, determined to end this and get on with his work, "if you'd like to send a message I'll take it. I'll see that Davis gets it. I'm sure as soon as he gets your message he'll start for Oregon City immediately."

Kitty took a deep, exasperated breath. "I am quite capable of handling my own personal affairs, Mr. Fletcher," she snapped, "and I would prefer they not be discussed in public. I see," she said icily, "that you are not a man of your word. You are all—all noise and a great deal of smoke!"

Curt's hands went swiftly to his hips and then moved up and down his thighs, slowly, in the unconscious, angry gesture of a man who has been challenged and who is ready and eager to fight. He walked toward her, and Kitty held her ground. Behind Curt four more men appeared, their faces both incredulous and delighted and now one nudged another meaningly with his elbow and grinned.

"What do you mean by that?" Curt's heavy eyebrows were a straight line across his forehead as he glared down at her.

Kitty motioned toward the signboard. "You advertised that you would take anything that could be hauled by bateaux, pack horse or kitchen mule," she reminded him. "For thirty cents a pound." She paused. "I did not expect you to take me without pay."

For a long moment Curt stared at her. Behind him Foster stopped chewing tobacco for the length of that look, and then resumed again, slowly. Curt turned to the clerk.

"Get that wheat off the scales," he ordered brusquely.

Homet leaped to obey. Curt motioned to Kitty.

"Get on," he said.

Kitty's face flamed. The crowd about her had increased and men were craning their necks to see. In the background a man stood on a barrel to get a better view. There was a ripple of laughter, but Kitty ignored it. She walked straight to the scales and stepped upon them.

"One hundred and eight pounds," Homet announced, in the ringing voice of an auctioneer.

"That will cost you thirty-two dollars and forty cents," Curt said coolly, "plus the weight of your gear. You'll be the only woman. You'll want a tent for privacy?"

Kitty bit her lips. "Yes," she said firmly.

"A tent, then," Curt spoke to Homet. "You'll need heavy blankets—you'd better get those at the Hudson's Bay store. And oilcloth and boots. Do you have heavy boots?"

Kitty lifted her skirt a trifle and thrust out her foot. She was wearing her storm boots, delicate, fur-trimmed. She glanced from them to Curt questioningly and again Curt met her eyes. The anger died from his own and he looked away and did not speak for a minute. Someone guffawed.

"Shut up!" Curt muttered. The innocence in the girl's face, the slim foot in the dainty, foolish little boots had stirred him oddly. "Look," he said, exasperated, "I'll get your boots. Don't take more things than you have to. There won't be room for luxuries—just the barest necessities. Ask Clara. She'll tell you what to take."

Kitty opened her reticule and took some money from it. "Here is fifty dollars," she said, and handed it to him on her snowy glove. "When you weigh my—my gear—if that isn't enough I'll pay the balance."

The coins gleamed and Kitty waited, determined. Finally Curt took them and dropped them into his pocket. There was complete silence as Kitty turned then and marched from the store.

The silence continued until the last fold of the swaying, russet-colored skirt had disappeared. Someone's long, low, expressive whistle broke the quiet.

"Well, I'll be damned," Homet said finally.

"Need a steersman on this trip, Curt?" drawled Williams. "I wouldn't mind joinin' you."

"Yeah, I'd like to take that trip myself, if my old shell'd let me go," jibed Foster.

"Allus did want to see Newmarket," remarked another, with a wink. "Cosy two-week trip, ain't it? Maybe longer?"

Curt picked up a heavy pack, tossed it on the scales. "You go to hell," he said to the grinning men.

THE WILLAMETTE RIVER WAS HIGH,
cold and leaden in the first faint light of morning. Charlefour was carefully checking the
distribution of weight in the first bateau, and
George, the Indian steersman, watched him
with sleepy eyes. Sunset stowed the last bedroll in a second boat.

"Curt, these two fellows who will be at the
first camp. They got their own grub?"

"If they don't they'll starve to death. I didn't offer to feed
them. . . . They've been hiding out across The River for three
days now."

"All right. We'll put them in this bateau. The river's rising
fast. 'Morning, Dr. Manning. Out pretty early, aren't you?"

Thomas pulled a heavy woolen shawl from his face and his
breath came like smoke.

"Yes, a bit early," he puffed. He put a big mittened hand on
Curt's arm. "Wanted to wish you well, men. And," he glanced
around surreptitiously, "thought you might need this."

"A medicine kit, Doctor?"

"Yes. Not for you. You'll never need it, Curt. But with Miss
Gatewood, well, you can't tell—accidents—fever—"

"Sure you can spare it?"

Thomas fumbled with the small wooden case. "Yes, yes. The
Sea Bird was stocked rather well with medicines and Captain
Craig shared a little with me. Look now. There's blister plasters,
rhubarb, calomel, elder flowers, spirits of hartshorn, a few bandages. Tell her not to bathe when she is exhausted."

Curt grinned slightly. "Dr. Manning, she'll bathe when she
dam' well pleases. No one tells that girl anything."

"Give this kit to Martha Sparks when you get to Newmarket. She might have use for it. And for you, Curt, and Sunset—" again Thomas looked over his shoulder guiltily, "a little—er—medicine—"

Curt opened the brown flask and sniffed. He looked at the label. "Apply as needed," he read. "Thanks!" He passed the bottle to Sunset and Sunset smelled it and laughed.

"Strictly for medicinal purposes, men," Thomas warned. "I'm allowed to prescribe only half a pint of whiskey at a time for each patient—but in this case—I made a little exception." He coughed.

"Mighty thoughtful of you, Doc."

"Here she comes."

Kitty, accompanied by Jeff and Clara and trailed by Jessie, was coming down the bank. The bonnet framing her face was of white fur and Thomas searched her face keenly. She was as composed as if she were starting off on a week-end expedition to Charleston, Thomas thought. She glanced at the boats and at the river, at the Indians and Charlefour, but if she were excited about embarking on this expedition she did not show it. She held out a little fur-mittened hand to Thomas and his big one swallowed it.

"How nice to see you, Dr. Manning!"

"I couldn't let you go without wishing you Godspeed," he said gently. He had intended giving her advice and warnings, but now, facing her, he decided only on "Godspeed."

Sunset took the packs, stowed them away. Kitty turned to Jessie Pearl. "You are to be helpful to Mrs. Linton," she ordered. The girl bobbed her head. "I'll be back—likely in a month. I think we can go home on the *Sea Bird*. Jessie, don't cry!"

"Miss Kitty—"

Kitty patted Jessie's shoulder. "I'll be all right, Jessie Pearl, I promise you, and so'll you." She brought her lips close to Jessie's ear. "And please, Jessie, guard my things carefully."

Jessie Pearl wept louder.

"Good luck to you, Miss Gatewood."

"Thank you, Mr. Linton. It is good of you to come this morning."

"You'll be all right," Jeff said. "Curt and Sunset will take care of you. They have a fine crew. There's no better boatman in Oregon than Charlefour."

"Give my love to Martha and the children," Clara said. She stood close beside Jeff and Kitty took her hand. "And I do hope you find Mr. Davis quickly and—and you are very happy."

"Thank you." For a minute the two girls stood together and then impulsively Clara bent and kissed Kitty's cheek.

"Ready, Miss Gatewood?"

Kitty pressed Clara's hand and turned toward the bateau. She felt warm and happy at Clara's kiss. She had made friends in Oregon—the Lintons and Dr. Manning, and, yes, Sunset. She took the seat Curt designated, but it was Sunset and Jeff who bent over her, shifting the bedrolls about her to give her greatest comfort.

Charlefour stood in the bow, his paddle ready, and Indian George, the steersman, took his place in the stern.

"Wait," Curt said suddenly. His ear had caught a familiar sound and he stared up toward Main Street. Sunset moved near to him.

"Lisa?"

Curt nodded. The white horse came into view, racing toward them, and the group beside the river exchanged glances. Clara began to talk animatedly to Kitty. Curt strode up the bank and stopped Lisa a few rods away.

The girl slid from her horse and the animal whirled, shielding Lisa and Curt. Kitty heard a cry "Oh, Curt!" and then Curt's voice, the words indistinguishable, and Lisa's muffled sobbing. Kitty kept her eyes carefully on Clara's face.

How perfectly disgraceful, Kitty thought, shocked and unreasonably angry; to keep us waiting while that girl— She heard a tiny tinkle of bells as Lisa moved in Curt's arms and the white pony tossed its head and set an echoing little shower of notes down the bridle reins.

Curt was back and the boat began to move. Lisa stood helplessly beside her horse. Her face was a mask of misery as her eyes feasted on Curt, and then, belatedly, she noticed Kitty and fury tensed her body. She spat out some evil exclamation and Thomas whirled on her with a sharp command.

"Watch your language, Lisa! For shame—and this the Lord's Day!"

The boat moved into the current smoothly and was river-borne. Charlefour's paddle flashed first at this side, then at that, sending back signals to George at the rear. Curt and an Indian oarsman settled into their places. Behind them Sunset's bateau slid out into the stream and Kitty heard the last calls of good-by from the shore.

They swept downstream then, feather-light despite their burden, and Kitty thrilled with the swiftness of their passage. Curt's broad back was toward her and only now and then did she catch a glimpse of his profile as he turned to right or left. What was it about the man that made her so aware of him? He was everything she despised. That half-breed girl, Lisa Le Seuer, was his mistress; Kitty was certain of it. And it was the attention of white men like Curt to Indian girls which made the savages take liberties with white women. Kitty had only searing contempt for any white man who associated with a girl of another race; of all Margaret's teachings that had impressed Kitty the most. It was an insult to all white women, and not to be condoned.

Yet Curt was respected in Oregon, and greatly admired. . . . It made it even more necessary, then, that girls of culture and good breeding be punctilious in their conduct, when they were on the unconventional frontier. That, at least, she could bring to Oregon. Though now, until she reached Newmarket, she was dependent upon him, she must be careful in all their dealings to be very dignified, very formal, and to let him know by her manner that she strongly disapproved of him.

The light of the morning was strengthening and Kitty settled back, knowing she must save her strength for the long days ahead. She felt at her neck for the little chain that lay against her flesh, and was reassured when her fingers found it, and followed it to the keys upon it. She ran her hand into the concealed pocket of her heavy skirt, touched a chamois purse and felt the weight of the coins within it.

The decision to take the money with her had been a difficult one. She had lifted her strong box from her trunk and had carefully counted her money. She had removed one-third of her treasure—five hundred dollars of it, and put it in the purse. The rest she had left in the box, which she had unlocked, and put in the trunk beneath her wedding gown. The key to the box and the trunk were both on the chain about her neck.

She would need money to hire a canoe to take her from Newmarket to Nisqually and to pay for her accommodations there. She had tried to prepare wisely for every possible contingency.

Thinking over her preparations she decided she had done well.

The boots Curt had bought for her felt awkward and heavy, but her toes, in the heavy wool stockings within them were warm and comfortable. The air was cold and damp on her face, and the sky was muddy gray, the river higher than it had been a week before. But the skill of the boatmen, the perfectly balanced little craft, gave Kitty a feeling of security she had not anticipated. Her buoyant young spirits rose in triumph for again she had had her way. Excitement warmed her and the speed of movement delighted her. They swept about a bend in the river and Charlefour, poised and tense, signaled unerringly, and Indian George responded. Charlefour's great voice rose suddenly, happily, in rhythmic river-music. . . . *"Sur la feuille ron-don-don-don—"*

After a long time Curt glanced at Kitty. Her face was alight, her magnificent eyes shining with pleasure, her cheeks rosy against the white fur that caressed them. She was happy now, he thought, almost angrily, supremely happy, because every hour brought her nearer to Philip Davis. And she was depending upon Curt, whom she openly despised, to take her.

◆ 2 ◆

THEY had passed Deer Island and Sandy Island and a multitude of smaller ones, and finally they had come to the mouth of the Cowlitz. They came close enough to Coffin Rock so Kitty could see the war canoes placed high on decorated scaffolds in the cottonwood trees, their sharp prows pointed west.

"Every paddle is in place in those canoes," Curt told her. "They wrap the dead in furs and put beads and trinkets with them. They put them in their war canoes so they will be ready for the flood of life they think will come one day with the tide. The land of the dead is *Memaloose Illahee*, in the direction of the setting sun. They point the canoes westward, so the spirit can find its way."

Then the real labor had begun. They turned northward to enter the Cowlitz, and they fought their way against its current. Early darkness crept upon them as they left The River. Kitty felt a sense of accomplishment that the tiny boats had successfully ridden upon the Great River of the West, crossed it safely and come at last into the Cowlitz. The Columbia was so immense, dwarfing its tributaries, and it rolled on, so relentlessly, to the sea. Kitty was cold and cramped and weary when at last they came to their night's camping place.

The bank was spongy and muddy and Kitty sank deeply into the mire as she stepped ashore. She understood now why Curt had insisted on the heavy boots, and she had to raise her skirts to keep them from tripping her as she struggled through the mud. The men stretched their tired arms, walked up and down to ease the muscles in their legs, and fell to making camp. Curt had not offered to help her from the boat. He had been courteous enough in pointing out landmarks along the way; but he had no intention, she saw, of exerting himself to help her. And that, she thought heatedly, as she scrambled up the bank, through a high wet tangle of ferns, was exactly the way she wanted it. She had no wish to be beholden to him.

She was glad when at last her tent was raised and she could escape into the privacy of it. Outside the campfires leaped high, and from within the tent she could see the men unpacking, hear the clink of the metal cups and plates they were bringing from their food kits. A load of evergreen boughs had been cut for her bed, and the fresh, clean, pungent smell of them filled the tent. Her bedroll had been tossed upon them and Kitty looked at it helplessly. The boughs were wet, the ground beneath her feet was soggy and the damp cold seemed to penetrate her very bones. She was hungry. She felt dirty and she thought longingly of Jessie Pearl, of a hot bath, of warm towels, of a soft bed and a heavily laden tray. She sighed wearily, dragged the bonnet and net from her hair and rubbed her aching forehead.

"Miss Gatewood?"

She pulled back the flap of the tent. "Yes, Mr. Fletcher?" Her voice was very cool.

"Do you know how to make a bed?"

"I can manage."

"Have you ever made one? In camp, I mean. There's a trick to it."

"I have never made a bed in or out of camp, Mr. Fletcher, but I don't think it can be very difficult."

For answer Curt entered and silently unrolled her blankets. He took the oilcloth from about them and spread it over the boughs. He put a fur robe on top of it, then two blankets, and rolled the entire bed in a large tarpaulin, forming a snug bag. He worked deftly and swiftly.

"Thank you," Kitty said when he had finished.

"Don't thank me. From now on you can do it yourself. I just don't want you to sleep cold and get sick, that's all. It would delay us. . . . There will be hot food shortly and after we have eaten you can have hot water if you want it. Dr. Manning said to tell you not to bathe when you are exhausted. It's some theory of his—take it for what it's worth. I'd advise you to try to sleep as quickly as you can. We'll leave before dawn."

"I won't delay you, Mr. Fletcher," Kitty snapped. How hateful the man could be! Unmoved, he looked at her mud-caked boots.

"Are they comfortable?"

Kitty's patience gave way. Even if they were making blisters as big as silver dollars on both heels she wouldn't tell him.

"As comfortable as anything in this frightful country can be!"

Curt paused in the tent door. The firelight behind him silhouetted his big frame, his dark head. His face was in shadow.

"You hate it, don't you?" he asked in a low voice.

"Every inch of it!"

He dropped the tent flap behind him, leaving her alone. She wanted to cry with exasperation and weariness, but she fought down the sobs in her throat. She tugged at the fastenings on her roll of clothing and finally she managed to free them, though her fingernails were broken in the process. He could have done that much for her, she thought, furiously. She found a brush and she let down her hair and began to brush it awkwardly, wishing for Jessie Pearl with every stroke. She twisted it to a shining, loose knot at the back of her neck and pinned it there. She wiped her face and then, more composed, left the tent.

Sunset handed her a steaming plate of food and she took it in both hands and sat upon a fallen log. The fire felt good on her face. She took up a fork and started to eat, and then she heard the disgusting sound of a man wolfing his food and she hesitated. Indian George was eating meat with his fingers and the unpleasant noises he made disturbed her greatly. She picked up the fork again, and again she stopped, as Charlefour's noisy coffee-drinking came to her ears. Her glance slid around the circle of men and she caught Curt's amused eyes on her. Her face flushed and stubbornly she began to eat.

"It's good," she said to Sunset.

"Ever eat venison before?"

"Is that what it is?"

"Yes. Charlie got it yesterday. You know, on the trail, Miss Gatewood, a person can eat much more than he can at home. We always figure on twice the usual amount of food for the people in the wagon trains. And the Hudson's Bay men, the *voyageurs*, like Charlie used to be, when they were on The River all day, they'd eat six pounds of meat a day apiece. We'll have hard goin' soon—portages. The Cowlitz is high and there are plenty of rapids and you'll be walkin' a good deal. So don't be surprised if you have a real appetite, too. Eat plenty."

She liked his steady, quiet voice. She accepted the coffee he offered and drank it gratefully. "Pretty beat?" he asked. She shook her head stoically. Her eyes felt heavy and the pleasant warmth of the fire was slowly stealing through the heavy boots. "Takes a little while to get used to it," he said comfortably. "We're expectin' two more men to join us here, Miss Gatewood, so if we have a couple of strangers here in the morning, don't be surprised. Or perhaps they aren't strangers to you. A couple of men who were aboard the *Sea Bird*."

"Joining us here? But why?"

"They're leavin' the ship. It's easier to get lost for a while north of The River—fewer settlers. So the men who desert the ships in The River stay to the north till the ships sail."

"But that's dreadful! Mr. Lee, why are you helping them?"

"Well, it's all in the way you look at it, ma'am. I know—you believe when a man signs to complete a trip he's bound to fulfill his contract. That's right. Man's word's no good, he's not much of a man. But often the men on the ships aren't there of their own will. Some of the best men in Oregon are off ships. Curt, for instance."

"Curt? Mr. Fletcher? He's a deserter?" I might have known! her tone added.

"The ship captain would call him that. He was shanghaied and put aboard the ship, the *Mary Lane*, out of New York. He left her in The River. He never signed with a shipmaster, Miss Gatewood. If he had, he'd have stayed with it. He's that kind of man. . . . These sailors from the *Sea Bird* figure to stay in Oregon. They asked to join us. We need Americans in this district so we're taking them with us as far as the Landing. We figure a man has a right to be free."

"But you, Mr. Lee, you didn't come by ship?"

"Will you call me Sunset, ma'am? Seems more friendly."

She could not take offense at his friendly, open grin. She smiled. "All right, Sunset. Is that really your name?"

"Not rightly, but it seems so, I've carried it so long." He stretched his long legs before him, cocked an eyebrow quizzically. "My Pa was named Daniel, and his father before him. They were Old Dan and Young Dan, and I grew so big they couldn't rightly call me Little Dan, now, could they?"

Kitty agreed, and the dimple appeared in her cheek. Sunset regarded her appreciatively. "And it didn't look like my grandad was ever goin' to die—reckon he's livin' yet. . . . So some way they began calling me Sunset. Cause all I could think of was goin' west."

Sunset bent toward the fire and expertly sought a coal to light his pipe. "Mind smokin', Miss Gatewood?"

Kitty shook her head. "You forget—I come from a tobacco state. . . . Would you—would you call me Kitty? My friends do."

His eyes twinkled and he looked at her a long time through the smoke before he answered. He took the pipe stem from his strong square teeth. "You musta got that nickname when you was mighty small," he said.

"Why?"

"We-ll, now, ma'am, I'd say you sort of stand folks off from a nickname. . . . But I'll be mighty proud to call you Kitty."

"You didn't tell me how you came to be in Oregon."

"Pa was a free trader. When I was small we lived in Illinois, then Missouri. Seems all the time I was waitin' for Pa to come home. He was a wanderer, and I guess I got itchy feet, too. . . . When I got big enough, thirteen, fourteen years old, I guess I was, he took me with him to the Rendezvous at Pierre's Hole. You don't know what the Rendezvous is, do you?"

Kitty shook her head and the dimples deepened. "I'm very stupid, I guess, Sunset. All this is very new to me."

"Reckon things back where you come from 'd be mighty strange to us, too," he said, politely. "Well, every year the fur traders met at Pierre's Hole. They come in from the mountains, from the north and south and west with their year's supply of pelts, and they met the buyers there and sold their furs and celebrated. It was a great show, Kitty, and a wild one—I, Dad! Pierre's Hole was the Rendezvous for the Rocky Mountain Fur Company—and there were others, where the Hudson's Bay men came, and the Free Traders. It wasn't an easy trip from Independence—that's in Missouri—to Pierre's Hole, and we were short of water and rations, but I remember how tickled I was to be headin' west. I met the men I'd heard about there at the Rendezvous—Sublette, and Kit Carson and Joe Meek and Black Harris. Mountain men. Seems I couldn't get it out of my blood. I just couldn't turn around and go *east* again."

Sunset's eyes had a faraway look and he was smiling, remembering. "Pa finally let me trap with him that winter, and the next. Taught me a lot about Indians and tradin' and such. I kept hearin' more about Oregon. It seemed to get into me, like a sickness, till I plumb had to see it for myself. Came a time I was old enough to prowl alone and finally I come west. Come through the Blackfoot country, and had my fill of Indian fightin', got to the Snake River after a while, then headed back for the Rendezvous. . . . But the next year I come all the way. I got across the Blue Mountains and to Fort Walla Walla.

"It was at the Cascades, three years ago, about forty miles up The River from Fort Vancouver when I first saw Curt. There was two other fellows with me and we were tuckered out. We had to portage at the Cascades, of course, and we'd made camp and was fixin' for a good night's sleep. Nest of river pirates, Cayuse Indians, jumped us. Our own dang fault. We'd got careless, bein' tired after a tussle with The River. We couldn't take to The River—not there. They had us penned in for sure, and we were almost out of powder and shot. Closest spot I've ever been in." Sunset was laughing now, and he rubbed the back of his neck slowly. "I could dang near feel that scalpin' knife. Then all of a sudden there was shots comin' from the left of us, and a couple of white men crawled into camp. They were Curt and Charlefour. We was too busy to talk any then. Curt handed me a powder horn and we both went to work, back to back. When it was over we turned around and introduced ourselves. Curt and me been together most ever since. . . . I value him, Kitty. I value him mighty high."

Kitty was quiet. She felt at ease with Sunset, but she did not agree with him. She did not value Fletcher. Sunset sensed the antagonism between her and his partner, she thought, and he was trying, with the kindness inherent in him, to explain his friend to her. She smiled slightly.

"Is there anyone you don't value high, Sunset?"

"Well, I don't rightly think there's many," he said thoughtfully. "Most people, if you know them well enough, or you know enough about what makes them so all-fired ornery, then you like them in spite of it. Or you understand them, anyway. There's a few, I reckon, I never could care for. One of 'em is a white man, Frenchman, name of Le Seuer. Bull Le Seuer, they call him. Him, I don't like. He's mean. It's born in him. He's no earthly good. I reckon he's the worst scoundrel unhung."

"Le Seuer?" Kitty repeated the name thoughtfully. "I've heard—oh!"

Sunset was not surprised that she suddenly recalled Lisa's name. He nodded. "Le Seuer was a Hudson's Bay trapper for many years. He works on the company farms now, sometimes at Cowlitz Farm, sometimes at Nisqually, sometimes at Vancouver. The farms are run by the Puget Sound Agricultural Company, but that's just a part of Hudson's Bay. . . . Well, Le Seuer is the kind of hunter who kills for the fun of slaughterin' things, not for pelts alone, nor meat. He'd skin an animal before it's full dead. He took an Indian woman and abused her and pleasured in doin' it and his torture finally killed her. Lisa is their daughter. She's a wild one—but knowin' what she come from, you'd expect no different. She stood up to her father. She was just a little thing when he took an ox whip to her and she flew straight at him with a knife. Le Seuer still wears two guns, but the right one's just for show. He can't shoot right-handed any more. Lisa cut his right hand across the palm and it healed stiff; she slashed his wrist and he like to bled to death. He likes to tell about it. He's right proud of her. You see, Kitty, a body doesn't know what kind of woman Lisa'd be, if she'd had a different kind of life. . . . She's had some hard things, too, full hard, for a woman." Sunset stopped abruptly, leaned back, stared up at the sky, narrowing his eyes against the pipe smoke. "Then there's Delaware Tom," he continued, after a while. "He's savage and cruel. But he's smart. More book-learnin' than I have, by a long shot! He's powerful bitter, but sometimes I think Tom's got a lot of right on his side.

I don't rightly value Tom, but I don't rightly hate him, either. Maybe we done the Indians a long wrong."

From across the campfire came the first notes from a fiddle. Charlefour was tuning up.

"Never see a *voyageur* without his fiddle," Sunset said. "Charlie spent seventeen years with the Hudson's Bay Company. Worked for seventeen pounds a year. Finally married Polly Careless and quit the company. He's no farmer and he likes Curt, so he stays with him." Sunset stood. "We have visitors. Indians. Ha! Dick Tom and his pals. *Klahowya, tilicum.*"

Into the circle of the firelight came three Indians and Sunset went to meet them. Two were middle-aged men and one was young and slim and strongly built. Their attention focused on Kitty and talk in Chinook began. Kitty sensed that she was the subject of the conversation but she could understand no word of it. Curt turned once and glanced at her. She took a pot of hot water from the fire and carried it to her tent.

Hurriedly she prepared for bed and finally she slipped into the cocoon that Curt had made for her. She lay in the soft darkness, listening to the men's voices. Through the crack in the tent-opening she could see their figures about the fire. The Indians squatted on their heels and Sunset and Curt sat near them, and the conversation went on and on. Drowsily, Kitty watched, and the hum of their voices lulled her near to sleep. She was not afraid. She was not easily frightened and, with the blind confidence of the privileged, she was calmly certain nothing unpleasant could happen to her. . . . To others, perhaps, but not to her. . . . Charlefour put his violin away. She hoped that tomorrow night he would play again, those rolling, gay songs of the *voyageurs*.

She was almost asleep when she saw Curt and Sunset rise and stare into the darkness. She heard new voices. She rose on her elbow to see the newcomers, likely the two sailors who had deserted the *Sea Bird*. She was not sure yet that she approved their desertion. She had to think about that awhile longer, when she was not so tired. There seemed to be many things accepted in Oregon which were contrary to everything she had known in the past.

One of the newcomers came into the firelight. She recognized him as a surly foremast-hand by the name of Evans, and then a

bulky, thick-necked man rolled into the circle of light and Kitty
caught her breath in surprise and displeasure.

Of all the men who had been aboard the *Sea Bird*, the last one
whom she had expected to see in this camp was Lige Read.

◊ 3 ◊

EVERY step was torture. The first portage, in early morning, had
not been difficult, for Kitty's healthy young body was rested and
fresh. Nevertheless, she had sighed with relief when at last the
bateau was launched again, above the rapids. But now, in late
afternoon, after a long, cold wet day, when again they took to
the river bank, she had to call on all her strength to keep going.
The mud dragged at her feet, branches whipped her face, scratching her soft skin, showering her with wet; ferns clung to her skirts
and her breath came hard and painfully as she climbed over immense fallen logs and ploughed through matted underbrush that
sometimes almost hid the Indian trail. She could feel her strength,
never fully tried before, draining from her. Even with their bur-
dens the men seemed to move tirelessly, and Kitty, determined
not to lag behind, drove herself mercilessly to keep the pace.

Sunset and Charlefour led the way with the Indians and bateaux, Lige and Evans followed, and Kitty trailed them, with Curt
bringing up the rear. Darkness was coming and the never-ceasing
sound of the raging river drummed in Kitty's ears. The rain came
intermittently and the wind moaned and wailed in the treetops,
two hundred feet above.

At midday they had stopped to eat; "nooning," they called it.
Kitty had been ravenously hungry, even for the cold meat and
hard biscuits. She had thought she could not possibly rise again,
once she had sunk to the ground to rest, but the food revived her
and the cold drove her to movement. She had caught a few low
words between Sunset and Curt and anger at Curt stiffened her
determination.

"Hadn't we better take it slower, Curt? She's not trail-broke
yet. She's apt to give out."

"She'll make it. It won't hurt her. Do her good."

The march was resumed. Not once during the long hours had
Curt offered his hand to Kitty. For a while she attempted to keep

the men ahead of her in sight, but as night crowded them the men swung on, eager to reach camp, and despite her efforts the distance from them widened.

Weariness made her step uncertain. She stumbled and put out her hand to catch herself and a sudden, violent pain pierced her palm. She smothered a cry, but, hearing Curt behind her, she pulled herself to her feet. She leaned for an instant, panting, against the great, rock-solid trunk of a tree. A sharp-pointed stick had pierced her mitten and her hand and she tried frantically to jerk it out. It broke in the flesh and the agonizing pain of it blinded her and she closed her eyes.

Curt spoke near to her. "It's only about a quarter-mile farther," he said. "It's better to keep moving, or you'll get chilled and stiff. The wind is increasing. We may be in for a storm."

Kitty made no move, waiting for the sick pain to stop, for her head to clear. She heard Curt swing his pack from his shoulders, drop it to the ground beside him. The wind mourned and a shower of rain came through the swaying branches. She began to shiver uncontrollably and she gritted her teeth stubbornly to stop their chattering.

"Look," Curt said brusquely, "have you had enough? You don't have to go on with this. I'll send you back. . . . I've been figuring on it. It's a long way to Newmarket. Only two days back to Oregon City."

Kitty's eyes flew open. He was standing easily, unwearied, and she was envious of his strength and angered at her own pain and weakness. "No, I won't go back! And you needn't be so hateful!" she flared at him. She glanced scornfully at the pack beside him. "I notice the rest of your freight isn't expected to walk!"

He stared at her for the space of a breath and then in one smooth, effortless movement he swept her up into his arms.

"I didn't mean—I didn't mean—" she protested breathlessly, "I can walk. Just give me a little time—just—"

His arms were like steel and now they tightened about her. In the fading light she could see his face, dark and intense, very near her own, and a flame had kindled in his eyes. He held her easily and he stood motionless, considering her.

"Put me down, Curt," she demanded, "put me down."

"Kitty," he said, "be quiet, Kitty."

The warmth of his low voice, his nearness, the vital, virile strength of him shook her, but she put her uninjured hand against his shirt and pushed away from him and forced herself to speak in her firm, normal voice.

"I will not be quiet. Put me down at once, Mr. Fletcher," she commanded again. "I am depending upon your sense of honor and decency to—"

He stared into her proud, angry little face and suddenly he laughed. "And yet you believe I have neither."

"I am not afraid of you, Curt Fletcher."

"No," he said slowly, "no, Kitty, I don't believe you are."

Curt's lips were so close to Kitty's he could feel their sweet warmth and he was not used to self-denial. The dark intimacy, the silence, the aloneness of the forest encircled them, and Curt held the beautiful, rounded, tired young body close. Kitty did not fight him. Her shining eyes, scornful, unfrightened, framed by their extravagant lashes, were wide open and she was passive, wooden. Her indifference challenged and excited him more than would either resistance or quick response. He would experience the full joy of awakening her, he thought, and he knew that if once the dam of Kitty's self-control were broken all else would pale in intensity.

His lips touched hers and he waited, curiously, deliberately, for some slight response, some sign of weakening. His skill at love-making was great and he was used to quick conquests. But Kitty's lips did not soften beneath the first light, experimental touch of his, her rigid body did not relax to fit his own. He drew back and their glances clashed like swords and anger darkened his face. Kitty heard his low, fierce exclamation and then his lips were urgent and demanding, punishing and bruising her own.

He released her finally and Kitty stood stonily, too proud to speak. Neither did she raise her hand to strike him, as another woman might have done—a futile gesture that would have pleased him, for it would have been a familiar feminine response. Curt put his hands on her shoulders, and his fingers bit into her flesh, and they faced one another for a long moment.

He would not accept defeat. She realized that as she studied his face, angry with frustration. He was used to taking what he wanted by force, but from Kitty, in the taking, he had received nothing. Yet that failure had only whetted his desire. Until that moment Curt had not made his decision, but now he spoke and his words were a promise.

"Yes," he said coolly, "yes. I want you, Kitty. You are going to belong to me."

"No." Her furious voice was as determined as his own. "I loathe you, Curt Fletcher. More now than, ever before."

"I want you, Kitty," he repeated, undisturbed. "And I make it a point to get what I want."

"And that, Mr. Fletcher, is not enough. *I* do not want *you*. You seem to forget, also—or perhaps in your code, or lack of one it makes no difference—I am promised to Philip Davis. You are paid to take me to him."

He laughed. "Davis?" His tone dismissed him as of no consequence. "I'll take you to see him. But you won't marry him, Kitty. You'll never marry anyone—but me."

He turned to pick up his pack and Kitty marched ahead of him, along the trail. She cradled her throbbing hand against her breast. Her thoughts were confused and racing. She had never seen fierce, frank hunger in a man's eyes before, never realized the primitive power of it. The wildness of Oregon was in this man, and, like the country, it held a fascination as well as a danger. She remembered Philip's kisses, carefully controlled. After all, she thought, a man of Philip's breeding would never be so coarse and terrifying. . . . And she thought also of the stolen caresses of other young men she had known. But they were nothing like this. The touch of their lips had never stirred her as had Curt's hard embrace. He stood for all the things she despised, the lax morals, the crudities, the rough hardships of the frontier, and he had taken advantage of her position as no gentleman would; and yet, for the briefest instant, he had stirred in her deep-buried, disturbing emotions she did not know that she possessed.

This awful, frightening, beautiful country overpowered people, she thought. It made them or it broke them, coarsening them, crushing out the last fineness in them, brutalizing them. Or it refined them, like Sunset, whetted their senses to razor sharpness, taught them tolerance and love for their fellowmen. There seemed to be no middle ground. Perhaps it was that Oregon, not yet veneered by civilization, still primitive, still near the days of Creation, simply revealed and intensified the qualities each person possessed. Certainly Oregon stripped everyone of all pretensions, made the strong stronger, the weak weaker, the evil still more evil.

She came at last to the campfires. Her tent had been raised and she went to it at once. Sunset had prepared her bed. She dropped upon it, the cold of the tarpaulin seeping through her damp clothing. Her hand throbbed, fatigue made wretched little drums of every nerve and muscle. But none of it compared to the turmoil within her and she lay still for a long time. She did not want to enter the frightening, wild world of Curt. She did not want her pride, her conventions, all the things that Margaret had taught her, erased by his touch. She wanted to hold tight to the safe, civilized life for which she had been trained.

And she would do it, she told herself fiercely. She was no savage like Lisa Le Seuer. She was proud that she had triumphed over Curt, that he did not suspect her own wavering.

And he could not dictate to her! That he dared to try infuriated her. . . . Soon this journey, which had more dangers than she had foreseen, would be over, and she would be safe. She would have proved to herself that she, too, had mettle, like that of Clara and the women of the Lost Company. It had seemed necessary to her to prove that to herself. She knew now that she had been groping toward it ever since she left Wildcliffe, the need to know herself, her own strength and limitations; and at Fort Vancouver that need had become an urgent demand.

Determination crept over her again, comforting, strengthening. She would not be thwarted by Fletcher nor by the covetous eyes of Lige, either; no, nor by exhaustion or hardship. She was a Gatewood and she'd prove to them that she was as strong and capable as any woman in Oregon, and she would earn their respect. She would be content then, able to return to Wildcliffe with her head high, feeling she had done the name of Gatewood proud, her self-respect intact. Already the horizons of her world—such a little world at Wildcliffe!—had widened, and she had reached heights and plumbed depths she had not known existed. She felt a momentary pity for the women at home who would never experience these things—the sweet taste of great and imminent danger and sweeter taste of magnificent triumph when the *Sea Bird* had plunged through the field of roaring breakers at the mouth of The River; the first glimpse of the mighty mountains of the Cascade Range—and even the hard, rough strength of Curt's arms. Oh, but she would not succumb to any of it.

It's only my second day on the trail, she remembered, her thoughts tumbling hazily. I wonder what it was like on the Plains, on the sixtieth day, the hundredth; the hundredth morning, knowing you had to push on, or you'd not reach Oregon before the snow and starvation overtook you. . . . Kitty rested, her thoughts foggy. She heard Fletcher again: "You don't have to go on with this. I'll send you back. I've been figuring on it." Damn him, she thought; she wouldn't go back if she had to crawl from Cowlitz Landing to Newmarket on her hands and knees. There was more to living than comfort and security, and she would not be wrapped in cotton-wool all her life. A woman, too, had a right to seek, to know. A woman had a life to live; she was not just a minor episode in the life of some man. What did he think she was? A quitter?

Lantern light seeped into the tent.

"Kitty?"

She raised her head. "Yes, Sunset," she said. Her voice was husky and she cleared her throat.

"You all right?"

She sat up dizzily and finally she pulled herself erect and went to the entrance. "Yes, I'm all right," she said, "except—I hurt my hand a little. It isn't important—it was just the pain."

Sunset drew her outside, held the lantern high. The mitten was torn, the once-white fur matted brown with mud and blood. He drew it carefully from her hand and uttered a low whistle.

"Come, sit by the fire," he ordered. He looked sharply at her white face and shadowed eyes and lowered the lantern quickly. "When did this happen?"

"Just a little while ago."

"Does Curt know it?"

She shook her head. Her knees buckled under her. Sunset caught her and eased her quickly to the place he had prepared for her. The blankets were warm and a fur robe had been laid across a log to give her a place to rest her back. He knelt beside her, examining the bleeding little hand.

"Sit still," he commanded, and smiled at her reassuringly. "We'll fix that up and get you something to eat." He was gone briefly and returned with a medicine case and hot water. He bathed her hand carefully. After a while Curt came to stand at his shoulder. He was frowning, looking down at the injured hand.

"Hold the lantern, will you, Curt? I think there is still a piece of wood in the palm. It's swelling fast."

Curt took the lantern and Kitty saw Sunset slip a knife from its scabbard. The blade was ugly-thin and very sharp; he held it over the open flame of the fire. She saw Read's beefy face peering over Sunset's shoulder, his little bright eyes watching her curiously and greedily. Kitty closed her eyes. She felt a warm, strong, steadying clasp on her wrist—Curt's fingers.

She bit her lips and the color drained from her face as Sunset's skillful probing began. Curt's fingers tightened, numbing her hand, seeming to take the pain into his own hard flesh. The roar of the river grew louder. It seemed to her that the storm came up suddenly and howled and stamped about the camp and its drumming and raging in her ears drowned out the low voices of the men.

She opened her eyes; the faces blurred before her. Behind them the campfire was a chimera. There was a spoon between her lips and hot, fiery liquid burned her mouth. Her world began to clear but her eyelids felt weighted and her body was too heavy to move. The faces finally swam into focus and the campfire became what it was, little tongues of flame, taking ineffectual licks and nibbles at the blackness of the night. Her hand had been neatly bandaged and the agonizing pain was subsiding to a dull ache.

"Thank you, Sunset," she said evenly. For answer Sunset held a cup to her lips. The coffee was strong and black and it poured down her throat in a welcome, warming stream. She managed a smile. "That's so good," she said, like a child, and she raised her shaking hands to clasp the cup.

"Think you can eat now?" Sunset asked. She nodded. She did manage to eat a little, slowly, and then she got heavily to her feet. The little distance to her tent seemed very long, but she managed it, without assistance, and the men, watching her, let her go alone.

She crawled into her bed, thankful for its warmth. Exhaustion was the best of all soporifics; pain and confusion could not keep her from merciful sleep. Dreams, shadowy, half-formed and tormenting, disturbed her, and now and then she moaned. Once she awakened to see through the crack at the tent entrance the figures of Curt and Sunset, in front of the fire. Sunset was whittling with the shining knife and it flashed in the light. Later she awakened again, and all the men about the fire were motionless, blanketed mounds—except one. Curt sat alone, staring into the fire. The coal in his pipe glowed as he drew upon it. Kitty turned, drew her blankets closer beneath her chin, sighed with the pain of her body. It was the slightest movement; he could not possibly have heard it, she thought; but Curt glanced at the tent quickly, alert, on guard, and then he came noiselessly to the entrance to the tent and waited, listening. Kitty made no further sound, and he went back to his place by the fire.

Kitty thought, I must sleep, so I will not delay him in the morning. . . . He is awake because of me. But I'll ask no favors from him, ever. She touched her wrist where Curt's fingers had clasped it and she willed sleep to come again.

◇ 4 ◇

THE little camp noises, a man coughing, hacking, the clink of metal against metal, awakened Kitty before dawn. For a minute she lay, dull and forgetful, not knowing where she was. The men's voices were subdued, still heavy and gruff with sleep, but a flame leaped high and made a pattern on the wall of the tent. Stoically Kitty pushed the warm covers from her, resisting the impulse to pull them over her head and drop back into the delicious world of sleep. Her muscles were stiff and sore and each movement of her hand made her wince. She yanked on her clothing impatiently, fastening her stays loosely, deciding to sacrifice a tiny waist to comfort. She put on her heavy, rain-stained skirt, ripped and snagged with branches and rocks, and she sniffed with disgust as she pulled on her mud-caked boots. She twisted up her hair and jammed her bonnet over it, not bothering to look in the small travel mirror that Jessie had put into her pack. She could not find her damaged mittens; she dragged a heavy pair of gloves from the tight roll of her belongings and drew them over her hands and she rolled up her bedding and cinched it tight with the straps provided.

Gray, wet dawn was a fine time to gain a proper perspective on the events of the previous night, she reflected. It had been only exhaustion and loneliness and pain, and the yearning for affection —after all, she had been loved and cared for and protected all her life, not only by her parents and Philip but by several hundred devoted slaves. It had been that need that had made her momentarily, but only momentarily, responsive to Curt's love-making. Fortunately she was sensible enough to look at it sanely now. It had been a natural and explainable reaction, nothing to be ashamed of and not to be exaggerated, and it was known only to herself.

She had started on this journey and she'd finish it, she repeated to herself, through clenched teeth. She'd show these Westerners the kind of stock she came from. After all, Wildcliffe had been a wilderness when her grandmother had arrived there—and now no finer estate existed in all the South. Curt needn't be so damned superior, she fumed, as she made the last knot in the strap around her bedroll.

Within her pack were the russet-colored dress and bonnet, which she would don before she met Philip, and a multitude of dainty, lace-trimmed petticoats and undergarments. They could stay there, she decided. She'd wear this ugly skirt the whole journey, even if it were in rags, and then she'd happily throw it away. She had no desire to impress Curt or any other of the men on this expedition with her beauty or fashion. The plainer she looked the better it would be. She was sick and tired of being looked at like a—like a—she refused to put her thoughts into words, even to herself.

She strode out to the campfire. The tantalizing odor of bacon came to her from the pan over which Curt was bending. He looked up at her in surprise and his glance traveled over her unhurriedly.

"Good morning," he said.

"Good morning," she snapped. His shirt was open at the throat and he seemed impervious to the cold and damp. She accepted the plate he handed her silently and forced down every mouthful of food, knowing she would need the energy it gave her. When Sunset appeared she nodded to him shortly. She knew the men were exchanging glances behind her back and she did not care. When the time came to move she was ready and waiting, and she swung off up the trail close on the heels of the men, and she did not look back at Curt.

Fortunately there were not so many or as difficult portages on the third day, and Kitty was able to keep the pace. She could feel

Curt's eyes on her, quizzical, amused, but it was to Sunset she turned in the evening. She sat beside him again to eat and to listen to Charlefour's gifted fiddle.

The Indians who had visited their camp on the first night returned and Kitty rested in the shadows, watching. The eyes of the young Indian, Dick Tom, slid toward her often and the talk went on with occasional long silences.

"What are they saying, Sunset?"

"They'll meet us at Cowlitz Landing with some horses. We've been bargainin' about the price of them."

"Is that all?"

Sunset looked at the fire. "We-ll," he said, "shall I tell her, Curt?"

"Sure." Curt waited, but Sunset, red-faced, said nothing. Curt regarded Kitty guardedly. "Dick Tom wants to buy you."

"What!" Kitty sat abruptly upright, her eyes wide with shock.

"Offers twenty-five blankets. Very good price, too. Usually girls bring fifteen at the most. Boys, five."

"Oh!"

"That price is for Indian slaves from other tribes. But because of your light hair you'd bring a higher price, though you're so small you couldn't carry very heavy packs. . . . Dick Tom promises also that you'd be treated as a princess in the tribe. He'd build a house for you, all your own. He even offered to consider giving up his other wives."

Kitty jumped to her feet. "You have a peculiar sense of humor, Mr. Fletcher."

Sunset rose, real concern on his face. "It's nothing, Kitty. They're savages. It's a custom. We listen so as not to anger them. It's—"

From the edge of the camp Charlefour called for Sunset and he left gratefully. Curt straightened slowly.

"Don't worry, Kitty," he drawled, "I told Dick Tom it was no deal. I told him I wasn't giving up my girl—to anybody. At any price."

"Between the two of you," she said icily, "I'd prefer the Indian."

Behind her Read guffawed and Kitty whirled and raked him with one furious glance. His laugh faded to an unpleasant grin, while his eyes went from her to Curt, knowingly, insultingly. Kitty went to her tent, chin high. She worked fast and skillfully, making her bed. How those men liked their vulgar jokes! She climbed into the bag of coverings she had made, pulled them close about her and determinedly closed her eyes.

In two or three days they would be at the Landing, and then they would leave the river and start overland by horseback. Irritated though she was, she was not afraid. She dismissed the Indians from her mind. Dirty savages, scum! Kitty slept.

She did not know what awakened her, but suddenly, hours later, she opened her eyes wide and lay rigid, listening, in the fearful quiet of the black dark. The light of the campfire marked a line between the flaps of the tent, but as she listened, every nerve alert, she could neither hear nor feel any motion about it. There was a soft drip, drip upon the tent. The rain had stopped but the branches still dripped slowly, like a metronome. Fear tingled along Kitty's limbs, prickled at the back of her neck, widened her eyes, held her motionless. Without turning her head she looked to right and left, but she could not see into the darkness.

They couldn't have gone and left me alone, she thought, suddenly frantic. They wouldn't just go—and leave me here! She tried to push the blankets away from her and realized that the covers, awkwardly made into a tight envelope, bound her. Protective, snug, warm, just a minute ago, now they were bonds, and she wanted to beat them away from her, stand free. She pulled her hands loose, finally, and her arms, and started to drag her body upward; but a soft sound stopped her and again she froze, listening.

The noise came from behind her head, outside the tent. Inch by inch she pulled herself to a sitting position, and turned her head to look behind her. She could see nothing, but she knew the thin canvas wall of the tent was there, the only protection between her and the forest. Was it some wild animal, brushing against the canvas? What animal—or what human—would crowd between the canvas and the tropical-thick underbrush which bordered it? The men had hacked with knives and hatchets to make a place for her tent and there had been little clear space about it.

Her eyes were more accustomed to the darkness now, and through the crack in the tent flap she could see vague outlines beyond the campfire—motionless figures of the sleeping men. Perhaps it is my imagination, she said to herself, holding her teeth tight together, perhaps it is nothing—a branch, a small night animal, scraping the canvas. *I will not scream, I will not scream.*

The sound came again, and it seemed to Kitty that she could hear breathing, short, heavy little breaths, through the canvas wall. And then she was certain . . . the unmistakable rasp of something, a hand, a body, against the canvas. Her hand went to her throat and she tried again to free herself from the blankets, holding her prisoner. She paused, breathing shallowly, to listen again.

There was a tiny, ripping sound, of canvas tearing. There was a quick movement behind her and then all the nightmares she had ever had materialized. A hand, rough and hard and evil-smelling, slid swiftly and surely out of the darkness, around her throat and up over her mouth, jerking her back, cutting off the screams rising in her throat.

Wildly, Kitty fought. She kicked the blankets away, struggled to her knees; she clawed at the hand that covered her mouth and twisted her face until she freed her lips. Savagely she buried her teeth in the hand. The hold loosened and she was on her feet, dragging a blanket about her, rushing to the door of the tent. She flung the flaps wide and the firelight shone into the tent. It caught the blade of a knife, sliding swiftly through the canvas behind the bed where she had lain.

Kitty's scream cut through the night. The men about the campfire jerked into life. Kitty heard a plunging noise behind the tent, saw the knife slip, slide across her bed. Her scream came again. She could not move, she could not escape from the danger she was sure was coming at her through that long slit in the canvas.

Behind her, Curt rolled from his blankets and was on his feet in one motion and reaching for his gun. He saw Kitty in the doorway of the tent and he passed her, running toward the river. Charlefour was after him, and there was a shout, then silence. Sunset brushed by Kitty, stopped, and turned back.

"There," Kitty gasped, pointed to the knife. She was shaking uncontrollably. Sunset's arms went around her and she clung to him frantically. He held her quietly, smoothing her hair, soothing her. Someone threw a log on the fire and it blazed high, throwing the camp into sudden light.

There was another shout from the direction of the river and Kitty shuddered. Sunset pulled the blanket close about her.

"It's all right, Kitty," he soothed, "it's all right, girl. You're not hurt?" She shook her head and he let his breath out in a long sigh of relief. He looked over her shoulder and then his big hand pressed her head back comfortably against his chest. Curt, striding back into the camp, saw them and stopped short.

Over Kitty's head Sunset grinned broadly, while his hand happily caressed her hair. Meaningly he pointed his chin down toward the girl in his arms, and one eye closed in a triumphant and delighted wink at Curt. Despite himself, Curt grinned.

"You lucky devil," he said, under his breath. At the sound of Curt's voice, Kitty straightened.

"Did you get him?" Sunset asked.

Curt shook his head. "Who got out of here ahead of me?"

"Danged if I know. When I was on my feet you was already running and Charlie right behind you. See anything?"

"Saw someone come around the end of the tent, head for the river."

Suddenly a shot rang out, and then there was silence. The three waited, listening, and Sunset pulled his own gun from his belt and examined it carefully. Curt picked up a lantern and lighted it at the fire. He passed Kitty and went into the tent and picked up the knife. Kitty and Sunset followed. Sunset examined the slash in the canvas. It was long enough to permit a man to slide through. Curt turned the knife over and his face darkened. He handed it to Sunset and then he held the lantern up and looked at Kitty.

"Did he hurt you—in any way?"

Kitty shook her head. Curt came closer to her and his eyes were dangerous, murderous. "You're sure, Kitty? Don't lie to me."

"He did not injure me. I heard someone brushing against the canvas and then I heard the knife, ripping the tent. I tried to free myself from the blankets, and then there was a hand over my mouth so I could not cry out—"

Her fingers went to her throat and her voice grew hoarse with the memory of terror. But, facing Curt, her defiance returned again to strengthen her. "I bit him," she announced.

"Good girl," Sunset approved.

Curt nodded shortly. "I'm sorry about this," he said crisply, "but there's no further danger tonight. No—nor any other night."

He left the tent abruptly and Sunset followed. Kitty began to dress. Now and then her glance slid to the damaged tent wall but she would not give way to hysteria. She dressed slowly, rubbing her cold feet with her uninjured hand, trying to bring warmth to them. Outside the tent were voices and she strained her ears to hear. What would happen to the man who had attempted to harm her? How did they deal with things of that sort on the frontier?

"Where's Read?"

"Evans, is this Read's knife?"

"Did anyone see Read?"

"He was already gone when I rolled out." Kitty recognized Charlefour's voice.

"Charlie, was that you who shot, down by the river?"

"No, Curt, I thought it was you."

"That's Read's knife, all right. I've seen him use it a hundred times."

The voices dropped and Kitty could not distinguish the words. She could see Curt's face as it had looked when he was questioning her. If that had been Read outside the tent—she shivered, remembering the rage in Curt's face.

The voices rose suddenly and she went to the entrance. Curt had his gun in his hand and was facing the path toward the river. Beside him was Sunset, and he, too, was fingering the revolver at his belt. Read walked slowly into the circle of light.

"So you came back," Curt said. His voice was flat.

Read walked by him, seated himself on his bed.

"Why shouldn't I?" he asked, insolently. There was dead silence in the camp. Curt walked to the big seaman, reached down and grabbed the front of his shirt. With one quick movement he jerked Read to his feet.

"Is this your knife?"

"Goddam you, what if it is?"

"If it is, you better talk. Fast."

Read's calculating little eyes went from Curt to Sunset. Curt's grip tightened and he gave the man a shake. Read's heavy neck grew dark red.

"That was my knife," he said, meanly, "but it wasn't me that tried to get into that tent. Though I guess I'm not the only man in this camp who's thought of trying."

"Keep talking," Curt ordered.

"I traded that knife to Dick Tom for some buckskin." He motioned to his pack and Sunset kicked it open and pulled the skin from it. "Something woke me—or maybe it was that I just couldn't sleep, thinking of—certain things." He leered at the men, then rolled his eyes meaningly toward Kitty's tent. "I heard somethin' back there, and when the girl screamed, I jumped. I took a shot at Dick Tom down by the river. Got him, I think. I'm a good shot."

With an abrupt, disgusted movement Curt threw Read away from him. The sailor stumbled back and regained his balance. The light had come, almost imperceptibly, while they talked, and now the world was gray, the firelight dimmer. Kitty saw Charlefour slip quietly down the path, and the voices went on, questioning, now with pauses between. Someone put a kettle on the fire, and Kitty drew away from the tent opening and went back to her blankets to sit, her hands tight together, waiting.

The motions of striking camp began. Sunset called to Kitty and gave her breakfast. She did not look at Read, but she was conscious of his watchful eyes upon her. After a while Charlefour returned and he nodded to Sunset and Curt.

"There was a canoe and there's a blood trail. It was Dick Tom, all right, but he's gone."

For answer, Sunset tossed the knife at Read's feet. "Here," he said, and Kitty had never heard Sunset speak so harshly before. "Take your knife. But don't be a damned fool. You better start prayin' you didn't kill Dick Tom."

"Why? Fletcher was ready enough to kill me—and so were you." Read sheathed the knife and his face was hot with anger.

"You're a white man, that's why. But you'd no call to kill an Indian. Scare the living begeesus out of him, sure. But not kill him."

Read stared, puzzled, and Kitty lowered her cup, amazed at this peculiar logic.

"It's fool things like that that start Indian wars," Sunset explained. "Kill one of them and they're like to have a whole tribe, or a dozen of them, down on us. If you've ever seen a massacre, Read—" He swallowed and then he turned to Kitty and his face was serious and tight. "Look, Kitty, it ain't I don't know how scared you was. It ain't that Dick Tom ought not to be strung up. But that's mighty unimportant to what a scalpin' party would be.

In this country, even if you'd been harmed, we'd have had to move carefully, if the man was an Indian. We'd have gone to the chief of his tribe and demanded he hand over Dick Tom, and we'd have tried him quick and killed him neat; but we would have parleyed, so's not to get the whole tribe on the war path. We're outnumbered by hundreds, thousands to one, here north of The River. One person might have to be sacrificed to save the rest of the settlers. We would have stalled till we got the families in a safe place, and then we'd have gone after him. We'd have got him, and we'd have made him pay—don't mistake that. But there's others to think about. Do you understand?"

The men's eyes were upon her and Kitty froze under their stare. She was horrified and shocked, trying to comprehend what Sunset was saying.

"If it'd been Read, here, or any other white man, he'd have got what was coming to him, and quick," Sunset went on, "but an Indian is different. We're in a dangerous spot here and it pays to tread easy. These are things you got to know, you and Evans and Read. You've not been in Oregon long. You got to know these things. Likely, Dick Tom ain't bad hurt, and nothing will come of it. He wants to do business with us. But after this, Read, and you, Evans, don't take pot shots at Indians, understand? Keep out of trouble with them, if you can. If they attack you, shoot, of course, and for the love of God, don't miss. But only when you've got to kill to save yourself or another. Don't send out invitations to a war party. They're touchy now; they're just lookin' for an excuse—some fancied wrong, and all hell will break loose."

Read shrugged. Kitty pushed away her plate. She felt small and unimportant. She was only one person, one life, and not a very valuable one at that; one that might be spent without hesitation, or traded for the lives of many. In Oregon no person was an entity. They were interdependent, whether they wanted to be or not. Read's impulsive shot at Dick Tom could cost the lives of Newmarket settlers who had never seen the sailor. . . .

Kitty's feet moved swiftly and surely up the trail, close behind the men. She had never thought such long thoughts before— things were all in different proportion in Oregon. But there was a certain pleasure in it, too, in being part of the whole great plan of settlement. If ill fortune happened to her or to any other

American in Oregon, the others would rally round her, protecting, defending, avenging, in a sane, sure, just way. Fiercely independent, these restless Westerners, but fully aware that in unity there is strength. . . . That was what made the powerful British hesitate.

The sound of the rapids no longer frightened her, the woods were not so strange. How odd, how quickly people adjusted themselves, began to take for granted things that grew familiar. You can get used to anything after a while, I guess, she decided philosophically, and in that lay a danger. If women accepted crudities and privations, it was likely that men would be quite content. It was up to the Oregon women to insist upon the niceties of civilization. Floors in their homes, proper furnishings, schools, decent clothing, books and music and flower gardens. The women who had been forced to give up their beloved possessions far back on the Oregon Trail, must insist their men replace them now. It would be bad for Oregon if the women ever grew content! They must work for law and order, for protection against the Indians, for more churches and community buildings; they must insist upon proper, conventional standards of behavior. . . .

So absorbed was Kitty that the miles dropped behind her swiftly. More accustomed now to the routine of the trail, she was not as weary as she had been on previous days. She noticed things she had passed by before: a brown rabbit, darting across the trail; tracks of small, sharp hoofs. At nooning she asked questions of Sunset and she was pleased that at the next short portage he waited for her and pointed out various marks that she had missed; the track of a cougar, signs where a raccoon had been along a little creek that emptied into the river. Once she caught a glimpse of a gray-brown body sliding like a shadow through the woods, a coyote, Sunset told her; and he told her to watch for black bear, for often they did not hibernate till Christmas time, because of the mild winters. He'd get a blue grouse for her dinner, or a native pheasant, he promised her, if she'd help him spot one; around the wild crab apple trees was the best place to find them. It became an interesting and exciting game, and her ill temper of the day before faded, and her spirits rose again. Sunset was completely at home in the woods, his knowledge unlimited, and her respect for him and his never-failing courtesy grew. His blue eyes were keen, and always they were kind, and he was not quick to reach for his gun when they came upon a wild animal. A saucy chipmunk scolded Kitty, and she laughed happily at him; she wrinkled her nose in distaste after a skunk had crossed the trail, and she shivered with delicious fear when she thought she saw in a shadow the tawny fur of a cougar. From the bateau she watched the river banks, and once she gasped with delight at the sight of three deer, poised motionless and breathtakingly beautiful, against the background of the woods.

They came at last to Cowlitz Landing, and on the high bluff above made camp. The Hudson's Bay Company's Cowlitz Farm was not far away, Sunset told her, and though there was no sign of Dick Tom and his horses, Sunset was confident they'd show up by morning. Kitty rested, watching Charlefour empty his fire bag of flint and steel and touchwood and skillfully nurse a spark into a flame. As he worked, Charlefour, glad of an appreciative audience, also began to talk, to add to Kitty's store of information. A raccoon skin, Charlie demonstrated, must be stretched square; a beaver skin as round as possible. Only the tail and liver of a beaver were considered good for food. His wife, Polly Careless, was a fine cook, Charlie bragged; he'd have Polly cook a real Oregon meal for her when they arrived in Newmarket. Charlie himself had toasted his moccasins, once, when he was hard-pushed. Kitty laughed and Charlie expanded under her attention and his tales grew more and more exaggerated and exciting. Charlie had shot the worst rapids, trapped the most beaver, killed the biggest buck, in all the Oregon Country.

Indian George shyly offered Kitty a small basket. It was beautifully woven and water-tight and Kitty accepted it gratefully. Little by little the comradeship that developed only on the trail began to fold about Kitty, and her beautiful face glowed with warmth and lively interest.

All day Curt had been measuring her. She was a girl who wore well, he decided. Her elegance and dignity and her careless disregard of her finery, so evident when she stepped ashore in Oregon City, did not mask an empty head, nor was her beauty dependent upon those luxurious trappings. She was alert and very intelligent, and every inch a lady; her great, altogether feminine charm did not mean that she was either helpless or frivolous. She was a girl who could be of help to a man, who would be a wife to be proud of, and she could adapt herself to Oregon ways, given a little time. Curt's decision strengthened. He was glad for her friendship with

Sunset. No one could do a better job of making Oregon interesting and beautiful than Sunset, and she was very responsive to beauty. It would be good, also, to have his wife and his partner good friends. . . . She'd been courageous enough in the face of Dick Tom's attempted attack. She had spirit enough to fight back and she had not given way to hysteria. Desire for her deepened. He had been a little surprised himself at the violence of the anger that had risen in him when he had believed that Read had attempted to enter her tent.

"Kitty."

Kitty's laugh died and her face grew still and guarded as she turned to Curt.

"Yes?"

"You can ride, I expect?"

"Of course. We have the finest horses at Wildcliffe. I have ridden them all."

All the casual friendliness that she displayed with Sunset and with Charlie, even with Indian George, was gone. She was again Miss Gatewood of Wildcliffe, a foreigner in Oregon, an impersonal visitor, bored and annoyed at the inconveniences and delays.

"That is fortunate. You'll ride astride, of course."

"Astride?"

"The women in Oregon ride astride. It's a hard trail. It's safer."

Kitty folded her lips. She remembered Lisa on her white horse, plunging down toward the river landing, the hawk's bells tinkling, her whip cracking brutally. Lisa rode astride; and Lisa, Indian fashion, had an ornamented tomahawk on one side of her saddle and a peace pipe on the other. The sudden, incredible picture of herself in such trappings flashed before Kitty and she stared at Curt in amazement. Kitty's riding clothes were in the best of taste, the most beautifully cut, the most conservative of pattern. Only the tip of her boot would show beneath the long skirts; her tiny, plumed hat had been designed to fit neatly over the gleaming crown of her hair; her sidesaddle at Wildcliffe had been especially made for her of the finest leather.

A few days ago she would flatly have refused to ride astride. She would have demanded that a proper saddle and mount be provided for her, and she would have expected it to be produced. But if Curt expected her to protest and if he relished the intimacy of an argument, he would be disappointed. She shrugged.

"If it is necessary to ride astride I will do so," she said, firmly, "though I'm not accustomed to it." She returned his gaze with frosty eyes and turned away. She would not prolong a conversation with Fletcher.

After Kitty had disappeared into her tent, Curt and Sunset sat beside the fire. Sunset had his knife out, working on a piece of wood, fashioning a little totem pole. Curt picked up one of the shavings and broke it into still smaller pieces and tossed them one by one into the fire.

"She's trail-broke now," Sunset observed finally, with satisfaction. "I, Dad, but she's game!"

"Yes," Curt said, absently, "she'll do."

Sunset's knife stopped abruptly and he shot a quick, sharp, startled look at Curt. After Curt went to spread his own blankets, Sunset sat alone, the wood carving unnoticed in his hand. He rubbed his chin slowly, thoughtfully, and his eyes were deeply troubled.

◆ 5 ◆

THE shouts were long-drawn, ending in a yelp on a high note. They were like nothing Kitty had ever heard before and they curdled her blood. They were punctuated by horrible grunts, as though a giant of a man or animal were being beaten in the stomach with heavy fists. It could be nothing but Dick Tom and a scalping party, Kitty thought, fumbling with the fastenings on her skirt.

But why were there no shots? Were the men already dead, and she to be saved for the last? Terrified, she peeked out of the tent, to see the camp deserted. The men's packs still lay about, but the fire smoldered, unattended. The noise was coming from a little clearing a few yards up the river, shielded from the camp by heavy brush.

The yells came again, and Kitty started toward them. They were wild and hideous—but they were also triumphant; and then she was certain that she'd heard laughter as well. There was a momentary lull, and then she heard Charlie's voice, loud with excitement and unmistakable delight.

"Ride him, Curt! Stick with him, boy!"

Kitty ran to the edge of the clearing and stopped, transfixed. The little field was ringed with men, and in the center of it was Curt, on a grunting, plunging bay cayuse. The animal reared, balanced, seemed certain to tip over backwards and to crush the man astride him; then suddenly his head was down and vicious rear hoofs were flying, as the horse tried to pitch Curt over his head. The yells came from Curt, as he rode, his long body undulating with the horse's gyrations; his arm was high and he waved his cap, and his heels, decorated with wide-roweled silver spurs, raked the animal's quivering sides. To Kitty's amazement, Curt was laughing, delighted with his dangerous sport, and the men watching were whooping encouragement.

The cayuse suddenly ceased his bucking and began blindly to run. He plunged toward the men and they parted, scattered, respectfully gave man and horse the right of way. Curt brought him back, and the animal finally quieted, acknowledged defeat, trotted docilely at Curt's bidding, and then stood still. Easily, warily, Curt slid from his back. He passed his hand down the animal's neck, petting him, speaking in quiet, soothing tones. Then he wiped his glistening face with his sleeve and turned the subdued animal over to Charlefour.

"He's all right now," he said. As he turned, Kitty saw the triumph on his lean face. It angered her and she wished the horse had thrown him, ignominiously, in the mud.

There were three more horses waiting. Indian George was leading one to the center of the clearing and he was grinning broadly.

"Want to try another, Curt?" he challenged. "This one, he a mean one!" Curt laughed and spat.

"What's the matter, can't an Indian break a cayuse?"

The horse snorted and plunged, lifting George off his feet. The men's laughing banter continued. "He's a devil, by God," Charlie announced, slapping his thigh. The animal rolled his eyes wickedly, evilly. Sunset picked up a saddle and approached the horse.

"I'll take him," he said. "Better blindfold him, George."

George slipped a heavy blindfold over the horse's eyes and the animal stool motionless, stiff, waiting, tense and ready to fight. Very carefully Sunset slid the saddle into position, reached gingerly for the cinch. The horse lunged and Sunset jumped back nimbly, out of reach of the flying, vicious hoofs, and he waited patiently until the cayuse quieted again. George hung on, and then Kitty saw the Indian had reached for the animal's ear and had clamped his teeth upon it. He held the grip until Sunset had drawn the cinch tight.

The animal stood with four legs braced, statue-stiff, as Sunset, ignoring the laughing advice of his onlookers, mounted. He settled himself in the saddle, gathered up the reins in one hand, and swept off his hat. In the bright sunlight his hair glistened like ripe wheat and Kitty caught her breath. Her hands gripped the cloth of her skirt spasmodically, in excitement and fear.

"Let him go," Sunset said suddenly.

Indian George dropped the blindfold and ran for cover. The horse shook his head, quivered, and then suddenly exploded into a whirling, squealing fury. The men's delighted shouts mingled with the protests of the angry animal and Charlefour threw his cap in the air.

"Look at that goddam sunfisher! Ee-yaw, he's an outlaw, that one! Ride him, Sunset, ride him, stay with him, boy!"

Another voice, from a man Kitty had never seen before, cut through the racket.

"Rake him, man, rake him deep!" A volley of obscenity followed.

It seemed to her a long time before the noise quieted and the shaggy cayuse gave up and stood with heaving sides and drooping head, while Sunset dismounted. Kitty went quietly back to camp. She heated some coffee and drank it slowly. Now and then she shivered. The sport these men enjoyed was violent and rough, and she had not liked the look on Curt's face when at last he had brought the horse into submission. How he likes to break their wills, she thought; he must be the master.

But Dick Tom had kept his bargain. He had sent the horses, though she had not recognized him among the Indians and Frenchmen who ringed the clearing. It seemed hard now to recall her terror of the early morning. The Indians had been enjoying the sport as much as the white men. If these men played together, bargained together, why should one be afraid? Dick Tom's attempt to enter her tent was only an isolated case, she decided. The Indians were like children, primitive, unused to the ways of the whites, but she refused to believe them dangerous. It was only necessary to exhibit authority and never to show fear. It was likely, also, she thought, with some rancor, that she would not have been annoyed by the Indian if the white men had not taken liberties with Indian women. Men like Fletcher, with his wild, half-caste mistress, actually were responsible for the insults that white women must undergo. The hot indignation that swept over her at the thought of Fletcher's mistress was discomforting. Resolutely she dismissed the thought.

The men trooped back into the camp, untired and pleased with their morning's work. The newcomers came with them, and Sunset, resting beside Kitty as he ate, pointed them out to her.

"See the Indian there on the right—the tall fellow who looks like he's lost his last friend?" Kitty nodded. She had noticed the stolid, morose man, the only one whose sour expression had not altered despite the laughter and excitement of his companions. "His name is So Happy."

"It can't be, Sunset!" Kitty protested.

They laughed together. Kitty's glance went on around the circle, examining the faces. The Frenchman who had shouted obscenities was a squat, bullet-shaped man, oily-faced, short-necked, his long black hair in greasy strings. He was sitting next to Read, talking with him as they ate, and he ran a great, grimy finger over his plate and lifted it to his mouth. He used his left hand, Kitty noticed, and then her attention was caught by the heavy revolvers he wore.

As she watched him he glanced up suddenly and met her eyes. His eyes were tiny, deep-set, in his round, pig-like face, and they were too sharp, too shiny. There was unmistakable evil and cruelty in them. Kitty glanced quickly away.

"The Frenchman next to Read. Could that be—Le Seuer?"

"Yes. That's Bull Le Seuer."

The humor had gone from Sunset's voice. He put down his plate with an impatient little movement. "He's working on Cowlitz Farm. If you can call it work. He and Read seem to get along. I reckon Read and Evans will leave us here, likely winter on Cowlitz Prairie. We'll be busy the rest of the day gettin' those horses in shape to travel. If we put a pack on any of them now they'd scatter goods from here to hell and back. That danged Indian sent us the meanest bunch of cayuses he could round up west of the Rockies. All but one. There's a beautiful little bay mare with four white feet, well-broken. Curt bought her for you."

He watched Kitty keenly as he spoke.

"That was kind of him," she said, but her lips straightened.

Sunset leaned forward, his hands clasped between his knees. His voice was low and his words reached only Kitty's ears.

"Curt's a good man, Kitty. He's hard, but he's a good man."

"I know," she said drily, "you value him."

He smiled slightly and reached for his pipe. "Rubs you the wrong way, doesn't he?"

"What does it matter what I think of him?"

Sunset drew long on the pipe before he answered. "On the trail it's easier, pleasanter, if folks get along."

Kitty did not answer. Sunset moved uneasily. "Kitty," he said, "I know Curt about as well as anybody'll ever know him. He needs friends."

"Sunset, I admire your loyalty to your partner. But frankly, I have never seen a man who seemed to care so little whether he had friends or not. He seems to me to be solely interested in Fletcher."

Sunset regarded her through the pipesmoke and grinned. "You're a stubborn one, for your size," he teased, "danged near as bull-headed as Curt, I reckon." Then, persistently, "Why?"

"If you are so set on knowing I'll tell you why I dislike him. First, when I arrived in Oregon City he was insulting to me. Then he fought Read on the river bank, and made me conspicuous."

"He shouldn't have beat up Read? Way I heard it, he was defendin' you." Sunset was plainly puzzled.

"But in such a rowdy manner!"

"What should he have done?"

"A gentleman would have called Read out."

"Curt couldn't. There's a law against duellin' in Oregon."

"Oh!"

"Funny thing, that law. Got passed in an awful hurry. Happened one day the legislature was in session in Oregon City. Fellow named Sam Holderness got in an argument with Dr. White, challenged him to a duel. Dr. White wouldn't have had a chance—yet a man can't refuse a challenge. Only way was to pass a law, quick. Jesse Applegate moved the rules be suspended and a bill be introduced to prohibit duellin'. They passed it in about thirty minutes and the Governor signed it right away. Made it against the law to give or accept a challenge to a duel. Saved Dr. White."

"You Oregon people make laws in a most informal fashion!"

"Just as we need 'em. We don't want any more laws than we need. Comes a time folks need lawyers to settle everything, things is getting bad, mighty bad. But there's no law against fightin', and that's a good thing, too; sometimes a good fight clears the air. But you see, Curt couldn't challenge Read."

"You do stick to the point. All right. Besides that, Mr. Fletcher antagonizes me because he dictates. He wants to rule, to crack a whip, to make others jump to it. When he rode that horse this morning there was more than just sport to it. He was triumphant—because he had broken its will."

She stopped, her face flushed. Sunset's direct eyes were on her, probing deep. "And," she went on, half angry, "it's his attitude toward women, as though they were so inferior. And—he's downright immoral. That Lisa Le Seuer. It's disgraceful! At least most men have the decency not to parade their—their—"

Sunset nodded. "I know what you mean. But Curt just isn't one to hide or to pretend—anything. I reckon it's hard for a lady such as you, to understand. Things is different in Oregon, or they were, Kitty, before the immigrants came in such numbers. Most of the Hudson's Bay men have Indian wives. They weren't allowed to bring white women to the posts. A man gets mighty lonely, Kitty. Some of the best men I know have married Indian women. Joe Meek's wife, Mountain Lamb, was a fine woman, she saved his life. Polly Careless is a good woman, despite her name. I reckon men, as kind of a defense, tried more or less to keep those women—unimportant, as you say. Didn't want to get too fond of them, so they couldn't break away. The custom, Kitty, was that when a man went back East again, he was automatically divorced. The Indian women understood that, and then they were free to take up with another man."

"And you ask that I condone such a practice?"

"No." Sunset blew the smoke high, watched it drift away. "No, but it might help you if you understood it. The thing is— the thing is—" he groped for words, "don't judge him too harsh, human nature bein' what it is. Like I said, a man gets mighty lonely—"

"I am not that liberal, Sunset."

"I reckon you're right," he said, after another pause. He smiled at her, cocked one eye quizzically. "I'm goin' to work now, little

Puritan. But Kitty—Curt has got the makin's of a great man. You can't stop him. You can't change his course, once he gets set on it. And that's what Oregon needs. He's a builder, Curt is. He drives hard and he gets results. Comes a time somebody understands him and he thaws out, maybe he'll change some. He's not one to trust many, and inside him, feelin's go pretty deep, and he's not one to talk much, about feelin's. If he seems hard on others—he's just as hard on himself. He's helped a lot of people, Kitty. Me, for instance. Reckon I'd always been a wanderer, a no-account mountain man, 'less Curt had teamed up with me, showed me the pleasure of buildin' a home, havin' a place of your own, buildin' a country. There's something about bein' first, first white man to cross a river, to find a mountain pass—Curt's got another way of dreamin', Kitty, of bein' first."

Sunset looked down at her, studying her, the shining, pale hair, the smooth, rose-flushed face, the perfection of her straight little figure. But the clear, velvet-brown eyes raised to him were unconvinced.

◆ 6 ◆

DR. WILLIAM FRASER TOLMIE, the Scot from the University of Glasgow who was manager of the Puget's Sound Agricultural Company and factor of Fort Nisqually, had gazed with amazement on the Simmons party when they were hacking a road from Cowlitz Landing to Puget Sound. With his own group of horsemen he had overtaken the Americans, and had watched their slow but continued progress toward the land they had chosen. When fallen logs across their path were too great to be cut, the Americans had built ramps over them and their wagons went on. Neither mud nor rain nor hard portages had halted them, and women and children had marched behind the men, each carrying their share. Dr. Tolmie had shaken his head with disbelief, and had declared the Yankees would take a wagon where an Indian would not try to take a pack horse.

Kitty believed it. Part of the way the going was smooth and fast and her sure-footed, white-stockinged little mare, named Mowich, the Chinook word for "deer," sped along, dainty and swift; and then all the obstacles that nature could devise seemed thrown in their path, and every mile was a test. Deep, miring mud entrapped men and animals, and the way over Mud Mountain was torturing for both horses and masters. Icy winds whipped them and driving, soaking rain drenched them and their packs and for three full days they did not emerge from the densest of forests.

The first night after they left the landing they spent in shelter, in the new cabin of John R. Jackson, who had just taken out a land claim on the prairie divide. Jackson was newly appointed sheriff of the Vancouver District and he called his place The Highlands. The protection of the roof and log walls gave Kitty a feeling of security. But from the time they left Jackson's until they came in sight of the first of the cabins in the Newmarket district, she had only her tent to shelter her and it was poor protection from the elements. The women and children in the Simmons party, however, had not had even that; they had depended only on brush shelters.

At any moment the rain would turn to snow. In early morning the ground was partially frozen, giving better footing, but by midday they wallowed in mud again. It was hard work. But Kitty was relieved since Read had left the group and each day was bringing her nearer her goal. She had plenty of time to think during the long days of slow progress. She pictured Philip's surprise at her coming, and tried to visualize their future. How happy Robert would have been, had he lived to see them together again!

She was increasingly aware of Curt and she braced herself against his presence. In numerous small ways he smoothed the way for her. It had become his habit to be at her stirrup at nooning, to swing her from the saddle, clear of the mud and filth of the trail. Kitty had tensed against him at first, and he had regarded her with slight amusement, fully aware of her mute protest, but paying it not the slightest heed. His manner and his touch were possessive and he cared for her almost as he would any inanimate possession of value. She hated his attitude, forced herself to look away when his gray eyes appraised her. He searched her face for signs of fatigue—with the same interest, she thought, furiously, that he examined his horses for injuries; there was no tenderness in him, only cool competence and confidence. His hand caressed the neck of a cayuse—but a whip would crack the next instant if the animal showed a will contrary to his. Kitty had decided to accept his help, to save her own strength. She would take from Fletcher whatever aid she could get, she decided, cold-bloodedly, but she would give him nothing; not docility and certainly not the stimulation of active resistance. She remained remote, a stranger, temporarily and impatiently in his company—but she gave him no indication that she wished to be friends.

Sometimes he walked beside her, leading his own horse, but their conversations were not satisfactory to Kitty. She was uneasy when he was near her, and, in her determination to be always on her guard, her tongue grew sharper than she intended. *I'll become a shrew*, she scolded herself; *he angers me so—and why should he? He should not have any effect on me at all.*

"Some day this trail will be as broad and smooth as the National Pike," he observed. "We'll have stagecoach service from Newmarket to the Cowlitz."

"Pooh! And who to ride them?"

"Americans, of course. From the towns and cities of Puget Sound."

"It isn't American, yet."

"It is. It will always be."

"Suppose the government compromises, and gives all the area north of The River to the British? Then where will you be?"

"We'll fight. We'll form our independent government. The Oregon Republic. We have everything—furs, timber, farm produce. We will build ships. We'll have the China trade."

"I'll read of you in the papers, no doubt."

The sarcasm in her voice caused Curt to look at her with some surprise and it pleased her that she had startled him out of his usual sureness. But only for an instant. Curt believed what he was saying. He was genuinely amazed that she should question him.

There was a bend in the trail before them and the rest of the party disappeared around it. Curt's hand brought Mowich to a halt.

He looked up at her, and unaccountably Kitty's pulse began to race. About them the silence deepened. Darkness was coming and Kitty remembered, not wanting to remember, that other evening, her second night upon the trail, when Curt had held her in his arms and forced his kiss upon her. Evidently Curt was remembering, too, for now he took her hand firmly and drew the woolen glove from it and examined the little scar on the palm. He reached inside his jacket and pulled out the white fur mittens she had worn when she had started her journey.

The jagged, blood-stained palm of the one she had torn had been carefully cut away and now the palms of both were of softest buckskin, neatly sewn to the white fur backs. Curt removed her other glove and put the mittens upon her hands. The gesture, the touch of his fingers, stirred Kitty strangely. It was an apology, and she recognized it as such. He would never tell her in words that he was sorry for that night, that he had not known she had faltered only because of her injury. Words of apology would never come easy to Curt.

Looking down at him, noticing, not for the first time, the way his hair sprang strong and crisply black from his forehead, his weather-darkened skin, his strong features, Kitty felt her resistance to him melting. Dimly she realized she had built up a barrier against him partly because she feared her own reaction to this man.

"Thank you," she said steadily, looking at the mittens, "I shall keep them for a souvenir."

"Around that bend is Newmarket," he said. "The Sparks cottage is first, and we'll stop there. Martha will make room for you. Newmarket is not a town. The settlers are scattered throughout all the area from here to Puget Sound, eight miles or so. My claim, and Sunset's, are six, seven miles on."

"Then I can get someone to take me to Nisqually tomorrow."

His jaw hardened. "I told you I'd take you to Davis," he said, "and I do what I say. I told you, too, that you wouldn't marry him, and I'll tell him. I meant it, Kitty. By God in Heaven, I do mean it."

"How can you be so sure?" Kitty's face flamed with indignation.

"Because that's the way it's going to be, that's all. I've watched you. You aren't a woman to marry a weakling like Davis. And that's what he is—and you know it. You came to Oregon. Whatever you believed your motive, you were wrong. You had the Oregon Fever. Do you know what Oregon Fever is? It's a desire for change, for improvement, for adventure, for something you weren't getting at home. It's a curiosity and a restlessness and a need for new and fresher and bigger things. Why do you think the immigrants came, risking their lives, their sanity, crossing the plains? Because they were looking for something—homes, opportunities, wealth, health, excitement, romance, maybe. You didn't know it, but you were a victim, too, of the Oregon Fever. You could have sent for Davis. You could have sent a messenger in your place. But you didn't. You came, because it was in you—the Fever. You'll never be content now, Kitty, to go back. From what I know of Davis, he'd never satisfy you, either. You're too hot-blooded, Kitty; you're not the kind to settle down and enjoy the fruits of someone else's labor—slave labor. You'd rather have the excitement of building for yourself."

"You have everything all figured out, haven't you?" Kitty blazed. "Well, there are some things you don't know, Mr. Fletcher. Some things you'll never know. I came to Oregon to find Philip and I intend to become his wife. You are very much mistaken; I shall go home very happily, and I shall remember only what I want to remember of Oregon, of—"

Without haste he reached for her, swung her from the saddle. His beard scraped her smooth cheek and the smell of buckskin, of tobacco, touched Kitty's nostrils. Her breath was short and sharp and painful. Her hand came up to push him away, but, without effort, Curt swept it aside, found her lips.

At last he spoke. "You won't forget, Kitty," he said, coolly. "That's why you won't marry Davis—or any other man. You'd be remembering me. Every time he touched you—every kiss—you'd be remembering. You're trembling, Kitty. Why keep on fighting? It won't do any good."

Kitty stepped backward and reached for Mowich. Words rushed to her lips but she could not speak them, not with Curt, unperturbed, watching her with that little flame of success in his eyes. She was in the saddle, swiftly, then, without assistance, and Curt watched her, unmoving.

Around the bend was Newmarket—and safety. She did not trust herself to look back. The mittens on her hands were soft and warm, but now, angrily, she dragged them off and threw them, furiously, over her shoulder, into the mud of the trail.

Before her, in a little clearing, was the Sparks' cabin, and the group of men and horses had stopped before it. Two children and a woman were running from the cabin.

She had reached Newmarket—but the lightness of heart she had expected was not there. At least a part of what Curt had said was true. She would remember him; forever she would remember the feel of his rough cheek, the stone-hard muscles of his chest, his lips; she would remember her own involuntary response, mounting into terrifying intensity, which, this time, she had been unable to control.

She could not help the emotions which Curt had aroused in her, for she had fought with all her strength against them. She would not even try to name them. She could not help her feeling toward this man of whom she disapproved so strongly and whom she had tried so hard to hate. But she knew that she could and she would govern her actions. She must trample out the fires his strange charm and power had kindled, for if she did not she knew that she would be forever lost.

FORTUNE SPARKS WAS A TALL, BIG-framed man, with a bony face and bald head and large, capable hands. He moved slowly; he was not a man given to hearty back-slapping. But the look on his face as he swung across the clearing toward the newcomers assured them of their welcome. He shook hands with the men with a brief "Howdy" and a smile which Kitty thought was rarely used; and then he turned to regard her quietly, estimating her with frank and kindly eyes.

But Martha was less reticent. Visitors were all too rare and the arrival of another woman to Newmarket was an occasion too great for reserve. She was a small, quick, wiry woman with snapping black eyes and weather-coarsened skin and her straight dark hair was fastened in a tight knot on the back of her head. Her laughter was quick and genuine and her words swift and to the point. Within a very few minutes she had greeted each in the party, had taken possession of Kitty, had reorganized her household and was already planning how she could "feed and sleep" the group.

The cabin was larger than the Lintons', and new. There was a loft, reached by a small ladder, above the main room, and a second small room had been built behind the fireplace, so the warmth seeped through. It was to this second and smaller room that Martha led Kitty, and where she directed that Kitty's possessions be placed.

"If I'd knowed," Martha said, for the tenth time, "if I'd just knowed you were coming I could have had everything redded up. Never occurred to me Fletcher and Sunset might bring back a girl with them. Families, sometimes, but a girl alone, no, save me, if I ever thought of it! When I saw you and Fletcher comin' down the trail together, I had a start; I thought, well, now, Curt's done it at last, he's got himself a wife." Martha laughed heartily. She was spreading the bed coverings, smoothing them, preparing them for Kitty. "I might have known! So you're going to Nisqually, now. Got kinfolk there, maybe? I'm surprised you didn't go by ship—the *Beaver* comes into the Sound now and then. You don't look English and you sure talk Southern. Kinfolks there?"

Kitty smiled at the friendly, bustling little woman. "No, not kinfolks. The man I am to marry."

"Law, save me!" Martha paused, her hands on her hips, and surveyed Kitty with even greater interest. "Now that is news! A fine thing, too, for a girl to come all this way to join her man, over that trail from Oregon City. I know that trail well. We came not long after the Simmons. Oh, but we had a time, wagon broke down or wore out, and why wouldn't it? I kept telling Sparks everything has to wear out sometime! Wonder it lasted long's it did. So we made sleds and dragged our goods through the mud. Save me, I thought we'd never make it. What now, Wealthy?"

The little girl, who had appeared and then disappeared shyly in the excitement of the arrival, peeked in. It was amazing, Kitty thought, that Martha and Fortune, neither of whom had any claim to beauty, could have produced this child. Her perfect oval face was that of a tiny Madonna; her fine pale brown hair was brushed plainly back from her smooth forehead, and braided very tightly; her eyes were wide and soft and clear and her mouth so sensitive it seemed on the verge of trembling. Kitty held out her hand to her.

"Come in, won't you, Wealthy? My name is Catherine Gatewood. You may call me Kitty, if you like."

The child edged into the room, her hands behind her. Martha smiled at her, and then suddenly her expression changed.

"Wealthy, I declare—you've got that chicken! Take it out now, this minute, you hear me? Miss Gatewood ain't interested in no chickens—"

Wealthy's seven-year-old face clouded and her eyes filled. Awkwardly she pulled the heavy hen from behind her back and clasped it in her arms, appealing silently and eloquently to Kitty.

Kitty laughed. "A hen? Wealthy, what an odd pet!"

Wealthy smiled and her small face was transformed. Her eyes lighted and she giggled and cast a mischievous, triumphant glance at her mother. The Madonna was gone, a delightful hoyden in her place. She edged a little farther into the room, and made way for the little boy behind her.

"Reason has the cock," Wealthy contributed eagerly.

Reason's face was as homely as Wealthy's was beautiful. A comical, round little face with overlapping freckles, eyes that squinted as though in harsh sunlight; his nose was upturned, and because some of his teeth were missing the new, front ones looked unnaturally large. He was a sturdy eight-year-old, and when the baby roundness left him, he would grow as big and bony and strong as his father; a shock of sunburned hair fell across his forehead and the paws that held the brown rooster were grimy. He squinted at Kitty suspiciously. Kitty felt it was very necessary that both Reason and his exquisite, small sister approve of her.

"Take them out, children," Martha commanded. "Law, those fowl are the trial of my life! But they set such store by them—"

"Let them stay just a minute," Kitty coaxed. Her eyes were dancing as she knelt and stroked the chickens. "They are very fine," she said softly, her face on a level with the children's. "Do they have names?"

"Why, of course," Reason said, with disdain. "Of course they have names. They're the only American chickens on Puget Sound. There's Hudson's Bay chickens at Nisqually and Cowlitz Farms, but nobody else in Newmarket has chickens!"

He made his momentous announcement slowly, his eyes solemn, to impress Kitty with the great importance of his words. Wealthy nodded seriously and hugged the hen.

"We keep them in the cabin because of skunks might get them, outside," Wealthy said.

"Yes," Reason confirmed, "and at nights we take them to the loft and they sleep on the foot of our beds. Ma doesn't like it much, but we can't let them stay downstairs, close to the chimney."

"But wouldn't they be safe there?"

Reason regarded her for a long moment, amazed at her ignorance.

"Course not," he said scornfully. "Owls."

"They might come down the chimney at night and get them," Wealthy explained. Kitty nodded with the solemnity the occasion demanded.

"Now take them out, children. Take them out." Martha shooed children and chickens through the doorway and turned, chuckling, back to Kitty. "I reckon you understand young ones, Miss Gatewood. The chickens are the only pets they have, you see. I don't rightly know what'd happen if a weasel or hawk got one of those fool chickens. Like to cry themselves sick. . . . I've hot water. Is it all right if I call you Kitty? My name is Martha. You can have a bath if you like. Maybe you'd like to wash your hair? Water's soft." She hesitated, "But I *am* right short of soap. Made a good batch of it—and Sparks up and took it, 'thout saying a word. Used it for axle grease. Made me so mad I didn't speak to him for two days. He didn't mind," she laughed heartily, "said it was a good rest!"

"I'd like to bathe and wash my hair, Martha. I have soap."

"I'll fetch a kettle." She leaned toward Kitty and added in a loud whisper, "The Necessary's out back. I made Sparks build a good one, first thing; won't have my young ones growing up like dirty Indians; I'll bring a lamp. We've a little whale oil, got it from Nisqually. Now I can have proper candles again! Fletcher didn't forget the molds. He's a man of his word, sure enough. You'll excuse me, Kitty, I'll have to stir up the fire and send Reason for water."

Martha bustled out and Kitty looked about her. The door opened a crack and she saw Wealthy's bright, curious eyes. "Come in," Kitty invited.

"We forgot to tell you their names," Wealthy said, her small chin tucked down into her neck, her words almost inaudible with shyness.

"And I want to know them. What is the hen's name, Wealthy?"

"It's Children."

"Oh?" Kitty waited for further enlightenment.

"We had a chicken before, in Oregon City. Her name was Mother. *Her* mother's name was Grandma. Mother laid some eggs but only one of them did hatch—this one. That was all the children mother hen had, so we named this one Children."

"That sounds very reasonable."

"But now this one laid an egg and I think she will have children, you see, so then we will change her name to Mother."

"I see. And the rooster is Father?"

"Yes."

Wealthy stepped aside to allow Martha to enter with hot water. "I just thought you'd like to know," Wealthy said politely, and Kitty nodded as the little girl disappeared.

Kitty was laughing as she bent to wash her hair. The water was like satin, foaming quickly into suds. It smoothed her skin and made her hair gleam and sparkle and it refreshed her immeasurably. The children's eagerness for friendship and their awkward little attempts to make friends by bringing to her at once their most treasured possessions were infinitely touching. Martha, too, was starved for companionship, and her wholehearted, generous offering of everything she had warmed Kitty.

From the outer room came a steady hum of voices and occasional laughter. Kitty took her time, bathing and dressing, brushing her hair dry. It was good to slip into clean clothes again and she unrolled the russet-colored dress and shook out the wrinkles. She was surveying it unhappily when Martha rapped.

"Supper's about ready," she announced cheerfully, opening the door a crack. "My land!" She spied the dress and the cascade of silk petticoats Kitty had spread on the bed, and she forgot her duties in the room behind her. As though drawn by a magnet she put her rough hand out to the beautiful, soft woolens and silks.

"The colors of them. And the quality!" Martha rubbed the materials between her fingers expertly and sighed with pleasure. "I'll fix an iron and you can press them. Coal's hot, and it'll take only a minute." She was back again almost instantly, carrying a flatiron and a carefully padded board. She tested the iron with a wet finger-tip. She released the handle of the iron and examined the coals within the hollow bed with satisfaction and then replaced it.

"Heat's about right, Kitty. Press the wool first. Silk won't take so much heat. Or shall I do it?"

"Would you like to?"

Eagerly, Martha pulled the garments toward her, clucking her satisfaction at the beauty of the materials. Her face was younger, softer, in the light from the tiny oil lamp. "Takes me back," she said wistfully, "it sure does take me back. Once before I was married I had a dress, not so fine as this, that's certain, but good woolen, soft, and a nice color, too, a woodsy green." Her fingers moved deftly and finally she held the dress up to Kitty and with a sigh relinquished it. She smiled then, and the quick, nervous movements ended and she stood motionless, watching Kitty as she donned the dress.

"I reckon," Martha said hesitatingly, "you don't figure to stay in Newmarket. I was of the idea when I first saw you that you was a settler. Thought you might be a new neighbor, seeing as you are to marry and all. But I see now—your young man is British?"

Kitty shook her head. The easy informality and eagerness that had emanated from Martha from the moment of her arrival had left her, and the woman looked awkward now, with some of Wealthy's shyness. She twisted her hands in her apron as though to hide their roughness, or to keep them from touching again the luxuries that belonged to Kitty. Kitty wanted desperately to recapture her friendliness.

"No, Martha, I'm not a settler. But you see—that is because I have a home, back in South Carolina. Or rather, Philip has it. My father died a year ago. He left Wildcliffe, that is our plantation, to Philip, for him and me. Philip must go back now to manage Wildcliffe and I must go with him. I have no one else, except Philip, though Philip has relatives there. My letters did not reach him in Oregon. I heard from him, from Oregon City. I had to find him, to tell him that Wildcliffe is his, and that father is gone. So I came. I came around the Horn, on the *Sea Bird*, and in Oregon City I found that Philip was at Fort Nisqually. We have been promised for more than two years. My father wished it, and he wanted so much for Philip to come home—"

She stopped. Why was it necessary to explain, to justify her presence here to this plain, suddenly quiet woman?

"Did you say his name was—Philip?"

"Yes. Philip Davis."

Still Martha stood, staring at her, pleating her skirt with her fingers.

"What is it, Martha?"

Martha took a short, sharp breath. "Nothing. I—I reckon that's a rather common name, isn't it? Isn't that funny, now! There's a Philip Davis, an American, come to Newmarket from Nisqually not more than a month ago. Took up a claim, right next to Sunset's. Built himself a stout, fine cabin, much the finest in Newmarket. But he keeps to himself, except for the British who go there to—well, I've seen him only once. Wouldn't it a-been nice now, if that were your young man, and you'd a-settled near to us? That woulda pleasured us all. But of course—"

"But that must be he!" Kitty said as she clasped Martha's arm in her excitement. "Tell me, Martha, what does he look like? Perhaps—"

"No, this couldn't be your young man." Martha clamped her lips tight together. "He's unsociable—and—well, now, I'd no call to gossip. He's a lean, thin-faced young fellow and dark; rides well, a fine sorrel horse. But—"

Kitty's heart pounded violently. Martha hurried back to the larger room and Kitty followed. Martha seemed greatly agitated, and the voices of the men stopped as she entered. Fortune stood awkwardly and offered her a chair near to the fire. Sunset, squatting on his heels nearby, rose, too. He seemed taller in the small cabin. He hitched up his belt.

She did not at first see Curt, but she felt him standing close behind her and then Sunset glanced over her shoulder as at some signal from Curt and nodded slightly. Curt moved toward the door and Sunset and Fortune followed.

"Supper's ready," Martha warned them.

"In a minute, Martha," Fortune said.

"There now!" Martha scolded. "Gone out to have a drink, most likely. Where Charlefour is, there's bound to be Blue Ruin. Just the same, I'm going to dish up."

It was several minutes before the men returned and took their places at the table. Martha had spread a worn cloth and laid out the few tin dishes she possessed. Curt had supplemented them with the familiar camp utensils; there was bread of coarsely ground or pounded wheat; there was a venison stew. Martha made no apology for the plainness of her fare and Kitty knew she had given her best. The children's eyes sparkled with delight when Martha placed a crock of berry jam upon the table. It was obvious it was an unaccustomed treat, saved for company.

Night had come. When the cabin grew too warm and the men relaxed with pipes of real tobacco, Martha opened a window—a sliding panel of oiled skin. The sky was clear and the moon nearly full and the night was like black glass; the cold, damp air poured into the crowded little room and Kitty drank it in, gratefully. She wanted to ask about Philip, but the men were deeply absorbed in talk important to them and she hesitated to interrupt. She listened with only slight interest, waiting till the conversation lagged and she could speak without rudeness.

"Dr. Tolmie finally agreed to let us have some blankets and clothing and a few other things; not much, but it'll help us to get through the winter. We made an agreement with him to hire Indian labor, and it's fair enough, though we'd got to promise not to trade for furs," Fortune said. From the mantel he took a small piece of paper and unfolded it slowly. "We all agreed to the rates and we promised Tolmie all the settlers'd stick by them, so his trade with the Indians wouldn't be unsettled. Hope it's all right with you. It was the best deal we could make."

He handed the paper to Curt and Curt read it aloud, thoughtfully.

"One day's work, one cotton handkerchief. One week's work, one hickory shirt; use of canoe to Nisqually and back, one cotton handkerchief; each Indian in canoe, one cotton handkerchief; one deer ham, one load powder and ball. One good horse, one musket . . . Yes, Fortune, I'll agree to that."

Sunset nodded thoughtfully. "Pretty cheap," he suggested.

"Yes. But Tolmie was set on it, said if we paid the Indians more he'd not give us goods, either for cash or credit. We finally got him to agree to a price of $3.50 a thousand for shingles delivered at the Fort. We're to get paid in groceries and goods. It'll mean we can make it through the winter, barring accidents. Simmons is fixing to have his grist mill ready by summer. He's using flat stones from the river bed. Couldn't get buhrstones from Nisqually, but he thinks he can make do."

"You figure to make shingles this winter, Fortune?" Sunset asked.

Fortune nodded. "Yes. Some of the men are going down to work at Cowlitz Farm. But I'd rather stay nearby, long as I can." He glanced at Martha and then at the children, half-asleep in the chimney corner.

"No Indian trouble around here?"

"No. Oh, they'll steal, of course, but no real trouble. Canoe Indians aren't like the horse Indians, you think, Sunset?"

"Seem more peaceable. But I wouldn't take too many chances."

"We got another worry, though. Seems the shipmasters, tramp traders, come in the Sound now and then, and they put ashore sailors who's gone mad at sea. Two or three of them, maybe more, roamin' this country now. We sight one of them once in a while. They're like wild things. They'd ought to be found and taken care of, some way, but I don't know who's to do it. They're no danger to Nisqually, so Tolmie isn't interested. But it's not good to have 'em roamin' loose. Poor demented devils; I figure they get hungry enough, they're apt to come around. Gabe Jones says—"

The talk of people she did not know, the recounting of the tale of the Lost Company, the news about the British and the Indian unrest to the east, would go on, Kitty presumed, far into the night. But finally Sunset arose, refreshed by the rest and the food and talk.

"I'll be moving on, Martha."

"Not tonight, Sunset! Stay till morning."

"Like to sleep under my own roof." He smiled at Martha and she could take no offense at his refusal of her hospitality. "Charlie's anxious to see Polly Careless and Fortune says she's still at our cabin. Glad she got a roof on it. Polly's a capable woman."

"She had a time! All the good Indian workers went to—went to others," she finished, lamely. "But it's right snug now. Sparks was over that way not two weeks ago; said Polly done right well."

Reason, drowsing in his corner, awakened with a jerk. His eyes were heavy and the room swam before him. His face was blank with sleepiness; he blinked manfully, and then his head nodded again, too heavy to support. Wealthy, a tiny, quiet bundle, was curled up beside him. Sunset grinned at them.

"I stay here and watch Reason I'll fall asleep myself," he said. "Got a little package here for 'em. Maybe you'd like to keep it till Christmas." He placed a clumsily wrapped bundle on the table and the worn wrappings parted, revealing a doll of fringed buckskin with popping eyes of bright blue beads, and a miniature hunting knife with a handle of deer horn; Martha clucked over them and Fortune's face pictured his gratitude and quiet pleasure. Sunset raised his pack to his strong shoulders and held out his big hand to Kitty. "So long, Kitty."

Kitty's hand was swallowed in his and she clung to him. She needed his reassuring presence, his quiet strength. Some of her need must have been reflected in her face, for he held her hand steadily, in no haste to go.

"I, Dad," he said, looking at the shining cap of her hair, her scrubbed, smooth skin, the soft rich russet of her beautiful dress, the smooth-fitting bodice, "you're a beauty, and I'll miss seein' you each day. I'm wishin' you luck, and happiness."

"Sunset, must you go? Can't you wait, till tomorrow? I wanted to ask—I know you're anxious to get home and I guess I've delayed you enough, but—"

"You've not delayed me," he said swiftly, "you kept up. Sick or well, tired or hungry or cold, you kept right on goin', and never a peep. It was a pleasure to have you with us, Kitty, and I'm glad you made it, safe and sound." He paused. "I reckon you'll be goin' back to Oregon City by ship. That would be easiest. Likely Davis can arrange it. I reckon you heard he isn't in Nisqually. He's here in Newmarket."

"I—yes," she said, "Martha said—"

"Kitty," he went on, and it seemed to her the cabin was very quiet, only the sound of his voice and the soft crackling of the fire marring it. "We think it might be better were I to stop by Davis' place tonight, late as it is, and tell him you're here. Likely he'll ride over, first thing in the morning—"

"Oh, no," Kitty said, breathlessly, "not—not here." Her face flamed. She could not meet Philip with curious eyes upon her.

"Only fair to give him some notice," Sunset persisted. He tried to keep his voice light. "Might be a shock to him, Kitty, not knowin' you were comin'. Be a shock to any man, have you appear like this, without warnin'. Only fair to let him know."

"Yes," she agreed, finally, "I guess you're right. But—please tell him I'll come in the morning. Tell him to wait for me there."

Sunset nodded and picked up his rifle. "Curt will bring you."

"I'm sure that won't be necessary," Kitty began.

"It's on his way. Davis' claim is next to ours. If I don't see you again—good luck, Kitty. Thanks, Martha, Fortune. See you in the mornin', Curt."

The men went to the door with him. Kitty did not want to see Curt again tonight and she excused herself swiftly and withdrew to the small room. But even then she was not to have the privacy she desired; Martha would share the bed with her.

Kitty lay silent and wide-awake when Martha slipped in beside her. She heard the older woman sigh wearily as she composed herself to sleep. But Kitty could not sleep. She heard Martha whisper her prayers, and suddenly homesickness for Wildcliffe, for Margaret, overcame her. The crowded quarters, her jumbled emotions, kept her wakeful and tense. She tried not to move restlessly, but every muscle seemed to cry for frequent movement. Would Sunset have reached Philip by now? Would Philip heed her request and wait for her, or would he, in his usual impulsive fashion, come dashing to the Sparks' cabin? What would their meeting be like?

How did she really feel about Philip? She had believed she loved him. She did have a deep affection for him. It had seemed natural and it had been pleasant to have her father's blessing, and she had happily looked ahead to spending the rest of her life at Wildcliffe with him. But the intense emotion she had felt for Curt—what was it? It was not love, she decided, for love must be based upon respect and admiration; it must be something more than a fierceness burning behind their talk; and yet she had not known a touch could mean so much, his fingers on her hands, his lips on hers. But that was all there must be between them—ever.

She was promised to Philip. And she could never overlook Lisa. Her conscience tormented her; she should have been strong enough to resist Curt, or at least to have hidden her own response. But her youth and her body had betrayed her. . . . It would never happen again.

Whatever had possessed Philip to leave Nisqually and build a cabin at Newmarket, she wondered? Why had Martha seemed so uneasy, talking about him?

She had believed Martha was asleep, but the thin, workworn body beside her turned cautiously, seeking more comfort. There was a rustling in the loft above—the chickens. From the outer room came a movement and then a few low-spoken words. Fortune and Curt were wakeful, too; Kitty's eyes closed but she could see Curt's face as it must appear there in the firelight, health and vigor in every one of its straight lines. Would he really speak to Philip? Would he dare?

He'd dare anything, she decided, wearily. He had always got what he wanted, but tomorrow, for the first time, he would find that could not last. She recognized that her exhaustion came not only from her journey but from the battle of her will against Fletcher's. His very assurance, that her marriage with Philip would not come about, was enough to disturb her, as though his words and his will could enlist the aid of higher powers to bring his wishes to fulfillment. How silly of me, she scolded herself; I am thinking like Jessie Pearl, that the man has bewitched me! He is only an arrogant and selfish man, who has no regard for the likes and dislikes of others, and no delicacy whatsoever. He'll discover tomorrow, that I, too, mean what I say.

But the cabin itself seemed wakeful, waiting; only the children in the loft above were asleep.

◇ 2 ◇

KITTY would return to stay with Martha until Philip made arrangements for them to leave. She was ready and waiting when Curt at last arose from the breakfast table and leisurely bade the Sparks family good-by. She had listened tensely, throughout the night and the early morning, for the first sound of horses' hoofs which might herald Philip's coming. But the sun was high and he had not appeared; he was gentleman enough to understand and to observe her wishes, she decided. He would meet her, likely, on the trail, and there would be few curious eyes—only Curt's sardonic ones—to witness their meeting. But Curt would have no further excuse to remain, then, once she were safely with Philip. She would not see him again.

The way was smooth, the trail more traveled from the Sparks' cabin toward the Sound. They rode in silence. But if Curt was uneasy he did not show it, and Kitty kept her face resolutely forward, straining for the first sight of Philip's cabin. She fancied she could smell the salt air from Puget Sound, and far in the distance she could see it, deep blue against the lighter horizon. Beyond were mountains and hidden in the clouded sky behind her was the greatest sentinel of all the Cascade Range—Mount Rainier. The Mountain was not visible today. Curt turned occasionally to see if the clouds had parted, but only the sky to the northwest was clear.

It was mid-morning when at last Curt spoke. "I think the cabin is just ahead," he said. His voice was level, expressionless, and Kitty did not reply. She urged Mowich forward, but suddenly Curt's large bay came alongside her and he swept down and grasped Mowich's bridle rein.

Something in his face halted the angry protest on her lips. He was leaning forward, standing in his stirrups, and he was listening intently.

"Wait," he said, almost in a whisper. And then Kitty heard it, too, a faint wail, an odd, eerie keening.

"What is it?" she breathed.

"If it's what I think it is—" he paused again, listening, still holding the rein. "Stay behind me," he ordered sharply. "If I tell you to stop—stop!"

They went forward, Mowich following the big bay obediently. The wail stopped and then it began again, louder, longer, and Kitty's hand crept to her throat. They came to a small, natural field; the edge of it, in the shadows, was still white with frost. At the far side of it stood a cabin, of raw logs, with a new shake roof. Behind it was a neat, stout barn and a corral of newly peeled rails. A sorrel horse and a smaller, shaggier Indian pony were within it and they raised their heads and whinnied softly.

There was no other sign of life about the cabin; no smoke came from the broad stone chimney. The door was closed; but the sound, the wail, rising now to a chant, came from within it. They came nearer to the cabin and Curt held out his hand, stopping her.

"Wait here," he ordered. "Don't come any closer."

He dismounted, dropped the reins to the ground. Kitty allowed Mowich to take a few steps forward and then she stopped, waiting. Where was Philip? What was that ominous, awful noise coming from the cabin?

Curt rapped at the door and there was no response but the noise from within stopped suddenly. He pounded again and finally he pushed open the door. He stepped inside, and then, almost instantly, he came out again, closing the door behind him.

He walked slowly back to Kitty and picked up the trailing reins. He wiped his face with his hand, his lips drawn back from his teeth.

"What is it? Curt—*what is it?*"

He looked at her then. The muscles on his neck and jaw were hard, and there were deep creases between his eyes. "It's the death chant, Kitty—of Indian women."

"The *death chant?*"

"Yes."

"This isn't—this isn't where Philip—Philip isn't here?"

"He's here, Kitty." For the first time Curt's voice was almost gentle. "He's—here. But he's dead. That's his squaw."

She stared at him in wild disbelief. "It's not true! He can't be! It isn't Philip! It isn't Philip!" Her voice rose to a scream and she struck Mowich suddenly with the ends of the reins and the horse leaped forward.

"Don't, Kitty! Don't go in there—for the love of—"

The sorrel horse in the corral whinnied again. Mowich came to a stop and Kitty slid off and began to run, stumbling, toward the door. Curt's shout followed her, but she paid no heed and he could not reach her before she flung open the door and stared into the dusky interior.

An Indian girl huddled beside the cold fireplace. Her arms were clasped about her breasts, and she swayed from side to side. As Kitty entered she raised her dark face and the wail came again, the awful, echoing chant of death that filled the cabin, reverberated from the walls, filtered out into the quiet morning.

There was a table there, carefully smoothed and polished white, and it was littered with papers and books; there was before it a single stout armchair, such as were used by the clerks in the British forts. In the chair slumped Philip Davis, his chin on his chest, his dark hair falling, partially covering his face. His hand hung limp at his side, his long, motionless, curling fingertips almost touching the revolver on the bare wood floor beside him.

Philip was carefully dressed in a black broadcloth suit, and a stock and waistcoat that had once been gleaming white. Now it was red, evilly, horribly red; the edges of the stain had dried black, but the center was still wet and crimson.

Kitty stared, refusing to believe what she saw. The dark hair was familiar, but never had she seen it in disarray before; it was not Philip, certainly, she said, her lips moving, but making no sound. Philip would not allow his hair to be so unruly; she took a step forward, bent to see the face; the straight, thin nose, the handsome, petulant mouth. Her horrified gaze traveled down the stained shirt-front, down the arm, seeming unnaturally long and limp, and came to rest on the weapon on the floor.

It was the gun which convinced her. The gun was a duelling pistol; it was one of a set from the gun room at Wildcliffe. Robert Gatewood had given it to Philip and on its polished handle was the tiny Gatewood crest.

◆ 3 ◆

DEATH has many faces. The one turned to Kitty now had nothing in it of the dignity of her mother's death, nor the grateful release of her father's. Death had come to them naturally, without violence. Their passing had brought to Kitty deep and everlasting grief, the ache of permanent separation which would be with her always; but it had been eased by the knowledge that they were the inevitable, natural endings, simply the quiet closing of beloved books at the end of the last completed chapters.

But to Kitty, Philip's death was tragic, sinful waste.

At first, numbed with shock, she was conscious only of a feeling of unreality, the natural, inevitable rejection of the living against the finality of death, intensified, now, because she had been so totally unprepared. The only words she could seem to form, and which she repeated constantly in the first tormented hours were "It can't be true, it simply can't be true—" and yet she knew that it was true and she must accept it.

If Robert had failed with Philip, Margaret had succeeded, nevertheless, in teaching Kitty to face realities, to do what needed to be done. Kitty's feeling that she was moving in a nightmare did not cause her to leave her duties to others. She had been taught that leadership was part of the Gatewood heritage; inexperienced as she was, unseasoned, and, until now, untried, she reeled, at first, from the awful and unexpected blow. But immediately she forced herself to come erect again and to go about the grim business that she knew she had to do.

At Wildcliffe, there would have been many to help her; servants to jump to her bidding, Judge Stuart, friends and relatives and officials, to do all the necessary, sad things. But Wildcliffe was half the world away, and at Newmarket there was not even an impartial, respectful official. The help Kitty received came not for pay nor from duty. It came because of that intangible something in Oregon that brought the fiercely independent settlers almost magically together in time of need; to Kitty, it was charity, which, because of Philip, she was forced unwillingly to accept. To the settlers it was a natural return for like favors they had received, or were any day apt to need.

Kitty selected the place where Philip would rest; a beautiful spot near Puget Sound, where the wind sighed softly in the treetops, and the waves lapped just as softly against the sand and gravel of the shore. It was a secluded, guarded and beautiful place, in earth undisturbed for centuries, and, if no one visited it, nature would kindly obliterate the grave itself, covering it over swiftly with lush undergrowth. Kitty asked Fortune if he would read over Philip. She prepared the brief eulogy, which was only a bare recitation of facts—the kindlier, impersonal facts; the year of his birth, his name—what more could be said?

Standing in the brilliant cold sunlight of the winter noon, listening to Fortune's halting, earnest voice, Kitty raised her heavy, tearless eyes and looked at the people about the open grave. There was a surprising number there. She had heard them greet one another, and the names were familiar—Simmons, Jones, Kindred, Crocket—but she could not yet put the names and faces together. She heard a woman speak softly to a restless child—Jackson January; and the name echoed in her consciousness, Jackson Jan-u-ary. These people had come on foot, on horseback, by canoe. How the word had spread, Kitty did not know. But they had laid down their tools, donned their best clothing, and taken precious hours to give to Kitty. She was, thereby, in their debt. She hated it.

Here and there a woman dabbed silently at her eyes. Were the tears for Philip, Kitty wondered impersonally, or were they for the memories Fortune's words invoked? Not a one of the settlers but had seen death before, and intimately felt its pain. Many a woman had lost her own and had endured the last, almost unbearable, heart-rending aftermath, the sight and sound of camouflaging wagon-wheels rolling over the new, deserted grave of her beloved. Kitty, bitterness gestating within her, envied them those memories. Their grief had not been weighted with humiliation and disappointment. At least their grief was sharp and clean.

Lingering in the background were several Indian faces; were they here because of curiosity about an American tribal custom, or had they been friends of Philip? On the outskirts of the group was the silent Indian girl, Melia; it did not matter to Kitty that she was there. To Kitty she was symbolic; the dark, intangible shadow of danger and evil and weakness that one must fight, within themselves or without. . . . Philip had not fought. Why hide it? Perhaps it was fitting that Melia, as well as Kitty, be here at the end. This was, after all, a summing-up.

She ought, she told herself, to be thinking only of Philip. It was odd how one's mind wandered; perhaps it was nature's defense, when the unadulterated facts were almost too painful to be borne. It was not easy to analyze how she felt toward Philip. Deep compassion for him and the torment he must have undergone before he was driven to the last cowardly extremity were overcome by her scorn for his weakness, and a resentment at what she considered a betrayal—of her, of Margaret, of all decent things. And perhaps Philip's torment had not, after all, been so great, she thought, uncharitably; Philip had less endurance than most. No, she thought, and her heart hardened. There was no mitigating circumstance. He had not taken a life, his own, to save someone else from grief or destruction, nor to free himself from unbearable, hopeless pain. Instead, without thought of the consequences to her, to anyone—even to Melia!—he had simply impulsively run away again as he had fled from Wildcliffe to avoid the minor embarrassments, the criticism and small unpleasantness that had arisen from his foolish duel.

She felt grief, of course. But now she recognized with cold clarity that part of her present extreme pain was disillusionment and shame. In the instant she had opened the door of Philip's cabin, she had lost forever the golden glow of romantic illusions. She had, in that one instant, left a precious, happy, girlhood innocence behind her. She resented the unnecessary cruelty of that abrupt change from the protected, genteel world to which she was born, to the harsh and sordid from which she had been shielded, but at which Margaret had hinted. She could find little tolerance in her heart for the man who had caused it.

It had been so vivid a portrayal, a garish, melodramatic painting, an indecent scene, which needed no words to explain: the swaying, wailing, dark figure of tragedy that was the Indian girl, who might, Kitty thought, ruthlessly not sparing herself, as well have been an octaroon instead; the revolver on the floor, where it had fallen from his beautiful, useless fingers; his incongruous, meticulous dress.

She knew very well what Philip had undergone during his last night on earth. She had known him thoroughly. It had been a secret, unworded knowledge of his weakness, demonstrated in the petulance and unhappiness in his letters, that had brought her to Oregon. How wise Margaret had been! And, if, after Margaret's tutelage, she had not known the innermost working of Philip's mind, an immature, erratic mind—the words of Sunset would have told her very well.

Kitty had sat on the bed in the little room at the Sparks', and she had heard every word clearly, through the thin, ill-fitting door, words that dropped one by one into her consciousness, like glass beads dropping slowly and singly into a china cup.

"There was a light," Sunset had said, "when I came by about eleven o'clock. Charlie and Indian George were with me. Davis came to the door. He hadn't shaved lately and was dressed roughly. He'd been drinkin'. There were bottles all around the room. Melia wasn't there. He was alone.

"He was mad at bein' interrupted—but drunks often are. Finally he asked us in and we sat down and he insisted we have a drink with him. I tried to lead up to the subject gradually. I knew about his drinkin' and gamblin' and Melia—Fortune had told us, and we thought it would be pretty rough for Kitty to go and find him like that, with Melia there. You'd understand, if you knew Kitty. We figured he'd want to clean up some, get Melia out of the way, and like that, before Kitty came. That's why I stopped by his place to warn him.

"The minute I mentioned Kitty's name he sobered up. He changed, right then. First he thought I had a letter from her. Then I told her she'd come to Oregon City by ship. He had a look on his face, full of hope and despair all at once. He sat for a while, sayin' nothin'. Finally he laughed, nervous-like, and said he'd decided, not hearin', that she'd given him up; that she'd married someone else, probably, being as beautiful and popular as she was. He couldn't seem to grasp the idea, that she had come to join him.

"He seemed all keyed up, then, like he was walkin' on top of the world. He strode about, gesturin', makin' plans. He'd have the cabin in fine shape by mornin', he said.

"I figured he was all right when I left him. He was excited and talkin' fast, but he was makin' plans. I figured he'd pull himself together.

"I went home. This mornin' Curt brought Kitty. She was stunned, she couldn't seem to take in anything. We left her with

Polly and went back to the cabin. I looked at the horse in the corral and found where Davis'd taken him out in the early mornin'.

"He'd ridden to the Sparks' place. I found where he stopped at the edge of the woods. He was there quite a while. Martha said Kitty went out early and stood just outside the door, tryin' to see The Mountain. But it was cloudy, of course, and the sun not high yet, and The Mountain was not visible.

"I think Davis stood there, hidden in the woods, watchin' Kitty. Even at that distance he couldn't mistake her, that hair of hers. I don't know why he didn't go on and speak to her. I think he meant to, for he'd dressed carefully and shaved. But he saw her, I'll swear to that. He came back home, then, to wait for her, I suppose, and Melia was back. Melia said she left when he started his heavy drinkin' bouts, crept back to take care of him when he was over them.

"He sat down at the table, Melia said, and began to write and then he gave it up and threw his pen across the room. She thought it was just the drink made him act that way. He didn't say anything to her. She went out to get some wood and water. While she was at the spring she heard a shot. When she came in she found him—like that.

"It was just that he couldn't face Kitty. He saw her, and when he came back to the cabin, there was Melia. It was more than he could handle."

Yes, that was the way it had been, impulsive, unplanned. Fortune was stumbling over the words Kitty had written for him to read but he was doing the best he could. . . . Why did you do it, Philip? There must have been some other way. What a waste. What an awful, sinful, tragic waste.

The people of Newmarket were too courteous to stare openly at Kitty, but they exchanged questioning and troubled glances. She had drawn apart from them. She stood, very fragile, very stiff, her stricken face unscarred by tears, and the women were undecided whether they should offer her condolences when the simple services were ended. The usual words of sympathy did not seem to fit here; this was more complex, unnatural, and the girl, remote, unapproachable, did not look like she would welcome any talk at all. The eyes of the men rested on her frequently. In spite of shock and grief she was still the most beautiful girl any of them had ever seen; with the sunlight glinting on her amazing pale hair, lighting the soft young curves of her face and figure, she seemed to them appealingly defenseless and admirably courageous. There were those who could not understand why any man would have done what Philip had done, had there been the most remote chance of possessing Kitty; but there were others, too, who could understand his desperation, for Kitty, despite her lush beauty, had a purity about her. There was a tiny white ruffle about her smooth throat, still finer ones about her small wrists; her daintiness and fastidiousness would be hard for a man to live up to.

Fortune's voice ceased, and then, at a sign from him, another man stepped forward, his head bared, and softly, beautifully, his voice, well-rounded and rich, rose in a hymn. It was a song beloved in Oregon—*Watchman Tell Us of the Night*—called by some Narcissa Whitman's song. Kitty regarded the singer without expression. He had Negro blood, reflected in the richness of his voice. But he did not have the deferential, closed face of a slave.

Ordinarily, a funeral, like a wedding or a christening, would be the opportunity for a rare, day-long visit among the settlers. But now they dispersed rapidly. It did not seem right to have a funeral feast, for after all, Philip had not been one of them, and Kitty, too, seemed alien; the crocks and baskets the women had brought remained unopened. They had done what they could. It seemed unnatural that the girl would not turn to the women of Newmarket; they would have been quick to offer homely advice and sisterly comfort, and Laura Trainor was heard to whisper to Sarah Hansen that it would be much better if Kitty "talked it out." But Kitty held aloof. There was in her manner a chilly, polite gratitude for their presence; but there was beneath it resentment that she should be here at all, and that she should be indebted to them. A few recognized her attitude for what it was, a defense against the hurt dealt to her. But most of them, direct and simple folk, were bewildered by her.

There was no privacy for Kitty in Newmarket, and this she missed most of all. Full darkness had come before they returned to the Sparks' cabin, but tears would not come to her in the night when Martha lay beside her. Kitty's head throbbed, her body felt heavy, lifeless. At morning she had no desire to get up from the bed. She was not hungry. When the children came to the door she turned her face toward the wall.

It would take more strength than she possessed now to force herself to enter Philip's cabin. Later on it must be done. For the first time in many days she thought of Jessie Pearl. She must return to Oregon City quickly if they were to go home on the *Sea Bird*. But lethargy claimed her. She knew she must get up, make plans, but she could not.

She awakened from a heavy sleep early one morning more than two weeks after the funeral. The children were shouting with delight, and another voice, Sunset's, mingled with them. Through the small window, which Martha had opened, brilliant sunlight streamed. Too brilliant. Kitty raised herself on her elbow, shivering with the sudden, sharp chill as she pushed back the covers, and peered outdoors.

The world was miraculously white. In the night the snow had come, softly, and every tree about the clearing was weighted with spotless, shining, diamond-trimmed white. Kitty caught her breath at the unbelievable, pure beauty of it. She dressed with trembling fingers, and stiffly she entered the outer room.

The smell of frying bacon was tantalizing and the good feeling of healthy hunger touched her. Fortune looked up with his slow smile and Martha, bright, bird-like, waved a happy, relieved greeting. The door stood open, despite the cold, framing the winter landscape. Outside the cabin the children romped, screaming with excitement, in the snow. Sunset leaned against the door jamb, watching.

"Mornin', Kitty," he said. He held out his hand. "Come here —there's somethin' for you to see."

She crossed the room to join him. She felt light-headed. He drew her outside and turned her toward the east.

Her whole sensitive body jerked with the shock of the beauty before her. There, so close it seemed she could touch it, so high, so magnificent, so mighty, dwarfing anything she had ever viewed before, in size or in beauty, was The Mountain, its great, snowy slopes gently descending in soft blue shadows and rosy highlights, from the truncated cone reaching high, high into the bright, un-clouded blue heavens.

"Looks near, doesn't it?" Sunset asked. "But it isn't. . . . You have to be at least fifty miles away to see the whole of it. Up close, you only see a part—the part right under your feet, like. Some things, real big things, are like that."

Kitty covered her sick, white face with her hands then, and at long last the healing tears came.

"That's your gift, Kitty," Sunset said, after a while, "a sight of The Mountain. It's Christmas, Kitty."

◊ 4 ◊

IT SEEMED only right, the settlers agreed, in the absence of any law to the contrary, that Philip's possessions be turned over to Kitty. The cottage had been cleaned and left locked after the funeral, and the team of oxen found in the stable and the sorrel horse had been taken by Sunset and Curt to await Kitty's direction.

On Christmas Day she rode back with Sunset as far as Philip's place. She hesitated at the door, and then she raised her head, her face ashen, her lips straight, and entered. Resolutely, at first, she kept her eyes away from the chair where she had seen Philip, but finally, standing in the center of the room, she forced herself to look; there were no stains, nothing, except her own memory, to remind her.

Sunset built a great fire for her and then he left her. She closed the door behind him, but after he disappeared down the trail she opened it again. Despite the chill she did not yet wish to be shut in those four silent walls alone. The brilliant sunlight streamed in, cheering her, brightening the ghost-ridden place, and, very gradually, Kitty calmed. It was good to be alone. The cramped quarters she had endured so long, aboard ship, in Oregon City, at the Sparks', had worn on her more than she knew. The quiet about her was protective and peaceful. The snow changed the appearance of everything, trimming the stable, putting little caps on the stumps; she was glad for the transformation. She felt the purity and whiteness of the snow had helped to wash the place clean.

She set at once to examining the cabin's contents, feeling this was business that must be attended to with dispatch. There was a chest which she did not open; it would be full of Philip's clothing, and she could not bring herself to touch it yet. The cabin was well-equipped, compared to Martha's or Clara's. Philip had brought many objects from the British fort, and had furnished it with considerable comfort. She was surprised to find real chinaware on the shelves; she caressed the smoothness of it, thinking how precious a piece of china was at Newmarket, where most utensils were of tin or iron. There was a variety of kettles and spiders and baking pans; even a bedwarmer stood upon the hearth. It made Kitty shake her head, it was so typical of Philip. He would have his comforts, even on the frontier.

He had also a good stock of tobacco and foodstuffs. The cabin itself was larger than some, one long room, with the fireplace centered on one side. The heavy door swung on massive iron hinges and had a stout lock. The windows were of real glass, small-paned and tightly set. Philip had built well and he had spared no expense to bring these simple luxuries from the British fort. The glass would have come around The Horn, all the way from England, as had the chinaware. There were chairs and benches of local make, with seats of woven rawhide strips, and Indian braided rugs upon the floor.

At last she turned her attention to the papers upon the table. She stood a little way from them at first, staring at them, trying not to remember that only a short time ago Philip had been handling them. . . . The duelling pistol was back in its case beside its twin and it weighted the papers now.

Firmly she picked up the pistol case and opened it. The guns lay in their velvet wells, clean, shining. She did not know which of them Philip had used. She was glad of that. She took one in her hand curiously, as though to test her own control.

A sound outside the open door startled her and she whirled to face the entrance. Instinctively she dropped her hand, hiding the pistol in the folds of her skirt and she waited, eyes wide, listening.

She had not long to wait. In the rectangle of the doorway an Indian appeared. Behind him were three others.

Kitty stood, her back against the table, watching them. She took a deep breath and then she managed a greeting.

"Hello," she said clearly, "what do you want?"

For answer the Indians crowded into the cabin. She stood unmoving. The leader looked her over carefully and then the four of them moved about the room, poking into shelves and boxes, fingering the blankets. They spoke occasionally to one another, in gutturals, gesturing, and then they came to stand in a semicircle about Kitty.

"Where your man?"

"What do you want?" Kitty repeated.

Again the four talked and one wandered off to raise the lid of the chest and to paw in it, among Philip's garments.

"Whose land is this?"

Warily, Kitty studied the intruders. She countered again.

"Is it yours?"

The question seemed to confuse the Indians. The leader's dark, glowering face became suddenly puzzled. "Yes," he declared, "our land. Our hunting ground. Not the white men's."

Kitty nodded. "That is good," she said.

Her agreement mollified the Indians. They drew together, gesturing, scowling. Finally one blurted: "You come with us."

"No," Kitty said firmly, as though that ended the discussion. She gripped the pistol tightly. "Since this is your land—will you sell it to me?"

"How much?"

"For the land, from here to the water, and back of me to the top of the hill, to that cabin yonder and as far the other way, —what will you take, to sell it to me?"

She had succeeded in diverting them. They began to argue. Their eyes searched the cabin for things of value. Kitty clutched the hidden pistol, moved tightly against the table to conceal the case and the second weapon behind her. She allowed her shawl to slip from her shoulders to the table top, further to conceal the case.

"Tobacco?" she suggested, quickly.

They found the tobacco and sniffed it with pleasure. The Indian who was investigating Philip's chest raised a coat, gold-braided, bright blue. Kitty caught her lip in her teeth.

"The clothing in that chest," she said swiftly, indicating it, "and the tobacco. I will pay you that for the land. But no more!"

The spokesman's face brightened with pleasure, and the four of them, childlike, went to the chest and pulled all the clothing from it. Boxes and papers fell upon the floor and were ignored. They decked themselves grandly; a coat here, a waistcoat there, scarves, which they tied about their heads; boots, too small for their great splayfeet. Laden with their loot, they started away.

The leader, however, remembered, and turned back to Kitty. "You come."

"No," Kitty said again. Her mind worked frantically. "I'm sick. Very sick." She put her hand on her chest and coughed.

The Indians crowded toward the door. They had experience with the sicknesses of the whites. The leader spoke again.

"You buy land," he approved, "you stay here."

They disappeared as quickly as they had come. Kitty watched them melt into the woods, toward the Sound. Her body went limp with relief. She closed the door, bolted it. She did not feel shut in, now; rather, the heavy door was protective, and the fire began to warm the cabin. She seated herself at the table, picked up the first of the papers before her.

It appeared to be part of a carefully prepared manuscript. Puzzled, she flicked over the papers until she came to the title page. *Philip Davis' Guide For Emigrants*, it said, in Philip's dashing penmanship; *Being a Compilation of Information for Those Attempting the Journey from Missouri to Oregon City.*

He had done a surprisingly thorough job, she thought, her glance sliding swiftly down each page. He told in detail what each immigrant should take with him; he would need a good rifle, a pair of long pistols, five pounds of powder—Philip recommended "Laflin's Best"—with ten pounds of lead and a few pounds of shot. . . . Oxen not over six years old and not too large; they must have stout sixty-foot ropes, and thirty-inch stakes, the heads shod with iron bands with eyes for tethering stock. Spare chains; a twenty-gallon well-bound cask for water—the lists seemed endless, and the cost of each item was painstakingly listed as well. Philip estimated that a party of four persons, with one wagon and ox-teams or mules, could cross the plains for $169 apiece— and their goods and stock would still have some value at the end of the journey.

There were small, carefully drawn maps, with the distances marked and waterholes, campsites, good grazing land indicated. There was a warning that worn-out oxen or mules could not always be exchanged at Fort Laramie or Fort Hall. . . . She had hardly expected to discover that Philip had spent his time at some constructive activity; she felt a momentary twinge of conscience. Had she misjudged him completely?

Hoping against hope, she examined the rest of his papers. If only they would divulge a mature Philip, of whom she could be proud! Her search disclosed a journal and as she opened it several pieces of paper fell from it. Each was a note to Philip, demanding substantial sums of money.

The journal began at Independence, Missouri, and it was an elaboration of his letters to her. He had kept a careful record of each day's happenings on the overland trail, perhaps not then recognizing it as an experience worth recording, but using the journal as an outpouring of his discomforts. "It is enough to try the endurance of any man," he had written, disgustedly. "It is actually more than an ordinary constitution can bear."

But he had been forced to bear it. He had taken a hasty look at the rawness of Oregon City and departed for the comfort and conviviality of the British post. His love for gambling had for a while eased his discontent and at first heavy losses did not disturb him. He was drinking heavily, and apparently was a great success with the daughters of the Hudson's Bay Company men. His journal recounted gay and expensive evenings, and he noted his enormous gambling losses quite cheerfully. "If my luck does not soon change I shall have to ask for credit, until I can get a letter to Robert. I have had enough of Oregon. I would take the next ship home, but I cannot go until I can pay my debts. . . ."

He had welcomed the invitation to visit Fort Nisqually. But the entry after his first visit to the British warship *America* was in a different, more thoughtful vein. "They really mean to fight," he wrote, incredulously. "I had hot words with Lieutenant H——, and the fact that I owe him a large sum of money did not make for better feelings between us. I cannot stay on at the British fort. It was a shock to me today to realize that they believed me sure to aid them if it comes to war. Me—Philip Davis—a traitor!"

Whether it was conscience, or his falling out with the British officers over his gambling debts, Kitty could not quite judge, but at last he had cut his ties with the English. He had hired the best workmen he could to build his cabin and used all his remaining funds to furnish and stock it well. "The only way I can keep my former friends from hounding me about my debts is to assure them that I intend to improve this claim and sell it to pay them. I think that can be done, in time. In fact, it is the only way out. I assure them that any day I will have mail, but they grow impatient. Melia is my only comfort. . . . She asks nothing. She never condemns me, she never says a word about my drinking too much. . . ."

Now and then there was a mention of Kitty. "She is so far away. How she would despise me if she could see me now! Kitty is as immovable as Margaret, and certainly Margaret has the strictest conscience of any person I have ever known. Kitty would be unforgiving. She is so contemptuous of weakness, and herself so blameless—how could she be expected to understand or to forgive?"

Kitty put down the journal. She was exhausted, spent with emotion, sick with his revelations. When she took it up again she read only briefly, for each of the later pages ruthlessly portrayed the gradual disintegration of the man. His accounts of debauches grew more frequent and were sometimes hardly lucid. Threats from his creditors were listed frequently and fear crept into the accounts, and then excuses and recriminations. Why did they hound him so, when he had been so unlucky?

And yet, Kitty thought, some way he had forced himself to write the *Guide For Emigrants*. He had tried to salvage something from his own miserable failure. For that Kitty gave him credit, but she could not force herself to read all of Philip's journal. She ruffled the pages to the last entry, written a few minutes before he died. "Everything I have—which is mostly debts—I leave to Kitty—"

She took it to the fireplace and abruptly tossed it on the flames. She would burn everything, she decided, reminiscent of the evil in Philip's life. His sin had been the failure to discipline himself, but no one other than herself need know. The journal was a filthy, horrible thing, she thought; it was best to destroy it. That much she could do for him. . . . She thought of Philip's relatives at home. There was his brother, Franklin, who lived in Charleston; his wife was a Gatewood, a cousin twice removed. Nothing could be gained by taking home to them any papers of Philip's that would reveal his sordid life and tragic ending. Let them remember him as the carefree and charming boy they had known.

His debts, of course, must be paid. She looked at the slips of paper again. Two thousand dollars at least were listed here as still owing. His plans for improving the land, however, were detailed and laudable. He had worked out a long-time program with more thought and talent than she had credited to him.

She studied his plans for clearing, planting, drainage, the use of timber, extensions on the cabin, more outbuildings. He had made sketches; the log cabin expanded into a gracious home, faintly reminiscent of Wildcliffe, the present great fireplace a beacon of welcome in a great central entry hall. Philip had dreamed of himself as an estate proprietor, a nostalgic carry-over from Wildcliffe, Kitty thought. He had dreamed of a wharf on the Sound for his own ships; of productive acres surrounding the house itself. He had made observations on the soil and seasons. Robert's training was evident here. Had Philip actually intended to carry out this ambitious plan, Kitty wondered, or had this been only a pastime, until he could go home?

Kitty, lost in thought, leaning back in her chair, tapping her chin with a quill, at first ignored the knock. It came again, more sharply, and she jerked at attention. She reached for the pistol.

"Who is it?"

"Fletcher."

"Oh," she said, without welcome, unbolting the door, "it's you."

"I came to take you back to the Sparks'. I have business with Fortune."

She closed the door behind him and laid the pistol back in its case. His eyes went from the weapon to Kitty's tired face.

"I frightened you?"

"No. . . . There were some Indians here today. I thought they might have returned."

"Indians? What did they do?"

"They pried into everything," Kitty said wearily, "they said they owned this land. So I offered them tobacco and clothing in exchange for it. We made an agreement, I guess. Anyway, they seemed satisfied, and went away."

Curt went to the fireplace and kicked the burning log. A shower of sparks rose from it and he waited until they disappeared before he turned to her again.

She had no intention of permitting a conversation with Curt to become personal. She spoke quickly, formally.

"I am glad you came. There are several questions I would like to ask." She motioned to a chair, almost imperiously, and seated herself behind the table. "I am anxious to wind up Mr. Davis' affairs as quickly as possible," she continued primly. "Perhaps you can tell me. Am I allowed to sell this land?"

"No. Not until you have clear title to it. The laws of the Oregon Provisional Government are patterned after those of Iowa."

"Why Iowa?"

"Two reasons. One—Iowa is a territory and has had problems similar to those of Oregon. But the main reason was that when the first legislature met the only law book anyone could dig up happened to be one from Iowa."

"Too bad it wasn't from South Carolina," Kitty said drily.

The wood in the fireplace fell, crackled, sprang into brighter flame.

"As I was saying," Curt continued easily, "you could sell the improvements, but not the land. It hasn't been proved yet. You'd have to live on it five years, a part of each year, anyway, and make certain improvements, to get final title to it. Our laws permit anyone to hold land, regardless of sex; but when Oregon becomes a territory, the Federal Government may change that. I don't know if they will permit a single girl to hold land or not. We hope our laws will be adopted—but Congress may alter them. That is one reason we are so anxious for government recognition —to clarify our land laws."

"I see," she said. "One other thing. The Indian girl. I suppose she expects something. Does she have any claim to this cabin?" She turned accusing brown eyes upon him. "I suppose that *you* would know."

"Melia will have no claim. She expects nothing."

He was very handsome, she thought detachedly, and imperturbable. She braced herself. *I'll never make the mistake Philip did,* she vowed. If it was necessary before for her to uphold the honor of the Gatewoods, it was even more imperative now, after Philip's shameful failure.

"At Wildcliffe it is customary to reward a faithful servant at the death of her master," Kitty said, biting off the words.

"As you wish. Though Melia was not a slave."

"As far as I am concerned she was Mr. Davis' servant," she said sharply. "What would you consider suitable for her? Perhaps the horse?"

"That would be very generous."

She detected sarcasm in his voice but she ignored it.

"I am staying here, for the time being," she said.

"You can't stay here alone."

"Do you think the Indians will disturb me again?"

"It's not likely. Unless there's a general uprising."

"Then what is the danger? I do not anticipate being troubled by whites."

Curt regarded her for a long time. "No, I don't think the settlers will trouble you," he observed. "I doubt that any of them will come more than once."

Kitty stood, her eyes flashing. "And that is all right with me!" she flared. "I paid you to bring me to Newmarket, Mr. Fletcher, and you fulfilled the contract. I think that is all the business I have with you—now or at any other time."

He shrugged. "The oxen," he said then, deliberately baiting her, "shall I send Charlie with them or do you prefer to come get them yourself?"

She bit her lip. "If you will send Charlefour I will pay him for his trouble."

"Charlie isn't used to being paid for doing a favor."

"I would like to buy Mowich from you. I would like to have her—for the little time that I am here."

"I paid ten dollars for her. But she's a better little mare than I thought."

"All right," she snapped, "I'll pay fifteen. Take it or leave it."

"I'll take it," he said. He laughed and Kitty whirled, turning her back upon him. She found her purse and carefully counted out the money. She laid it on the table beside him, avoiding the contact of his fingers. He pocketed the coins, and turned toward the door.

"Just a minute," she said, and Curt paused. "Would you mind —taking some things to Martha? It's—it's Christmas—and perhaps I can find something for the children."

She went to the shelves beside the fireplace. From the supplies she took a bag of corn and she took two of the china cups and filled them. She hesitated, then, and she looked back into the bag to measure how much corn was left. She sighed softly and Curt waited, watching. She was unaware of his regard as she raised one of the cups and started to pour the corn back. Again she stopped, tossed the bag back upon the shelf, impatiently, and turned to him with the two full cups. Her face softened, became sweet, appealing, betraying her dreadful loneliness.

"The children might like the corn for their chickens," she explained, "and maybe Martha would like the cups." She raised the lid of the chest and found a scarf which the Indians had scorned. She wrapped her gifts carefully within it. "And the scarf for Fortune."

The big bay horse that Curt rode covered the miles to the Sparks' rapidly. Curt, frowning, was still thinking of that movement of Kitty's, her impulse to save a portion of the corn, when he came in sight of the Sparks' cabin. Born to wealth, extravagance was natural to her; and her impulse to send the gifts had been quite genuine. Why, then, had she suddenly acted like any prudent immigrant, carefully weighing her stores and trying to decide how much she could safely spare?

Well, he thought, give her a night in the Davis cabin alone, and that will cure her; she'll seek companionship then. He'd give her time, he decided, to recover from the shock of Davis' death—and then he'd gather her in. . . . But she had met him at the door with a pistol. Curt was not so sure she did not know how to use it. No, Kitty would not be an easy conquest, after all, and that made the game, to Curt, more worthwhile. He grinned as he recalled that she had negotiated what might well be the first Indian treaty north of The River.

Behind him, Kitty bolted the door, and then she looked at the windows. Outside were miles of forest and the Sound beyond; but she knew the Indians' childish disregard of privacy, and she would not have been surprised to see a curious dark face pressed against the panes. She shivered, as she recalled Fortune's words about the mad seamen wandering in these woods. She took blankets from the bed and fastened them carefully over the windows. She put another log on the fire, remembering, gratefully, that Sunset had brought a large quantity of wood inside the cabin, and she took the last remaining robe and draped it about her and sat close to the stone hearth.

Philip's debts must be paid. She had some money—but not nearly enough. She twisted Philip's ring on her finger. It was much looser now than when Philip had placed it there. She clenched her teeth tight together. There was no use looking back. There was no use thinking about what might have been. She must decide about the future.

Owning slaves was not all profit. One had obligations, too, and

Margaret had sternly impressed upon Kitty the responsibility of a slave-owner. She had to take care of Jessie Pearl. Kitty twisted the ring. . . . It was a long way, reckoned in miles, or in time, to Wildcliffe.

She loosened her bodice, pulled the pins from her hair, sighed with relief at the blessed privacy. She loosened her boots, pushed them off, stretched her toes toward the fire. "I will not be afraid," she said firmly, aloud. "I will *not* be afraid." From far off came the cry of a cougar and Kitty tensed and looked at the covered windows, the heavy barred door. "There's no danger," she assured herself. And of course it was the wind, not stealthy footsteps, around the cabin. But the loneliness—

It's always worse at night, she decided, practically, but her eyes were wistful. How different she had planned it—and it was Christmas.

Then she saw them. They were placed neatly, primly, side by side on the hearth. They had not been there before Curt came. They were tiny, new, inviting. She sat erect and stared at them and then she picked them up, soft Indian moccasins, the small rounded toes intricately beaded.

Slowly, experimentally, she slipped her little foot into one of them. It fitted like a fine glove, soft, yielding, it was like wearing nothing at all, and yet it was warm. Kitty smiled, and though she did not know it, her dimples twinkled; she twisted her foot and her pretty ankle, and her expressive eyes sparkled. The moccasin was flattering, very flattering—and very comfortable after the heavy boots. Almost guiltily she drew on the other and lay down again, admiring, girlishly, the shimmering, multicolored beads on the tiny toes of the little Indian slippers.

She had received two Christmas presents, she considered, drowsily—Sunset's, the sight of The Mountain, an experience she would never forget; and Curt's, the little moccasins.

Tomorrow would be time enough to think of big problems, money, debts, wars; now it was the little things that loomed important. She was cosy and warm, and very young, and the moccasins felt like gentle handclasps on her little feet and she was so sleepy. So sleepy.

◆ 5 ◆

"I KNOW she done wrong, and it goes hard on all of us. But I'm not of a mind to hate anyone out of the community."

"She's takin' food right out of the mouths of your children, Martha, and you sit there and defend her! There'll be trouble of some sort, long's she's *in* the community!"

"I don't care," Martha repeated stubbornly. "It could be she didn't know."

"Fortune said himself Curt read the agreement out loud to Sunset and her. She was sittin' right here in your very own cabin, Martha Sparks, and she heard the men agree to it."

"All right, Laura, so she did. But then she didn't even give a thought to hirin' Indians herself. I doubt she even heard him, or, if she did, that she took it in."

Laura Trainor sniffed, unconvinced, and Sarah Hansen nodded in agreement with Laura. "Haakon woulda had twice as many shingles to trade at Nisqually if those young Indians hadn't quit when he needed them most," Sarah said bitterly. "Haakon said they was the best workers he'd found yet, and was just gettin' into the swing of it, and one mornin' they just didn't show up. Deaf Wilson come by, and said how did it happen Haakon's Indians was workin' for the Gatewood girl, snakin' logs. Then afterwards he saw one of the Indians, proud as a peacock, wearin' silk handkerchiefs. Silk, mind you!"

"I'd like to know what she'll have to say for herself," Laura said grimly. "John says it ain't so much that our help left us for her, bad as that was, as it is that she'll make Dr. Tolmie mad, violatin' the agreement, and then none of us'll get any more goods at Nisqually. The men was pushed hard to get an agreement with Tolmie in the first place. If'n they don't live up to it, Tolmie'll not buy our shingles, and he won't trade us no groceries, and I don't rightly see how any of us are goin' to get through this winter, 'thout some trade. Our stock's mighty low. Gettin' so a meal of hog and hominy would sure look good to me."

Martha jabbed her finger with a needle and pressed it quickly against her teeth to stop the bleeding. "I agree she made a mistake, overpayin' the Indians," she said. "But could be she needs help. From us, I mean. Lots of things she doesn't know. She's mighty young and she's had folks to do for her all her life."

"How we goin' to help her if she stands us off, like she did at the funeral? And I don't know as she needs so much help from us! All those Englishmen keep callin' on her all the time. Deaf says there's one there every day or so. Don't look right, her without a husband. Don't look right no way for a single girl to be livin' there alone."

"Polly's with her."

"That's another thing. I should think Sunset and Curt'd be mighty sore, way Polly up and left them. I bet Charlie's not been a mite a good to Curt since Polly moved over there. And have you seen Polly? You'd think she was that girl's slave! And the airs Polly puts on—for an Indian!"

"Kitty has a way," Martha said calmly, "makes folks want to do things for her."

"Pays 'em double, that's why," Sarah said tartly, "or, if it's a man, she just looks helpless and flaps her eyelashes at him and he spends the whole blessed day cuttin' firewood for her. Accordin' to what I hear, folks in Oregon City didn't cotton up to her uppity ways one bit. They didn't like the way Jeff Linton was shinin' 'round her either."

Martha shot a sharp look at Sarah. "Now Sarah, just because the girl's pretty don't mean she's not got feelin's like the rest of us. I reckon a girl with a beautiful face and shape feels pretty much like the plain ones do. Gets her feelin's hurt, same's you and me."

Sarah flushed. "I'll thank you, Martha Sparks—"

"I'm a plain woman and I know it," Martha continued calmly, "but I allus did think I had the feelin's, inside me, of a beauty. Allus did think that if I'd only had the looks to go with the rest of me, then maybe I'd be a—well, you can't tell. I mighta been a real hussy, hadn't I been so plain."

"Martha!"

Martha bit her thread, her dark eyes dancing. "Well," she finished, "thing is, I don't reckon just because Kitty's so pretty we ought to hold it against her. Could be she's just like the rest of us—outside her looks."

"Martha, you a respectable, God-fearin' woman, to talk so!"

"Could be," Martha said calmly, "that I'm respectable not so much because I'm God-fearin' as because I'm plain-lookin'."

Laura sputtered and Sarah tried to calm her. "Now, now, Laura, don't make no never mind. Martha's plagued you ever since you left Independence. She don't mean but about half what she says. Don't cock your eyebrow at me, Martha; you know you take fun in pesterin' Laura. It's nigh on to three o'clock. Wasn't she supposed to be here at three?"

"Think Kitty Gatewood cares if'n she's on time or not?" Laura snorted. "Sure as you're born she'll come an hour late, and the men'll listen to her, her talkin' in a voice you could pour on a pancake, and they won't know *what* time it is."

"I think a girl alone's got a right to use any advantage she has," Martha said, looking at Laura out of the corner of her eye. "I know I would. Hard in this country to get along without a man. Hard sometimes to get along *with* one. She's got no one to do for her, less'n she hires, or coaxes somebody. If she can get old Deaf Wilson to do an honest day's work, then more power to her, I say."

"She's got money. Charlie said she even had a slave. Left her in Oregon City."

"Don't rightly think we oughta judge too quick, Laura. Let's hear her first."

"You can hear her soon. Here she comes. And Polly with her."

"Land alive! If she ain't dressed up! Ain't she pretty, though!"

Laura bridled. "Satin ribbons and dimples aren't going to feed us this winter, Martha."

"Likely they'll feed her," Martha murmured, and then, more wickedly, "It's your John who's helpin' her off her horse." There was a stony silence.

Kitty had been invited to the gathering only after long consultation among the settlers. The agreement on the rate of pay to Indians had been arranged with the factor at Fort Nisqually only after prolonged negotiations. That Kitty had flagrantly violated it and thus cornered the best of the labor supply, which had resulted in swift improvements on Philip's land claim, had been overlooked as long as possible. But now, six weeks after her arrival, the situation had grown serious. All trade with the Hudson's Bay

Company was threatened. It had been decided that Kitty should be called to account before a representative group of settlers.

Curt, lounging in the Sparks' dooryard, talking with Sunset and Fortune, Haakon and John and Deaf Wilson, watched Kitty coming up the trail, Mowich, her beautiful bay coat shining in the sun, taking her usual dainty steps. Behind Mowich came a nondescript Indian pony, and on it was Polly Careless, once a valuable addition to the household of Sunset and Curt. Polly, who was almost as broad as she was tall, and who had a round, smooth face with round eyes, had attached herself to Kitty. It might be, Curt thought, the magnificent green silk petticoat that Kitty had impulsively bestowed upon Polly; it could be Kitty's soft, lavish praise of Polly's cooking. Charlefour had not exaggerated when he said his Indian wife knew all there was to know about Oregon cookery; she knew how to bake camas root so it tasted and looked like mealy chocolate. She knew that alderwood was best to barbecue fresh salmon; she did not insist that the delicious Sound huckleberries swim in a saucer of fish oil, and she knew magical tricks with shell fish. She also had friends at Cowlitz Farm who were generous in passing on to her rolls of butter and bags of real flour, filched from the Company warehouse.

Kitty's coming had opened up to Polly a new world. She was no longer only Charlefour's devoted mate. If Charlie wanted to live with his wife, he would have to work for Kitty, too; so Charlie, drawn also by the occasional sips of fine liquor Kitty allowed him from Philip's store, and himself smitten with the pale-haired girl, had also become a part of Kitty's household. Charlie drove the oxen, keeping them moving with his colorful and profane vocabulary, and he bossed the Indian workmen. A full acre behind the Davis cottage had been cleared. A second room had been added, and this room Charlefour and Polly now occupied. There was a shelter ready for sheep, there was a pig-house. There was space laid out for a kitchen garden and for a patch of corn and wheat. Moreover, Kitty's Indian crew had delivered several thousands of shingles to Fort Nisqually.

Actually, Curt had been relieved when Polly Careless and Charlefour had gone to live with Kitty. It was not safe for the girl to live alone, and he knew how helpless she was; he doubted that she had ever cooked a meal. Certainly she did not know an ox-yoke from a plough; he could not picture her pitching wild hay to feed her stock. She was a hard one to help. She had given no indication that she ever wanted to see him again, and Sunset, Curt knew, visited her very infrequently. It was better, Curt thought, to have Charlie and Polly with her than for her to be alone.

But she had an amazing way of using what talents she possessed, hiring others to do what she could not. She had surprised them all.

As she slid from her horse now and approached the cabin, her small hand barely touching the forearm of John Trainor, Curt saw her turn abruptly toward the east. Curt smiled slightly. It was the unconscious gesture of all who lived in the shadow of The Mountain. Only Mt. Rainier was "The Mountain," as only the Columbia was "The River"; it was one of those rare days when it was unveiled, a treat for the faithful, and Kitty gathered from it strength and poise and beauty.

She looked exceptionally well, Curt reflected; the drawn look of grief had gone from her face, but she was noticeably thinner and her eyes seemed more deeply set. She appeared neither self-conscious nor guilty, but Curt suspected that behind that sweet demureness she was wary. It was hard to tell about Kitty; she was full of surprises, and that was one quality which made her so intriguing. He wondered if she would stand up to the settlers in defiance, and flay them with a tongue sharpened by her hot temper, as she had him. She was quite capable of it.

Little Wealthy came to cling to Kitty's hand and Kitty smiled upon her. It was a pretty pose, Curt thought skeptically. In the yard Polly Careless tethered Mowich. The fierce loyalty which Kitty seemed to instill in people was phenomenal, Curt thought, and certainly, now, to Kitty's great advantage. It was difficult for anyone, watching her, to remember that this lovely, defense-less—or was she?—little creature could jeopardize them all. Curt was curious to see how Kitty would get out of this predicament. He followed the group into the cabin.

It might have been a very awkward moment as Kitty stood before her reluctant accusers. But Kitty, to their everlasting gratitude, spared them all.

"Martha, I'm so glad to see you—it's been such a long time! And Mrs. Hansen and Mrs. Trainor! I've been meanin' to come to see you, but you know how it is, with all the things there are to do! Wealthy, child, how's Children? Run out and tell Polly

Careless to give you that little parcel for Martha—some soap, Martha, I got at Fort Nisqually. Dr. Tolmie gave it to me yesterday. Oh, yes, I been meanin' to tell you—"

Breathlessly, Kitty's soft voice rushed on. Curt leaned against the wall, watching her, his tongue in his cheek, but Kitty's wide, innocent eyes carefully avoided him. Sunset watched her, too; his face betrayed nothing.

"I heard a couple of days ago I been causin' you good people some worry, and I just can't tell you how sorry I am!" Kitty's lashes rose and lowered, and Curt remembered his first glimpse of her at Oregon City, when her critics had been silenced with just such a potent weapon. "I didn't realize what a trouble I was," Kitty went on, penitently, "but when I heard I went right to see Dr. Tolmie, and told him it was jus' me to blame—none of the rest of you."

Kitty's clear, candid eyes rested on each in turn, asking understanding and forgiveness. Very obviously the people thawed. She had courage, this pretty lass, to go direct to the stern old factor himself and make a clean breast of it. "Dr. Tolmie understood and he told me it wouldn't make a mite a difference. I had dinner with him and he gave me the soap. . . . He's the nicest man!"

Her ripple of laugher echoed through the room, and Curt had a mental picture of her discussion with the dour Scot. "The thing was," Kitty went on, "I just didn't have any *cotton* handkerchiefs to pay the Indians." She clasped her hands together earnestly. "All I had was—was—my—" her face pinked, "my underthings, my petticoats. I had to cut them up and—"

There was a pause. "You see," she said sweetly, and Curt knew that she knew that she had won. "I'm so used to having colored help, and I feel they are my people if they work for me. When I have a very good worker, one who is superior to the rest, I just naturally feel like doin' somethin' nice for them—like givin' them a little extra. It is just because I feel friendly toward them who feels friendly towards me. I don't reckon you can understand how it is, hardly. But if you ever owned slaves you'd see. You feel responsible for them, and you don't count out each little bit you give them. Now I feel like that about Polly Careless. Sometimes I have to scold her. But when she does a very good piece of work then seems to me she should have somethin' extra. Polly doesn't *have* to stay with me."

That was true enough, Curt agreed—but try to lure Polly away!

"And if you worried about Dr. Tolmie, you needn't. He's just as friendly! Martha, will you let Wealthy stay with me a couple of days next week? I'll be leavin' for Oregon City soon and Wealthy and I have some visitin' to do, haven't we, Wealthy?"

As Kitty left the cabin she glanced once at Curt out of the corner of her eye and there was a hint of a grin about her pretty lips. It was a glance of defiance and triumph and it told him that she had neither forgiven nor forgotten him.

It had been a clear victory for Kitty, Curt had to acknowledge. She had gently taken the weapon from the hands of her accusers and fired it in the other direction, handed the empty gun back with a sweet, forgiving smile—and now she was going home.

Sunset, too, had seen Kitty's knowing glance at Curt. He did not move as Curt left the group and mounted his own horse and galloped down the trail after Kitty; but his big hands clenched inside his pockets and Deaf Wilson had to speak twice to get his attention.

"I say, Sunset," the toothless old fellow said, in his high voice, slapping his thigh and cackling, "I say—first time I ever hear of a *respectable* girl turnin' her petticoats to good account!"

◆ 6 ◆

Kitty rode hard on her way home. Polly's cayuse could not keep up with Mowich and Kitty raced on, finding some release in her reckless pace down the narrow forest trail. She was not proud of her performance at the Sparks' cottage; it was more than the cold wind that made her cheeks crimson.

She was within sight of the cabin when she heard pounding hoofs behind her and looked back to see Curt on the big bay. She did not slow her pace, but Curt came swiftly alongside and shoulder to shoulder they raced across the clearing. At her door she leaped from her horse, dropped the reins to the ground.

Unhurriedly, Curt dismounted. He pushed his hat back on his head and stood, hands on hips, regarding her. At the door, Kitty glanced back at him. He wore a new black shirt, she noticed, and it fitted his big, lean figure very well. Perhaps, she thought, Lisa had made it for him. She could almost see Lisa's brown fingers measuring the long line from his shoulder to his waist.

"Well?" she said, defensively.

"That was a nice little performance you put on back there, Kitty." She made no reply. "They let you off very easily. This time."

"You may save your advice, Curt."

"You'll listen to me, Kitty."

She tapped her foot irritably with the switch that had served her for a riding crop.

"Maybe they believe you. But I don't. You knew you were violating that agreement. You didn't give gifts out of the kindness of your heart. You're a calculating little lady, and you measured to the quarter-inch every one of those silk squares you gave in place of cotton handkerchiefs, and you knew just how much work you could get in return for them."

"Are you quite finished?"

"No. I have a personal interest in this. I intend to live on Puget Sound for many years. I'm not going to let you upset my plans by antagonizing the other settlers. I've let Charlie and Polly stay here—because when our places are combined it will make no difference, and I don't want you here alone. But your conduct is very unbecoming in the girl I am going to marry."

Kitty gasped. It was bad enough to have him put into blunt words her own secret knowledge of guilt. But this was going too far. She opened the door and would have slammed it behind her but Curt put his hard arm across it. Kitty glanced into the small room, hoping that Charlie was there. At her obvious uneasiness, Curt grinned.

"You can relax, Kitty," he said, in that infuriating, assured drawl. "I'm not going to take advantage of you. I've just told you I want my wife to be above reproach." Kitty fumbled with the ties on her bonnet and was irritated that her hands were shaking. "Don't be disappointed," he added, wickedly.

That was unforgivable. So he did know. She had convinced herself that Fletcher, self-centered as he was, was unaware of her own response to him when last he held her in his arms; she had forced herself to believe she had concealed it well, and that in the intensity of his own emotions he had not noticed the first break in her own control. But that he should taunt her with her momentary and unmaidenly weakness! Confusion and humiliation and pain stunned her and for an instant she could not retaliate. She stood, small and defenseless, clutching her bonnet helplessly; her hair was mussed, her cheeks crimson, her eyes brimming.

Suddenly the grin disappeared from Curt's face. He came to her quickly and his arms were about her and there was tenderness in his voice for the first time. "Kitty," he said, "I didn't mean—"

Her desire to hurt him overcame all else, and, feeling the unaccustomed tenderness in his touch, she recognized her advantage and deliberately played it. She moved her head slightly, so his face was brushed by the silken veil of her hair and touched, for a brief, searing instant, the warm, smooth flesh of her forehead; she relaxed, softly, sensuously, in his arms, as though on the verge of complete surrender, and she turned slowly, very slowly so that the man became conscious of each of the delicious and enticing curves of her beautiful body.

"Aren't you—Curt?" she said huskily. "Aren't you—going to take advantage of me?" Her hands came up to his shoulders, then to his face, her fingers caressing, and, quite coldly, through her long, wet lashes, she watched the deep tan of his face flush. She felt his arms tighten as she raised her face. He had a handsome, hard mouth, she thought dispassionately, and her own lips almost brushed his.

She drew back deliberately, her eyes veiled and vindictive.

"Aren't you, Curt?" she repeated in that husky whisper, and she watched the iron-hard mask of his face begin to soften. And then, sharply, she spoke aloud. "What a pity!" With one swift movement she twisted herself from him and was across the room, her slight body tense, her eyes blazing. "Think," she said clearly, with stinging sarcasm, "what a great experience we both have missed!"

He started toward her then, and she watched him come, her head high, her hands gripped at her sides in tight little fists. And then she used her most potent weapon against him. She laughed.

He stopped in his tracks.

Beyond the open door there were voices. Curt relaxed suddenly, but his eyes were glittering with anger even as he laughed.

"You're lucky, Kitty. But," he promised, very softly, "you'll pay for that. How you'll pay!"

◈ 7 ◈

"You don't condemn me, Sunset. Why?"

Sunset turned the wood over in his hand and carefully considered the raven's head he had carved and the bear's head below it.

"I got no right to, Kitty."

"But Sunset—" Kitty protested. She studied the little totem pole on which he was working and then her brown eyes tilted up to him. "You think I did wrong. Don't you?" she challenged.

"Don't know as anybody knows right and wrong exactly, Kitty," he said. He fashioned a bear's paw neatly, carefully put the tiny shaving in the fire. "What's deep wrong for one is small wrong for another. It depends on where a person starts from, see? For instance, Dr. Manning refuses a drink. No feather in his cap. Deaf Wilson or Charlie refuses one—that's winnin' a big battle."

Kitty drew a burned twig from the fireplace and, with the charcoal, made geometric figures on the stone of the hearth. "Sunset, does that mean—even if I make mistakes—you still value me?"

For a fraction of an instant Sunset's fingers paused. "Kitty, ain't nothin' you could do—ever—that'd keep me from valuin' you. Valuin' you—high."

The beautiful, pale-gold head was on a level with his knee and Kitty's lowered face was invisible. Only her muffled voice came up to him. "Sunset—I knew it wasn't fair."

Suddenly she raised her head and her eyes met his straightforwardly. "I was paying for haste, Sunset. I don't want to stay here. I wanted to get as many improvements made as I possibly could, in a short time. I—I had to. Philip left a lot of debts. I paid them, and I haven't any money left now—only a little in Oregon City. I'll have to get enough out of the improvements on this claim to pay my passage and Jessie Pearl's back home. I thought I had plenty when I came, but I didn't foresee—" She paused to steady her voice. "The British officers kept coming and demanding—oh, very politely—but reminding me of Philip's obligations. Naturally I had to make his notes good. I gave them everything I had—including my ring. And actually, I never *did* agree to that rate of pay for the Indians. No one ever asked me to. I guess it's no excuse. But—I didn't want anyone to know about Philip's gambling. I thought—the rest of you are going to be here all your lives. You can plan far ahead. I can't. I just have to hurry, to get out of the Oregon Country."

Sunset studied her lovely, earnest face and he smiled.

"You took on a big job for a little girl. And all this is new to you. I guess all of us understand that, and no one holds one mistake against you. If you was to stay, I reckon you'd soon understand the importance of everyone workin' together, for the protection of us all. These people came over the Trail. There's nothin' like crossin' the plains with a wagon company to teach folks to get along together, even if they don't like each other. Personal troubles in a wagon company caused more failures, made more folks turn back than all the rivers and mountains and deserts from here to Missouri. These folks are strict, Kitty—but they are fair, too. They're willin' to give you another chance."

Finally Kitty smiled, a little shakily. "I, Dad!" he said softly, "I never knew you'd taken on all Davis' debts." His glance went from her appealing face to her small bare hands. He took one in his own and turned it over. The nails were broken and there were calluses on the palm. It was a pathetic, red, hard little hand now. "Kitty, forget what happened today. It's behind you. Tomorrow's the important thing."

She nodded. For the first time in many weeks the nagging whisper of her conscience was stilled. She had made a mistake and, finally, frankly confessed it, and Sunset's understanding brought her peace.

"Tomorrow," she said steadily, "I must make plans to return to Oregon City. I will file this claim in my name there. Then I'll try to sell the improvements. It would help, if only we knew for sure the British wouldn't seize this land north of The River. Maybe it won't be easy to sell, Sunset, if folks are scared this'll go to the British."

"That's right. It's a gamble. But I think the odds are on our side. Likely there'll be somebody willing to take that chance. That is—if you're in a hurry to go. Might be, if you'd wait till the boundary is settled, you'd get a sight more for it."

"That may be months—years even. And it may mean war. I want just enough to take us home. One thing you folks from free states don't understand. Owning slaves is a responsibility. I got to take care of Jessie Pearl. I got to get her out of Oregon before something happens to her, the way the folks in Oregon City feel about the coloreds. Wildcliffe's her home, same as mine."

Sunset picked up his carving again, studied it intently.

"Reckon there's no chance of your stayin', then."

"Staying? You didn't really think I would *stay* here, did you?"

"I thought maybe—Curt would convince you."

"Curt!" Kitty's lips folded tightly. "Every time I see him I quarrel with him. I never quarrel with anyone else like that."

Sunset's knife moved slowly. He glanced at her out of the corner of his eye. Her face was flushed and her composure gone.

"Curt's a man who likes to be leaned on, Kitty. Bein' stood up to is a challenge to him, and he'll fight at the drop of a hat. If he'd a known—if you'd told him about Davis' debts, and what you were tryin' to do, he'd have helped you. He'd have protected you, Kitty. There's nothin' on heaven or earth he wouldn't do for you if you asked him."

"I don't want his help!"

Sunset rose, brushed the shavings into the fire, and reached for his hat. Kitty came to her feet and smoothed her hair with both hands and smiled up at him.

"Thank you, Sunset, for coming, and for helping me. You did help me, you know. I feel easier now. You never sit in judgment on anybody, do you?"

"Well-l Kitty, I try not to. There's so danged many things a fellow doesn't know about other people, their reasons, what they're aimin' at, what they're thinkin'—things like that." He turned his hat in his hands and then shot a sharp look at her. "Never seemed to me a body could go wrong if he just listened to his heart, Kitty, and followed what it told him to do. . . . But fightin' what your heart tells you is a pretty good way to destroy yourself."

Kitty watched Sunset ride away. He halted his horse at the edge of the clearing and waved to her and then was gone into the black shadows of the woods. *There's just not a bit of meanness in him*, she thought; *he's the kindest man I've ever known.*

APRIL WAS THE MOON OF LEAVES, Polly Careless said, and Kitty, depressed by weeks of gray days, with alternate driving and drizzling rain and snowstorms, and constant icy mud or slush underfoot, was startled and delighted by the almost overnight change. For long weeks her cabin had seemed, in her own disgusted words, as dark and isolated as the back of the moon; and then suddenly the Chinook winds came, the contented sighs of the awakening world, and all live things, rested by the winter's sleep, stretched and burst forth in new and dazzling spring dress. Kitty, unused to the excitement of sharply contrasting seasons, considered the warm south winds magical, and they seemed to release her, too, from the dull, mechanical movements of the winter.

For the first time in her life she had labored like a field hand. But with the coming of spring she felt an upsurge of energy and hope. The days became as brilliant and clear as new-minted coins, and, without warning, shrubs and trees were in leaf and the first of the wild flowers came to blooming. Trillium lilies appeared and striped coralroot, starflowers and wake-robins covered the forest floors. The vine maple, a mass of weak and crooked stems throughout the winter, came forth now in leaves of gorgeous rose-red, and the first greenish-yellow flowers of the dogwood began miraculously to appear.

Birds, seemingly eager to make up for their winter's absence, worked and scolded and flirted without ceasing. Shore birds, both delicate and powerful, swarmed upon the beach, glittering in the brilliant light of sun and water. Kitty saw her first cinnamon-teal ducks, marveled at their brilliantly polished coats and chestnut bills and wished she might see them at their game of leapfrog, which Polly said they played at mating time. Charlie told her, too, that the ungainly cranes had a peculiar and beautiful love-dance, a dipping, sidling and shuffling as precise as the figures of any reel. She learned to recognize the noisy kingfishers and the great blue herons, and tiny and beautiful songbirds awakened her with a great and joyous chorus of true, golden notes. The spring sun drew blades of green through the black, wet soil and warmed the evergreens, and the air seemed weighted with fresh fragrance. Anything could happen in the Northwest in the spring, Kitty thought; the whole world seemed on tiptoe with happy anticipation.

Although the winter had seemed endless to Southern-born Kitty, Charlefour declared it had been very mild. The newcomers who had crossed the Plains the previous summer ought not to be fooled by their first winter, Charlie warned; he had seen the thermometer drop 'way below zero as early as two weeks before Christmas, and choke the Columbia with ice. He had seen The River and its tributaries crest at dangerous, raging heights, taking great, fierce bites from their banks, sweeping all before them in spring floods. Kitty, remembering the feel of the outgoing tide and the powerful pull of The River on the stout *Sea Bird*, shivered at the thought of those multiplied tons of water roaring down to the Pacific.

Charlie, perversely, had been content throughout the winter, enjoying his role as adviser to Kitty, happy with amenable Polly Careless, relishing his position as boss of the Indian workmen. But now, with spring, Charlie grew restless, and when Kitty suggested they prepare to leave for Oregon City he responded with alacrity. To ride down river on the flood tide of spring was not only exciting and swift but safe, Charlie told her eagerly; deep waters, he explained, were safe. Shallow waters were not.

With the spring, too, the *America* left, and the *Fisgard*, with her forty-two guns and three hundred and fifty Englishmen, sailed imperiously into the Sound to take the *America*'s place before Fort Nisqually. Kitty was glad the *America* was gone. She prayed the British would advise their government against haste in attempting to capture the Oregon Country and she was relieved to see the last of Philip's creditors.

On her way down the Cowlitz now, Kitty felt an unexpected little twinge of regret at leaving the Puget Sound country. She would miss that great inland sea and she would miss the majestic

Mountain. Her accomplishments were very small, when one considered the tiny change she had made in the unlimited forests of Puget Sound; but the effort had cleansed and comforted her. It was only the work, she knew, that had made the long months bearable. If she had not been forced to enter Philip's cabin again, all her life she would have been haunted by her memory of him; but now she would remember that cottage in the woods as a place in which she had triumphed over fear. She had laid the ghost.

There were fields blue with blooming camas; the high cliffs between which the Cowlitz flowed had taken on new and vivid colors. The legends the Indians told entranced her, lulled her into a feeling of security and beauty. Resting, letting the river carry her, Kitty wondered why anyone should fear this simple and poetic race. How could one fear people who had music in them? For they had quaint and lovely names and legends. Mt. Rainier was "The Mountain that was God" to them, and Idaho, or El-da-how in the dialect of the Snake Indians, was "Sun Marching Down the Mountains," and they had stories to explain the creation of the natural wonders of the Oregon Country; the tale of Wishpoosh, the Beaver, accounted for the various tribes; a battle between the mountains had resulted in the natural rock bridge across The River, called the Bridge of the Gods; and up-river at Wishram the Indians had long ago painted on Witch's Rock a great and evil face of a witch. The eyes of that witch, Polly said, in subdued and awestruck tones, would follow an unfaithful woman. Many a young Indian had paraded his sweetheart before The Witch's Face and watched The Eyes. It was an infallible test. . . .

Wild strawberries bloomed in every sun-struck clearing; wild cherry and red currant and blossoms for which even the Indians had no name. The venturous had approached The Mountain, and before some dire evil had befallen them had found a riot of flowers growing clear to the snow itself in those glacial meadows. But no man approached The Mountain and lived his life out in peace and contentment. Humans must revere The Mountain, worship it from afar, but never approach it. Kitty, awed and humbled by its great size and brilliance, when it shone like a multicolored jewel against the sparkling clear sky, wondered if the Indians were not wiser than the whites credited them. Polly told her other stories, too; hinted at strange, dark secrets, at incantations and barbaric rites that bordered upon hoodoo and witchcraft, and Kitty could almost believe it was Jessie Pearl talking, with her superstitions and her visions.

Kitty deliberately kept her mind on Jessie, because she did not want to think of Curt. She had left while he was at Fort Nisqually, and Sunset, too, had been up the Sound. *Of course I'm not running away,* she told herself, proudly. *I simply wish to avoid another unpleasant scene. I am not afraid of him and I certainly do not doubt my own self-control. I'm a little older now, and much wiser than when I came to Oregon, less impressionable —and stronger, too.* Remembering her first tortured days on the trail to Newmarket, she smiled. She was "trail-broke" now.

They reached the mouth of the Cowlitz and Kitty gazed upon the mighty Columbia at flood and shuddered. They decided to inch their way along The River's north shore to Fort Vancouver. It was presumptuous of man, Kitty thought, no matter how skilled, to dare that awful, relentless, impersonal current with only a shell-like craft and puny paddles. Charlie, his eye shining, longed to attempt it, but nothing would persuade Kitty to dare crossing The River in a bateau. She would go in the Hudson's Bay Company sloop at the very least, she declared, and even that stout little vessel seemed ridiculously inadequate against the pounding, rolling weight of The River.

It was twilight when she finally stepped ashore at Oregon City. How different it was, she thought, wistfully, from her first arrival here! Unbidden, the memory of Curt as he had stood on the river bank, Lisa beside him, came back to haunt her. Resolutely she picked up her own blanket roll, drew a heavy dark shawl, worn for comfort and not for decoration, snugly about her shoulders and made her way up the river bank toward Main Street.

She knocked on Clara's door and eased her burden to the ground. How wonderful it would be to be ministered to again by Jessie Pearl!

"Kitty! Kitty Gatewood—whatever happened to you? You aren't alone?"

Clara drew Kitty within the cabin. Kitty loosened the heavy shawl tiredly and smiled. "Yes, I'm alone. Where's Jessie Pearl?"

Clara stared round-eyed at Kitty. She could hardly believe that this plainly dressed, weary woman, carrying her own pack, was the glorious and fashionable Miss Gatewood who had swept so regally to her door only a few months before. Clara swallowed. A tiny sound caught her attention and automatically she touched the cradle by the hearth with the toe of her slipper, set it to rocking gently, and the noise ceased. Kitty's eyes followed the movement and she dropped swiftly to her knees to look at the child.

"Clara, he's lovely! It is a boy, isn't it?"

Clara knelt also. "Yes, and such a boy!" Proudly she drew down the blankets so Kitty could see the chubby, rosy little face.

"You darlin'," Kitty crooned, and then she asked again, "Where's Jessie?"

"Kitty—she's gone."

"Gone? Gone where?"

"She left Oregon City. On the *Sea Bird*. She married that Negro sailor, Ben."

Kitty's lips parted and her eyes widened with shock. "Why, how could she? She wasn't free, she belongs to me!" Kitty began stupidly. "I came back to get her, to take her home."

Clara clasped her hands nervously. "She left in the night. Ben had been here to see her off and on. Others came, too. Some threatened her. Others came to preach that she was free. Allie Johnson and Tildy Snider told her she was not a slave in Oregon. We treated her real good, Kitty."

"I know you did," Kitty said swiftly. She took a long, deep breath. "My—my things?"

"They're all here," Clara said eagerly. "At least, I think they are. Of course Jessie cared for them, and I'd no way of knowing if she took anything she shouldn't. They're in the lean-to."

Kitty began to pull out her trunks and cases, and then, suddenly a cold suspicion gripped her and frantically she tugged at the trunk that contained her wedding gown. Clara, sensing her urgency, helped her to drag it into the larger room and Kitty knelt before it, fumbling with a key she took from a chain about her neck. But there was no need for the key. Her nervous fingers discovered that the lock hung loose and broken.

She turned back the lid. The gown lay as she had last seen it, scented with rose petals that fell to the floor as she lifted it. Clara gasped at the beauty of it and she took it from Kitty's impatient hands and laid its snowy, foaming, jewel-encrusted length upon the bed. Kitty plunged her hands deep into the bottom of the trunk, beneath the rest of the bridal finery. Her fingers clutched the strong box.

There was no need for a key here, either. A string held it loosely together.

The box was not quite empty.

There had been a thousand dollars in that box when she had left Oregon City. Now there were only a few scattered coins. Beneath them was a slip of paper and Kitty held it up to the light.

Jessie had learned to write at Kitty's side in her own schoolroom at Wildcliffe. Kitty would have known that writing anywhere.... She had been proud that few Negroes wrote as well as her Jessie Pearl.

"*Dear Miss Kitty,*" Jessie had written. "*I tuk the money. Don blame Mr. or Miz Linton. They good folks. Ben told me to tuk the money and other folks they said I urned it and I need it to pay Captain Craig. I know it won't mean much to you this little bit. Mr. Philip will care for you. Folks say everyone in Oregon is free. I am going to marry Ben. I am sorry not to be at your wedding and do for you. You been good to me, Miss Kitty. Please tell Mr. Philip and all the people at Wildcliffe good-by. Don't think hard of me, Miss Kitty. I feel for Ben like you feel for Mr. Philip. I lef a few dollars becuz people say there is not much coins in Oregon. I didn tuk nothing else except the gloves you throwed away. I would not go except I got to be with Ben. I miss you Miss Kitty my heart hurts but seems like it tell me to go. They dont want Negroes in Oregon Miss Kitty. They tol Ben they whup us both didn we go on the Sea Bird. Jessie Pearl.*"

Kitty shook the strong box. The coins made a pathetically small pile within it and panic chilled her as she counted them once, and, unbelieving, again.

Jessie had left her exactly ninety dollars.

Kitty sat very still, fighting back hysteria. She raised her eyes and stared around the cabin. When she had first entered this room she had been a girl of great wealth, on her way to her betrothed, a careless and pampered beauty, off on a high adventure, with her slave to care for her. And now—

Oregon had done this to her. The free air of Oregon had been too heady for Jessie Pearl. Oregon had taken Philip from her, too, for he had been unable to withstand the rugged isolation of it. Oregon had robbed her of her passage home.

Home. Yes, Wildcliffe still was home. But it would take six hundred dollars to get her there. *Six hundred dollars!* Suddenly that amount seemed enormous. It might as well be six thousand, or six million.

Clara's timid hand on her shoulder aroused Kitty. Kitty managed a remote, polite little smile, which failed to reassure Clara. Kitty stood and shook out her skirts and turned to the gown on the bed. She folded it, her teeth set against the memories it brought, and put it back in the trunk.

Jessie's desertion was a stunning blow—but how great a blow no one else in Oregon would be allowed to know. A Gatewood did not publicly bemoan misfortune.

She dropped the coins into her reticule. Ninety dollars, she thought wryly. Ninety dollars—a doubtful claim to a piece of land which the British or even an American land-grabber might snatch from her at any minute. And her wits. Some way that would have to be enough.

◆ 2 ◆

THE *Liberty* was a shabby vessel, an aged, tired tramp, scarred by seas and tropic suns and Arctic ice. It had been a long time since her rigging had been replaced or blacked or her deck holystoned. Such repairs as had been made were patchy and makeshift, "for stout and not for pretty" as her captain and owner, Jonas Kemp, admitted. Kemp matched his vessel; he was slovenly and unkempt and weather-beaten.

He was very unlike the stern and immaculate Captain Craig of the beautiful *Sea Bird*, Kitty thought, dismayed. She stood on the wet and littered deck, and her delicate nostrils flared at the unpleasant odor that rose from the ship—what was it, fish, fertilizer, spoiled goods—or just age and moldy damp? She clung to her tiny ruffled parasol and stood very straight, a beautiful, immaculate little Dresden-like figure amid the filth and clutter.

"I wished to ask about passage home, Cap'n Kemp," she said carefully. "To Charleston, South Carolina."

Kemp hawked, spat noisily and thickly over the rail. Kitty held her breath and closed her eyes in disgust.

"Not goin' round the Horn, Miss. Goin' to the Sandwich Islands, then to Chiny. Sailin' by way of Yerba Buena, San Francisco Bay. Figure to pick up a load a hides and tallow, maybe. You could sail with us to Hawaii, get a ship there for the States, after a while."

His eyes roved over Kitty and he stroked his wet, tobacco-stained chin. "Guess we could fix you up all right, though we don't generally have ladies. Missionaries now and then, with their wives. They don't ask fer much."

A great clatter behind her startled Kitty.

"Nothin' to worry you, ma'am. Just a bit of bad luck. Fellow in Hawaii, he had a shipload of furniture—furniture, mind you! Wanted to get rid of it bad, so I took it. Got it here, thought maybe the settlers'd have need of it, but we had bad weather and it was packed none too careful. Ain't a whole stick of it left. Ain't a bedstead or a dresser all in one piece. Fit'n for firewood, maybe—but if there's anything Oregon don't need, it's firewood." Kemp's disgust deepened the grimy crevices in his face. "Better get rid of it, I says, so they're dumpin' it ashore. . . . I'll take you to Hawaii, Miss. Cost you three hundred dollars."

"Three hundred dollars! Why the very idea!" she exclaimed, indignantly. "Captain Craig brought me all the way from Charleston for six hundred!"

Kemp shrugged. "All a us have to make a livin', Miss."

Kitty opened her parasol with a snap. "Good day, Cap'n Kemp."

Alone that evening in the Linton cabin with Clara's baby, Mathias, Kitty sat in the small rocker before the fire, deep in thought. She had placed on the bulletin board in Abernethy's store a notice offering for sale the improvements on the New-market claim, now registered in her own name. She had hoped to secure enough from their sale to pay Captain Kemp's fee for her passage home. But she would not sail on the *Liberty*—not at any price, she decided. Unfortunately, though, the news from Washington was ominous. The *Polynesian*, the Hawaiian newspaper which the *Liberty* had brought, stated that the United States Pacific fleet of nine ships and 322 guns was moving toward the Columbia. Also that the French government, in return for England's tolerance of French pretensions in the Pacific, would support the claims of Great Britain in Oregon. The war clouds were thickening.

It was not likely she would have even a small offer for a claim at Newmarket with war so near. . . . But, on the other hand, she thought with youthful optimism, word had also sifted over the plains and mountains that thousands of stubborn, homeseeking Americans from the East and Middle West, undaunted by rumors of war, were now on the Oregon Trail, headed west. Moreover, it was said that fifteen thousand Mormons were migrating west. The Oregon settlers feared the Mormons were headed for Oregon City, and were much disturbed by the rumor. In any event, Kitty reasoned, with great numbers of immigrants arriving in the fall, surely someone would want her snug little cottage and its sturdy outbuildings.

She could not leave now, at any rate. If her stay was to be prolonged she might as well benefit by it. She decided to change her notice in Abernethy's store to "For Rent" instead of "For Sale." Let someone occupy the claim in exchange for certain improvements upon it during the next few months, she decided, since money was so scarce. She had Philip's long-term plan and Charlie's advice to guide her. She would decide just what clearing and building she would demand in exchange for occupancy of the cabin, and when the immigrants arrived in the fall the claim would bring a higher price.

She could send letters on the *Liberty* to Hawaii, to be transferred to the next vessel bound for the States. She must advise Judge Stuart of Philip's death. She would also ask him to send her money, though she hoped to be on her way before it arrived. She would send him also Philip's *Guide for Emigrants*, and ask him to arrange for publishing it. It would be a nice memorial to Philip. As always, her lips compressed at the thought of Philip. She would do her duty by his memory, but as yet, contempt for his weakness and hurt at his betrayal burned very deep.

Clara and Jeff had been kind, she thought, as she went to search for her writing materials. They had insisted that she remain with them in their cottage, which Jeff had managed to enlarge by one room during the winter months. And she liked to stay with tiny Mathias on these evenings when Clara and Jeff went to visit neighbors or attend evening church services. The baby whimpered now and Kitty, settled in her chair again, with a quill and inkpot beside her, stretched out her foot and rocked the cradle gently.

The baby cooed and Kitty glanced at the tiny, dimpled, waving fists and smiled. The firelight shimmered on the polished wood of the cradle. Suddenly her foot stopped and she caught her breath.

The cradle. The beautiful spool bed in the shadows behind her. . . . All the magnificent furnishings that homesick, heartsick Oregon women had been forced to leave beside the Oregon Trail. How they missed them, those lovely, well-rubbed, well-waxed treasures they had hoped would grace their new homes in Oregon! Jeff was a woodworker, a magnificent craftsman, perhaps the only skilled cabinetmaker in Oregon City. Hundreds of homes would be erected in Oregon in the months and years to come. War or no war, determined Oregon women would make those backwoods cabins into gracious and beautiful homes as fast as they could.

Kitty thought of the shipload of ruined furniture which Captain Kemp had discarded on the shore at the townsite of Portland. Mathias whimpered and she rocked the cradle absently, and now her eyes were shining with excitement. Jeff was well enough to work some now; he could work faster if he had his tools—the tools in the warehouse at Abernethy's, where Curt had left them. Jeff owed Curt money on those tools.

The ninety dollars in the chamois bag wouldn't purchase her passage home. She had to face that. But it might serve as partial payment to Curt, to persuade him to release Jeff's tools to him. If she could get those tools, if she could gather up the furniture Kemp had thrown away, if Jeff could salvage it, and if she could make friends among the Oregon women and sell that furniture to them—

There were so many *ifs*, Kitty thought. But she could win over the women if she put her mind to it. She could have the ruined furniture for the taking. And Jeff—with no effort at all she could wind Jeff Linton around her little finger.

The biggest undertaking would be to approach Curt and to attempt to do business with him. Above all, he must not know of her desperate plight. She'd give no one the satisfaction of seeing her stranded, worried, forced to grub for a living!

I wonder if Curt is very angry with me, she thought. She remembered his face in that one instant of gentleness, which she had so quickly erased by her flash of temper. That might have led, at last, to an understanding of the man; likely she'd never see it again. It was just as well, she decided, finally, for that closeness, which had been imminent, was dangerous ground.

◈ 3 ◈

THERE is a long, lingering twilight in the Northwest in summer, a gentle easing into darkness, a chance to adjust, appeasing the tireless ones who are reluctant for day to end, encouraging those who long for the quiet of the night. The approach to night was to Kitty the most pleasant part of the day; not as vivid as the early morning, which seemed tense as a newly-wound spring, but a slow dimming of light, a gradual relaxation of taut nerves. It was like the luxury of the velvets and soft pillows which she loved, after the practical, soap-and-starch, plain gingham day.

Kitty guarded that twilight hour jealously. She needed that time to review her progress and her mistakes, to plan her future. Every day was crowded, from sun-up to sun-down, with hard, poorly-rewarded labor. Only the coming of darkness halted her work.

Late one July afternoon she left Abernethy's store and started slowly toward the Linton cottage. Weary and troubled as she was, she decided to take the long way home, along the river bank. She was empty-handed, for there had been nothing in the store that she could afford to buy. Despite her efforts, she reflected soberly, her little supply of money was dwindling rapidly.

She had managed to sell several pieces of furniture, but not for cash. She had taken wheat in payment for orders early in the summer, and it had dropped sharply in price as the year progressed and no vessels came to relieve the overstocked granaries of Oregon's golden harvest. Then she had managed to secure several orders on the stores—but they did not solve her problem. Enterprising merchants would accept only cash for the most precious items, and for other things the orders were discounted as much as fifty per cent. Her first attempts at barter had been expensive lessons.

She had taken part of a choice beef in payment for a table and chairs and had congratulated herself on the bargain. Clara, she thought, would salt the meat and it would supplement their tiresome diet of salmon. But when she offered store orders for salt she learned that it had risen to $2.00 a bushel, and could be bought only for cash. She had to dip into her thin purse to buy it. The meat became an expensive luxury.

It was costly, too, she reflected, to travel up the Willamette in search of orders for furniture, and it was expensive to deliver the finished pieces by ox-cart. There was a great deal about business that she did not know, she admitted, and she had to face the fact that money was almost non-existent in Oregon.

But the scarcest item of all was women's clothing. She had learned to guard her dresses and shoes carefully, and secretly to darn and patch her cloaks and skirts. She was determined to give the impression of gentility and affluence. She vowed she would never wear buckskin, as most men and many women were now forced to do.

She thought ruefully of the armload of Philip's clothing which she had given the Indians at Newmarket. She might have satisfied them with a single garment apiece, and a man's jacket now would bring forty dollars in government scrip.

But I didn't lose much, she decided, philosophically. *Government scrip isn't much good, either, with the colonial treasury so nearly empty.* At least she had been able to pay her taxes in wheat.

Mentally, and for the hundredth time, she counted her possessions, which now seemed so pitifully meager. The temptation to sell them off, one by one, was great. How she would like a good cup of tea! But tea had gone to a dollar and a half a pound. She could sell a pair of sheets to some woman to make shirts for her husband—but for what? More wheat. Or orders on the stores.

Kitty sighed softly. There was no use deceiving herself. She must anticipate even harder times. If she should lose her claim at Newmarket she would have to rely on the business she was trying to build with Jeff. Yet—if only they could weather this winter, things were bound to be better. Everyone said so. Everyone was in the same predicament. The people were short of everything but hope.

The children of some of the foremost families were reduced to a single cotton garment apiece, made of coarse sheeting and home-dyed. Many a man was both barefooted and bareheaded and even the most cultured women wore patched, odd-looking garments. They found wry humor, however, in the fact that Indians on the lower Columbia were better dressed; that squaws, in fact, were decked in fine silks and warm woolens. A ship had been wrecked on the Columbia River bar, and the Indians had salvaged some of the precious cargo.

Kitty paused to look down at the river, molten silver in the soft lavender twilight. . . . She might as well admit that she must spend the winter in Oregon, and she knew well that this year, 1846, was the year of crisis. A second British vessel, the *Cormorant*, now guarded the entrance to Puget Sound. If war came, the Sound would be a battle area. Yet to hold her claim at Newmarket she would have to return to it for a part of the year. She would stay in Oregon City till after the harvest, she decided, hoping that a ship would come with news and goods, and she would try desperately to get a winter's supply of foodstuffs on hand to take back with her to Newmarket.

Everyone in Oregon felt the tension, she reflected. All about her she saw signs of it. Small arguments flared into quick fist-fights. The men of the *Modeste* continued their private war with Tommy Dundee, who had heard the Englishmen cheer their flag and had roared at them: "Hurrah to hell and damn your country!" Even close friends and neighbors had misunderstandings.

Yes, one worried about international problems and the threat of war and Indian uprisings. But until those things actually occurred, Kitty considered, the immediate, daily battle for subsistence, the next meal, a new pair of shoes, a batch of soap, were much more important. If Mathias had a fever it was a greater worry than a rumor of war. And actually, malicious gossip troubled Kitty more than the sight of the guns of the *Modeste*.

Kitty's cheeks pinked as she walked on, and righteous indignation swept over her. She had made an honest effort to make friends with the Oregon women, she thought. Yet a few were still hostile toward her and caused her great embarrassment and heartache. Jeff Linton's devotion to her was no secret and busybodies remarked upon it openly. She had not lacked for escorts to any social event of the entire summer, and that fact was not overlooked by the gossips either.

Once—and her chin came up and a satisfied little smile touched her lips as she recalled the incident—she had had four escorts in one evening. That was when the British officers of the *Modeste* had presented Oregon's first theatrical performance. They had offered a prologue and three plays—*Three Weeks After Marriage, The Dance Is In Him,* and *The Mayor of Garrett.* Kitty had a different escort for each part of the program and at each intermission her escort had been replaced with all the formality of changing the palace guard. Tongues had wagged. But Kitty had enjoyed it.

Oh, well, she thought—there have to be a few waspish women, like Allie Johnson and Tildy Snider. They can't all be saints, just because they crossed the Plains. And, actually, the greater majority of Oregon women had begun to accept her. When she thought of these kind and worthy women, Kitty blushed at the memory of her own arrogance when she had first arrived in Oregon City. She marveled that none of these women considered themselves heroines, although the tales they told of their journey west revealed amazing depths of courage.

And if she had hardships and worries, she must remember that there were other women on the Oregon Trail now, longing only for the end of that journey.

All summer Clara had talked about the immigrants now on the Trail, and lived over again her own westward trek, until she had Kitty thinking of them, too, and mentally following their progress. In May, they'd be camped around the towns of Weston and Independence, Clara said, gathering supplies, and painting signs on their wagon covers *On To Oregon*. The women would be writing those last letters back to their folks in the States; they'd have meetings and organize the companies and gradually everything would be readied. Then, at last, they'd make the crossing, across the Missouri, into Kansas. That was the final break with the past and they were on their way, then, headed west. That was the big moment, Clara said, and there was no use trying to describe how a body felt, when the men cracked their whips, the trains formed, and at last the wagon wheels began to roll—to Oregon. . . . Only time to equal it was when they'd passed the halfway mark, and they knew for sure there was no turning back.

"The first ones'll be at Fort Laramie about now," Clara had said this morning. "They're past Scott's Bluff and the Black Hills, there's Sioux Country—and the awful alkali dust; they'll lose a lot of stock there. Then Independence Rock. And the Rocky Mountains. They'll be coming through South Pass in early August, and late in the month they'll make Fort Hall." Friends and relatives of many settlers were coming this year and Kitty remembered to say prayers daily for the people now out there on the rutted, grave-strewn Trail.

Coming for free land, Mary Mawson had said, laughing mirthlessly. Kitty took a long deep breath. There was nothing free about Oregon land. None ever came so dear. Kitty believed it now, and she was beginning to understand why the settlers so longed for government recognition, why they were even more anxious to clarify their land titles than for protection against the British and Indians.

The walk was doing her good, Kitty decided. She could feel a lightening of her spirits already, and a relaxation of aching muscles, and, now that she had thought over her problems she could look at the other side of the ledger and see all the good things, too. In a few months she had seen great progress in Oregon. Oregon City had a newspaper now, the *Oregon Spectator*, first newspaper to be published west of the Rockies. Kitty approved the announced editorial policy, to promote science, temperance, morality and general intelligence. The editor also advised the citizens of Oregon to "be sure you are right, then go ahead. Dig up the stumps, grade the streets, tax dogs, prohibit hogs—and advertise in the *Spectator*." Kitty had followed this advice and had inserted in the paper a small discreet advertisement of "Furniture for sale" by Catherine Gatewood and Jefferson Linton.

Dr. McLoughlin had resigned as factor of Fort Vancouver, and was building a real mansion in Oregon City. He had likewise begun construction of a canal about the falls, and had presented the town with land for parks and schools. . . . Kitty had enjoyed the trips up the Willamette in the new keel-boats, the *Mogul* and the *Ben Franklin* and the *Great Western*, and she had come to know the men who ran them and the people along the banks who hailed them. She had gone down to Portland and upon The River in the new-built sloop, *Calapooya*, and watched houses and settlements a-building, and in exchange for furniture she had bought a riverfront lot at Portland. Portland now boasted of sixty residents, and she thought it wise to plan a warehouse there, both for the salvaged furniture and for the produce she took in trade. And she really had guessed correctly on what the women longed for, and had been quite successful in persuading their husbands that fine furniture was almost as essential as a plough or saw. If only money weren't so scarce—

She remembered, with growing optimism, that there would be certain improvements on her claim at Newmarket when she returned to it. She had rented her cottage there to the Missourian, Frank Hatch, in return for some work to be done on the claim. Certainly she hadn't wasted the summer—even if the six hundred dollars passage money home seemed farther away than ever.

Kitty came to the end of the trail and reluctantly she turned back toward Main Street. . . . It didn't pay to be downhearted. Few Oregon people were. Despite anxieties and back-breaking labor, the colonists played with the same zest with which they worked. Certainly romances flourished. It seemed to Kitty there had been a wedding and infair and charivari every week throughout the summer. Many of the brides were very young. Some of the couples were genuinely in love, Kitty judged, but many of them also based their marriages only on practical considerations. *Oregon marriages*, Kitty privately termed them. The girls married for protection, and for independence, and to get out of the crowded family cabins. The men needed wives to work with and for them, and husky sons were the most valuable crop a couple could raise. If one were condemned to live the rest of her life in Oregon, an Oregon marriage, to a strong and decent man, was the only sensible choice.

But she, fortunately, was not so condemned.

The biggest event of the whole summer had been the Fourth of July celebration—and at the memory of it, Kitty's heart leaped. That day would not be forgotten in Oregon, for it was the first Independence Day celebration there. Dr. Manning had been busy from early morning till late at night, patching up the injuries of the celebrants. The spirit of '76 had been rampant in Tommy Dundee and Jimmy Correll, and they had challenged the men of the *Modeste*, claiming they could lick the entire British navy single-handed. Then the Indians, attracted by the white men's celebration, had got into the spirit of the occasion, and had turned the town into an uproar, racing down the streets on their half-wild ponies, and yelling "Potlatch Blue Lu!" which, roughly translated, meant "Give me some liquor!" Sheriff Meek had his hands full, stopping the sale of liquor to the Indians, jailing the troublemakers. A posse had finally dumped Dick McCrary's still into the river, and would have tossed Dick in after it if he had not taken to the woods.

It had been a great day in Oregon City, with patriotic toasts being greeted with rousing and defiant cheers; and there had been a thirty-one gun salute for the thirty-one states, and Dundee and his friends had fired an anvil for good measure. Weedy little Grandma Burns had almost collapsed with the heat and excitement, and there had been inspired oratory and a Liberty Pole.

But the highlight of the day had been the ball in the evening.

At first Kitty's thoughts shied away from the memory of the ball. She had promised herself that she would not think of that evening—or of Curt Fletcher—again. For three weeks she had been trying to discipline herself, and, by deliberately occupying her mind with other things, she had managed rather well. It was true she had not been able to avoid watching for Curt. As she passed the billiard parlor or the Main Street House, she had watched, out of the corner of her eye, and she had walked a little faster and a little straighter. But Curt had not appeared—not since the night of the Fourth of July.

If twilight was the most peaceful part of the day, it was also the loneliest. Kitty, face averted, studied the dusty path now. . . . She had worn one of her loveliest gowns to the Independence Day ball. It was a fine white dress with tiny rosebuds scattered upon it, and it had a very tight bodice and very full skirts. She had thought she looked quite well. Certainly her two escorts told her she did, and when she had entered the hall there had been a general craning of necks and a buzz of voices—the sort of thing every girl is aware of but always pretends not to notice. Bert Thomas was the caller. Bert interspersed the usual calls with booming personal greetings—and that was part of the fun. He had just finished calling the *Grapevine Twist*, and as she entered he'd started *The Girl I Left Behind Me*.

The set nearest the door was not complete. Clara had motioned for Kitty and one of her partners to join them. They had run to their places, laughing, and Kitty had politely given all her attention to her partner. She had bowed and automatically swung happily and carelessly into the dance, paying no attention to the others who made up the set.

There had not been enough girls to go round. There never were, at the Oregon dances. So a number of men tied white handkerchiefs on their sleeves, to indicate they would take the places of girls, and one huge fellow nearby had simpered and pointed his toe in grotesque and good-natured imitation of little Kitty, and a roar of laughter had followed him. Kitty had laughed, too, and at

Bert's roar, "Pass right through and balance, too!" she had held out her hand—and Sunset Lee had taken it.

It had been a real surprise to look into Sunset's steady blue eyes. She had not known he was in Oregon City, and in her preoccupation with the clown who was imitating her, she had not noticed him. And then she suddenly jerked to attention and glanced beyond him, wondering if Curt also were there. Bert had sung out—"And swing that girl behind you—"

Curt had turned, and the music had swiftly whirled her into his arms.

It had been a great shock to see him there; a greater shock to feel his touch, and she found herself trembling now, remembering it. She had thought that Curt's face had paled slightly as he had put his arm about her. His eyes were narrow and bright, and he did not smile. . . . But she was sure, now, that she had been mistaken. Seeing her had meant nothing to him, apparently; for he had disappeared later in the evening, and she had not seen him since. She was much too proud to inquire, even casually, where he had gone. But she knew he had left Oregon City. Surely she would know if he were there. . . .

I won't think about him any more, she decided. *But he did look at me in a most possessive fashion, and it angered Jeff, and everyone noticed it.* It had been embarrassing, and yet, in a strange way, pleasing, too; and more disturbing than she liked to admit, to see Curt again. . . .

So absorbed was she that she did not at first notice that someone had fallen into step beside her. She glanced up to meet Curt's bold gray eyes and she started violently, wondering if he could read her thoughts.

He was in high spirits, she noticed, and well-dressed. The only people she knew who were making money were the merchants who were charging exorbitant prices for goods. Some of her resentment toward them transferred itself instantly, and for no logical reason, to Curt. Why should he be so gay and self-possessed? Where had he been, anyway? She was irritated that he had caught her off guard, angry at herself because his sudden appearance had shaken her.

"Well, Kitty?"

Her first impulse was to flounce on to the Linton cabin and to slam the door in his face, but then she hesitated, remembering Jeff's tools. Curt had them, still, at Abernethy's store. She needed them.

"Well, Curt?" she answered coolly.

"Let's walk up the bluff. I want to talk to you."

She considered for an instant, then shrugged. She had often wanted to climb the hill to the top of the bluff, particularly at sundown, but she was afraid to go alone. Sometimes Indians, on their horses, were silhouetted there on the bluff above the town, sitting statue-like, brooding, looking down upon the activities of the whites; and from the bluff in wintertime the wolves howled. Now it was peaceful, warm, somnolent, heavy with the scent of evergreens and sun-heated grasses, and with Curt she was safe. *He's so big*, she thought, regarding his powerful shoulders, his height; *I wonder if he has ever feared anything*.

"All right. The afternoon is wasted anyway."

Curt laughed and he drew her hand beneath his arm and imprisoned it very tightly with his own. She darted an angry look at him. She could not struggle with him on Main Street, he knew, and he was taking advantage of it. They walked on and Kitty bowed and smiled to acquaintances but she spoke to Curt through clenched teeth.

"Let go my hand, Curt."

Curt ignored her and politely tipped his hat to Grandma Burns and the old lady's bright glance swept them meaningly. The dimple in Kitty's cheek deepened as she set her lips with annoyance.

"I don't think you'll believe this afternoon wasted, Kitty," Curt said, after a while, as they started the climb up the bluff. "You've not heard the news?"

"What news?"

"Wait. You'll hear—and see—very soon. Great news, Kitty!" He studied her critically. "You're thinner. What's this talk about you being in business with Linton?"

"I am. Jeff is a furniture-maker. The Lintons have been very kind to me. As long as I must remain in Oregon, waiting for a ship, I thought I'd do what I could to help them. Jeff has to work. Clara can't travel around talking to people, not with the baby to look out for, and she has to help Jeff a lot because he isn't very strong yet. So I just—"

"So you travel the Willamette valley, selling furniture, taking meat, wheat, potatoes—"

"There's no money in Oregon. We have to take what we can get."

The climb was steep, the sun was warm, and Kitty loosened her bonnet ties. She was breathless when they reached the top and glad to stop and look down at the little city and the Willamette, silvery in the sun, threading its way toward The Great River.

"It's beautiful, isn't it?" Curt said, finally.

"It's cruel and dangerous!" Kitty flashed back. "It's just not worth the price! People working, slaving, dying, women losing their children, half-starving, not enough clothing to cover them! Living in log cabins too crowded to turn around in—and going on crazy, wild hope. Look at the British—with three warships in Oregon waters right now—and look at us. Granaries filled, more lumber than we can sell—and no ships to take it away. And I don't think it will ever be any better—not for years, anyway!"

"Look at me, Kitty."

With an effort Kitty turned her head and raised her eyes. They were alone here, on the bluff. Kitty took a firm grip on herself, steadied her voice. *I must be very business-like*, she reminded herself.

"Curt, you have some of Jeff's tools. When he gave them to you in return for the loan, he wasn't well enough to work and they meant nothing to him. Now he needs them badly. I'd—I'd like to—I wonder if—"

Curt put his hands on her arms and studied her face. His own was serious now, and Kitty's heart beat faster.

"I saw the way Linton watched you, dancing," he said slowly. "I've heard a lot of talk since I've been back. What's going on here, Kitty?"

"There's nothing going on. And I wish the silly gossips would mind their own business! If you must know it—I have no money. Only a very little bit, that is. Some of your fine Oregon people think nothing of persuading a slave to run away—though Jessie was my property, my very own! Father gave her to me, and she was worth a great deal of money. They urged her to desert me, and she took my money with her—a thousand dollars, that's what she took! You fine upstanding people who believe in freedom for everybody and a fair chance for everyone—you haven't been fair to me! You've robbed me, that's what you've done, of my legal property. And so I *have* to work, but I'll show you, I'll show all of you! Those tools aren't doing you any good in that warehouse. We can use them, and maybe Jeff can pay back your loan if he can work that much faster. And—as soon as I can—I'll leave Oregon, I'll get out of this awful place where—where—"

To her fury she was choked with sobs and tears rained down her cheeks. She covered her face with her hands. Curt's hands dropped from her shoulders and he stepped back. She wiped her face finally and raised her head.

"I just don't have the faith in Oregon that you have—or the interest either," she said bitterly. "I don't care *what* becomes of the place!" She glanced at him then. He was leaning against a tree, his hands in his pockets staring down at the town below them. His face was expressionless, and she stared at him, puzzled. His lips curved in a sardonic little grin and then he spoke, almost absently, tossing the words at her across his shoulder.

"Of course you can have the tools, Kitty."

She frowned with surprise. From far below them came the boom of cannon fire, and her whole sensitive body jerked. Curt straightened quickly, his face suddenly alight.

"What is it, Curt?"

"The news I told you was coming, Kitty. See the boat—there at the landing? It comes from the schooner *Shark*—an American schooner, with twelve guns. She tried to cross the bar at the mouth of the Willamette today but couldn't make it, so she lies in The River. That small boat brings her officers—Neil Howison, commander. One of our fighting ships has, at last, arrived in The River!"

Kitty's eyes went wonderingly from Curt to the scene below. People were rushing toward the landing place and again the cannon boomed in salute and the sound echoed from the bluff. Curt laughed aloud.

"That'll show the British! The *Shark* will take the *Modeste* out of The River when the time comes! Well, Kitty," he took a long, satisfied breath, "the time you said would never come is here. Right now. The government has given notice to Great Britain that joint occupancy of Oregon is over. It's what we've been waiting for, praying for, what we *knew* was coming. They haven't forgotten us, Kitty, after all."

"You—you knew about the ship."

A greater explosion than cannon fire rocked Oregon City and again Curt laughed. "The boys can't make enough racket with the cannon. That was Dundee firing an anvil. . . . Yes, Kitty, I knew about the ship. I met her down river early this morning. I wanted you to see the arrival—from here, with me."

Why, he planned this for me, Kitty thought, suddenly dismayed. He wanted me with him when this great news came. It means so much to him; he thought it would to me, too, and I've spoiled it, by being ill-humored, by saying I didn't care—

I don't know, I don't know—she whispered to herself. Maybe I've underrated him. There is power in him, and faith, and vision, as Sunset said. His dreams are big. A sudden flash, like the click of a shutter, gave her a momentary insight into Curt's mind. She felt that she was on the verge of discovery, of understanding him—and then it was gone. If we could just be friends, she thought, if there were not always conflict between us—

She put her hand on his arm. It was the first time she had ever touched him voluntarily and he glanced at her sharply.

"I—thank you for bringing me here, Curt," she said gently. "You were right and I was wrong. Maybe—you're right about other things, too. That Oregon will grow, and Puget Sound—maybe even the railroad you and Sunset dreamed about will come." She tried very hard to keep her voice level, friendly, but suddenly she was breathless, hurrying. "I hope, for your sake, that it all comes true. I—I thank you for the tools. Jeff will pay you back. I—I hope you and I can be friends, Curt."

His eyes grew hot and hard and angry and there was a hard ridge along his jaw. He swept her into his arms then, lifting her from her feet, and his lips were close to hers as he answered.

"Friends, Kitty? We'll never be friends. *Friends* is a mighty weak word for what is between us and you know it. You're just afraid to admit it. You're so damn anxious to be a lady you try to forget you are a woman. . . . Of course I was right about the Oregon Country. The coming of the *Shark* proves it! I want to see towns on Puget Sound, and shipyards, and ships of every nation in the docks. I want to see a railroad into Oregon. I want you, Kitty." He was hurting her, his hard, muscular body pressed tight against her, and Kitty could feel the power and force of him, his body and mind and will. Despite herself, her hands moved up yearningly, and her arms went around his neck, and at last she gave him her lips.

For a long instant Kitty forgot where she was, floating in time and space. Curt's words shocked her back to her surroundings. He had not been swept away—not this time. He was thinking, planning, sharp and clear, even as he held her, even as his lips had drained her of all strength.

"And you're damn right Linton will pay me back, Kitty," he said tightly, "every cent of it. But if he so much as touches you, Kitty, he—or any other man—I'll kill him, so help me God."

He meant it. Kitty, with awful certainty knew that he meant it, as she saw his face, rigid with violence and jealousy and desire, watched his lips, barely moving as he spoke.

A shout from the crowds below drifted up to them.

"They're raising the flag," he said, his arms still tight about her. "We'd better go down now. . . . There she goes, Kitty—the Stars and Stripes!"

"What does it mean, Curt?" She would stay for just one more minute, just one short minute, in the safe circle of his arms.

"Mean?" His eyes were glittering, frightening, the eyes of a fighter, ready for battle, and they were narrowed against the setting sun. "It means a showdown with the British. That flag will stay there. The British will get out of Oregon. Or—it's war."

◈ 4 ◈

THE excitement in Oregon City at the arrival of the *Shark* overshadowed the Fourth of July celebration. When Kitty at last made her way through the crowds to the Linton cabin she had forgotten her exhaustion in the wild joy that had swept the town. The news spread and grew and it was good. The United States squadron, the frigates *Congress* and *Savannah*, and the sloops of war, *Cyane*, *Portsmouth*, *Levant* and *Warren* were on the coast of Mexico and California while the store-ship *Erie* was in the Islands provisioning for the fleet. Uncle Sam was coming to the aid of his people in Oregon. Plans were under way to establish military posts along the Oregon Trail; even to provide a monthly overland mail service to the colonists who had occupied Oregon and held it for the United States. Mounted riflemen would be sent west. Land laws were up before Congress. A territorial government would be formed, backed by government money, government credit.

The nation was fulfilling its manifest destiny. The Stars and Stripes flew from sea to shining sea. No force on earth could stop the western tide now—Texas, Oregon—and then California! There remained for the actual northern boundary line to be settled—by treaty or by war; and the settlers took up the old shout "Fifty-four forty or fight! Oregon—all or none!"

Their faith had been rewarded, their sacrifices justified. They'd blazed the trail, they were first, they had gambled and they had won. Uncle Sam had served notice on the British. . . . American sailors and marines mingled with the jubilant settlers, and the welcome was one that only lusty and rugged frontiersmen could give.

Kitty dropped into Clara's rocker. Her eyes were like stars, her heart light. If only the boundary were settled soon, and the land laws clarified, so the Newmarket claim would be undeniably hers! Thousands upon thousands of people would head west next year. The prophecies of Sunset, the dreams of Curt, fantastic as they had seemed, would come true. Cities would rise on The River and on Puget Sound, and the powerful Hudson's Bay Company which had ruled Oregon so long, would at last admit defeat and withdraw. What a triumph!

"Kitty."

Jeff spoke softly. Clara had stepped outside, holding little Mathias in her arms, pointing toward the flag that flew over Oregon City.

"Kitty, I saw you walking with Fletcher."

"Yes, Jeff, I walked with him, up the bluff," Kitty answered absently. Again her heart leaped. Curt—the excitement within her was so intense that she could not conceal it. To share a moment of triumph with a man of strength—with Curt— Her face was radiant as she forced herself to bring her attention back to Jeff.

The man's face was pale. "Why, Kitty?"

"Why did I walk with Curt? Why, Jeff—" Kitty frowned. His face was tormented and pity for him touched her. There were many problems to work out, she thought, hazily, and she would think about them, one by one, when she was alone in the dark. She would allow herself to remember Curt, there on the bluff, and she would try to organize her thoughts and decide what she must do. It was wild, insane, to feel like this, she thought, trying to compose herself, and yet—

"Why, Jeff," she tried again. He's sick, she thought, very sick. He ought not to be upset. I must try to help him and Clara. I must be kind. "I wanted to talk to him, Jeff, about getting your tools. I thought they would help us."

Jeff's face cleared. "Kitty, forgive me. I thought—"

Kitty smiled comfortingly. "We are business partners, Jeff, you and Clara and I. We have to work together. Curt will let us have the tools and we'll pay him off as rapidly as we can. Times should be better now. I know you don't want to be in debt to him."

"I see." Jeff was reassured. "I'm glad, Kitty. He's not worthy of you. He's attractive to women, I guess. His kind usually are. I didn't want you to be hurt, Kitty."

"Me be hurt?" Kitty laughed in supreme self-confidence. She jumped up and started for her own room. "Jeff, today no one could hurt me. No one!"

"I'm glad," Jeff said again. "I didn't know if you knew—Curt keeps Lisa. He left here on the Fourth, after the ball—with her."

Kitty stopped and turned slowly back to him. He did not look at her. "What did you say?"

"He's been up The River the past three weeks. He went to the Whitman mission. Everyone knows about it—but it's one of those things no one talks about. He makes that trip at least once a year. He always takes Lisa with him. She lives in the village at Fort Vancouver, but she's here, whenever Fletcher is. She was waiting outside the hall that night of the ball, while he danced with you. Lisa lives all year for those weeks with Fletcher."

Kitty put her hand against the door jamb to steady herself. Curt's promise at Newmarket came back to her. She had forgotten. She had been a fool to forget his words: *"You'll pay for this, Kitty. How you'll pay!"*

What was he trying to do? Deliberately to break her heart, to force her to humble herself, to go to him, on his terms? How dare he come to her today straight from Lisa? He wants to break me, as he broke that wild horse, she thought. He cannot bear to be defied, ever. Will he be satisfied now? Has he had his revenge? Humiliation and anger seethed within her. That moment of revelation, when she had thought she saw beneath Curt's armor into the shining dreams that drove him, was gone; it had been her imagination, purely. Because of the physical attraction of his magnificent body, because of her own youth and loneliness, she had read into him a nobility that was not there. It was a mistake as old as woman. She should have known better. Margaret had warned her—

"So I'm glad it was just the tools."

She spoke heavily, quietly, trying not to hate him for this revelation. "Yes, Jeff," she said, "it was just the tools."

◊ 5 ◊

THE meeting was in the long room over the granary of the Methodist Church. The leaders of the Oregon Provisional Government were there, and many other leading citizens as well. As Dr. Manning approached the building he glanced sharply at the faces of the women who clustered about the entrance.

They had been standing there since early morning, despite the chill autumn rain and now it was after noon. They were a silent crowd, depressed and anxious, but there was nothing beaten about them. Their faces were defiant and grim, reflecting the faces of the angry men gathered within.

"Good afternoon, Dr. Manning."

Kitty's soft voice made him pause, and he turned to take her hand. She smiled at him, but her hand was very cold and the heavy dark shawl framed a tired, thin little face. Her eyes, heavily shadowed, looked enormous and sad, Thomas thought, but she was none the less beautiful. The childish softness had been erased from her face in her year in Oregon, but the strength in her jaw, the sweetness of her lips, were intensified.

"Kitty, I thought you'd gone to Newmarket."

"We're leaving in the morning, Jennie and William Hines and I. I thought I'd take the latest news I could back to Newmarket —whatever word comes from this meeting."

Thomas nodded, chafing the cold little hand with his big warm ones.

"You're all right, child? You have enough provisions?"

"Oh, yes." The smile came again and warmed him, despite the rain. "The Hines will stay with me until they get their own claims staked out, and build their cabin—and that may take most of the winter. So I won't be alone. The Hatch family have moved on, you see, to their own place—and I don't dare leave my cabin empty."

"Right. Right, Kitty. It's a pity but there are those who'd be quick to claim it was abandoned and take possession of it. No news from inside?" He motioned to the building. Kitty shook her head.

"Sometimes a voice is raised, an argument starts, and then it dies down again. Some are still demanding that they take matters into their own hands and run the Hudson's Bay people out. And once someone shouted: 'It's not a compromise—it's a betrayal!' and it caused quite an uproar, but it quieted again and the discussion continues."

Thomas nodded. What a pity, what a pity, he thought, frowning, looking at the patient women. They had waited so long; they had known such blessed relief when the word came that war with England had been averted and a compromise had been reached. But when the actual terms of the final treaty reached Oregon, by way of the bark *Toulon* from the Sandwich Islands, the joy had turned first to disbelief and then to anger.

The Oregon boundary was settled—but at the 49th parallel, instead of fifty-four degrees and forty minutes. The government of the United States had relinquished to England a part of the Pacific coastline and of Oregon, though by far the lesser and poorer part.

In itself, that was bad enough, the settlers declared, though the boundary still lay far to the north of Newmarket and Puget Sound. But a second article in the treaty was worse, and it brought a real roar of protest.

The Hudson's Bay Company was to be permitted, under terms of the treaty, the right to use The River for the duration of its charter, and to keep their lands and stations in Oregon. The unpopular monopoly of the Company, protected by international agreement, appeared to be stronger than ever!

It was an impossible situation, the Oregon men said, and showed how little the Congress really understood conditions in Oregon. The wealthy Hudson's Bay Company *must* withdraw from Oregon, the settlers declared. They could not stay, trade with the Indians, keep the savages under their influence as a threat to American settlers, drain the country of wealth, keep the best town- and power sites and farm lands, have free access to The River, compete in business with American colonists. Treaty or no treaty, the Oregon men would run them out; they'd form their own republic, if necessary, withdrawing from the United States entirely. Their long-tried patience was worn thin. It was time for revolt.

Thomas opened the door. The deep steady voice of a speaker within rose in volume, was muted as the door swung to. It was Fletcher's voice.

Kitty turned to look toward Mt. Hood. The mountain had not been visible for many days now, hidden as though the pall of gloom that hung over Oregon veiled the glory of it, too. To the south, war raged in California, for Mexico, anticipating war in Oregon, had declared war on the United States. Kitty's jaw set stoically; there was nothing to be done but keep doggedly plodding, hoping for the best. But violence seemed to have swept the entire Pacific Coast. Perhaps it was the violence of labor pains, she thought, in the birth of a new country.

It would not be a pleasant winter, she reflected, sadly. The cabin would be crowded—and still, for her, it would be lonely. Worst of all she dreaded the day when Curt would come back to Puget Sound.

She was glad he had been kept busy throughout the autumn—too busy for her. He'd been up The River again, meeting the immigrants, telling them of the advantages of Newmarket. Sunset had gone still farther, far out into the Cayuse country. Curt probably took Lisa with him, Kitty thought, sickly, to watch for his comforts, to make his clothes, to cook for him, to share his camp. And when he was ready he'd come back to Kitty, and expect her to be waiting for him. The unspeakable—

Suddenly there was a stir in the crowd and puzzled glances among the waiting women. From the room in which the men were gathered came a startling and altogether unexpected sound —the sound of laughter, deep laughter, that grew and swelled, laughter of genuine mirth and delight. It was the most welcome sound the anxious women had ever heard, a rich and healthy, wonderful sound, and the women, hopeful, not knowing what had caused it, began to smile, too. There had been too little laughter from those men since they had turned their faces west.

"What is it? What are they doing? What happened?"

The door opened. The laughter boomed amid wild cheers. John Homet emerged, chuckling, his face red, and the crowd surged toward him, firing questions.

"It's the wording of the treaty!" he said, when he could talk. "The men were all studyin' it. Abernethy and Lovejoy and Burnett, and Fletcher. And—do you know what the treaty says?" He paused, laughing again, and slapped his knee. "They overlooked it—those smart British diplomats, and our cute, generous politicians in Washington! They made a mistake! They slipped up, by gad, and it's there in writin'—signed, sealed and delivered! It's true, by the old Harry, it's true!"

Someone shook his arm in impatience and he held up a paper and read in a loud, delighted voice, his eyes moist from laughter. "It says here, it says: the Columbia River is to be left free to British traders *on the same footing as the citizens of the United States*. Well, folks, citizens of the United States have to pay duty on imported goods. So every item that comes in here from England or Montreal to the Hudson's Bay posts, to Vancouver or Nisqually or whatever, will be subject to duty! They can't provision their forts in Oregon under this treaty—the one they already signed! They got to move north of the border!"

At first many of the women did not grasp the full import of what Homet was saying. They sensed only blessed relief that a crisis had passed. But Kitty savored and digested each of Homet's words. It was incredible, fantastic, that a colossal, diplomatic blunder had ended the glory days of the Hudson's Bay Company in Oregon, she thought—but, accident or merciful Providence, it was true. Her eyes were stinging with tears and her heart was full of gratitude as she turned away, giving thanks that the lusty laughter of the Oregon men, not gunfire, was the fur company's death knell.

◈ 6 ◈

Up The River in the land of the Cayuse Indians, Sunset squatted in a smoke-filled hut. His host, Five Crows, put a live coal on the tobacco in the long-stemmed pipe, puffed it and passed it to Sunset.

Sunset smoked in silence. Near him a squaw, who had been huddling with her head down on her knees, raised her face, and a long, low, eerie wail came from her. It started on a low note, grew into a nerve-torturing keening, and then it faded, died, and silence entered the lodge again.

Five Crows was a tall, powerful, handsome young chief, his black braids hanging low on his chest, his head decorated with eagle plumes. He was a wealthy man; hundreds of horses and cattle roamed upon his lands and a dozen slaves were at his call. He was Sunset's friend.

"These are the last?" Five Crows asked, in his own language. He was sure of an affirmative answer. "There will be no more Boston men come?"

"Not this year. But next year, many, many more."

Five Crows regarded Sunset with anger and suspicion.

"But there can be no more! There will be none left in the lands to the east."

"They are as many as the stars in the heavens, the leaves on the trees. There will be more next year, and the year after that. They will bring guns, bigger guns than you have seen before. It is wise to make friends with them. Do not try to stop them, Five Crows. Obey their laws and they will leave you in peace."

"They wish to make slaves of us. They wish to take our lands. Already they are taking land from the Mexicans to the south."

"And Delaware Tom—who is a wise Indian—and Yellow Serpent, your own chief, ride beside our leader, Colonel Fremont. They are friends to the Americans."

For answer Five Crows glanced at Sunset from half-closed eyes and he almost smiled. Sunset, too, nearly grinned. Despite his words neither he nor his Indian friend believed that the Delaware or Yellow Serpent, for all that they fought with Fremont now, were loyal friends of the Americans for all time to come. The

Delaware and Yellow Serpent had ridden southward, as they had warned Sunset they would do a year ago, to avenge the murder of Yellow Serpent's son, Elijah, at Sutter's Fort. Fremont had met them in council, appeased them, promised them redress. And so the Indians had joined him and gone to battle against the Spanish.

But Sunset and Five Crows both knew that Delaware Tom, whose prying, vengeful eyes had noted every lock and bolt and gun in every fort and settlement in Oregon, would return with information on the ways of fighting of the Americans; and this knowledge would be used against the whites when the time came. Now the Oregon settlers had a respite, while the Indians brooded, muttered, orated. But Sunset knew that it was only temporary peace. The unrest was too general and too intense.

Nor had Delaware Tom's evil influence left the Cayuse country with him.

"Tom Hill says we are not to believe the missionaries—neither the Protestants nor the Black Gowns," Five Crows said finally. "He told the Nez Perces they might have as many wives as they liked, and one hundred lodges then named him their chief."

"Are you a Catholic, Five Crows?"

The Indian shook his head. "No. But my brother, Tauitau, believes the priests. He says the illness comes to us because we do not follow them. The Catholic ladder frightened my people."

Sunset frowned. The zealous battle between the Protestant and Catholic missionaries for the Indian souls was not well-timed. Already uneasy, threatening, the Indians were still further confused and aroused by the opposing doctrines of the white men.

Across the lodge another dark figure moved, swayed, and the death wail rose again. It seemed to Sunset it went on and on; even when it ended the echoes of it continued as another woman, far away, took up the chant, passed it on through the winter night to another lodge far out on the rolling prairie.

"For whom do they mourn, Five Crows?"

"Their children. Their sisters. Ten, twenty, lie ill in each lodge. Most of them die." His eyes glittered. "The white men brought us this disease. But the white men cannot cure us of it. Yet the white men do not die of it."

"Dr. Whitman has explained it to you. The sweat baths are not good for people sufferin' with measles. Your plunge into icy water from the sweat bath makes the illness worse."

"It is our custom. It has made us well in the past," Five Crows answered stubbornly.

Sunset dropped the argument. It was true that diseases seldom fatal to the whites were taking a heavy toll among the Indians. Pestilence had come with the wagon trains and the suffering in the lodges was very great. Dr. Whitman labored among the stricken savages, but he received small thanks. Each time a patient died the mutterings grew louder.

Five Crows continued to recite his grievances. "I offered skins, many rich skins, my finest horse, fine blankets. I built a house—with glass windows. But though I camped for many days beside the Trail and talked to many men, none would sell a white wife to me."

Sunset looked at the proud, bitter young chief. He had seen Five Crows during the immigration, waylaying every wagon company, trying to barter for a white wife. Time after time Sunset had stepped softly into the conversations, tempering an immigrant's angry refusal, counseling forebearance. Often, after those unsuccessful attempts of Five Crows to buy a white girl, there had been swift, sudden raids on the wagon trains and stock stolen and scattered and killed.

"They do not pay us for crossing our lands. They do not pay us for lands they have taken."

"Our government will pay, Five Crows. It takes time, for this country is very large and it takes a long while for messages to go to our Great Father and return. You must be patient. You must obey the laws and you must not kill and steal the stock. You will be punished, Five Crows, and all your people destroyed, if you try to stop the white men. Live in peace with us. Be our friend."

Five Crows fell silent and for a long time he stared into the flames of the fire. "You are my brother, Sunset Lee," he said, finally. "I believe you tell the truth. But this land is ours. It is a big land; it was free until the Boston men came. The English did not bring their women and their ploughs. They bring trade goods and they live among us and marry our women and are buried beside us. They do not try to drive us away or to spoil our hunting grounds. Now you say the English will leave and the Boston men alone will rule."

The infinite sadness in the Indian's voice held all the tragedy of a proud and threatened race. Pity for him, for all his people, swept over Sunset. It was true that the whites were invaders. It was hard to beg the young chief not to resist. In his place, I'd fight, too, Sunset thought; and this understanding showed through his words of careful counsel to his friend.

But there was deep hate in Five Crows and hurt pride, and, though he listened, Sunset knew he was not convinced.

After the usual ceremonious parting, Sunset left the lodge and started down river, to the camp of the immigrants. The Walla Walla wind was icy and sharp, and it sought holes and thin places in his buckskin jacket. He carried only his long rifle and he traveled fast and light, soundless as a shadow, and his pace kept him warm. At last he came to the silent camp, spoke softly to the young sentry, and settled himself in his blankets. But he did not sleep.

He breathed long and deep, every one of his trained muscles relaxing to his will, and the earth beneath drained him of fatigue. He was thankful that this was the last wagon train to come over the Trail this year. Already it was nearly Christmas time, and fine light snow blanketed the earth each morning. The exhausted people about him slept deeply, feeling themselves safe now that they had reached, and passed, Dr. Whitman's mission at Waillatpu, that outpost which meant they had successfully crossed the Plains and their journey was near an end.

They had been harassed and robbed and insulted by the Indians, but there had been no slaughter. Sunset stared into the black blanket of the sky; if they knew what he knew, he thought, all the information he had gathered from Five Crows tonight, and from other Indians in the hundred nights since he had left Oregon City, these people would not sleep so soundly.

He moved restlessly on his bed. I, Dad, it was hard to know right from wrong, and it was hard for him to hate! He was certain it was only a matter of time before his Indian friends would be his enemies. They were too proud a race, their freedom too precious, to let it go without a war. Isolated raids could not stop the westward march of immigrants; but a concerted uprising of all the Indian nations, led by the brilliant renegade, Delaware Tom, and his brothers, could wipe out every settlement and wagon train and cut the Oregon Trail. The Indians in Oregon must outnumber the Americans by five to one, Sunset figured, and if ever all the tribes rose as one—

There was a slight movement here and there in the camp. People like these, Godfearing, home-seeking, bravely heading west to what they believed a bright new world, would be the victims if the Indians struck.

At Oregon City, messengers said, there had been a great celebration, and optimism reigned, for the crisis over the treaty had passed. The worst was over, Oregon won from the British. Sunset knew it would be hard to convince them that the dangerous, dozing giant, the Indian menace, at their backs, was awakening and pulling himself together. The deep beat of war-drums would come as no surprise to him. Pillaging, slaughtering, burning, torture—Sunset tossed uneasily. A man could fight them. Many of the colonists had fought Indians before. But a woman—

Sunset knew too well what would happen to a girl—a girl like Kitty—if ever she were in the path of an Indian raid. He felt the sweat break out all over his body as he thought of her, and remembered the things he had witnessed in the past. It was hard to say whether Indian men or squaws were worse fiends at torture; but it was at the hands of the squaws that girls, and girl-children, after the men had finished with them, suffered the ultimate in agony.

He tried to put the thought away from him, for there are some things too horrible for a man to contemplate. Yes, his sympathy was with the Indians, for they were the innocent victims. But he would fight them, the men who had been his friends, with all his strength and skill and endurance, his life, if necessary.

In his mind's eye, he saw this country like a relief map laid out before him. They must keep the fighting away from the settlements, out on the rolling bare hills from the Columbia to the Clearwater, he figured. They'd have to hold The Dalles. The Dalles would be the Gibraltar, protecting the settlers to the west.

Perhaps, Sunset thought, it was written in the stars that no country as beautiful, as magnificent, as rich as Oregon could be won without paying a price of blood.

At last he slept. But one thought threaded through his troubled dreams. When would it come? Not during this winter, for the snows would hold them back. In the spring? When the first immigrants came next year? When Delaware Tom and Yellow Serpent returned from the Mexican war?

The sentry, so young that only the first light fuzz covered his square chin, leaned on his rifle, absently rubbed the aching muscles of his arms, and yawned. The muscles were sore from wrestling with the lithe young Indians who trailed the wagon train, challenging the white boys to fight. The sentry grinned. He had pinned an Indian's shoulders to the ground today, but the redskin had inflicted considerable punishment upon him.

Suddenly he jerked to attention, raised his gun, listened intently. The wild, thin distant wail that floated into the camp was only the cry of a wolf or coyote, he decided, and he relaxed again. He had not been in Oregon long enough to recognize the chant of death.

THE PURPLE BLOSSOMS OF THE TALL fireweed carpeted the cut-off land on Kitty's claim at Newmarket in the spring. The pod-like buds at the top of the three-foot stalks opened first in May, and then, as the season progressed, the flowering descended lower on the stem. Kitty watched the slow, regular procession of its flowering, saw the blossoms fade and drop, like leaves torn from a calendar, and, at last, the ripened seed pods burst into silken gray tufts. The summer was over.

On a late September evening she sat at the table in her cabin, a tiny, whale-oil lamp spreading a fan of light over the paper before her. The scratch of her pen was loud in the quiet room.

"I will return to Oregon City in a month, Clara," she wrote, "and I pray there will be mail for me there. On the whole, however, it has been a good year at Newmarket. We have many new settlers and they find it much easier traveling from Oregon City. There is a shelter at Cowlitz Landing now, and the trail from the Cowlitz to Newmarket is being widened. Simmons' sawmill is in operation here. He managed to buy an upright saw from the Hudson's Bay people for twenty cents a pound, so the cutting of lumber has begun.

"We have fared very well. Never have I seen such berries as we had this year! Martha taught me to make Boston clam chowder with Oregon clams. The Puget Sound oysters are a great delicacy. In March some Indians brought to Polly a great many smelt from the Cowlitz River.

"I now have two hogs, two little pigs, one cow, and one of the nicest kitchen gardens in the precinct. Polly is a great help in the garden. We had corn and beans, pumpkins, squashes, potatoes, peas, cabbage, melons and cucumbers. I got the seeds from George Bush, the colored man who lives about eight miles away, on what is now known as 'Bush Prairie'. It is odd to have such plenty! Charlefour keeps us well supplied with game.

"But the biggest news of all is that I have new nearby neighbors. They are Edmund Sylvester, a bluff and hearty fisherman, and Levi Smith, a very cultured gentleman, a Presbyterian divinity student, I believe, who came by sea from Maine. They talk of establishing a town here on the southern tip of Budd's Inlet. Mr. Smith has a neat cabin near to the winter camping ground of the Duwamish Indians. I do not know if Chief Seattle will welcome his new neighbors. There were about 300 Indians wintering there last winter. They call it the 'place of the bear'. Polly says though the Indians were of the Duwamish tribe the land is really of the Nisqually nation. They gave us some trouble, begging and stealing when their requests were not granted. It annoys me very much when they enter without knocking and poke into my cupboards. I have become used to sweeping Indians out of the cabin with a hazel broom!

"The Sparks family are well. Reason and Wealthy have seven hens and a cock.

"Tell Jeff I have busied myself during the evenings sketching some pieces of furniture we have at Wildcliffe. They are very beautiful and he might like some day to copy them. I hope you all are well. The Hines family moved on to their own claim, but there is so much travel now, and shelter so scarce, that I never lack for company."

Kitty signed her letter, added her address with a flourish: *Newmarket Precinct, Lewis County, Oregon Territory, September, 1847.* She smiled with satisfaction. That address made Newmarket seem quite a civilized place. She picked up Clara's letter to which she was replying and read it again, although she almost knew it by heart.

It was odd, she mused, how one had to readjust her thinking as well as her habits of living in Oregon, and how quickly one did accept these new thoughts and new ways. . . . Clara wrote that cattle-raisers in the Willamette Valley had gone to California in spite of the fighting there, and driven back more cattle and horses. They came by paths beaten down by the autumn fur brigades of the Hudson's Bay men in the old days—the trail that

Curt had followed when he made the first cattle drive from California into Oregon. They had been harassed by Indians a good share of the way, Clara said. Westerners blandly disregarded distances, Kitty thought, and she had likewise become used to this coastwise travel, which would increase when the Mexican war ended.

There was no "North" and "South," here on the Pacific Coast, as there was on the Atlantic, she reflected. No great rivalries or political differences separated the area. It was simply—the West, with the same problems; the distance from the capital, the lack of adequate roads and communications, the need for government protection and funds. In South Carolina, she reflected, a twenty-five mile journey seemed to her a long trip. Now, in Oregon, it seemed quite natural for men to journey seven hundred miles south to Sutter's Fort, or to sleepy little Yerba Buena, and one merely mentioned it in passing, much as she would once have mentioned a drive to Charleston. Perhaps, after the Oregon Trail, no distance seemed great to Westerners; and ties with California were strong because many who had started out together in the wagon trains separated at the fork of the Oregon and California trails. These friends kept up correspondence still.

Actually, transportation being what it was, Oregon was closer to the Orient than to the Boston State House, Kitty mused. That fact had been brought home to her forcibly when a tramp vessel had put into Puget Sound, and had taken on lumber and as many fresh vegetables as the settlers could spare. The vessel was for China, and the skipper had spoken with such familiarity of the fabulous Oriental ports that they seemed very near. He had left Kitty a small lacquered table as a gift. But he had left the Newmarket people an unwelcome gift, also. He had put ashore two demented and diseased sailors, and Deaf Wilson had been forced to shoot one of them when he had attempted to attack him with a club. The other, a powerful man who believed himself the Messiah, had disappeared, but Kitty kept a close watch when she rode to the Sparks or to the Smith claim.

But one did not write of those things to one's friends. And she would not write to Clara, either, of the Indians who had terrified Martha by demanding that she sell little Wealthy to them for a slave.

How odd it will seem, she thought, to live without constant

vigilance. She glanced about the cabin. She would remember every detail of it when she returned to Wildcliffe. Even if no mail awaited her at Oregon City she would have enough money this fall to buy her passage home. Her improvements on the land claim were of value, doubled now by the boundary settlement and by this year's record immigration. Clara had written that the first immigrants of 1847 seemed to be people of means. Many of them, it was said, had sizable sums of money sewed into their patchwork quilts.

There was a rap at the door and Kitty automatically reached for a pistol. She rose, a slim, straight, alert little figure, and went to the door and spoke through it, before she lifted the latch.

"Who is it?" Her soft, sweet voice was silvery and clear in the night quiet.

"Name of McNair. Kentuck McNair, ma'am. And my wife, Lissa, and two young ones. Sparks, down the way a piece, said you'd give us shelter."

There was no mistaking the voice of a Kentuckian. Kitty threw back the bolt and opened the door wide, with the graciousness and hospitality inherent in the mistresses of Wildcliffe.

◈ 2 ◈

To LISSA McNAIR, exhausted and ill and terrified by the wildness of the rugged country to the north of The River, the sight of Kitty in the door of the cabin, and the glimpse into the comfort and homely charm within, was a view of paradise. The child Lissa carried was heavy, but she gripped him to her with a clasp so tight that the little one awakened and raised a sleepy head. Kitty was trim and immaculate and beautiful, with strength and purity in her perfect face, and the warmth of her smile was reassuring and as welcome to Lissa as sunlight after storm. Lissa had never seen anyone so lovely as this small, golden-haired lady who welcomed her into her clean, tight little cabin.

Deftly, without confusion, Kitty bent at once to the fireplace, placed another log upon the flames, and swung the kettle over it. Every move she made was graceful, Lissa noted, her sick eyes wide and worshiping; the tiny collar about Kitty's smooth throat was snowy-white; her shining hair was piled smoothly on her proud little head.

Lissa's glance went from Kitty to the room itself. There was a print bedspread of dark blue and white upon the bed in the corner, and a second, matching spread made curtains, to assure the sleeper genteel privacy. There was a trundle bed beneath it. A footwarmer—Lissa had not seen one since she left Kentucky—stood beside the fire, and there was actually a silver candle-snuffer on an odd and delicate lacquered table. Kitty poured a basin of warm, soft water and put it beside the silent Lissa, and with it she brought soap and a clean linen towel. Lissa could not believe her eyes.

"You'll want to wash your hands and wipe your face before you eat, perhaps," Kitty said softly, looking down at the weary woman. Lissa was no older than she, but the lines in her worn face were deep and profoundly tragic. "I'll have food for you in just a few minutes. I have milk for the children."

Kitty took the little boy from his mother's arms and laid him gently on the trundle bed, where sleep claimed him again. Lissa's arms felt empty, for she had clung to the baby during long days and nights and for an instant her hands followed the child. Her second son stood at Kentuck's side, shyly clasping the tail of his father's jacket.

Kitty disappeared to a room at the rear, and Kentuck put one great, hard hand on Lissa's hair. "All right?" he asked, clumsily. Lissa's dark eyes, enormous in her white, gaunt face, lifted and misted, and then she nodded dumbly.

Hours later, Kitty and Kentuck sat by the table, talking. Lissa and the children, clean and fed, had fallen into deep sleep in the room adjoining.

"She'll rest now. She's had a bad time," Kentuck said finally, after he had listened for movement from the room beyond. He stretched his long legs in front of him and sighed. "We had some trouble, back on the Trail, above The Dalles." He hesitated, studied Kitty, and made up his mind she was not a woman given to hysteria. "The Indians attacked us. There were just two wagons of us traveling together after we left the Whitman mission. Our cattle strayed and my partner and I went to search for them. While we were gone, this party of Indians came down on the wagons. They stripped the women and burned everything. There wasn't nothing left. We came back to find them—well, Lissa was bad-treated. She hasn't been herself since. It was somethin' we hadn't none of us figured on, some way. The Indians stole, and always wanted the young fellows to wrestle or race with them, but they'd not been full bad—and we was near The Dalles. I reckon I wouldn't a come, had I known that would happen to Lissa. But they spared her life, and the children. She was pretty sick and near out of her mind for a while. I'm tellin' you so's you'll understand if she don't talk much."

Kitty caught her breath with shock and pity and horrified understanding.

"We wrapped the women up the best we could in our own coats and shirts and what was left of the wagon covers, and another wagon came along within a few hours and gave us blankets. . . . There was an awful lot of sickness in the company we started out with and a lot of folks are down sick at the Whitman mission. We'd been lucky not to of took sick before then. We figgered it was safe enough to leave the others and go on to Oregon City, though I can't say we wasn't warned not to be mighty careful. But there was measles and smallpox and mountain fever and some said cholera in the trains. Lissa was afraid for the children, and we figured to get away from it. Well, we finally got to Oregon City, but seemed like Lissa didn't want to stay in town. She wanted to get away where she'd not see anyone, she was that shamed. I reckon that's harder for a woman than all the starvin' and thirstin'—"

Kentuck rubbed his harsh hand over his bearded face. "So— I brought her to Newmarket. Thought we'd start out all over again. We got little money, ma'am, havin' lost our wagon and goods and stock thataway. But I'll work for you for shelter, till we can get our own cabin up, if you'll let us stay. Lissa'd maybe get well, and forget—here. We're honest folk, ma'am. I've got letters—"

He fumbled beneath his shirt and brought out a stack of papers and extracted some from it and laid the rest on the table. "That there's from the county judge, ma'am, testifyin' to my character—"

Kitty did not hear. The small booklet that lay on the top of the pile of papers had caught her eye, and now her hand went out to it. It was a worn little booklet, that had been handled much, but a portion of the printed cover still was there.

Kentuck's glance followed Kitty's hand. "That there's a mighty valuable book, ma'am. Haven't you seen it? No, I reckon not, for it was printed just in time for us who was comin' west this year. Everybody on the Plains—and there's five thousand of 'em —is carryin' a copy, I reckon, and a good thing, too. You're welcome to have it if you like, ma'am. You say you already been here two years?"

Kitty's slim fingers closed about the booklet. "Yes," she said absently, "almost two years."

Long after Kentuck left her and slid into his bed, his arms strong and protective about Lissa, Kitty sat staring at the slim little book. She could not bring herself to open it for a long time.

"A *Guide for Emigrants*," the title page said, "*Being a Compilation of Information for Those Attempting the Journey from Missouri to Oregon City. By Philip Davis.*"

◈ 3 ◈

KITTY crossed The River, not in the Hudson's Bay Company sloop as she had on her last trip to Oregon City, but by a ferry kept by an American, John Switzler. The *Modeste* and the *Shark* were gone, but these were only a few of many changes that had taken place during her months at Newmarket. As she proceeded up the Willamette she was surprised and pleased at the growth of the settlements. Portland boasted two frame buildings now, in addition to numerous log cottages and stores, a brickyard, a tannery, and a cooper shop.

On both sides of the river there were signs of new settlers, thin threads of smoke from cabins hidden deep in the woods, fresh ax marks along the shores. Both on The River and the Willamette there was much traffic, and at Oregon City itself Kitty was astonished at all the activity.

Three ferries operated across the Willamette at Oregon City— one horse-drawn, two drawn by hand—and all of them were busy. Kitty stood on the river bank, ignored by the crowd, watching the comings and goings. She saw no one whom she knew, and even the falls themselves looked different. The canal which Dr. Mc-Loughlin had begun around the falls was finished; McLoughlin's grist mill and sawmill seemed to be running at top speed, and the

Island mills as well. As Kitty started up the path she was pleased to note that stout planking had been laid, and she had no need now to wade through the mud. She walked slowly, toward the center of town, noticing several large, new frame houses. Abernethy's was no longer the only brick store on Main Street.

The street itself was crowded as it had not been even after the big immigration of 1845. There were new signs in the windows of the business buildings, announcing the offices of doctors, lawyers, surgeon-barbers. A Hat Manufactory, operated by John Travers and William Glaser, advertised they would accept wool, beaver, raccoon, wildcat, muskrat and mink skins in exchange for hats; a great many horses, many wearing the rawhide saddles with the wooden stirrups and horsehair cinches to which Kitty had become accustomed, and others bearing magnificent, silver-encrusted Spanish trappings, lined the hitching rails. Wagons and ox-carts moved toward the mills, the cracking of whips, the shouts of the drivers, punctuated by the creaks and groans of the vehicles. From the open door of a smithy came men's laughter and then the ring of hammer on anvil, and as Kitty passed the tenpin alley she heard the click of balls and a hum of voices.

Farther down the street, at 10th, was a new Catholic church, and the path which she had walked with Fletcher to the top of the bluff was widened and smoothed and apparently now much used. There were buildings on the top of the bluff, too; Oregon City had crept beyond its old boundaries, with the mills on the river below it, its stores and offices drawing settlers from all the rich Willamette valley.

The extended streets were straight, the lots true, Kitty noticed. The town, then, had been re-platted, for when it had been first surveyed the line used was a rope which shrank when it was wet by spring rains. No one had cared very much then. But Kitty cast a businesswoman's eye over the town; lots must have skyrocketed in value and likely a foot or two each way was of importance to the owners today.

The legislature was in session, Kitty remembered, as she neared the granary of the Methodist Church. Her heart jumped as she passed it, for Curt was within. She had not seen him for many weeks, and the thought that he might at any moment step into her path set her blood to racing. Actually she had planned to avoid him, and, womanlike, she was piqued that there had been no need. She would have preferred that the choice be hers, but Curt had not sought her out.

She had seen him once at Simmons' mill. He had nodded to her from the group of men with whom he had been talking—and that was all. Once he had stopped at her door, but he had not dismounted. He had given her a message from Martha and his sharp eyes had looked her over carefully; then, hurried, and apparently satisfied, he had galloped away.

She knew that he and Sunset had spent most of the summer in surveying the country north of The River; they had gone to find out for themselves how much snow was on the summit of the pass through the Cascades which the Indians called Snoqualmie. They had returned convinced that a road could be put through the mountains. They had held long discussions with Simmons and other settlers about the possibility of a road from Fort Walla Walla directly to Puget Sound. With the Barlow road opened around Mount Hood, and a southern route opened by Jesse Applegate, the Willamette valley and the southern Oregon valleys would attract immigrants more and more. If the Puget Sound area were to prosper, routes must be found from the immigrant trail straight to Newmarket.

He's too busy and interested in building Oregon even to think of me, Kitty thought wryly. *He's like a man possessed. He thinks women's role is just to wait while men build a country. It's just as well.*

She turned toward Clara's cottage, dropped the burden she carried on the step. *After all,* she admitted finally, not without bitterness, *he never said he loved me. Of all the things he said— he never said he loved me.*

◊ **4** ◊

THE discussions droned on; there was argument about collection of taxes in wheat or specie, and there was discussion about regulating liquor sales, now that prohibition had been repealed. There was an announcement that the fifteen thousand Mormons whom Oregon people had feared would be their unwelcome guests, had turned toward the Southwest. Plans were offered for the Oregon State House. It was agreed that for a payment of a five dollar fee a man could hold his claim while he was gone to the States for a wife—even though the trip took him two years. It was suggested that a committee be appointed to visit the Cayuse and Nez Perce chiefs in the spring and attempt to get payment for goods stolen from the wagon trains. Curt found the discussions windy and tiresome, and he grinned slightly at Joe Meek and quietly walked out and went to Burton Lee's ten-pin alley next door and called for refreshment.

Meek and several other delegates joined him. The talk ranged from the Donner party, which had met disaster on the road to California last season, to the price of wheat and the possibility of snow before morning.

"Sunset came in late last night," Curt said. "Guess he's still asleep over at the Main Street House. Indians getting mighty saucy, he said, all the way from the Blue Mountains. He's really worried about them. He was too beat to talk much."

"Government's taking long enough to send soldiers out here," a settler observed.

"They raised a company for Oregon but sidetracked them into California instead," Meek explained. "Soon's the war's over down there—what you lookin' at, Curt?"

Curt's hand had stopped with his glass halfway to his lips, his eyes on the street. Carefully he put down the glass and picked up his hat. He did not answer and the men exchanged glances and grinned as Curt's big figure disappeared.

"It's Kitty Gatewood," Tommy Dundee said, from the doorway. "She must have just got in from Newmarket. She's headin' for the Lintons. Say, there goes Sunset now. Charlefour's with him. Hey—Sunset!"

But Sunset did not pause. He turned and waved, and hurried on toward the river, Charlefour half-running to keep up with him.

"Now what is he in such a hell of a hurry about?" Tommy wondered.

◊ 5 ◊

"KITTY."

Kitty's small fist, raised to knock at Clara's door, dropped and she turned to meet Curt's eyes. He had approached silently and he stood very near to her. She put her hand behind her on the door to steady herself. Her knees seemed suddenly weak and she could feel the hot blood rush to her face. It was as though her thoughts had conjured him up, and for an instant she was not quite sure he was real.

She could not deny the delight that swept over her at sight of him, and she could not keep back the smile that deepened the dimple in her cheek. Her face was radiant, her eyes shining, and Curt, watching her, smiled too.

"Clara said you were coming," he continued, in the same low voice. "I've been watching for you. I was going to send for you—then I learned you were already on your way."

"You were—going to send for me?"

"Yes. I think we've waited long enough, Kitty."

"I—I have hardly seen you all this year."

"I've never been far away, Kitty."

She watched the movement of his lips as he spoke. No—he hadn't been far away. She had been aware, all the long months, of Curt's nearness. *When he is here it is hard for me to judge him fairly*, she thought now. *An instant ago, before he came, I hated him. Now it seems right that we should be together. I have never been so uncertain before. I have never vacillated like this. Why cannot I reach this man, understand him, know him thoroughly? What is the truth about him?*

"It's been a busy year, Kitty," he said slowly, watching her face. "We've made great progress. You've had time enough to adjust yourself now, to know what it will mean to live in Oregon. I've watched you, Kitty; you've done well. The Hines, the McNairs, speak well of you. You've grown up."

Kitty's chin came up. "So I have been on trial, have I?" she asked drily.

"Yes," he said calmly. "There was one moment when I doubted —that day on the bluff, when the *Shark* came. I was disappointed in you, Kitty. But only for a moment."

Anger flickered in Kitty's eyes, but Curt ignored it. "Would you like to have Dr. Manning marry us?" he asked. "The legislative session will soon be over. We'll have Christmas and New Year's. Then back to Newmarket. Your cabin is more comfortable, of course, but I prefer we live on my claim. It's the better of the two. We'll fix up the cabin. Sunset's gone most of the time anyway."

"This is the strangest proposal," Kitty sputtered—"if it is a proposal, Curt Fletcher, that I've ever received!"

Curt laughed. "And you've had many, of course."

"I have, indeed. But not like this. I'm not sure that it is not insulting. I—"

"Let's not quarrel, Kitty. I've no time now." Calmly he put his finger beneath her chin and kissed her lips. "There's another reason I stayed away from you, Kitty—there's no preacher at Newmarket. It seemed safer to stay away."

Kitty caught her breath and Curt stepped back, bowed. A boy was running up the street gesturing frantically and he gasped out:

"Mr. Fletcher—they're—callin'—for you—sir—"

"What is it, son?"

"Message—just—came—to—the Governor. He just read it—at—the—meeting. The Indians struck, Mr. Fletcher. It's a massacre—at the Whitman mission. The whole mission is wiped out!"

"Good God!"

Curt started to run. Kitty, frozen on the step, stared out at the street. Men poured from the buildings, streamed toward the church as the word spread, and women, too, joined the throng. The church bell started to ring, loud, uneven at first, then steadily. Before the church two riders mounted, bent low to receive some last minute instructions, and then dashed off, up the trail to the bluff.

Dr. McLoughlin, surrounded by men and boys, was hurrying toward the meeting-place. He was bareheaded, his white hair blowing in the wind, his face set and grim. Behind Kitty the door opened and Clara joined her.

"Kitty!" Her attention went from the girl on the threshold to the crowds milling in the street. "What is it? For mercy sakes, what is it?"

Her hands dug into Kitty's arm.

"The Indians," Kitty said. "It's a massacre. At Whitman mission."

◈ 6 ◈

THE call for mounted riflemen volunteers and for money and supplies for the Oregon Army went out from the aroused, grief-stricken capital. The government leaders went sleepless, planning their campaign, and through the night couriers spread the word through the valleys to the south. By morning armed men began to pour into Oregon City.

They came by horse and canoe and bateaux and on foot, carrying their guns, and with what ammunition they could gather strapped about their bodies. The December rains and snow flurries beat the streets into rivers of mud and swelled the streams; but all the furies could not halt the swift preparations for war. In less than twenty-four hours after the word reached Oregon City, the first rifle company was ready to march.

Kitty, her eyes smarting from lack of sleep, her body aching with tension, still suffering from the nausea that had overcome her when she heard the horrible details of the Indian attack, stood with other sleepless women at the entrance to the City Hotel, watching the crowd of men and horses. Forty-five volunteers, the Oregon Rifles, were in this vanguard of the fighting force. They would move to The Dalles and establish headquarters there. They must keep the fighting away from the main settlements west of the mountains.

Other troops would follow and they would sweep on into the Cayuse country, after the murderers of the Whitmans. Rumors flew thick and fast, but not even the most imaginative could conceive horrors worse than the facts. Thirteen Americans had been killed in a prolonged orgy of killing and burning and looting, and from forty to sixty-seven—no one knew for sure—had been taken captive. There was no doubt that the entire mission had been wiped out and that Dr. Whitman and his wife, Narcissa, the first white woman to cross the Plains, were among the victims.

The captives, mostly women and children, had been scattered among the Indian lodges. Already sixteen Hudson's Bay men were on their way up The River to meet with the chiefs in an attempt to ransom them. Peter Ogden, successor to Dr. McLoughlin as factor of Vancouver, led them.

Fresh snow had blanketed the mountain peaks late yesterday and by morning it had crept down on the town itself. Kitty, drawing her cloak close about her shivering body, looked at the white hills and the leaden river. It would make the going hard for the Oregon Rifles and it would delay sending a messenger over the Sierras to California to ask for aid. But, Kitty thought, it would also help to keep the Indians out of the Willamette Valley until spring. And by spring—

The legislature had voted to send Sheriff Joe Meek direct to Washington to seek government aid. Meek had resigned his seat in the legislative body to take the new assignment. He would travel with the Army as far as Walla Walla, and then he would head east, back-tracking the Oregon Trail. It was a desperate mission, and many said not Meek, mountain man though he was, or any other could get through the hostile Indian country in mid-winter. But Meek would try; he would pick a few seasoned men to accompany him to the Missouri.

A bugle call pierced the noise of the crowd and a drummer boy began a blood-stirring tattoo. Kitty recognized most of the riders. Tommy Dundee, Correll, Tim Mawson, Foster and Williams. Tommy reined his horse beside her, grinned down at her.

"You know, Kitty," he said ruefully, "I'm plumb sorry now I run the *Modeste* out of The River. Those British sailors were good fighters. We could use five hundred good fighters about now."

His horse reared and he was gone again. Nerve and bluff and Irish laughter, Kitty thought—that was Dundee.

Curt was talking with Joe Meek. Kitty's eyes followed him constantly. He was outstanding in any crowd, she thought, big and broad-shouldered, sitting easily on a high-spirited black horse.

The drumbeat quickened, the horses pranced, pawed the earth. Mawson leaned from his saddle to speak to Mary. Kitty looked at Mary's chiseled face. There was a kind of hard beauty in it, a cold, steadfast beauty that would not change with the years. It was odd that she had never noticed it before. . . .

"Don't fret if you don't hear right soon," Mawson said. "We figure to make a stand at The Dalles, but—" he cast an uneasy eye at Meek and Fletcher—"there's those ain't goin' to want to stop there."

Mary nodded. "Any word about the survivors?" How often had that question been asked during the last hours!

"No. Ogden'll travel night and day till he gets to Fort Walla Walla, but it'll be hard going on The River in the storm. Like to take ten days, a week at least. Did you know Sunset is with him?"

Kitty started. "It's danged near suicide for an American to go up The River now, even with the British." Mawson's lips drew back from his teeth and he frowned, making no attempt to hide his deep anxiety. "I was talking to a man from the fort a few minutes ago. Fletcher was questioning him close about Sunset. Seems that Sunset heard of the massacre before we did. He saw the messenger from Vancouver on the way to the Governor. He was Pierre somebody—a friend of Charlie's, and he blurted out the whole story to Sunset. Sunset sure didn't waste any time. He's a man who thinks fast and acts direct. He and Charlie were gone, halfway to Vancouver, before we even heard the news. He got to Vancouver just as Ogden was ready to push off, and asked to go along. Him and Ogden are old friends, you know.

"Ogden refused at first, said the only chance to get the captives out of there was to take only Hudson's Bay men and try to bargain with the Indians. But Sunset pointed out he'd need good boatmen if they had to get down The River in a hurry, and he promised to lie low, so Ogden finally took him and Charlie. They was wearin' the Hudson's Bay blue—same's the others, but Sunset's well known among the Cayuses and Walla Wallas and Nez Perces, and those renegade Palouses, too; and if they spot him they'll know he's an American fast enough, and God knows what they'll do to him. But the thing that persuaded Ogden to take him was when Sunset pointed out the Indians might demand an American as hostage."

Mary gasped. "Sunset offered himself?"

"That's right."

Kitty stood with her hand on Mawson's stirrup now, listening, horrified. "But they'll never let him go!" she said. "Once they get him—they'll know how valuable a man he is—"

Mawson looked over the heads of the women and his eyes were narrow. "That's what Fletcher fears, Kitty. It was a brave thing to do. But the Indians set a lot of store on the importance of a man, and it's true they might accept him as hostage when they wouldn't take just anybody. They value Sunset as a chief, and if he can trade himself for some of the women and children—"

Mawson wiped his face on his sleeve. "Sunset agreed with Ogden that the only chance to ransom the survivors is to get there before the Indians know this army is on its way. After the shooting starts those prisoners won't have the chance of a snowball in hell. Yet we can't wait—we got to hold The Dalles. . . . Even if they let those prisoners live, God Almighty—"

"Sh-h," Mary warned, motioning to a woman nearby. Mary whispered to Kitty. "Her daughter is there—*was* there, at the Mission. She was helping Mrs. Whitman care for the little ones who were sick. There's been no word, whether she was captured or killed. Look at her, Kitty."

Mary's last words were almost a moan. Kitty's eyes rested on the woman. Her shawl was drawn tight around her gray face; she was chewing her lips, unconsciously and continually, and she plucked the wool of her shawl with stiffened fingers.

"Tim, I'm surprised Sunset didn't tell Curt, at least, before he left."

Tim leaned both hands on the pommel of his saddle, glanced toward Curt. "He's the last one Sunset'd tell," he said. "He knew Curt would hear soon enough, and would be on his way, guns in both hands. Curt ain't a man to negotiate. He wants to wipe out every Indian between here and the Blue Mountains, and damn me, if he won't get plenty of them I miss my guess. He'll personally find the one that got the children—"

"Him and Meek's got plenty of reason for killing," Mary said grimly.

Kitty's eyes followed Curt. If only he would look her way, speak to her, she thought. The guns on his hips were huge and wicked and she saw him bend and check a knife, a "skin-dew" someone called it, in his boot. But it was his face that frightened her. Since the word had come that drawn look of cold fury had never left him. His was the face of an avenger, an avenger without mercy.

The column was forming now and Kitty stepped back so Mawson could say good-by to Mary. Down the line, Curt stood in his stirrups, looking back over the crowd, and then he saw Kitty. He rode toward her.

The drumbeat grew louder. From the hotel the flag was being carried, the flag that the women of Oregon City had made. Kitty had given some of her sheets to make the white stripes in that flag, and some of her stitches were in it. There was one great lone star on the blue field, one star for Oregon, for this was Oregon's war and Oregon, encircled by snow-clad mountains, would fight it alone. This was the flag these men would defend. . . . Kitty's throat ached painfully as she saw it. She gripped her skirts hard, and gritted her teeth. As Curt reached her and leaned down from the saddle she managed a smile and her heart raced as his face came close.

"You all right, Kitty?" he asked. She nodded.

"Of course, Curt." How dear of him to be concerned about her, she thought, when it was he who was going into war.

"Did you hear about Sunset?"

Kitty nodded and the notes of a bugle drowned Curt's next words. His big gloved hand came down on her shoulder and tightened strongly. It was a reassuring, comradely grip, saying more than words. She put her hand on his boot, wanting to touch him, just once; her fingers rested on the cold handle of the knife.

He touched his hat and was off, to the head of the column.

Kitty moved higher on the stairs to see above the heads of the crowd. The flag was being presented to Captain Lee of the Volunteers now, and the crowd quieted while the presentation speech and acceptance were made. A sob, loud in the quiet, burst from the mother beside her.

The ceremony was over, and movement began again. There were shouts and cheers and men walked their restless mounts in circles as they awaited the order to march. Kitty searched again for Curt and then she saw the black horse loping down the street.

Curt was riding to meet a girl on a white horse.

The white horse was running and the girl upon it was screaming to Curt and holding out her arms to him. Curt's big arm encircled her and he swept her from her horse as the white horse raced by. He held her in front of him on his saddle.

The bugle called and Kitty saw the other men leaving their wives and sweethearts, forming an orderly column, the flag at their head. She watched Curt ride toward his place, Lisa still in his arms. The girl had her face hidden on his chest and she was clinging to him frantically, sobbing convulsively, and as Curt lowered her, gently, to the ground, Kitty saw her face. It was a mask of tragedy, contorted with grief, her eyes red and bloodshot, her full, moist lips working, her wild black hair blowing back from her forehead.

They were gone then. Only Lisa stood in the mud alone, her shoulders drooping, her body swaying. She made no attempt at control, and she did not care who saw her grief. Her body went limp and would have slid into the mud and groveled there if Dr.

Manning had not hurried to her and supported her. She went with him blindly, stumbling, to the walk. Her sobs had subsided into a pathetic mewing with every labored breath. She passed Kitty, her red skirt brushing Kitty's cloak.

Mary's face was wet and her lips were trembling as she took Kitty's stiff arm.

"Even if she is a—a—" Mary began, and then stopped and swallowed. "She loved her child, just as she loves Curt. Why did those savages have to kill children, too? Curt's little girl, and Joe Meek's little Helen—they never hurt anyone—"

"Curt's—little girl?"

Mary nodded miserably. "Kitty—I supposed you knew. He took her away from Lisa when she was born. He wouldn't have her raised in that beast Le Seuer's house, and Lisa—well, she's just a common prostitute. She'd never be any different, raised as a savage—and she's just that kind. Curt took the baby to the Whitman's, and Mrs. Whitman, saint that she was, cared for her, just as she did for Meek's little girl, Helen." Tears flowed down Mary's cheeks. "Helen's mother was an Indian too, a Shoshone, I think. The men wanted the children raised as whites. Curt took Lisa to see the child once a year, but he wouldn't let her have the baby. I don't think he saw Lisa any other time—but he promised her that, and he stuck to his promise. And now this awful thing—I should think Lisa would hate him for making her leave the child there. But she doesn't; she's always loved him, in spite of her carryings-on. She—she's just stricken, like the rest of us."

Kitty could never remember, afterwards, walking the blocks from the City Hotel to the Linton cabin.

◊ 7 ◊

Sunset sat in a small, dimly lighted room at Fort Walla Walla. He was not a nervous man, but occasionally he arose and paced noiselessly from one wall to the other, and then stood, listening intently. Voices came to him faintly from beyond the barred door. He recognized the deep voice of Peter Ogden, the grizzled trader, and of several of the chiefs in council with him.

Ogden had carried on many a parley with the Indians in his long life. He had bargained for furs worth, literally, millions of dollars. He knew how to talk to the dark-skinned warriors with whom he sat now, using the flowery phrases, the long pauses, the parables and similes which they loved. But never had any trader, American or British or French, bargained for such great prizes as Ogden bargained for now—forty-seven American lives.

The council had begun at early morning and now it was dark night. Sunset went to the small window that opened on the inner court and pulled back the blanket which covered it. Snow was falling and the ground was white. He went to the door and listened again. He could distinguish no words but presently there was a little scratching on the door and swiftly he lowered the bar and opened it a crack, standing behind it, well out of sight.

Charlefour slipped in and the door closed behind him. The two blue coats came close together in the far corner of the room, as Charlefour brought his lips close to Sunset's ear.

"They bargain now. Ogden's got a pile of blankets, guns, shirts, on the floor there higher than this table. They are asking much. Some refuse any offer."

"I, Dad! I wish I could hear what they're sayin'," Sunset breathed. "What did Ogden tell 'em in that long speech?"

"He said he come to ransom captives, that is all, not to punish, not to seek the murderers. The chiefs want two or three great Americans to come in the spring for a peace parley. They say they will then give up the captives if the Americans promise not to war against them, and if no more Americans cross their lands."

"Hah! They expect us to ignore the massacre?"

"Yes. They say to remind the Americans of the murder of Elijah, the son of Yellow Serpent, at Sutter's Fort. They say Yellow Serpent and Delaware Tom did not go to war because of that, against Fremont, but became his friends. If the Oregon men overlook these murders then the Indians will give up the captives—and no more trouble."

Sunset shook his head slowly. His face was lined, his eyes very tired. The trip up The River had been a hard one and anxiety had kept the men sleepless now for most of the two nights they had been in the fort, waiting for the chiefs to answer Ogden's summons to council.

"So they figure to hold the captives as hostages, to keep the Americans from warring upon them?"

"That is right. . . . But Ogden is very smart. He told the old chiefs they were weak, that they could not control their young, hotblooded men."

Sunset nodded in approval. "That is good. . . . And what else?"

Charlie grinned suddenly. "He told them they were not men, not even women, if they could not control the sub-chiefs who do this thing. He told them they were hermaphrodites. That got them!"

Sunset smiled reluctantly. "Peter has courage. They respect that. He has not promised them peace if they give up the prisoners?"

"No. He is very plain about that. He just tell them it better for them to give them up, that already they have gone too far, and the Americans will wipe them out unless they try to right their wrongs. He has them worried, I think. Some want to give the captives to Ogden and seek peace. But they want much ransom. Five Crows is worst of all. Blankets, guns, mean nothing to him."

"And the captives? They are alive?"

"The chiefs say there have been no killings since the massacre. But some were ill with the fever and maybe have died."

"They killed them, damn their black souls, whether with tomahawks or fright or exposure or starvation," Sunset said hotly. "The murderers, Charlie, do you know who they were? The leaders?"

Charlie nodded. "The chiefs will not say. But—" he brought his lips close to Sunset's ear again, "a slave of Five Crows tell me. He said Tomahas, and Tiloukaikt kill Dr. Whitman. They come to the Doctor's house to ask for medicines and when he turn to get it Tomahas struck him down from behind."

Charlefour was breathing heavily with outrage as he thought about it, for he, too, had revered the Whitmans. It was not easy to sit in council with the very chiefs who had led the attack, Indians whom the Whitmans had befriended. "Mrs. Whitman was wounded first by Ishalhal, and then by others as she try to get to the mansion-house." Sunset's fingers gripped into fists, relaxed, gripped again.

"And Five Crows. Did he take part in the killin', Charlie?"

"He say not. I do not know. He is rich and has no need for loot, so perhaps he say the truth. But he take a prisoner for his wife, and he refuse to give her up. She is that beautiful, light-haired schoolteacher, Miss Bewley, the girl who look like Kitty Gatewood. She was sick at the Mission when the attack come.

Afterward Five Crows speak for her and take her to his lodge. She beg, and the other women beg—but he take her."

Sunset was silent. Only the muffled sound of voices from the big room adjoining came to them for a long moment. "I go back —I let you know," Charlefour said in a half-whisper. Sunset let him out and he risked holding the door open a crack, to look at the scene in the room beyond.

The pile of goods Ogden was offering as ransom was indeed large, and as Sunset watched an aide added more blankets and more guns to it. Sunset saw Yellow Serpent stand and begin to speak in his usual slow and impressive fashion, then Tiloukaikt. A few of the words drifted down the long room to his ears.

Dr. Whitman had poisoned the Indians, the chiefs charged. The measles, smallpox, mountain fever, which had taken such a heavy toll were man-made illnesses, they declared. Ogden denied this vehemently and pointed out that many whites were ill and had died also, and silence settled over the gathering again. Five Crows, proud and defiant, his carven profile silhouetted against the roaring fire, neither moved nor spoke.

Sunset closed the door and bolted it again. A plate of bread and meat sat upon the table. He went to it and broke off a crumb and chewed it thoughtfully. The Indians were changeable, shifting, touchy, suspicious—and they were also worried. The pauses were longer, the Indian voices not quite so arrogant. Sunset listened—and some sixth sense, developed in his years of association with the savages, told him they were beginning to weaken before Ogden's courage and his convincing arguments.

He ate the rest of the bread and the cold meat. He would be in need of strength. If Ogden was successful in persuading them to give up the captives, they would have to get them down The River before the army of Americans launched their attack.

Time was running out. It would take a few days to gather up the scattered prisoners, even after negotiations were completed. Indians moved so slowly and you could not hurry them; they would also have to bring in the Spaldings, the missionaries at Lapwai in the Nez Perce country, and any other Americans isolated in this hostile area. Waiting here at Fort Walla Walla for the prisoners, knowing that every hour was bringing the Oregon riflemen nearer—Sunset rubbed the back of his neck. I, Dad, it was apt to be a tight squeeze!

His forehead was wet and he wiped it with his scarf and settled the red belt around his lean waist. He went to the window again, regarded the snow. . . . Curt would have wasted no time in starting up The River, he thought uneasily. The storm might delay him a little, but he was certainly on his way.

He walked the floor again, flexing his fingers. If only Curt's boats would break down, or his supplies be delayed—anything, to hold him back, just a few days longer, until the captives were safe! Damn Five Crows for his stubbornness and his determination to have a white wife! As wealthy an Indian as he cared nothing for the trade goods Ogden offered. Sunset considered; if he could talk to the young chief himself—

He shook his head. No, that would not do. Only the pressure of the older chiefs to fulfill a pact between them and Ogden would persuade Five Crows to give up Lorinda Bewley. Sunset carefully kept his thoughts away from the girl in Five Crows' lodge, and all the other tortured women and terrified and suffering children in the Indian huts tonight.

The scratching at the door came again.

"It is done," Charlie breathed. "They agree to bring in the prisoners. They still argue with Five Crows, and one or two other chiefs now try to make separate deals and to buy their prisoners. But the pact is made—they pass the pipe. Pete paid sixty-two three-point blankets, sixty-three shirts, a dozen guns, six hundred loads of ammunition, seven oxen, twelve flints, and God knows how much tobacco and flour. But the Cayuses will wipe out all the captives, if the Americans attack, or if any American other than a peace commissioner come into their lands. The prisoners were decreed against already, and they delayed only because Ogden call this council. He get here just in time."

Sunset and Charlie gripped hands in triumph.

"You get some sleep, Charlie," Sunset advised. "I have a feeling we'll have to move fast—mighty fast—when it's time to go."

◈ 8 ◈

Dr. Manning entered the church late and slipped quietly into a rear pew. All the churches were crowded these days, for the anxious Oregon people were in need of the comfort of their faiths, and they were in need, too, of companionship. Adversity had at least had the advantage of bringing them closer together, Thomas thought, bowing his head. A short time ago feeling had been high against the Hudson's Bay Company people, who already were beginning to withdraw north of the border to new headquarters on Vancouver Island, and the loyalty of the French-Canadian settlers, former company employees who had elected to remain in Oregon, had been openly questioned.

But now, with Peter Ogden himself heading the rescue party—pray God he would be successful!—and with French and half-breeds wholeheartedly answering the call to arms and forming their own company to go to war for Oregon, public sentiment had changed. Dr. McLoughlin's counsel had been sought and freely given, and the venerable old man had contributed heavily to supplies for the army of volunteers. There was nothing like common peril to unite a country, even a country settled by individuals of such varying beliefs and backgrounds.

Personal arguments had seemed to dissolve, or at least to have been postponed, too, Thomas noted. A settler and a member of the mission group who had been involved in lawsuits over a land claim both attended the services this morning; and Allie Johnson and Tildy Snider were sitting in the same row with Kitty.

Kitty's eyes were on the minister, her profile still and flawless against the wide brim of her bonnet. Her gloved hands were quiet in her lap. Thomas allowed himself the pleasure of regarding her beauty and composure. There was no sin, he decided, in appreciating the beauty of a woman, God's most noble creation, during church services.

The women of Oregon City had certainly rallied to the cause, Thomas thought. They had been quick to organize a society to support the army in the field, and all the maidens, including Kitty, had pledged themselves to treat with avoidance and contempt all able-bodied young men who would not march at once to the seat of war. They had sworn also to see that the soldiers' land claims were respected during their absence, and Thomas almost chuckled as he visualized the fate of a claim-jumper faced by the militant maidens of Oregon City. By resolution they exhorted the men to fight on, be brave, obey their officers and never quit their posts until the enemy was conquered, and they promised them their sympathy as a reward. Thomas, who had attended that meeting to enlist the women's help in gathering supplies for the Army, had caught the flicker of amusement in Kitty's brown eyes as she added her vote to the rest, making the resolution unanimous. Kitty smiled rarely now; too rarely, Thomas thought.

He wriggled uncomfortably on the hard seat. . . . The girl had not disappointed him. He remembered his first impression of her, spoiled and lovely, peremptory and arrogant as she had been—even then, her strength and intelligence and genuine sweetness had shown through. She had matured very much in the two years she had been in Oregon, Thomas thought, but she had not yet found happiness. The old conflict which Thomas had recognized in the beginning—the battle between her heart and her senses and the demands of her beautiful, voluptuous body, opposed by her strict conscience and intolerance, as deeply ingrained in her as in any fanatical man of the church—that conflict had not yet been reconciled. It was a pity, Thomas thought—a pity; and then he jerked himself up sharply. No, it was not a pity. It was stupid to sympathize with Kitty. She was becoming a far greater and bigger woman through the challenge of hardship and suffering. He should be thankful that these opportunities for growth had been given to her. She would weather the storm. She had inner strength. She was a person to depend upon in a crisis.

Governor Abernethy was attending the service, too. He showed the strain of this past month. Thomas bowed his head again and repeated the prayer all the settlers voiced day and night—for the rescue of the survivors and the success of the Army. Peace enfolded him and for an instant he almost dozed. He needed these few minutes to restore his strength, he thought, gratefully, for his work was heavy and would be heavier still. He wished he were younger so he might have gone with the volunteers. Five hundred were to rendezvous at Portland this very day, to proceed up The River. But all Thomas could do was to take care of the ills of the settlers of Oregon City, to join the Home Guard, to help in gathering provisions for the Army and to be ready to care for the survivors—if they came.

On the list of supplies he had checked this morning he saw that Kitty had made another contribution. She had given—now, let's see; Thomas kept his eyes closed, mentally picturing the list. Kitty had given three pounds of powder, eight pounds of lead, twenty bushels of wheat and an order on the store calling for one hundred pounds of flour. A big contribution for a single girl, he approved.

There was a sudden commotion in the church and Thomas came slowly to attention. People were standing, as though drawn to their feet against their will, and Thomas lumbered to his feet, too. The minister had stepped aside and the governor, his face very white, was in his place.

He held a paper in his hand and the room grew very still. Thomas could hear the heavy breathing of the woman beside him. The wind whistled around the corner of the little church and somewhere, up on the bluff, a dog barked.

The letter, the governor said, had just been handed to him. It was considered of sufficient importance to interrupt the services. It was from James Douglas at Fort Vancouver. He read it to the congregation.

"Sir: Mr. Ogden has this moment arrived with three boats from Walla Walla and I rejoice to say he has brought down all the women and children from Waillatpu, Mr. and Mrs. Spalding and Mr. Stanley, the artist."

A wave of sound like a soft moan swept over the church. The Governor paused until it subsided, then read on.

". . . Mr. Ogden will visit Oregon City on Monday and give you every information in his power respecting the Indians in the interior. The Cayuses, Walla Wallas, Nez Perces and Yakimas are said to have entered into an alliance for mutual defense. In haste, yours respectfully, James Douglas. . . ."

◈ 9 ◈

"I CAN'T bear it," Clara whispered, "Kitty, I simply can't—"

"You have to bear it," Kitty snapped. She gripped Clara's arm until it hurt and gave her a short little shake. Clara swallowed her sobs and cast a frightened glance at Kitty.

Kitty's face was like marble. Her eyes were dry. She did not turn away nor hide her face as the litters moved by her, one by one. Here and there a woman turned her back, unable to view the stark suffering in the faces of the rescued survivors, but Kitty stood immovable, waiting, ready for any task that was assigned her. Clara could see the pulse throbbing in Kitty's white neck.

One by one they were carried or supported from the boats. A young woman stepped ashore and someone called her name "Miss Bewley!" and a wave of sound, of indignation, of pity, swept up the bank. Her friends closed about her, barred her from sight and Kitty turned back to the boats.

"Kitty—Clara—"

"Yes, Dr. Manning."

"This girl. Can you care for her?"

Kitty looked down at the litter and despite herself she recoiled from what she saw there. She caught herself and nodded. "Yes, Dr. Manning." She moved swiftly ahead of the litter and bearers and Clara followed.

"Bring her in here," Kitty said at the Linton cabin, motioning to her own room. Her bed was fresh, the Gatewood sheets newly laundered. She looked again at the girl on the litter. "Wait," she said, and quickly spread a blanket and another sheet upon the floor. "Lay her here, first, please."

Silently the men lifted the slight little figure from the stretcher. Kitty felt for the girl's wrist. It was thin and bony and very hot to the touch, and it was caked with dirt. She could not be more than fourteen years old, Kitty decided.

"Bring the basin, Clara," Kitty commanded, "and soap—quickly." Clara hurried to her bidding. "Now help me get these rags from her. We'll have to burn them. They're infested."

Very gently Kitty raised the girl and suddenly the still, emaciated figure galvanized into action. Her hands came out like sharp claws, scratching, fighting, vicious as a wild creature, and Kitty stepped back out of reach, waiting. The blue eyes staring up at her were unblinking, glazed, and for an instant Kitty closed her own. Clara put her hand over her lips.

"It's all right, dear," Kitty said, her voice very soft, "I'm going to care for you. Let me make you comfortable and clean—"

The girl's eyes seemed gradually to focus on Kitty and the blank look dissolved slowly and consciousness of her surroundings seemed to come to her. She stared at Kitty and then her voice came, heavy, deep, hoarse, too big a voice, too weary and too old a voice, for such a tiny, abused child-body.

"I'll never be clean," the girl said, "I'll never be clean again."

Kitty caught her lip in her teeth. The girl's eyes closed and Kitty, after a moment, tried again. The patient did not resist; Kitty drew the rags from the violently trembling little body and dipped a cloth in the soft warm water, rubbed soap upon it.

"Help me turn her, Clara," Kitty said finally.

"Kitty, I'm going to be sick," Clara gasped.

"Go in the other room then," Kitty said, without sympathy, "and hurry up and get it over with." She set her teeth as she started to tend the deep, foul-smelling, suppurating sores on the girl's back. She washed her patient's hair, carrying tub after tub of water, determined to free her of the torment of vermin. Gently she rubbed mutton tallow in the cracked and bleeding hands and put soothing salve on the crusted, swollen lips.

At last Clara returned and helped Kitty to lift the girl to the clean bed. She was clothed in one of Kitty's own fine lawn nightgowns; she was little and pathetic, her thin hands lying idle on the soft down quilt. After a while her fingers began to move, caressing the soft smoothness of the coverlet, and then she looked down at it, unbelieving.

"That's better," Kitty said encouragingly. She raised her carefully, trying not to hurt her, and held a cup of soup to her lips. The girl drank gratefully and when she lay down again she thanked Kitty with her eyes. A little color crept into her face. "Soon you'll be rested and well again."

"I'll never be clean," the girl said again and the fierce and wild look came back to her eyes. "Do you know what they did to me—do you—"

"Yes," Kitty said firmly. "Yes, I know. But that was to your flesh only, not to *you*." The girl stared at her, tormented, unconvinced, and Kitty saw in the young face the same torture that had been in Lissa McNair's. "Look." Kitty pushed her own sleeve high and with her fingernail made on her own arm a deep red scratch. "That hurt my *flesh* but not me—me, inside. I'm no different now, am I, with that scratch on my arm? The mark will go away. That is what happened to you, my dear, only much, much worse. But the body will heal. You *are* clean, you are clean *now* and free again."

The girl's thin fingers clutched Kitty's, imploringly, and in her despairing eyes there came the first faint flicker of hope. But a shudder suddenly wracked her body and she began to talk rapidly, hysterically.

"They butchered my father and my brother," she said, jerkily.

"I saw them. They dragged me right over their bodies—only my brother was not yet dead. He lived a whole day, lying there in the blood and water, and they held me when I tried to go to him. They scalped him and they made me watch. His blood is still on my clothes."

Clara and Kitty stared at one another. Kitty drew a chair to the bedside and sat down.

"Try to sleep now," she said levelly.

The girl shook her head. "I can't sleep," she said, and her eyes glazed again. "They were going to kill my mother and my little sister too, if I did not go with the chief. They showed me my brother and they said that was what they would do to the others if I would not go to his lodge."

"Yes, dear, I know."

"No. No, you don't. No one knows—except those who were there. You don't want to know, do you? You can't stand to hear, can you?" Her voice rose, thin, almost to a shriek. "You don't want to know—how they killed Mrs. Whitman? She was lying there, still alive, and the Indian Ishalhal picked her up by the hair and beat her across the face with a whip. I saw them. I *heard* the whip on her face!"

Kitty took the wildly waving hands in her own. If only she would cry, Kitty thought, if only she could cry and then could sleep. Once she had been pretty and rosy and strong, untouched and gay. Kitty's heart ached and tears were a hard lump in her throat.

"You're safe now," she soothed, "your mother and sister are safe, too. They are resting, and warm and clean and fed."

"My mother's insane," the girl answered. "I'm not. I kept saying I would not go crazy. My mother did. She went crazy when the Indian took me. She doesn't know me now. I am not crazy. I will remember. I will never forget, never, never—"

There was no way to stop her, Kitty decided. Perhaps she should not be stopped. Perhaps she should purge herself of all the horrors burned into her heart and soul and body, put the awful weight she carried on other, older shoulders. Kitty braced herself and then she said carefully:

"Do you want to tell me all about it? From the beginning to the end?"

"Yes," the girl said. "No one would listen. Except my mother. She would listen—only she does not know me now."

Hours later Clara sat beside the fire, her sleeping child in her arms. The voice of the girl in the next room had gone on and on, without ceasing; Clara had been unable to stand it longer. Her own eyes were swollen and smarting from tears that she could not stop and she was exhausted, spent. Dr. Manning had come and gone; he had looked in upon the girl and Kitty, holding her hands, listening, and then he had quietly withdrawn and closed the door.

"That is the best thing for her," Thomas said, "if Kitty can stand it. It may save her sanity. The girl's mind will give way if she does not get some release and sleep. If she can hang on to Kitty—"

Thomas shook his head. He had seen sights this day unequaled in all his long years on the frontier, in his longer years in the practice of medicine and ministering to sick souls. And he was getting old. His will was as strong, his mind as clear—but his body would no longer respond quickly to his will. Gratefully he accepted the tea that Clara brewed for him, taking it from her small and precious store, and then he left. There were many others scattered throughout the city that he must visit during the night.

Clara entered the sickroom once, and placed a candle beside Kitty. She had sprinkled salt upon it till it touched the black part of the wick, to assure a steady, tiny flame through the long hours of the night. Kitty had thanked her with a silent glance. That glance had shaken Clara; occasionally during the day she had thought that Kitty was hard, unfeeling. But the deep compassion in those suffering eyes belied any such notion and Clara felt humble and ashamed before it. Kitty's hands seemed to be drawing the poison from the little girl upon the bed.

"Miss Bewley fought and wept, but it did no good," the girl's dead, expressionless voice continued. "Five Crows took her just the same. He acted like he really was in love with her, though. When he brought her to the boats he brought her on a beautiful horse, with a new buffalo robe upon its back, and he begged her, even then, to stay with him. Some said he even offered to leave his own people and come to live with her among the whites.

"I heard the squaws. They were savage, like a pack of wild dogs;

they were angry because we had been decreed against, and then the chiefs changed their minds and said we were not to be killed. They screamed and shouted and waved knives. I was hoping they would kill us quickly. I tried to find a knife myself but they were very careful. They made me cook and clean up after them. I was so sick.

"We got to the boats. Finally we got to the boats."

The girl's voice hesitated and then the barest flicker of a smile touched the mask-like face. "An American was there—Sunset, they called him. He was big and strong and he lifted me into the boat.

"We thought we were safe, then. We had hurried so. But just as we were ready to go there was a great commotion on the bank and we heard horses running and Indians yelling again. They were the Cayuse Indians, the worst of all, and they were painted and ugly and huge and hideous! It sounded like the massacre all over again, those awful war whoops. I lay very still in the boat and the American—I knew he was an American from the way he talked, he smiled and told me not to be frightened. He didn't act frightened himself."

"Yes," Kitty whispered, "that would be Sunset."

"Do you know him?" Kitty nodded. The girl on the bed considered her thoughtfully, her sick mind veering for the briefest instant from the awful memories, and then they came back, with a rush, and she shuddered convulsively.

"I thought it would be—the same—all over again." Her chin began to shake as she remembered that final terror. "But the boat shoved off. Sunset had an oar and a Frenchman he called Charlie was in the bow. There were more Indians on the bank and someone said they'd just learned the American army was coming, and they did not want to give us up after all. If we had delayed another hour we would never have got away. I was sure they were going to take us again—"

"But they didn't," Kitty reminded her softly, "you're safe now."

"Yes. Sunset suddenly shouted to the man in the bow. He yelled, 'Sing, Charlie, for God's sake, sing!'"

The girl closed her eyes and her breast rose and fell in a long sigh. "It was so odd—" her eyelids fluttered—"Charlie started to sing in French, a funny song, it seemed to be mostly *Ron-don-don-ron-don-don*—but it had a beat to it, and all of a sudden the boat picked up speed and it was very smooth, and it fairly shot down The River—"

The eyelids fluttered once again, the girl's breath came evenly, and Kitty sat, afraid to move. Of all the things she had poured out, the girl's tired, tortured mind had fastened on that last scene now; she twitched and moaned in her sleep, seeing again the warriors on their painted coursers, wildly racing along the river bank, their faces evilly striped with vermilion and violent yellow and blue, cheated of their prizes.

And then gradually the girl's body relaxed and her lips moved slightly, once "Ron-don-don—" and Kitty knew she was seeing Sunset's reassuring smile and hearing Charlie's great voice in his wonderful river song, bringing all the oars into unison. She was feeling the comforting, mighty power of The River, sweeping her swiftly out of hell, into safety.

Kitty arose, her limbs stiff and cramped, and limped to the door. Clara put down the sleeping baby and poured Kitty a cup of tea.

"How is she?" Clara whispered.

"She's asleep," Kitty said. "For the first time in weeks, I think, she is in a really natural, deep sleep. . . . Have you seen Sunset? Did he come with the boats?"

Clara shook her head. "No, Dr. Manning said he met Curt and Meek somewhere above The Dalles. Meek asked Sunset to try to get through to the Missouri with him. Sunset will team up with Curt again—they've fought side by side before—until Meek is ready to go, and then they'll head east. It looks like getting a messenger to Washington is almost more important than bringing in the Whitman murderers. The immigrants this year, Kitty—will they dare head west, straight into the Cayuse War?"

The two women stared at each other, and then they looked away. They sat side by side throughout the rest of the night, and only the girl in Kitty's bed, and little Mathias, slept.

◆ 10 ◆

THERE was no shelter at Waillatpu—*the Place of the Rye Grass*. The adobe house that had been the home of the Whitmans for eleven years and had welcomed many an immigrant, was now a pile of rubble; and the mansion-house adjoining, which had contained a large Indian room, a kitchen, sleeping room, schoolroom and church, had all been systematically leveled. Twisted remnants of wagons and household furnishings and tools, blackened by fire, were strewn about the enclosure, and here and there a man picked up a book, a shoe, a toy.

Curt leaned upon his rifle, surveying the scene. Even the orchard had not escaped. The trees had been hacked and burned in a diabolic frenzy of wanton, useless destruction. There had been other and still more horrible remnants of the massacre, for the shallow graves into which the victims had been placed had been torn open by wolves. Those parts of the mutilated bodies had been mercifully reburied now, and the new mounds heavily weighted with protecting stones. A service had been read, but despite the presence of the Oregon Rifles, the place still was gripped in the silence of desecration and death.

Curt passed his hand over his bearded chin. His face was gaunt, his eyes sunken. Two months of marching and fighting in winter storms, with the hardships attendant on an untrained, inexperienced army, had left their mark, and the first glimpse of the scene of the massacre was enough to shake even the toughest-fibered man.

They had fought their way up The River, established Fort Lee at The Dalles and Fort Gilliam at the Cascades, and pressed on into the Cayuse country, and always the murderers they sought eluded them. They were reported here, there and everywhere—and nowhere. It was like seeking ghosts. They had learned much of the exasperating Indian method of warfare. They marched ready for battle, prepared for an engagement, and found no enemy; the Indians had melted into the earth, only to rise behind them, painted demons multiplied, making the air hideous with their warcries.

They had learned not to trust any Indian—even professed friends. Approaching a lodge, believing it sheltered one of the men they sought, they would be met by a peace envoy, an old man, unarmed, with one hand on his heart and the other on his head, and he would tell them vaguely that Tomahas—The Murderer—or Tiloukaikt, or Ishalhal, had fled with his people and his herds into the Nez Perce country—or the Blue Mountains—or southward—and that the people in this lodge wanted only peace;

that as peaceful Indians they must have guns and ammunition for the hunt.

The chiefs called for long councils which accomplished nothing, but which gave the Indians time to slip away, ahead of the whites, deep into their own lands, drawing the Americans farther and farther from their source of supplies. And then the young Cayuse warriors, surrounding them, seeming to spring from the earth itself, would shout their taunts: they would kill every white man; in the spring they would go into the Willamette valley, burn their homes, take their women, burn their towns—

But the volunteers still stalked their prey ruthlessly. They were after the murderers, and they let it be known that anyone who protected or aided them was to be considered equally guilty. They'd find them, they told the Indians, if they had to annihilate every Indian in the Oregon Country. As the Army came on, never stopping, never turning back, the Indians' taunts were silenced. The Oregon men learned swiftly to use the Indians' own methods of warfare. They discarded their cannon. This was a war to be fought with rifles and with knives.

The latest and fiercest battle of all, at the crossing of the Umatilla, had been a clear-cut victory for the Oregon men. The Indians had boasted the whites would never drink of the waters of the Umatilla—but the chief, Great Eagle, had been killed in that battle, and Five Crows had retreated with a shattered arm. The Americans had drunk deep, for they had been without water for two days, and as they stubbornly forded the river they heard with grim satisfaction the death chants rise and fall.

Yes, they had made progress in the winter campaign, despite heavy losses, short supplies, scanty ammunition—but still the murderers were free, somewhere in these rolling hills. As Curt, standing in the midst of the desolation of Waillatpu, thought of them, still alive, still free, the desire for vengeance again rose within him.

He straightened, picked up his gun. Broken china and glass grated beneath his boots. The sound set his teeth on edge. He mounted his horse, turned toward the camp nearby. A sadness such as he had never known before had settled upon him. Though he had known what to expect at Waillatpu, the full impact of the tragedy had not struck him until he had actually viewed it. Even the sight of the survivors had not affected him so deeply; they, at least, were alive. Here at Waillatpu there was only death—the odor of it, the feel of it, the loneliness of it.

He had never known loneliness before, he realized, as he dismounted at the camp and began to care for his horse. Heretofore, dreams and ambitions had been enough. He had been building, planning, exploring, since he came to Oregon. And he had had Sunset's friendship. He had never fully appreciated it until now. It would be a good thing for a man to have a friend beside him tonight. . . . But Sunset was out on the Trail, headed east, sleeping by day, traveling by night. Meek's party had left as soon as the burial was over.

Curt squatted on his heels before a campfire, watching the cooking meat, feeling no hunger. He wished he could put into words, to himself, the things he was feeling. When it came to cold reasoning, to logic and bargaining, Curt could talk with the best of them. But when it came to analyzing or expressing emotions, he was inarticulate. There was a dam there that he could not break. The words would not come.

His child had died back there at the Place of the Rye Grass. A five-year-old, black-haired girl, a child he had not known very well, but who had looked, in an odd and touching way, something like himself. He had not been attached to the child, but he had wanted her to be brought up decently. He had thought he had chosen the best path for her. He had closed his ears to Lisa's wild pleadings—Lisa's home was no place for any child. It was a nuisance, he had thought, in passing, that she must rant about it; but it was a thing that had to be done, and he'd paid Lisa well. If he had thought of it at all he'd supposed the grief of a woman of loose morals did not go very deep. The pure agony she had endured because of him had not touched him until the day the army had marched.

Because of his decision the little girl was dead. Her body was there in that common grave. A child of tragedy, not born of love, and dead by violence, and not allowed, even after death, to rest. . . . It was a hard thing for a man to feel responsible for, to remember, all his life. By God, he'd see those savages hang for it if it was the last thing he ever did! And he'd beat their tribesmen into submission with his bare fists, if need be. He cursed them under his breath and the man beside him glanced at him, understanding.

Curt threw his plate down with a clatter. There was no taste to the food and he could not swallow it. He walked to the edge of the camp, rubbing the palms of his hands on his thighs, and finally he rested them on his guns. He had worn the heavy side-arms so long he did not notice their weight.

At last he pulled his blankets over him, tried to find release in sleep. The camp was quieter than usual tonight. . . . He tried to think of his land claim at Newmarket, of the progress he had made there, of the things that he would do, when Meek came back with United States soldiers to protect the settlers. But the heavy weight of sadness and tragedy and loneliness would not lift.

Finally, reluctantly, in the silent sleepless hours of the night, Curt faced his need, admitted and named it.

A man could not always walk alone.

He had believed he was self-sufficient, dependent upon no one, and he had reveled in his strength and complete independence. True, he valued Sunset's friendship, but even that was not indispensable. But to satisfy this new need, this deep yearning within him, was essential, and only one person could do it—Kitty. Only Kitty could crowd from his mind the ugliness, the remembrance of killing, the savage slaughter, the burning, at Waillatpu. He needed her, her beauty and purity. He needed her presence, the soft, slurred voice, the clean, washed smell of her skin, the incredible softness of her moonlight hair. Only with Kitty could he be complete and whole and cleansed again; only with her could he savor to the fullest his accomplishments and his dreams.

His hunger for her, his great need, was so violent and deep that he turned on his face, and dug his chin into his blankets, fearing that he would shout it aloud. . . . It was her presence he needed, not only her beautiful body; it was her understanding, the deep, sweet goodness of her—and without her there was nothing.

Her beauty and spirit and complete femininity had interested him from the first. He had coldly and calculatingly looked at her as he regarded any attractive woman, and he had decided, almost without emotion, that she would make him an ideal wife; she had quality, and intelligence and refinement, and he would not tire of her easily. . . . Once that decision was made, violent possessiveness followed. His desire for her had grown, stimulated by her own resistance and the barrier of respectability and convention which, for him, had been both new and tantalizing. He had believed that she needed him, his strength and his protection, and he had been pleased and triumphant, but not surprised, when he had forced her to reveal that need, for he wanted her helpless and dependent upon him.

But now, lying there in the army camp, his powerful body covered by coarse blankets smelling of saddle leather and the sweat of men and horses, his hand resting on his rifle—there, near to silent, ravaged Waillatpu, Curt realized his own need, his own complete dependency upon her for happiness. He, like Oregon, rugged and violent, had to have the beauty and delicacy and fineness of a woman—and it had to be Kitty. That was the strange thing about it, he considered; the realization, for the first time in his life, that one woman, and only one, would do.

◇ 11 ◇

A NEW legend grew about Curt at the battle of the crossing of the Touchet.

"I tell you, Jimmy," Dundee said hoarsely, at the end of the thirtieth continuous hour of fighting, "that man Fletcher's a whole goddam regiment. You know a quicker way to get yourself scalped than waitin' for a lousy Indian to do it? Just try sayin' to hell with it, and start home when your enlistment is up. If the Indians ain't whipped by then, Curt'll scalp you himself. I'm glad," Tommy continued with feeling, "that he's on our side."

"He's not a man," Jimmy Correll groaned, his hands on his empty, aching stomach. "He hasn't even got a belly, let alone a heart. I bet he could drink a gallon of Indian liquor—rainwater, dog-leg tobacco, red pepper and all—and never even shiver. Tommy, we've had nothin' to eat but one little old colt for two days, and I think I got the shinbone a that. Curt ain't even tired, from the looks a him. This is a hell of a war."

Tommy's grimy, bearded face creased in a grin and he ran his tongue over his dry lips as Jimmy's words recalled his own hunger.

"Jimmy, you look as forlorn as an unmated 'coon," he observed, cheerfully. He rammed a new charge into his rifle-barrel. "It's one hell of a war, all right," he agreed, raising his rifle again and taking careful aim, "but we're winning it. Me—and Curt."

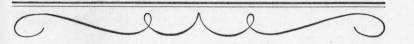

 IT WAS SPRING AGAIN AND KITTY, who had worked mechanically throughout the winter, found the Linton cottage unbearably confining. The Cayuse War had drained the country of its produce and money, and prices were high and goods were scarce. For many weeks there had been no work for Jeff, and finally he had convinced Clara he was strong enough for a three months' enlistment with the volunteers.

But if the energetic women of Oregon City could not buy furniture this season they could nevertheless carry on their program of civic betterment. They had begun to herd the reluctant youngsters of the town into schoolrooms and Kitty helped occasionally at the Female Seminary, Mrs. Thornton's private school for young ladies. Mrs. Thornton, the wife of the judge, taught all branches of a thorough English education, and Kitty found pleasure in directing classes in plain and fancy needlework and drawing. It was nice to know that the young girls of Oregon City, in spite of war and privation, were being properly taught the maidenly arts of painting in mezzotints and water colors.

Kitty picked her way along Main Street, a portfolio of drawings under her arm. The breeze was soft on her cheeks, and she looked longingly up the road to the bluff. It was time she was home after her work at Mrs. Thornton's—but— She turned up the path, and began the climb.

I'm twenty years old, she reflected. *An old maid. But I don't feel so old today.* For the first time in many weeks she felt glad to be alive. There was much work for her besides the teaching. There was the never-ending job of sewing for the soldiers, of packing and checking supplies, and very often Dr. Manning called her to help out in a home visited by sickness or tragedy. She had performed her duties efficiently and without emotion. For a long while she had believed herself incapable of ever feeling deeply again.

But today she was restless, impatient—even hopeful. Any day a ship was sure to come, now that it was spring, and certainly it would bring her money and news from Wildcliffe. Regardless of the age or condition of the next vessel, she was determined to sail upon it for home.

From the bluff she looked down on the little city and she allowed herself to think of the day that she and Curt had stood there, and watched the welcome to the officers of the *Shark*. There was a quick, sharp pain in her heart at the thought of Curt. That had been a day of such great rejoicing, followed so quickly by disappointment and anger at the terms of the treaty. And then again there had been triumph and high spirits—until they were dashed to the ground by the awful blow of the Whitman massacre which began the war. Oregon was a land of extremes, Kitty thought; of deepest depths and highest heights. She turned to glance behind her and was rewarded. For the first time in many long cloudy days, Mount Hood was visible, and, as always, Kitty caught her breath as she drank in its beauty.

From the height she had a good perspective of the town. She remembered Sunset's words when first she had seen Mount Rainier from Newmarket. *"You have to be at least fifty miles away to see the whole of it; up close you only see the part right under your feet, like. . . . Real big things are like that."* Maybe, when she was gone far from Oregon she could look back upon it, understand it, find some reason for the suffering that had been visited upon her here.

She watched the ferries at work on the river, and then her attention was drawn to the little wooden blockhouse that was the jail. It stood above the falls, almost on their edge, and a narrow walk led from it to the mainland. A thin line of smoke was coming from its small windows and Kitty started; as she watched the smoke was cut by little red tongues of flame.

Almost at once men began running from the mill, but before they reached the jail the entire building was wrapped in flames. They worked rapidly. The door to the building was opened, the walk drenched with water, and soon the flames were gone and the blackened little building emerged from the smoke. Kitty relaxed. No great damage had been done, but the conflagration had caused quite a crowd to gather. They were moving away now, down the river, but the crowd seemed still to hold its shape. The people were headed for the river near the horse ferry landing.

A boat was docking. Kitty caught her breath and her face lighted with excitement and hope. A boat could mean only one thing—news. Perhaps it would tell of the Volunteers, or of Joe Meek's party—or, most wonderful of all, perhaps a ship had come to The River. A ship—with news of Wildcliffe, with money for her passage home, a ship that would carry her away from hardship and tense anxiety and tragedy, into luxury and comfort and leisure and affection. The very thought of it made Kitty's throat tighten with tears of homesickness and desire and hungry anticipation. A ship was Rescue and Escape. Kitty picked up her skirts and ran.

◈ 2 ◈

"It's the United States transport *Anita*, from California," John Homet said. "Sent up here to recruit men to fight the Mexicans. We told them we had a war of our own on our hands. First they'd heard of it. . . . There's a letter here for you somewhere."

Kitty tried to control her impatience as John fumbled through the mail with his crippled hand. He dropped a letter, slowly picked it up and put it back in the pile. He read each address carefully before passing on to the next, speculated upon its author. It seemed to her it was hours before he found the right envelope and even then he was reluctant to let it go, peering at it, turning it over once more to study the heavy seal upon its back.

She snatched it from him, her hands trembling. She would not open it here in the store, her first letter, her first word from home in more than two years. She hurried toward the privacy of the Linton cabin, clutching the precious paper.

In her room she broke the seal. It was pleasant just to look at the familiar, fine writing of Judge Stuart, and she relished every careful curve of it. It brought back with a rush all she had left at Wildcliffe, all the beauty and safety and luxury to which she would return. She unfolded the heavy paper, and the gold certificate she had expected dropped from it. Her expressive eyes shone with pleasure. Money was wonderful! The certificate was for one thousand dollars, one thousand beautiful dollars, redeemable in bright, shining gold, a slip of paper that any shipmaster, no matter how greedy, would be delighted to accept.

She sighed happily, carefully laid the precious certificate on the bed beside her, tapping it once with happy, dancing fingers. She turned to the letter. It began with the Judge's usual "My dear Kitty—"

She could hear him say it, his kindly hand outstretched, his courtly old head bowed—"My dear Kitty—" A wave of homesickness swept over her.

The Judge expressed his shock and grief and great sympathy at Philip's death, his concern for her welfare, and his indignation at Jessie Pearl's perfidy. But what was she to expect in a wild country like that? the Judge asked, petulantly. Kitty laughed aloud—it was so like the Judge, to write pages of argument, his anger at the Free-Staters who robbed Southerners of their property. The Judge recounted the arguments that had been going on in Congress, and that had delayed the formation of a territorial government for Oregon. Her eyes sparkled. *I will be a great success, back at Wildcliffe, for I will have so much to tell them all! Even men—older men, will listen to me.* For an instant she contemplated devoting her life to politics, behind the scenes, of course, as a woman must forever be. A talented hostess with a great fortune behind her could be a powerful influence, and certainly she was prepared now to discuss the Oregon Question. She might even write pieces for the papers!

She turned back to the letter. It was filled with bits of gossip of relatives and friends—how nice to hear of them! Weddings and christenings, balls and barbecues—how they had missed her! All the county was awaiting her return—

She came to the last page of the letter and she read it first through a dreamy mist, still visualizing those happy scenes, and then, puzzled, she turned back and read it again. Judge Stuart had left the actual business of the letter for the last.

"Philip's older brother, Franklin, being his nearest of kin, is, of course, his heir—in the absence of any will to the contrary. Isn't it fortunate that his wife, Sue, is a Gatewood, and your cousin, though several times removed, so, after all, Wildcliffe will still be in the Gatewood family. Franklin and Sue beg me to send you their love and to tell you how glad they are to send you this money for your return. They want you always to consider that Wildcliffe is your home. Franklin has made a few changes in the estate.

"As you probably know, Kitty, a single girl is at a disadvantage in the courts in proving property rights. Since your father's will specifically bequeathed Wildcliffe to Philip, Franklin's right to the property seems quite sound. Unless, of course, Philip left a will leaving Wildcliffe to you. There was none among his effects here and you mentioned none. However, it is my duty to state that I believe that your father did not intend the estate to fall to other heirs than you. He specifically told me that he was bequeathing Wildcliffe to Philip in anticipation of your marriage to him. It is possible if you had the means to fight this matter, that you might, in some far-off day, regain Wildcliffe, or a portion of it, if you wished to contest your father's will in court. Mind you, I say *might*; and the amount required to carry such a matter through the courts would be considerable and the chances of success doubtful.

"I do not anticipate, however, that you will wish to contest this matter, and likely you will be happy enough to be relieved of the responsibility of the estate. Franklin and Sue promise you a home as long as you live, and a liberal allowance—and I am sure Franklin will be generous in bestowing upon you a reasonable sum in case of your marriage. This seems the better way, to accept this and be thankful. In fact, I see no alternative at this time, considering your present unfortunate lack of means, and I advise you to accept this arrangement. The decision, however, rests with you."

Kitty dropped the letter in her lap. A will. Philip's journal. "All that I have—which is mostly debts—I leave to Kitty"— She had tossed that journal into the flames, thinking only to protect his memory, shield Franklin and Sue from pain. What a fool she had been! She had always considered Wildcliffe hers, for it was her home; she had naturally supposed that, with Philip's death, it would belong to her. What an ignorant, trusting little soul she had been!

She looked at the gold certificate but she did not touch it. That money was charity. Franklin and Sue had been *glad* to send it to her! She, Kitty, who had never asked for anything from anyone in her whole life—and who never would! Offer her a home, did they, a poor relation, to subsist on their bounty? "Oh, yes, that's poor Kitty, our little cousin. She lives with us."

To sit by and watch Franklin making changes in Wildcliffe— *her* Wildcliffe! To see Sue in her mother's place at the Gatewood table, giving orders to servants, wearing her mother's keys at her belt! Pure outrage swept over Kitty and she clenched her fists. Robert had not intended it that way. He had told her that a single girl was practically a nonentity in the eyes of the law; legally she did not exist. But Robert had intended her to have Wildcliffe, though Philip might be the master in name. He had depended upon Kitty to preserve it.

The day would come, she thought, the day would certainly come, when women would not be treated so, when they would have equal rights with men, when they would have control of their own property, and when they would have a voice in the way laws were made and enforced. Even here in Oregon, a new country, uninhibited by many of the old traditions, women had no voice, no right to vote. No wonder women made marriages of convenience! What else could they do? The injustice of it infuriated her and she pounded the bed with her fists.

I won't take this lying down, she vowed, I won't. There must be some way. I won't be a charity case. I won't creep back there and be patronized by Sue and Franklin and say thank you prettily for any little handout they may wish to give me. I'll starve first! I'll fight them! There must be ways of making money. I'll go into the courts and demand my rights. I'll tell them about Philip's journal and I'll make them believe me. I'll tell them that Father intended me to have Wildcliffe, that he left it to Philip only to bring him home. I'll raise such a fuss that women everywhere will be behind me, and men will have to do something about it!

But it had been all she could do to keep body and soul together in Oregon. She had not been able to lay by very much. She looked at the certificate and caught her lip in her teeth. Angrily she folded it and started to tear it across and then she hesitated. No, she would not destroy it. She would keep it, use it, and everything else she could get her hands on, to fight for Wildcliffe. She would demand that she be repaid the money she had paid out on Philip's debts—and she realized sickly that she had torn up and burned those canceled notes to the British officers, too. She had been so eager to finish that unpleasant business, to forget it. How stupid she had been!

She was aroused from her thoughts by a tapping at her window and curiously she slid back the pane.

"Kit-tee?"

"Polly! Polly Careless! Whatever are you doing here?"

The wide dark face of Polly was barely visible in the dusk.

"I come meet Charlie."

"Where is he? I haven't seen him. Is he in Oregon City?"

"He was here. He burn down jail. Now he gone down river to Dick McLa'ys place. He awful drunk on Blue Lu."

"Polly! Was that Charlie who set the jail on fire?"

"Sure. Kit-tee, you come home."

"Polly, you'd better get out of town. They don't like Indians here after dark. How are things at Newmarket?"

"M'Nay people, in your house, they go own place. Sparks, he tell me tell you come home, somebody take your place."

Kitty reached out and squeezed Polly's arm.

"You're good, Polly. Even if you are an Indian. Listen. You go down river and find Charlie and you wait for me, understand? I'll be there in the morning. You wait, at McCrary's place. And you make Charlie stop drinking—hear?"

"You come home—Kit-tee?"

"Yes, Polly, I'll come home." She turned from the window and immediately began to gather her possessions together. Now and then she muttered with anger. "Land-grabbers. Trying to take my place when my back is turned. They took Wildcliffe. But they won't take my claim. And some day I'll get Wildcliffe back, too. I'm not whipped yet! Not by a long shot!"

◈ 3 ◈

SUNSET put his foot on the wagon wheel, rested his arm on his knee. He pushed the skin cap, too warm for the Kansas sun, far back on his head and looked up at the deeply creviced face of the man on the seat above him, and at the sun-bonneted woman beside him. She was a spare woman and strong; she had made no comment during the men's conversation.

"This here book is right enough?" the man said. He tapped a dog-eared copy of Philip Davis' *Guide For Emigrants*.

"Mostly," Sunset answered, "it'll be all right for your company, being the first to cross the Plains this year. Later on in the season, those waterholes won't be there, and the 'good grass' the book mentions will be gone. But it's fair help."

The man nodded. He looked ahead, over the ears of his mules and Sunset straightened, stepped back. "About the Cayuse War," Sunset added, "I didn't figure to fright you, ma'am. But it's only fair to warn you what's ahead. Better keep mighty close together, folks, and under arms. . . . That is, if you still are of a mind to go. There's still time to change your minds, and turn back."

The man shifted the wad of tobacco in his cheek, rolled the whip in his hand, and turned to look at his wife. She met his gaze steadily. There was a long moment of silence, and then he turned away, his eyes shining. He spat over the wheel, sharply, contemptuously, and the whip cracked, defiant and unafraid.

The wagon moved—west. Sunset grinned, unsurprised, and saluted as it passed.

◈ 4 ◈

CHARLEFOUR was sick. At first Kitty believed it was only the results of his prolonged drinking bout, and she had no sympathy for him. But as the days wore on the deep crimson of Charlie's face did not fade, and his movements grew slower. She watched uneasily as he doggedly fought his way up the Cowlitz and she saw him stumble when he tried to shoulder his packs at the portages. Somewhere he had found Indian George, and Kitty noticed that George, too, as well as Polly, was watching Charlie with anxious eyes.

But the Frenchman would not admit that he was ill. He told Kitty he had taken a ball in the shoulder and the wound had not healed well. He stubbornly insisted that was all that was wrong with him. He explained that Fletcher had sent him back to Newmarket to hold his claim. Sunset would not return for another month or more, and Curt would not leave the Cayuse country till a truce was reached or victory was assured. Rumors of land-grabbers had come to Curt also, and so he sent the ailing Frenchman home. Charlie was proud of the paper which Fletcher had given him, naming him his agent.

Kitty was relieved when at last they reached the Landing and left the canoes for horses. Once Charlie was home he could rest, and surely his recovery would be rapid. But now he was forced to hold the pommel of the saddle with both hands to keep his seat, and when he dismounted at evening he sat for a long time holding his reeling head in his hands.

"Charlie, you're very ill," Kitty said in desperation. "You can't go any further."

"Sh-h, Kitty." Charlie managed to raise his head and glance around the camp. Polly was tending the fire some distance away and George had gone for water. Charlie kept his voice low. "Let them think it is just the wound. When we get home, I stay in the cabin so I see no Indians. Already there is sickness in the camp of the Duwamish, and the Indians are restless. If they think I come, bringing more sickness, it will be no good for us. I get home, I get out of sight—I get well."

"Charlie, what about Polly? She's your wife, but—"

"Polly is loyal. She was an Indian slave. You know about that?" Kitty shook her head. "When a child is orphaned the Indians make her a slave, even in their own tribes, sometimes. Polly was orphaned. If the master die, the slave is buried alive with him. Those bodies on Mt. Coffin—they were not all corpses when they were put there. Polly's master die, and they would have sent her to Memaloose Island with him, but I buy her. She is grateful. The whites have been kind to her. They teach her about cooking and things at Fort Vancouver. She has no love for the Duwamish Indians, or the Nisquallys. She stay with us."

Kitty swallowed. How could she ever have thought the savages a harmless and poetic people, placing their dead on Mt. Coffin to await the return flood of life?

"And George?"

"He is a good Indian and long my friend. But I do not want George to know I have sickness."

Charlie would not stop at the Sparks' cabin. He was close to delirium. He wanted only to reach home. He would go to Kitty's place, he agreed, with Polly, for he was too sick to be alone. Kitty, stopping in the Sparks' dooryard, watched Charlie and Polly disappear down the trail.

The door opened before she could reach it and Martha emerged. She did not run and shout her greetings. She walked with great effort and her face was pallid. She held up her hand, though, and her bright smile lighted her face.

"Kitty, I'm so glad you're back." She leaned weakly against the fence. "Don't come in, though. The children and Sparks are sick. I guess it's measles, though it acts different than what I'm used to. I'm just getting over it, though I had them once, when I was a youngster. Kitty, you look healthy enough. Try to stay away from it, if you can. We'll see you, soon's we're up and about again."

"But Martha, you need help!"

Martha shook her head. "We'll make out now. It was hard for a while. Wealthy's been powerful sick, but then she's so little and frail. She's better today. Sparks' been tryin' to do three men's work, and went from here to the Hansens and Trainors, carin' for their stock, for they was all down with it, too. No men to spare—all them that could is off with the Volunteers. But the Trainors and Hansens are all right now, able to do for themselves. But it's sure been a hard winter. The Indians been awful saucy lately. Stole a couple of cows from the Trainors last week; there's been some talk we ought maybe to build a blockhouse, just in case. We're keepin' in close touch with Dr. Tolmie at Nisqually. He's strengthened the fort some, and he'll let us all in, in case anything happens, though it's a good piece away. Best way to avoid trouble, everyone says, is not to antagonize the Indians if'n you can help it, till folks get well and the men come home. That Dick Tom's been hangin' around your place."

"Dick Tom! Oh, Martha!"

"He's mean. I got to tell you though, Kitty. There was two white men through here a couple weeks back and they looked over your place some. Sparks told them the place was yours, and McNair did, too. I guess they decided to strike out for their own selves, but they weren't very friendly. They might be back. I didn't like their looks much. They poked around Curt's and Sunset's place, too, but when the men told them whose claim it was they left, quick. They heard about Curt's shootin', I think, and they want no truck with him."

"Martha, that seaman, the man who was insane. Is he still around?"

"Yes, but he's harmless enough. I been feedin' him. He's nothing to fright you, poor soul. He thinks he's Jesus Christ. Kitty, we ain't heard from Deaf Wilson lately, and I can't leave the folks to go see him. It's on your way. Will you stop and see if he's all right? Might be he's down sick, too, and all alone."

Kitty nodded. "Are you sure the children are all right?"

"Fever's broke. I brewed some tea of dogwood bark. Seemed to help. What of the war, Kitty?"

"It's going pretty well for the Volunteers. Charlie thinks this summer they will declare the Cayuse lands confiscated to us, and will force the Indians to deliver the murderers. They will leave forces at The Dalles and the Cascades and at Waillatpu and send men to escort the immigrants through the Cayuse country. They think Sunset and Meek made the Missouri, all right. We know they got as far as Fort Hall some time ago. Everyone figures Sunset will come back with the first immigrants."

Martha pondered the information for a long moment. She smiled hopefully. "That's good, Kitty. That's right good. It'll cheer Sparks a heap. I reckon the trouble won't spread this far, then, if they've got the Cayuses stopped east of the mountains. There hasn't been no killin' this side of the mountains yet, but they are mighty bold. Sparks said to tell you not to let Dick Tom in the house, no matter what. He's lookin' for trouble. You better keep Charlie and Polly with you. They can keep an eye on Curt's place from there. You hadn't ought to be alone, nights, especially. Mr. Smith's been ailin', too; Sylvester's gone."

"I'll be all right." Kitty leaned from the saddle and patted Martha's arm. "I'll come back to see you in a day or so. I'm sorry about the sickness, Martha."

"Better hurry, before it gets dark. Don't forget to stop and see about Deaf."

Kitty's horse loped off down the forest path. She wished she could catch up with Charlie and Polly. The stillness of the woods settled about her, and every tree seemed to shelter an unnamed danger. She feared to glance behind her, and she was afraid not to. She spurred her horse as she came into the clearing surrounding Wilson's small cabin.

It was a ramshackle place and there was no sign of life about it. She rode to the door and called out. There was no horse behind the snake fence that formed a small corral. Deaf had gone to help the Trainors or Hansens, or Mr. Smith, she decided. She started on, and then hesitated and turned back. If the old man was sick and helpless within— She had promised Martha to make sure.

She called again and her voice echoed, eerily. She dismounted and approached the door. She hoped that it was locked. She did not want to enter that dim interior alone.

She knocked sharply, waited. Only silence greeted her. She tried the latch and the door swung inward, creaking loudly on rusty hinges. She pushed it full wide with her foot, peering within. She saw Deaf's bed in the corner. It was empty. He was not ill, then, and she breathed a sigh of relief.

The light from the open door made a big square upon the table. There was a piece of paper upon it. Deaf had left a note for any chance passer-by, she thought. Briskly she stepped into the tiny room, picked up the note and held it to the light.

It was carefully written. It was certainly not the awkward printing of old Deaf Wilson. It was the writing of an educated man—but the words held no meaning for her. There seemed to be a verse, or a part of a verse, of Scripture. Kitty frowned, trying to make some sense of it. "I will work a miracle to convince— that I am the Messiah—" the note ended. She shrugged, put it back on the table and turned to leave the shack.

The door swung slightly, creaking loudly, and she put out her hand to stop it before it closed. And then she stopped, transfixed, her eyes, accustomed now to the gloom, widening in horror and terror.

Behind the door, against the wall, was a man, crouching.

Kitty tried to scream, but no sound came from her frozen lips. She did not know how long she stood there, rooted to the floor, unable to move, unable to speak. The figure had his back toward her, his face toward the wall, and he was on his knees, one arm stretched high above his head.

The man did not move. Kitty's terrified eyes went from his bowed head to the arm, on, up to the hand. The arm was brown with dried blood, that had streamed its full length, and spread upon the floor around the crouching figure.

Nausea swept over Kitty and she clung to the door for support. The hand, flat against the log wall of the cottage, was impaled there, a heavy spike driven through it, deep into the heavy log behind it. Beside the huddled figure, within inches of the other hand, lay the heavy stone that had been used to drive that nail through the living flesh.

At long last Kitty began to recover from the shock. She was still too numb to feel, too weak to flee, but she tried hard to reason. She had to ascertain if the man was dead, if he was past human aid. She forced herself to approach him, touched him once, gingerly, and had her answer. There was nothing she could do for him. A little gust of wind fluttered the paper on the table, the message the insane, tormented man had written so carefully before he had crucified himself.

Some way Kitty got out of the cabin, closing the door against the horror within. Her horse was nervous, jumpy, snorting, and it took all her skill to mount him, and then she was lying low on his neck, to avoid being lashed by outthrust branches, as she raced down the narrow trail toward her own cottage and the comforting presence of Charlefour and Polly.

At least it wasn't Indians, she said aloud, half-sobbing. At least —it wasn't the Indians that did it.

◆ 5 ◆

KITTY's arms ached and it seemed to her the weight of the water pails must pull them from their sockets. She had to coax and to battle with Charlie to make him take food, and even though she managed to feed him a little each day his big form was wasted and very weak. Only occasionally did he rouse enough to recognize her, and Polly now lay beside him, the dark skin tight and crimson across her broad face, her eyes hot and feverish. Kitty had forcibly to restrain Polly from running from the cabin. She told Polly that it would kill her if she were to go to the Sound and throw herself into its icy waters to cool her fever. She compromised with her by carrying pails of cold water, and bathing her burning face.

When Polly was well, Kitty's strength would have been no match for her; but Polly grew more feeble each day as the disease coursed through her veins. Kitty watched the trail anxiously, praying that someone, anyone, would come to help her. Surely a settler must ride by; surely Fortune would be well enough soon to come to see how she was faring; surely Deaf Wilson would return and pass her cottage and stop to see her. She remembered that she had not told Martha that Charlie was sick. Perhaps Martha, too, was bedridden again, and was wondering why Kitty did not come to her aid.

Kitty managed to feed and water the stock and to prepare some kind of food for herself and her patients. She lost track of the days and the nights. She never left the cottage without a gun, and she was certain, more than once, that she saw a dark shadow at the edge of the clearing. She had a feeling she was being watched, and her old fear of Dick Tom returned, multiplied now a thousand-fold by the knowledge of the atrocities at Waillatpu. It had been more than a month since she left Oregon City. It had been a month-long nightmare.

She put down the water pails, turned to close the door behind her. She wiped the sweat from her forehead and, dizzily, looked across the clearing. . . . That was no shadow. In the twilight she caught a full glimpse of the Indian standing at the edge of the woods, watching the cottage.

I must not lose my head, she told herself firmly, and I must not let him know I am afraid. She controlled her impulse to slam the door and bolt it. Her temples were throbbing and again the dizziness swept over her. By sheer force of will she pushed it aside. She felt for the pistol, was reassured by the hard coldness of it, in the deep pocket of her skirt. From the room behind her came Charlie's restless moaning, and then a low, sick, sleepy sound from Polly.

Deliberately, Kitty stood in her doorway, staring at the Indian. He watched her for a long time, and then he approached a few steps, coming into full view. She recognized Dick Tom with a sudden mighty thump of her heart. She stepped outside the door and faced him.

"Stop there," she commanded. Her voice was sharp and clear. The Indian stopped, regarding her speculatively, and then he came on a cautious yard or two. Kitty raised the pistol. "Stop—right there, Dick Tom!"

Again he paused, his bright, insolent eyes going from her face to the gun. For a long moment they measured each other, and Kitty prayed silently, desperately. Don't let me get dizzy now. Don't let me faint! She felt herself swaying and she gripped the pistol harder and took a step toward the Indian, trying to steady herself. To her great relief he stepped back.

She gestured again with the pistol. "Leave here. Go away. Go now—or I'll shoot."

Step by step, Dick Tom withdrew, very slowly, drawing back into the shadows of the woods, animal-like, silent. Kitty waited until she could see him no longer, and then she moved back to the door, walking backwards, feeling her way carefully. She closed the door, dropped the heavy bar and stood, breathing heavily, her eyes closed; she could feel the sweat running down her body in tiny, tickling streams, between her breasts, between her shoulder blades.

She would not have to leave the cabin again until morning, and some way, tomorrow, she must get help. There was no use denying it longer; she, too, was ill. Black cotton wool seemed to float before her eyes in big soft masses, and she had to push it away before she could go to the hearth. She put a cup into a pail of water and drank deeply, forgetting it was the cup she had used to feed Charlie and Polly.

She could not eat. She sat at her table, rested her aching head on her arms. If I were not sick I would not be so frightened, she reasoned. I'm just imagining that I hear footsteps around the cabin—

She jerked to attention, listened. Far away a cougar cried; another, farther still, answered. Or was it an animal? An owl hooted, another replied, and then there was heavy silence. Were the Nisqually Indians gathering, perhaps to descend on her cabin, angry that Charlie and Polly had brought the whites' illness here? Was Dick Tom still out there, waiting, ready to carry her away as Five Crows had taken Lorinda Bewley? Kitty could no longer draw the fine line between reality and her own feverish imaginings. She forced herself to rise and she took the long rifle from the deer horns mounted over the doorway, and laid it across her lap. It seemed extraordinarily heavy.

She began to shake with a chill, violent, convulsive; her teeth chattered like castanets, and she was no longer certain if it was herself or Charlie or Polly who moaned. She thought she slept, and then she found herself standing rigid, tight against the door, breathing short and hard, listening with every nerve. There was no mistake this time. There were footsteps, running footsteps, without. They were coming nearer, they were on the step, and there was a pounding at the door. She could feel the door vibrate with the force of that demand for admittance. She reached for the gun, but her weak fingers would not bear its weight. Then she was falling, falling, into a deep and bottomless black pit, and that was all she knew.

◈ 6 ◈

How long she was ill, wavering between sleep and semiconsciousness, she did not know. But when at last she did awaken and her mind was clear she knew that it had been for many days. Sunlight poured into the cabin. The fire burned steadily on the clean-swept hearth, and on the table was a bowl filled with the pure gold of wild flowers. The sheets on her bed were clean and smooth, and beneath the covers her body felt wasted and weak. There was no sign of Dick Tom, and the pistol case was closed and in its accustomed place on the mantelpiece. The door to the adjoining room was open, and Kitty could see that the bed was neatly made.

She lay still, trying to remember, to sort reality from the nightmares that had tortured her. She could remember talking to someone, perhaps incoherently and at great length, and she had been wild with fear. But now in the orderly little house there was nothing out of place, nothing to remind her. It was normal, peaceful, safe.

The door opened softly and Sunset entered. He put down his long rifle carefully and glanced quickly toward the bed. Kitty met his eyes and his smile transformed his face. He came to her softly, his feet making no sound, and stood, hands on hips, looking down at her. His blue flannel shirt was open at the throat, and Kitty remembered, drowsily, the feel of that shirt beneath her cheek. Sunset dropped on one knee beside her bed. She studied him. His face was so near that she could see the tiny weather-lines about his blue eyes, the texture of his clean, sun-browned skin, the tiny scratch on his lean cheek where a razor had nicked it.

"You're better," he said. She could see a little pulse beat in his strong neck, and a tiny, involuntary twitch of his smiling mouth.

He took her hand carefully, as though he feared to hurt her, and his anxious eyes were begging her to speak.

"Yes," she said, "I'm—much better, Sunset." Her voice sounded husky and weak tears misted her eyes. Sunset wiped them away with a corner of the sheet.

"Now, now, Kitty girl," he chided, "you're all right. Dr. Tolmie came from Nisqually. Your fever's gone and all you need to do is rest, and eat, and get strong again."

"Where's—"

"Polly and Charlie? They're well again and back at work. Martha has been here, too, to care for you. You had us mighty worried."

"And—Dick Tom?"

"That blasted Indian! You scared hell out of him."

Kitty sighed with relief. "I don't remember very well," she said slowly, "but I'm glad I didn't kill anybody. I was so frightened—"

His hand tightened on hers. "I know, Kitty. But it's all right now. Don't talk and tire yourself."

"I'm—glad you came," she whispered. She closed her eyes. "Sunset?"

"Yes, Kitty?"

"You—you came alone?"

He did not answer right away. She opened her eyes, questioningly. He was looking at her hands, smoothing her small fingers between his own big ones. The smile was gone from his face. "Yes, Kitty, I'm alone," he said quietly. "Curt's still in the Cayuse country—still fighting."

"Oh. . . . Sunset, I don't—I don't ever want to see him again."

Sunset raised his head then and studied her searchingly. "You're sick yet, Kitty. And weak. Wait till you're well—"

"No, I mean it. You always tried to convince me, since the first time I came to Newmarket, that Curt was—that he was—"

"A good man. I still say so, Kitty."

"But not for me. He's not good for me, Sunset."

Sunset took a deep breath. "Maybe not, Kitty," he said finally. He looked down at her hands again. "I guess there's no use tryin' any more to persuade you. Kitty—I knew you loved Curt. And he loved you. I kept thinkin' if you'd just see it the right way, you wouldn't have to fight your heart no more. I figured that would bring you happiness, Kitty, if you could follow your heart. If your conscience would let you. But if it won't—then I guess he's not good for you. A woman like you, I reckon if you'd feel guilty, as if you weren't doin' the right thing—then there'd be no happiness for you, no matter what your own desires. Kitty, I kept thinkin' there'd come a day when you'd change; when you'd admit you loved him, and you'd forgive him the things he's done, and you'd go to him, no matter what."

Kitty rolled her head on the pillow. "No." Her thin face hardened. "Not after—not after seeing him and Lisa there—in Oregon City—and knowing—"

"He's suffered too, Kitty. He's suffered full long."

"He brought it on himself."

"I don't reckon that makes it any easier to bear."

She was silent. Sunset stood and released her hands. He was very tall, very big, there in the low-ceilinged cottage, she thought, looking up at him. And good. She needed that strength and goodness now; he had sheltered her; he had warmed her with his own body. His face was naked now, his eyes upon her, his lips unsmiling, his hands clenched. "Sunset," she whispered, "don't leave me. I can't—I can't go on alone!"

For a moment he hesitated, the struggle within him plainly pictured on his face.

"No," he said, "no, you can't go on alone."

He turned his back on her and went to the fire and leaned against the mantelpiece. He was looking into the fire as he talked, sensibly, evenly. "It's no good, goin' on alone, Kitty. You've made a good fight; if it hadn't been for the Indian war—and all the other things out of your control, maybe you'd have made it. You were doin' right well, and we all admired your grit. You're a person, we said, could paddle upstream.

"But it just ain't in the cards for a girl to be alone in Oregon. There'd be no peace for you, Kitty. You're lovely—there'll be men wantin' you all your life, and out here—no, it wouldn't work, Kitty. I know you're tryin' to prove this claim, to get some money, to go back to Wildcliffe. I know you need a sum of money to put up a legal fight for your home there. You told me all that, and other things, while you been so sick. It was on your mind so much. I guess that's what you need to make you happy, to make you easy in your mind. I kept thinkin' you'd change your mind about that—that you'd decide after all it was Oregon and

Curt you wanted. I thought after you'd lived awhile near The River and The Mountain that you'd not want to leave. . . . I guess I was wrong."

He began to pound his left hand softly with his right fist. It was the only gesture of strain she had ever seen him make. "Truth is, Kitty, I don't know for sure if you can even hold this claim or not, alone; law isn't clear yet, about a single girl's legal rights. Even after you've improved it, cleared and planted it, put your heart and strength into it, some schemin' son-of-a-gun might be able to take it away from you. That hadn't ought to happen to you twice. . . . I think you got a chance to get Wildcliffe back, if you had the money to put up the fight. There was several of us here who investigated Davis' death who saw that journal. We could get sworn statements—"

Deliberately he put another small log on the fire and his face flushed. He came back to her bed then, and spoke softly, earnestly. "Kitty, there are feelin's won't fit into common talk like mine. I reckon you know you gave me a heart-stir, the first time I saw you, and I reckon it ain't no secret to you that it's been growin' on me ever since. I guess you know—I'd cut off my right arm rather than have you hurt, or sick, like you been these last weeks, and I been prayin' mighty hard—"

His voice grew husky, remembering. "Don't seem right," he went on, "you so little—bein' hurt, or sick, or scared. When I finally got in here that night you were lyin' on the floor, hangin' on to that gun. It was Charlie who heard me and let me in, finally, though he had to crawl to the door. I, Dad, Kitty—when I saw you there—"

There was a white line around his mouth now. "When you came to, you started to talk, and it wasn't easy to quiet you. I held you, Kitty—I held you in my arms all night. Seems as if you—wanted to be there.

"Seem'd as if the sun'd go out, Kitty—if you didn't get well."

The silence in the cabin was heavy, waiting. "Kitty, if it's Wildcliffe you want, if that'll make you happy—I'll try to get it for you. If you'll let me take care of you, Kitty, let me work for you—together we can do it. We'll get title to this land. We'll sell, trade, we'll manage it, some way. It'll take a little time. There's still trappin' to be done, there's money to be made in town sites, likely, and in lumber, now the mill's operatin'. It ought not to be too long—if we put our minds to it."

"You'd leave Oregon—for me?"

"I'd go to hell for you, Kitty—if it would make you happy."

The man's face was naked, all the love in his great, kindly heart, so long unspoken, was revealed there, and in the intensity in his voice. But he would not touch her now, not trusting himself, waiting her answer. Sunset would never force her, he would never demand, he would ask nothing for himself, only the privilege to give to her, his strength, his knowledge, his loyalty, his protection. How different, how completely opposite he is, from Curt, Kitty thought.

And then the words which Curt had never spoken, the words that, from Curt, would have changed everything, came from Sunset's lips. No other man, knowing Curt, would have dared to speak them to Kitty. But Sunset had waited. He had given Curt his chance; and now, with the full knowledge of what he was doing, Sunset firmly took the future from Curt's hands. "I love you, Kitty. I only have everyday language to say it—but I love you, Kitty Gatewood.

"The moment I saw you at Fort Vancouver, your hair like a moonglade and your eyes dancin' above your fan, the glory-glow on your face and the dimple in your cheek—and your little waist so tiny I could span it with my two hands—I loved you then." He was smiling down at her, remembering. "And at the pier, when the Lost Company came, and you were watchin', hurt with the pain of them, and there were tears on your cheeks. I wanted to gather you up and keep you away from that, away from all pain. On the Cowlitz trail, when I took the piece of wood from your hand, it was hard to hurt you—such a little, soft hand. And it wasn't easy not to tell you, Kitty, all these months between. I've watched you and Curt—and I kept still, thinkin' your heart was with him, and that some day the two of you would come to understandin'.

"When I came back to Oregon City and I found you'd come to Newmarket, I had a scare like I've never had before. I heard the Sound Indians were risin' and there was sickness. I couldn't get back here quick enough. I reckon nobody's ever come up the Cowlitz any faster'n I did to get back here to you."

He knelt and slid his arm beneath her shoulders and raised her face, his hand beneath her soft chin. "I love you, Kitty," he repeated. "I reckon now I've said it—I'll never get through sayin' it. Kitty, is that enough? Will you marry me? Will you marry a rough mountain-man?"

"Yes," she said thickly, "yes—"

◈ 7 ◈

"Dr. Manning's too old for circuit-riding, but I reckon he thought it was about time to bring God's word north of The River," Martha said briskly. "And warn't it wonderful he and the Lintons all came in the same party? Seems if all nice things happen at once, the fightin' done, and those danged Indians quiet, and Clara comin' to visit, and Dr. Manning comin' to hold prayer meetin's, and the weddin'!"

"Yes." Kitty was counting the brush-strokes on her hair, and she spoke around the pins in her mouth.

"And the infair! I declare, it's been a long time since we've had any celebratin'! Folks need a little pleasurin' now and then, to store up, against the bad times, and I never feel like folks's really had a weddin' less'n there's music and dancin' after. Course some now, they'd think it sinful."

Martha paused, holding Kitty's dress, regarding the beauty of it with pleased eyes. The Gatewood wedding gown. Kitty's glance slid around to it and there was a little tug at her heart.

"Quaker weddin's different," Martha observed, thoughtfully. "But then—they sure do last, Quaker marriages. I mind my mother tellin' me about her wedding. You know, they didn't have a priest or preacher or even a judge. They married themselves. Of course," she added, "took them three months to do it."

"Three months!"

"Yes, three months. Likely it'll take Dr. Manning about three minutes to name you and Sunset man and wife. Land sakes, Kitty, this gown is the most beautiful thing I ever *did* see! . . . Ma said the churches each had two departments, one for the women and one for the men. The first month, each of them, the man and the girl, rose in their own departments and announced they were going to be married. Let's see, how did Ma say it?" Martha rolled her eyes ceilingward. "'My beloved sisters, John

Ryan and myself have concluded to become man and wife.' Yes, that's the way she said it. 'If there is no objection and we do not change our minds within the time allotted.' I wonder," Martha mused, "if that was a good idea. I wonder how many of us woulda gone through with it if we'd had to think it over for three months."

Kitty bent her head to pin up her hair and did not answer. Martha looked at her out of the corner of her eye and went on. "Pa said the same thing in his department, and the next month they got up and said they got no cause or wish to change their minds, and if nobody else had any objections they'd go on with it. Third month, Pa got up and went into the ladies' department and sat down beside Ma. After a while they threw open the door between the ladies' and men's departments and the couple got up and declared theirselves married."

Martha chuckled. "But me, now, I don't think I could stand the strain. Not for three months. Land alive, I was so nervous when Sparks and I was married I was that limp when it was over—I was sure I looked like the last of pea-time! And of course, Fortune mighta changed his mind, had he time to think it over. Maybe he took me jack-at-a-pinch at that. No, I reckon this way's best."

Kitty straightened and reached for the gown. Her face was pale. Martha watched her as she slipped the dress over her head and it fell in soft, shimmering folds about her. Martha began the chore of fastening the multitude of tiny buttons up the back, pulling the bodice very tight about the little waist.

"But you're not a Quaker, Martha?"

"Can't say I am. As Dr. Manning'd say, many of the brethren fall into temptation after fightin' Satan some years in Oregon . . . but I ain't rightly a sinner, all ways. You know," Martha chuckled, "Ma was a talker, like me. Don't rightly see how she kept still all those three months. It was easy for Pa. Pa allus was a quiet man—though his gettin'-up holler was second to none."

Kitty frowned and turned to Martha, a question on her lips. Was Martha trying to advise her to delay this marriage, give it more thought? Martha was the wisest woman she knew.

"What is it, Wealthy?"

The little girl slipped in and closed the door behind her. She

stared at Kitty with awe and admiration, forgetting what she was
going to say.

"Yes, child?"

"Mr. Fletcher's here," Wealthy said absently, walking around
Kitty. "Wants to see Kitty. He looks mighty mad."

Kitty started and Martha straightened with a jerk.

"All right, Wealthy, all right." Martha ushered the child out
quickly and turned to Kitty, her back against the door.

"Oh, no, Martha. No. Why did he have to come now? How
did he know—"

Kitty twisted her hands together and the two women stared at
one another. There was a sharp rap on the door.

"You'll have to see him, Kitty. I guess," Martha said, doubt-
fully, and jumped as the sharp rap came again. "He'll bust the
door down," she added, in a whisper. Kitty bit her lip.

"Do you suppose he's seen Sunset?"

"Likely not. Likely he just come. Bet he stopped at our place
and Sparks told him. Or maybe he heard it farther down the
line. Kitty—what you goin' to do?"

Kitty stood very still. "I'll see him, Martha," she said finally.

Martha jerked her head in a nod. "Just a minute," she called,
through the door. "Don't let it upset you, Kitty," she begged,
herself obviously upset. She put her hand on the girl's shoulder.
"Kitty—are you sure—yourself?"

"Yes."

Kitty's face froze and Martha dropped her hand. She opened
the door.

"Why, Curt," Martha said, feigning surprise, "I didn't—"

Curt did not answer. He brushed by Martha and entered the
small room, and closed the door.

He had been riding hard. His face glistened with perspiration
and he held his broad-brimmed hat in his hands, gripping it
fiercely. He stared at Kitty, his glance starting at the top of her
shining head, dropping, inch by inch, down her face, down her
figure in the magnificent wedding gown. He glanced from her to
the veil upon the bed beside her, snowy white, virginal.

"What do you think you're doing?"

His voice was tight, furious, and his breath was short. Kitty
was silent. I'd forgotten, she thought, I'd forgotten how he looked
—how big he is—how strong his face—how black his hair, how

angry his eyes can be, and his mouth. I'd forgotten what it was like to be near him, to be in the same room with him—oh, Curt!

He took a step or two toward her and his hands clamped down on her shoulders and he shook her slightly. "What do you think you're doing?" he said again, the words coming hard through his teeth.

Some way Kitty found the words. "I'm going to be married, Curt. To Sunset."

He stared at her, wordless, for a long minute. "I didn't believe it," he said. "Fortune told me. I didn't believe it. I was sure he was lying. Now you—you tell me—you and Sunset—"

His voice thickened. "I told you—" he went on, "I told you, Kitty, you'd never marry anyone else. I told you—"

"I am going to marry Sunset, Curt."

"Marry him—when you love *me?*"

She did not answer. He shook her again, aching to hurt her, and then his hands slid down her arms, to her waist, in that possessive, magic touch of his and he drew her close. The folds of her wedding gown were crushed between them.

"You love me. You know it, Kitty. You'll never love anyone else. You belong to me."

"I am going to marry Sunset, Curt," she kept repeating the words, hanging on to them. "Please don't do this. You only make it harder—for all of us. My decision is made. It will be a good marriage. Don't hurt me any more, Curt."

"You damned little fool! You cheating little fool! You and your virtues! You won't marry me because of Lisa. Don't think I don't know! But you'll marry a man you don't love—because it will be a 'good marriage' for you. What can you take to Sunset? Love, passion? How in the devil do you reconcile that, with your conscience? Why don't you be honest, Kitty? Why don't you tell him, Kitty, that you can never give him your love—never give it—to anyone but me?"

"That's not true. There is more than one kind of love. I do love Sunset—in—in a way, a good way, Curt. A good way on which to found a marriage. I'll be a good wife to him."

"If you marry him, Kitty," he gripped her tightly, hurting her, "if you marry him—"

He is beginning to accept it, she thought, holding tightly to her own control. It is right, no matter what he says. He'll accept it. It will be all right. *An Oregon marriage,* she thought—*I'm making an Oregon marriage—*

"I could kill you, Kitty. I could kill you. And Sunset, too. By God I'll—"

She could feel him shiver, suddenly, and panic leaped within her. He strained her to him then and kissed her. She was crying now, the sobs deep, the tears burning her face. He drew away from her to look at her face and the anger went out of his own. "I knew you wouldn't, Kitty," he said, "I knew you couldn't—"

"Curt—"

She buried her face in her hands, steadied herself, and raised her face again.

"Curt—I am going to marry Sunset. It is the right thing for me. I know it. He loves me. I'll be a good wife—"

Incredulity crossed Curt's face and he moved toward her again. "You mean—"

"Yes. I mean that I have promised Sunset to become his wife and I intend to do so. There'd be no happiness with you, Curt. You want to mold things to fit your own purposes. You're selfish. You would not give—only take. You would never change; you're made of granite and steel, and a woman would wear herself out and break her heart, beating against that hardness of yours. Lisa appeals to something within you—some wildness; you'd not give her up, not permanently. I couldn't stand it, Curt. I'd be betraying myself—and all the decent women in Oregon. I'd be as weak as Philip was. This will be a clean and decent marriage, something to build on, something to be proud of. There's no finer man than Sunset. You know that."

"Yes." Curt's laugh was short and contemptuous. "Yes—Sunset's a good man. And you're damned right you'll be a good wife to him. If you marry him, Kitty, I'll see to that. You'll not cheat us both."

Kitty's hand came up then and she could not stop it. With all her strength she struck him across the mouth. All the outrage and hurt that had built up within her was in that one blow.

"But you're not his wife yet." Curt was smiling now, a twisted smile, as he moved toward her, the red mark of her hand livid across his face. Easily he pinioned her wrists behind her, and he kissed her again, her body arched, his weight against her. "Remember that, Kitty. Remember it—after you're married," he said.

His eyes were hard and bright and narrow as he slowly let her go.

He had to bend his head a little to go through the door. Kitty stood where he had left her, and after a while Martha tapped questioningly.

"Come in," Kitty said steadily. Two bright spots burned in her cheeks and she held her head high. Martha looked at her anxiously. "It's all right, Martha," she said. "Will you help me with my veil?"

"Sunset and Dr. Manning is comin' up the path," Martha said. "Are you—are you sure you're all right, Kitty?"

"I'm sure."

"All the folks' here now, I think. Clara's ready to stand up with you."

Kitty went to the window and glanced out. In the dooryard a large group of people stood, talking and laughing; horses and carts lined the hitching rail and Sunset, his golden head uncovered, looking strange in his broadcloth suit, was coming up the path. Curt was going to meet him.

Kitty could not see Curt's face, but as the two men neared each other she saw Sunset throw up his head and hurry forward. He was smiling and holding out his hand. Kitty saw Curt's hands moving on his thighs in that nervous gesture of anger that meant his hands itched for the feel of a gun. Curt's long figure was tense, and, Kitty thought, with a pang of compassion, why, he's very tired, tired and shaken; the war, the trip, the shock to him— and her heart turned over. I can't help loving him, she thought. I can't help it—and then, steeling herself, but I can help what I do about it. . . .

Sunset's glance did not waver as the two men came together. For an instant Kitty held her breath and then she saw Curt's hand go out, slowly, too. Kitty closed her eyes with a breath of relief as the hands of Curt and Sunset met.

Sunset knows, Kitty thought. He knows all about it—and he's not afraid of Curt.

"Ready, Kitty?"

Kitty turned to Martha, her face calm. "I'm ready, Martha."

There was noise in the outer room as the guests trooped in. Charlefour's fiddle music, softly, sweetly, filled the cabin and then there was quiet. Martha opened the door.

Kitty walked straight and slim to Sunset's side. There was a gasp of admiration as the bride appeared. Sunset watched her and his face flushed as she came toward him. Beside him Curt stood, stiff, immovable.

Kitty was conscious of Curt standing there, watching, his dark face stony, his eyes hot and shining, when she raised her face and turned back her veil to receive her husband's first kiss.

◈ 8 ◈

THE infair was at its height. Dr. Manning, his white head bowed, his chubby hands on his fat knees, nodded, and Wealthy and Reason, on either side of him, nodded, too. Charlefour's fiddle was replaced by Deaf Wilson's banjo, and Charlie went outside to take a drink from the jug that was being passed from hand to hand among the men in the dusky dooryard. Clara glided and dipped in the Virginia Reel and Money Musk; the tunes of *Pretty Betty Martin* and *The Girl I Left Behind Me* echoed, and re-echoed from the rafters. In the small room, Clara's Mathias had gone soundly to sleep, hiccoughing now and then with the memory of the exciting day he had finally, and with reluctance, completed. Mathias had nearly brought disaster upon the company, for he had drunk an entire bottle of cherry pectoral from Dr. Manning's bag. There was either too much or not enough prussic acid in it to kill him, Thomas had said, calmly putting his finger down Mathias' throat, but it had made Mathias very sick for a little while. As soon as he had recovered he had been found solemnly and thoroughly mixing green coffee beans and rice together and pouring the mess into patty pans that Kitty kept especially for making sweet cakes for Wealthy and Reason.

No, sir, it'd be a long time before Newmarket would see another wedding like that of Sunset and Kitty Lee, Martha decided, fanning herself, though she allowed she was so tired she felt like a scalded shoat on the last day a hog-killin'. It wasn't the work. Martha'd put in lots of harder days than this, though she'd been cleaning and cooking since before dawn—but it was the tense excitement in the air. She'd hardly taken her eyes off Curt the whole blessed afternoon and evening, and she specially watched him every time he came in from outside, after the jug had been passed around. Curt was a man who'd hold his liquor well, under ordinary circumstances, she reckoned; she couldn't recall anyone who'd ever seen him drunk, or even actin' like he'd had a drink. But men under a strain sometimes did some funny things, and in spite of herself she'd heard some of Curt's words to Kitty before the wedding.

"I could kill you, Kitty. I could kill you and Sunset, too—"

Martha had felt obliged to tell Fortune, but Fortune hadn't said anything. In his quiet way he had nodded and he'd been watching Curt, too, but he wasn't one to interfere. Martha had a feeling Sunset was aware, too. Couldn't say she'd ever seen a happier groom than Sunset; his happiness shone out all over him and when he looked at Kitty it was enough to make tears come to any woman's eyes, but Sunset was mighty aware.

And Kitty herself was the most breathlessly beautiful bride anyone could have imagined. Her smile never left her face—not even when she danced a set of figures with Curt and her fingertips touched his. Curt was formally polite to Kitty. He had even kissed the bride—on the cheek. Jeff had kissed her, too, a little more slowly than a married man oughta, maybe, Martha had thought, her bright eyes measuring him, but she didn't know as she could blame him, and even Fortune's leathery cheek had reddened as he bent over the pretty little satin-clad figure. Martha had chuckled at that; she hadn't thought Sparks'd have the nerve! Kitty herself had reached up and pulled Dr. Manning's big head down and smacked him firmly, and the doctor had been delighted. All this kissin' and dancin'—Martha sighed happily. Nothing like a wedding and an infair, she thought.

She came out of her dreams with a jerk. Outside the night was fading, and it was time, certainly, for the guests to be on their way. Too bad it had to end, but after all, Sunset and Kitty—

Briskly Martha got to her feet and began to marshal her forces. She beckoned to Clara and Laura Trainor and Sarah Hansen and Lissa, and they nodded meaningly and spoke to their men. They began bundling children into their wraps and Deaf Wilson, taking the hint, put down his banjo. There was not a scrap of wedding cake left, and from Charlefour's gait, Martha surmised there wasn't a drop left in the whiskey jug, either.

Martha kept an eye on Curt as the guests began reluctantly to depart. She managed to fuss around until they were 'most all gone and Fortune, for once, didn't hurry her. They bid Sunset and Kitty good night and they bundled Dr. Manning into the cart, and Martha wondered, fleetingly, whenever they'd get a proper buggy at Newmarket.

Charlefour was singing loudly; he climbed upon his horse, lurched uncertainly, righted himself miraculously. Martha paid no attention until the words of the song registered suddenly and she turned around with a shocked expression.

"Land's sakes, Curt, shut him up!"

Curt was tightening the cinch on his saddle and did not look up. Fortune followed her glance.

"Charlie," Fortune said, "shut up—or else sing in French." Obligingly Charlie, without missing a note, put the words of his bawdy song in his own language and lumbered off, up the trail. Curt swung into his saddle.

"Good night, Curt," Martha said, hesitatingly. Again he did not reply. He sat upon his horse, his hat on the back of his head, his face hard and drawn and grim in the gray morning light. There was no gaiety, no polite mask on his face now. He held the impatient horse back for an instant and his brooding eyes rested upon Kitty and Sunset in the cottage door, silhouetted by the light behind them.

Martha saw Curt's free hand rubbing slowly on his trouser leg. Then, without a word, he spurred his horse deeply, and the animal leaped and disappeared down the trail toward the cabin he and Sunset had built.

Fortune stood for a minute, deep in thought. Then he handed the reins to Martha.

"Take the kids and Dr. Manning home," he said briefly, "I'll be comin' along."

"You walkin'?"

"I'll borrow Mowich."

He disappeared around the corner of the cottage and Martha clucked to the horse and the cart began to move.

It was full daylight when Fortune got home. He slid into bed beside Martha and sighed softly as he let his big body relax.

"Sparks?" Martha whispered. "Is everything all right?"

"Yes," he answered, also in a whisper.

"Anything happen?"

"No. . . . I trailed him. He rode hard down to the bend and

then he stopped and sat on his horse and looked back at Kitty's cabin. . . . He stayed there, till the lights went out."

"Then he went on home, with no fuss?"

"Well," Fortune said, "yes."

There was no use, he thought, to tell Martha, and he had no words for it anyway, to explain. He couldn't tell her how he'd felt, standing there in the shadows, watching Curt. He'd seen Curt swing down from his horse, and he'd heard the click of his pistol as he'd taken it from his holster and checked it. It was at that moment that the light in Kitty's cabin had gone out. He heard Curt's choked exclamation and Fortune knew that the tortured man in the dusk was fighting a fierce battle with himself; Fortune had felt the sweat coming out all over him. He'd drawn his own gun, noiselessly, had it ready, praying he'd knock the gun from Curt's hand the first shot. And then Curt had suddenly shoved his gun back in his belt and leaped upon his horse. He'd hesitated again, and he'd muttered something and his breath came hard and labored and then he'd ridden on down the trail, following Charlie, whose song wafted back to him through the dying night.

"Reckon if there's no trouble tonight then there won't be none," Martha whispered, after long reflection. "I pity him, Sparks, I sure do. Land alive, is she sot in her ways. . . . Couldn't budge her nohow. And so's Curt. Sunset's sure got sand—never let on, the whole evenin'. . . . Sparks, you think she done right?"

She could hear the rasping sound as Fortune's rough hand stroked his chin.

"She done right," Fortune whispered, after long consideration.

9 THE BREEZE FROM THE SOUND WAS cool, the sun was warm and Kitty walked slowly down the forest path, swinging her bonnet. The Mountain had been visible all day today, and it seemed very near. She raised her eyes to it and smiled and then glanced back at the cabin.

Sunset had planted rhododendron and dogwood about the house and had greatly enlarged the clearing, cutting out underbrush to give her a view clear to the Sound. Behind the house the wheat was a thick carpet, just beginning to turn, and the kitchen garden grew in well-tended rows. A comfortably large pile of house logs lay nearby, ready to enlarge the cabin. The fence was stout and new, the walk flower-bordered. It was a bright and cheery place and Kitty, with a rush of thankfulness, marveled at Sunset's accomplishments.

He never seemed to hurry, she thought, walking slowly, watching for him. He would interrupt his work during the day to take her hunting, or to bring the horses and to insist that she ride with him, toward The Mountain, or down the Sound. Or, in the early evening, he would take her in a canoe, paddling softly along the shore, identifying the little night noises for her. He guarded her carefully, watching her for the first sign of fatigue or worry. He had dedicated his life to her happiness, and Kitty, grateful and comforted, tried always to be lighthearted for him.

The space for the orchard would be cleared by spring, Kitty reflected. Philip's sketch had placed the orchard there, and Sunset had approved it. Sunset had told her of the Lewelling family, Seth, and his brother Henderson, who spelled his name Luelling, and son Alfred, who had brought to Oregon two wagons loaded with eight hundred fruit trees, planted in charcoal and earth. Kitty never tired of that story of astonishing accomplishment. It was hard enough for men to keep themselves and their stock alive in crossing the arid plains; but the Lewellings, experienced orchardists, had managed to save the greater number of their precious trees as well, and soon it would be possible for settlers to buy stock from them. In the spring, Sunset promised her, he would take her to the Lewellings' land claim, at Milwaukie, six miles from Oregon City, where she might view those eight hundred trees and put in her order for the ones she wanted. She could already see them, their blossoms and fruit a riot of color there to the east of the enlarged house. . . . She would have Seek-No-Further and Golden Russet apples and Rambos; and maybe a tree of Winesaps. She'd want Bartlett pears and Winter Nellis, and Martha said she should have a Fall Butter, too. Philip had put a question-mark after peaches; he was not sure they'd do well on the Sound. But she'd have a Black-Heart cherry tree.

It was time for Sunset to be home from Nisqually. Kitty came near to the Sound, shaded her eyes for the sight of his canoe. She could see it, a far-off speck, coming around the point.

Philip's grave was near the path. Recalling it, she walked on, slowly. It must be just about here, she thought, a few feet back from the trail. She searched for it—and then she found that a new trail had been cut, at right angles to the path, and she followed it.

Philip's grave had been cleared; a stout, neat paling surrounded it, and a headboard, carefully carved, marked it.

Kitty was still standing there when Sunset came. She turned her head and raised her cheek for his kiss.

"You were—very good—to do this, Sunset," she said slowly. "I—I thought I wanted to forget. I was going to let the underbrush erase it entirely—"

She choked, turned and hid her face on his chest. He smoothed her shining hair with a big, understanding hand. Kitty felt her resentment, so long harbored against Philip, leaving her at last. Sunset had given Philip new dignity, paid tribute to his contribution, for the headboard said "Philip Davis, author of Davis' Guide For Emigrants." That was the way it should be, she thought, humble and ashamed. To remember the good, forget the bad. It seemed to her that Sunset's whole life was a silent sermon, a gentle leading toward tolerance and forgiveness. He was a preacher who never preached, a man who conquered by love, who created beauty, not for himself, for he found beauty in all things, but for her.

"Here, now, Kitty girl," Sunset said. She raised her head and wiped her eyes.

"You make me ashamed, Sunset," she said frankly. "I've—hated Philip. I blamed him for being weak, for—deserting me, as he did. I don't, not any more. Sunset, the longer I live with you the more I cease to hate and to judge, the more I learn to love—"

She stopped. Something in his face, an intense hunger, a yearning, struck her with a powerful impact, and was, as quickly, veiled. She stood still, appalled, realizing for the first time that in her own selfish problems she had been blind to the aching need of this patient, strong, unselfish man who was her husband. Her attempts at gaiety had not deceived Sunset, and he had not mistaken docility and gratitude for love. Her words had brought to his eyes for a moment a sudden flicker of wild hope, and the revelation was a stunning shock to her. He had hoped she was going to say "—the more I learn to love you."

A shaft of late sunlight shone down the little path, the cleft in the woods that Sunset had made to Philip's grave. It touched Sunset's face, the goodness, the gentleness, the strength of it; a new and strange excitement stirred within Kitty and her pulse began to race. He watched her silently, and she could feel her cheeks grow hot.

"The more I learn—" she said again, and her hands came up to his shoulders.

"Kit-tee! Kit-tee!" Polly's mournful Indian voice wafted down the trail. Kitty and Sunset turned their heads and their cheeks came together for one quick instant and then he released her.

"Here, Polly! What is it?"

"Indian runner come with letter for Sunset from Curt. Said bring it to him very damn quick."

◇ 2 ◇

"WELL, I'm of a mind to think it's true. Curt's not one to go off half-cocked, and he believes it right enough." Sunset referred to the letter, which had been read and re-read a dozen times throughout the evening. "Curt says Samuel Brannan—he's the Mormon editor in San Francisco—doubted it too, and he went out to prove there was nothing to the story. He come back with a bottle full of gold and yelled it all over town and within a coupla days there was only seven men left in San Francisco. Curt says Oregon City's gone crazy. Every man that can walk is figurin' to head for the American River. There's Indian trouble along the trail south, but men will get through, all right."

"I remember Jim Marshall well," Fortune said. "He was a carpenter, from New Jersey. Went down to Sutter's Fort a couple years ago. Quiet sort of fellow. Moody. Ain't heard of him since."

"That's him all right," Sunset said, referring to the letter again. The men in the crowded cabin were quiet and attentive as Sunset read: " 'Marshall went up the American River late last year, about twenty miles from Sutter's, to build a mill. He had to deepen the lower end of the race and they dug and blasted during the day, turned the water in at night. One morning, last January, in the tailrace, about two hundred feet from the mill, he found gold. They tried to keep it quiet but the story got out. The captain of the schooner that came to Oregon City a week ago bought up all the knives, spades, picks, pans and flour he could get his hands on—and it was only when he was ready to sail that he held up a sack of gold dust, and told us the hills of California were made of it. We tested the dust. It's gold, all right. The soldiers in California are deserting, heading for the gold fields, and they're afraid to send men after them for fear they won't come back, either.' "

"Fightin's all over down there?" Deaf Wilson asked cautiously.

"Yup. California belongs to the United States and Yerba Buena is named San Francisco."

Deaf spat a stream of tobacco juice into the fireplace.

"Here comes Hansen and Trainor," Sparks said. "Guess they just heard about it. Howdy, men."

Sunset arose to greet his new guests. Again Curt's letter was read, and the talk went on. Kitty, sitting quietly in the shadows, waited, listening. Almost from the moment the Indian runner had put the message in Sunset's hands, the neighbors had begun to gather. The rumor of the discovery of gold in California had swept into Oregon, spread swiftly, and the Newmarket men came to Sunset to confirm it, to hear the letter from Fletcher from

Oregon City. Kitty watched the faces in the firelight, thoughtful faces, with excitement in their eyes, and she could not suppress a smile. They made a great show of doubting and considering the news; of being logical and composed about it. They weren't going to be stampeded. . . . But no man hardy and adventurous enough to head west for free land was going to sit by and pass up an opportunity to make a quick fortune in California gold. By morning, Kitty knew, these men would be on the trail south. Nothing could stop them.

"You reckon it's safe enough here, now, Sunset, for the women and kids?"

The men waited hopefully for Sunset's reply.

"Yes, I think it is. The Volunteers trounced the Indians good, and they won't start trouble again right away. They've promised to bring in the murderers of the Whitmans if the Volunteers'd lay off. Curt says they left a garrison at Waillatpu and they're havin' parleys, but won't talk peace till they get the murderers. But the fightin's stopped, temporarily, and the immigrants are comin' through without much trouble. Mind you, I don't say the Indian war's over; Indian trouble is like a forest fire. You think you got it out—and it starts up again, some place else. But Curt says the word is that Joe Meek got to Washington and went straight to the White House and talked to the President. He musta bummed his way because he was stone broke when I left him at Independence. Anyway, Congress is still arguin' and fili-busterin' over Oregon and slavery, but it does look like we'll have a territorial government here any day, with Indian agents and an Army, too. When Uncle Sam takes over it ought to be safe enough. Meantime, they'll stop fightin' until they bring in Toma-has and Tiloukaikt and their helpers."

There was a silence. Finally Sparks spoke guardedly. "You figure to go, Sunset?"

Sunset stood and hitched up his belt. He glanced at Kitty and she smiled, knowing his answer, and Sunset grinned. He was the first to commit himself.

"Reckon I'll have a try at it, Fortune," he said, trying to keep his voice casual. "Curt's waitin' for me in Oregon City, and he's strainin' at the bit. He's got tools and horses. He says some figure to take wagons. Pete Burnett is figurin' on takin' a lot of wagons, with planks for gold rockers. But I think Curt and me and

Charlie'll travel fast and light. I don't aim to be gone too long. . . . Soon's this word reaches the States there'll be the biggest rush west you ever *did* see. Every Tom, Dick and Harry will be headin' for the gold fields. We Oregon men have a head start."

Fortune's deep-set eyes were sparkling. "Reckon I could be gone a few weeks, 'thout puttin' the work back too much," he drawled, "though it's nigh harvest." He stood. "Guess I'd better be goin' —got a few things to do, 'fore mornin'."

"How much you figure a man could make, Sunset? I never did any minin'," Trainor asked.

"Your guess is as good as mine, Trainor. Figure an ounce of gold dust is worth $14—$16, well, I think a man ought to make good wages, if he has any luck at all, and is willin' to work."

"And if he found a pocket of the stuff, with a big nugget or two, say ten or twenty ounces all at once—"

"Ounces, man? Hell, I heard there was pounds of it—big chunks!"

The voices came fast now, excitement no longer concealed. Charlefour rolled into the room, dropped a pack on the floor.

"When you ready, Sunset?"

"Soon's I get my blankets," he said. Again his eyes turned toward Kitty.

"They're already packed, Sunset," she said.

◇ 3 ◇

Kitty rode with Sunset as far as the Sparks'. Fortune would join him and Charlefour there, and Kitty surmised that Martha might not be reconciled to her husband's sudden departure. She was not mistaken.

"Wild goose chase, that's what it is," Martha grumbled. "We'll go west, Martha, Sparks says, we'll go to Oregon, take up some free land, and be independent. Gets us all settled here, then he takes off for Californy, figures to find gold and get rich quick. He'll lose a season's work, and we'll be just that much farther behind, that's what'll happen. Ain't enough for him to bury us out here in the wilderness—then he has to desert us, go off to Californy. Who's to cut the wheat, Kitty? Who's to lay in the potatoes for winter? They'll be right good and glad to get back, I'm thinkin'—*if* they come back. Never growed up, that's all. Reason, now, I can understand. He's been bawlin' all night cause Sparks won't take him gold-huntin'. But grown men! Oughta have more sense. I never figured Sparks to be a flighty one, but you might as well talk to a stone wall. He's sure got gold fever bad. Never figured I'd be a half-widow!"

Trainor and Hansen rode into the dooryard and Martha's gloomy face brightened. "There now, I bet Laura and Sarah carried on something handsome this mornin'," she said, with satisfaction. "Bet they're cryin' still. Laura's scared to death to stay alone anyhow. Kitty, looks like there won't be a man left in Newmarket. Maybe not in Oregon. They've all gone plumb crazy, that's what."

"Kitty?"

Sunset took her hands. She managed a smile. "Kitty, sugar," he said, very softly, watching her face, "this is our chance. We'll get Wildcliffe for you—sooner'n we figured. I'll come home with so much gold—you can dress in cloth made of it, if you want to. But it won't make you any prettier."

"You make it sound true, Sunset." The dimple appeared in her cheek. "You work magic. I think you will make it true!"

"Things that are right just naturally come about, Kitty. It's right that I'll find gold. It's right that you'll have everything you need to make you happy. I promised you, didn't I?"

She nodded. Laughter and whimsy and strength and simple faith—Sunset was such a mixture of them, she thought. He did the most incredible things, like going with Meek all the way to the Missouri, returning safely with the immigrants; like coming to her when she needed him most, when she had prayed for help; like finding the Lost Company. Like giving her this new understanding, a new warmth in her heart, a freedom from hate and bitterness and fear. Despite the people about them, Sunset took his wife for one long moment in his arms. He held her so carefully always, as though she were something so fragile, so precious; he made the word "cherish" a tangible and wonderful thing. Kitty's arms went about him tight and he bent his lips to hers.

"My girl," he whispered, and his eyes were shining with the warmth of her kiss, "my girl. It won't be long, Kitty. Keep happy. Promise me, you'll keep happy?"

She nodded, dumbly. At the bend in the trail he stopped and waved to her again. *When he comes back,* she thought, *when he comes back, I'm sure I'll be able to tell him I love him. When he comes back, I'll tell him.*

◈ 4 ◈

KITTY lowered the heavy ox yoke to the ground and wiped her dripping forehead on her sleeve. She glared at the quiet, unsuspecting oxen, and then, balefully, at Martha. Martha sat on a stump, her knees far apart, her hands planted on her hips, a picture of disgust and exasperation.

"They're supposed to come under when you say 'Come under!'" Kitty said furiously, "and they just stand there, the stupid, old—"

Martha removed her bonnet, wiped her face and clapped it back on her head.

"Pa always said a good man oughta be able to yoke and hitch four teams in twenty minutes," Wealthy contributed brightly in her high treble. Kitty and Martha frowned at her and she subsided.

"I wish Reason'd come home from Trainors'. He could help," Kitty said hopefully. "I never paid much attention when Charlie yoked them. He just did it so easy." She labored again to get the heavy yoke to her shoulder, her pretty face creased with worry and earnestness. "He always laid it across his shoulder, like this," she panted, "and he carried one pin in his mouth and the other in his hand—hand me that pin, Wealthy." She clamped the pin in her little white teeth and edged toward the ox.

"Come under!" Martha shouted. For answer the animal moved away a step or two and the full weight of the yoke slid back on Kitty. She dropped the pin from her teeth and yelled at Martha and the beasts.

"Judas Priest!"

"Kitty, that's small swearin'." Martha pursed her lips primly.

"I don't care if it's real swearing," Kitty fumed. "Martha, if we don't get these beasts yoked we can't get that grain to the mill, and you'll eat boiled wheat all winter. And I don't aim to eat boiled wheat, not after what I've gone through to get that grain cut and threshed. You think I stood on that stump and fanned that wheat with a sheet, and then am going to eat it boiled? My arms nearly fell off!"

Wealthy tripped around the team, came back to stand before Kitty with wide eyes. "Kitty, when you said that—what you just said, what Ma said was small swearing—they moved. . . . I think you got the off ox on the wrong side."

"Does it make any difference which side they're on? Do you mean those stupid beasts know the difference?"

Martha chewed her lip thoughtfully and shot a guilty look at Kitty.

"Kitty, I think I know what's the matter. Those animals aren't so stupid. They know a few things. Charlie—well, I don't reckon he talked to them polite like you do. When he said 'Come under,' did he say it that way?"

A great light broke over Kitty's worried face. She wiped her moist hands on her dusty skirts and reached for the yoke again.

"Martha," she announced firmly, "if you don't like small swearing, you better cover your ears. Wealthy—"

She motioned the child to her mother and Martha put Wealthy's head in her lap and covered her head with her apron. Martha looked desperately at Kitty and then she put her fingers in her ears. "Go ahead," she said, bravely.

Kitty's lips moved, and, Martha thought, she actually seemed to relish the words that had rolled so easily from Charlefour's lips. Martha uncovered one ear experimentally, winced, and covered it again.

"Come under you—" Kitty ordered, and in Charlefour's manner she commented upon the oxen's ancestry and affectionately consigned them to warmer climates. Immediately, obediently, the big, patient animals moved, and, triumphantly, Kitty got the yoke across the neck of the off ox and managed to maneuver the bow beneath his neck. Martha's eyes widened and she jumped up, spilling Wealthy, to insert the pin.

"Come under you—" Kitty demanded happily of the near ox, and the beast moved obediently.

With a triumphant flourish, Kitty cracked the whip, and the cart began to move, down the trail toward the mill.

"Times like this, I appreciate Sparks," Martha conceded, after a while. "I reckon I'll be that glad to see him I won't care a pickle if he's saw the elephant or not."

Kitty stumbled over a projecting root and smothered an exclamation. Martha looked at her anxiously. "Swearin' to get the oxen started was one thing, Kitty," she said sternly. "Then, I reckon the end justified the means. But you aren't going to get the habit, now, Kitty?"

"Of swearing?" Kitty laughed. "No, Martha. I promise. But I do get so furious—these everlasting trees, the underbrush, the roots and stumps, seems like it grows faster than you can cut it."

Martha nodded. "Yes," she said, thoughtfully, "but I never complain about the trees, Kitty. I'd feel guilty. Thinkin' of the Plains—sand and prickly pears and prairie dogs—and not a tree, nary a one, for miles and miles and miles. Couldn't fix an axle or a wagon-tongue, no wood to do it with. When we got here to the Sound, I used to sometimes just put my arms around these big old trees, I was that fond of them. No, sir, I'd rather live in timber country than any place else on earth."

Kitty trudged on, only partially convinced. "Martha, I've been thinking. We don't know how the men are getting along, and likely we won't hear till they come home, and heavens knows when that'll be. But I'm not going to waste this winter. I can't do this kind of work—and neither can you. It's taken us a half a day to yoke these oxen. It'll be dark night before we get home from the mill, and then with only a teeny bit of flour."

"What you aim to do, Kitty?" Martha asked cautiously.

"I've some money put by. I'm going around and buy all the wheat I can get, and I'm going to store it in that warehouse at Portland where we used to keep the furniture. They say there are ships coming into The River every day after produce. It's going to be scarcer and scarcer, with all the men gone, and the crops short, and no matter what I have to pay for it now it'll be worth more before spring."

"We-ll," Martha demurred.

"And another thing. The master of the ship in the Sound wants lumber. Says they need it badly in San Francisco. I'm going to try to hire a man today to take my house logs to the mill."

"Your house logs, Kitty!"

"Sunset will cut me more when he comes home. I can wait.

We'll never again get a price for lumber like we can get now."

Martha's eyes began to sparkle and she chuckled. "Kitty, like as not we'll do better right here to home than the men will in the diggin's!"

"It could be," Kitty agreed. She felt light and happy as she walked, and Martha, watching her, thought she had never seen a woman so governed by her emotions. When Kitty was light-hearted she was never weary. She was like quicksilver, Martha thought fondly. There was nothing stolid about her. She was stimulating to be with and she was always "thinking up" something. Things happened when Kitty was around, and Martha liked to have things happening.

"Wealthy, how many chickens do you have now?"

"Twenty-two hens and two cocks."

"They'll lay in the spring if you feed them right. I'll bet you can sell those eggs for a pile of money."

"To take them all the way to San Francisco?"

Kitty nodded firmly. "Pack them in sawdust, from the mill. I wouldn't be surprised if you could get a half a dollar apiece for them."

"A half a dollar apiece!"

"She never had a half a dollar all her own in her life," Martha laughed.

"She will," Kitty said confidently, "and so," she continued, "I think I'll go to Oregon City. Sunset promised me some fruit trees in the spring, though they'll probably be very dear. If he comes home by then, we can bring them back with us—"

Martha smiled and her kind eyes were gentle as she regarded Kitty's flushed and eager face.

"Couldn't be you want to be in Oregon City so you'll see him just that much quicker, could it?" she teased, and then she bit her tongue and wished she could have taken back the words. The light left Kitty's face, left her troubled, quiet.

I'd swore, Martha said to herself, *when she told Sunset good-by she'd never give another thought to Curt. But maybe she never will get over him. Martha,* she added fiercely, silently, *you got less sense than that off ox. At least he keeps his tongue quiet.*

◆ 5 ◆

CALIFORNIA gold poured into Oregon in a beautiful, stimulating yellow stream, a trickle at first, as the shipmasters carefully measured the shining dust and left it in payment for lumber and wheat, and then in greater and greater amounts as the 48'ers began to return home. Kitty could hardly believe her eyes when she saw twenty or more ships in The River, waiting at Portland for cargoes, and when she saw that Oregon City was now a feverishly busy and prospering town of women and children.

If most of the men were in the gold fields, digging out fortunes with picks and shovels, or sometimes with knives alone, their wives in Oregon were also reaping a golden harvest. Kitty was not the only resourceful woman to see the opportunity, and in many a case the earnings of the women at home would make up for the failure of an ill-fated Argonaut.

Clara's talents did not run to trading. But she had made a deal with the mate of a schooner, making periodic trips to Oregon, to do laundry for San Francisco men. Some shipmasters were taking dirty clothes to Hawaii for laundering, she explained to Kitty, and Oregon City was no farther. Clara was up to her elbows in soapsuds from morning till night, but her earnings were substantial; men thought nothing of paying an ounce of gold dust for even the slightest service, and very carefully Clara examined the bottoms of her tubs for any sign of the magic yellow metal which might have clung to pockets and seams.

Women and children kept the business establishments going, but the legislature had adjourned for want of a quorum. Judge Peter Burnett had declared court adjourned, also, while he went off to the gold fields. The *Spectator* was suspended because of lack of printers. One hundred and fifty of the Hudson's Bay men remaining at Fort Vancouver deserted and headed south. Already headquarters of the Company had been shifted to Vancouver Island. The gold rush completed the abandonment of the post by the British.

Jeff had gone with Burnett's party, a group of fifty wagons and a regiment of a hundred and fifty Oregon men. They took provisions with them for six months, Clara said. Tommy Dundee, all his worldly possessions on his back and in his saddle bags, rode off with Jimmy Correll, after promising half the girls of Oregon City that he would bring back to them nuggets as big as hen's eggs. Pettygrove, it was said, sold the townsite of Portland for a pile of leather and joined the rush.

From all that Kitty could learn, Curt and Sunset and their party were among the first and were believed to have headed for Sacramento City, that tent town that had sprung up at the junction of the American and Sacramento Rivers. From there the men followed the Sacramento, the American or Feather River to the "diggings." Kitty traveled with the men in her mind, up the Willamette, through the valleys of the Umpqua and Rogue River, over the Siskiyous and down the Sacramento, an ever-widening trail. The Indians, led by Cutface Jack of Rogue River, swarmed along that trail to California now, harassing the gold seekers; but, fearing reprisals, they stayed away from the depleted settlements.

Kitty bought wheat, had it ground and barreled at a cost of seven dollars a barrel. In a month it was worth nine dollars, in two months, twelve. She sold it finally at a profit of six thousand dollars on eight hundred barrels. She opened a provision store at Portland, the shingle-camp that had become a boom-town almost overnight, and as she weighed out gold dust, handling it like bran, she asked constantly for news of Sunset and Curt.

It was March before she heard. She was packing the day's receipts in a pickle jar when John Homet appeared.

"Great news, Kitty!" he sang out. Kitty laughed softly. All news in Oregon was great these days. Everyone talked in superlatives. The wildest dreams were being fulfilled. Nothing was impossible. And to Oregon people, who had never been short on dreams, the sudden change in fortunes was no great surprise. Six months ago they had been in great poverty and greater peril; and now, as though Nature was making up for her hard treatment of them, she was pouring into Oregon wealth that would have taken generations, perhaps centuries, to develop by any other means. It was a miracle, Kitty thought, sometimes, as she watched the settlements boom, under the magic touch of gold—and it could happen only in the fantastic, roaring West.

"John," she said practically, reaching for another pickle jar, "I wish there was a better way of handling gold dust. Every time I measure it I lose a bit."

"Haven't you heard? We've got the mint operating at Oregon City. Some of us have formed the Oregon Exchange Company. We got Mr. Rector to make some dies for five- and ten-dollar pieces, out of some wagon rims, and a blacksmith to turn them out. Nice design, too, a minister did the engraving, and he's pretty good at it. It's got a beaver on one side, and the initials T.O. for Territory of Oregon, on the other. Easier to handle. Wait, I got some here. I'll trade you now, take the dust back with me."

Kitty was pleased. "That's a comfort. I've got dust in coffee pots and pickle jars and sacks and—" She poured the beaver money from one hand to the other, admiring its color and weight. John cached the jar of dust in a commodious pocket.

"But that's not all! The ship is in—the *Janet*. She came over the bar forty-eight hours ago, and is coming fast up The River. The news is that Joe Meek's aboard, and the new governor! Oregon's got a territorial government at last, Kitty!"

Kitty spilled the money on the counter before her. "The *Janet* —Captain Dring, from San Francisco?"

"Yes. Meek and the new Governor, Joseph Lane, came west by the Santa Fe trail, it being near winter when they started. Then up the coast to San Francisco. Kitty, there's a hundred Oregon men on that ship. They was waiting in San Francisco for passage home, and finally they got together and chartered the *Janet* for ten thousand dollars. They are loaded with gold! Story is not a one of them has got less than ten thousand, and them only worked for six weeks. Some of them got as much as forty or fifty thousand."

Kitty grabbed his sleeve as he turned to go. "John, is Sunset with them? Have you heard?"

John slapped his thigh. "Kitty, I plumb forgot. That's what I come to tell you. I'm that excited— No, he isn't aboard. Dundee is, though, and you'd ought to see him—messenger said he was decked out in silver trappings like a Spanish don. He said he left Sunset and Curt near Placerville, and Sunset was minin' more gold than any other three men in California. Tommy said it's the gol-dangest thing—

"Sunset'll be home on the next ship. Due any day."

◈ 6 ◈

OF ALL the beautiful homes that had risen in Oregon City, Kitty believed that Rose Farm, the home of William Livingston Holmes and his wife, Louisa, was the loveliest. It was a two-story house with a wide fireplace at each end, and a long, pillared porch with a balcony above. It was sturdily built, of handsawed and hand-hewn fir, put together with wooden pins and mortised joints and set on stones, and lapped, narrow weatherboard finished the out-side. Kitty loved to go there, for it proved that more than a plain log cabin could await immigrants at the end of the Oregon Trail; and it demonstrated well how a cultured woman could bring grace and beauty to the West, combine it with Oregon's natural gifts, and make a home of charm and permanence and dignity.

Rose Farm had chairs with laced rawhide seats—particularly of Oregon origin; and it had Chinese matting on the floors, re-minding visitors of the nearness of the Oregon Coast to the Orient. But it likewise boasted a walnut sewing-machine which had come around the Horn, and in the parlor was a square piano. In many ways, Rose Farm, which took its name from a great garden of roses that stemmed from bushes in France, reminded Kitty of Wildcliffe, with its comfort and sturdy beauty and open-hearted hospitality.

It was quite natural that Rose Farm should be selected as the setting for the inaugural ball for Governor Joseph Lane. Kitty had been pleased to be invited to the Holmes' house early in the day to help with the preparations for the festivities. She had carried her ball gown in a big package tied behind her saddle and her dancing slippers in a small bag hung from the pommel. A barbecue would precede the ball, and a dozen happy women had worked all day in preparation. By evening a quantity of fresh butter had been lowered into the well, cakes and pies and cookies covered the tables in the big kitchen, and outside the roasting meat had begun to give off wonderful odors.

But of all things Kitty loved most about Rose Farm, she was fondest of the big sit-in bathtub of tin. She luxuriated in it now, taking her time relaxing in the soft warm water. A half-dozen other excited and laughing girls were waiting their turns at this rare luxury, but Kitty was quite sure that none of them would enjoy it more than she. She had twisted her gleaming hair high on her head, and now she soaped the back of her neck and her smooth shoulders and slim arms and sighed deeply in pure contentment.

It had been just a week since the *Janet* arrived, and Oregon City was still delirious with excitement and happiness. The old colonial days and the rule of the Provisional Government, were over, and with Governor Lane's proclamation the Oregon Country had become a full-fledged Territory of the United States, the first step towards statehood itself.

Any day another ship would come—bringing Sunset. Tommy had sworn solemnly that Sunset was taking a king's ransom out of the hills of California.

"You're a rich woman, Kitty Lee," Tommy had assured her, and Kitty had dimpled, wondering how much to discount Tommy's tales. But Tommy himself had brought back great wealth, so Kitty's hopes were high. It would mean so much to Sunset, she thought, to succeed for her. She doubted that he cared a fig for wealth, for himself.

She was glad, too, that Curt was successful, though she could not imagine him otherwise. She was happiest, however, that the two men were companions again, on this, the greatest of all their adventures. But she would not think of Curt. She was a married woman now, and thoughts of another man were unseemly and wicked. She refused to examine her heart, to measure what part of her tense expectancy came from the knowledge that when Sunset came, Curt would likely come, too.

And Charlefour, loyal, happy-go-lucky Charlie had found gold, too. He had incredible luck at cards, Tommy said, so he spent more time in card-playing than in mining. His companions were not of the best—Bull Le Seuer and Lige Read were in the same camp, and the camp itself was a riproaring spot, to hear Tommy tell it.

Kitty turned in the tub, letting the silky water stream from her shoulders, and she stood reluctantly and reached for a towel. How wonderful it would be if only Sunset were here tonight—and Curt. If she could look up and see them approaching her in a cotillion or reel, as she had on that long-ago Fourth of July at Oregon City.

What a shock, and what a delicious, wonderful feeling it had been! But—Lisa had been waiting for Curt that night, just outside the hall. The old anger simmered in her brown eyes and the muscle on her jaw knotted. Perhaps Lisa was waiting for him tonight, too, in a tent somewhere in that mining camp. She had traveled with her father, Tommy said, in a careful aside. Women like Lisa were flocking to the mining camps and tent towns—

Kitty began to dress. The dress had been brought from Wildcliffe—my goodness, she thought—it's four years old! But it showed no wear. There had been few occasions for a formal ball gown these past years in Oregon. She regarded it thoughtfully; she had worn it last at Fort Vancouver, the night she had met Sunset. Dr. McLoughlin had ruled there then; now the Fort was to be a United States Army post. That night, she recalled, she had thought the British so mighty, the Oregon men so ill-prepared, the survivors of the Lost Company so wretched. Today some of them, like Tommy, were men of wealth.

From the garden came the gay and longing notes of a fiddle. Her foot began to tap. Each year the immigrants brought lilting new songs, and this year it was *Oh, Susannah!* the greatest favorite of all.

She coiled her hair, fastened it carefully. What a welcome they had given Joe Meek and the new Governor! Joe had plenty of stories to tell and he told them well. She could imagine the amazement of the people in the national capital when Joe, dressed in his buckskin and furs, marched into the Willard Hotel and registered as plenipotentiary from the Oregon Country to the White House. Joe's description of the clerk's reaction was hilariously funny. Lots of folks took him for an Indian, Joe said, and let him travel on public conveyances free. How the Oregon men had roared at that!

Joe had gone to the White House and asked to see the President. His audacity caused a great stir—but it would have surprised the people of Oregon if Joe had taken any less direct measures. He had succeeded. He'd been received by both the President and Mrs. Polk, and the President had listened to him with great courtesy and interest. Joe had become the sensation of the capital, and he had been wined and dined to his heart's content. He was United States Marshal now, and he wore his new badge proudly. The President had presented it to him personally.

Meek couldn't get over the fact that when he'd arrived in San Francisco with the new Oregon Governor, that Oregon men, many of whom had been very nearly starving to death when Joe left, or had been fighting the Cayuses, now wore fortunes in gold dust strapped around their waists. Aboard the *Janet*, too, had come a messenger from Sutter himself. To Dr. McLoughlin's amazement he brought gold to settle an old debt; McLoughlin had loaned supplies to Sutter long ago, and had given up the idea of ever being repaid. But now, not only Sutter, but many an Oregon settler whom the old Canadian had trusted, paid his debts.

There was gold dust in tea canisters, in milk pans, in sacks, in kettles, on the shelves and under the beds in a great many cabins in Oregon since the *Janet* came in. One would have to see it to believe it, Kitty thought. Doubtless Easterners considered all the stories of the gold discovery fantastic tall tales; you could hardly blame them, for there'd been nothing like it before in history. Judge Stuart, clucking over her most recent letter, likely branded her a colossal story-teller, Kitty thought, sighing happily. That wealth would be poured back into Oregon industry and farms and homes, and there would be more lovely places like Rose Farm, more tin bathtubs, more square pianos and fine pieces of Linton furniture. Jeff had returned with a substantial sum, and with Clara's earnings he could establish himself now as a real manufacturer.

Of course some gold-seekers had failed miserably. Some had died on the way. But for the most part the 48'ers, already hardened frontiersmen, had profited in the gold fields beyond their dreams. Outside of California itself, it seemed the Oregon Territory was to profit most by Jim Marshall's discovery.

The music called her. She hurried down the stairs, humming the words to the tune *Oh Charlie Is My Darling*. A group of men stood in the hallway and conversation stopped as she approached. Kitty had that special look that beautiful women have when they know they are looking their best. Her fingers danced lightly along the stair rail and the crisp mauve silk of her skirts rustled richly.

The men watched her—but there was something wrong with their smiles. Her glance went questioningly around the familiar faces. What a pity something should dampen their spirits today, she thought, disappointed. They ought to be so happy tonight, at the inauguration, the justification of all the stubborn years they had held Oregon, waiting for government recognition. But even Tommy Dundee was quiet. She tipped her head to peek up at Dr. Manning and her dimples twinkled. That gesture, pure flirtation, delightful and daring and sweet, always brought a smile from the old man and it brought a shaky smile now.

"Kitty," he said, "little Kitty Lee—"

She stared at him, deeply concerned, for he was greatly agitated.

"Kitty—there's someone waiting to see you. In the parlor." Dundee spoke hastily, awkwardly, motioning to the closed parlor door.

Puzzled and apprehensive she went toward the parlor, and as she opened the door she heard Dundee speak behind her: "We'd better find Clara. She'll need someone—"

The door closed behind her, shutting out the little group of men in the hallway.

Curt was standing at the window, looking out on the crowded garden. He turned as she entered. He was not dressed for an inaugural ball. His black shirt was old and stained, his boots scuffed and worn, his buckskin trousers ragged. His face was bone-thin and he looked older, much older than when she had seen him last.

"Curt!" She glanced swiftly around the room. "But where is Sunset? Isn't he with you? Didn't he come?" She hurried toward him, hands outstretched, imploring, and Curt watched her silently. Her words hung in midair, and she paused in front of him, bewildered, frightened by the look on his face.

"Where is he?" she demanded.

"He's—not coming," Curt said. His voice was heavy, without expression.

"Not—coming?" She wanted to grasp Curt's shirt front, to shake an explanation from him, but she knew that would be futile. She clutched the whispering silk of her skirts with frantic fingers and waited. Curt looked down at her, the delicate brows, the wide, innocent eyes, the full parted lips, the magnificent gown, missing no detail of her breathtaking loveliness. His eyes were brooding, his mouth twisted in bitterness and grief.

"No, he's not coming," he repeated again, "but I brought his gold. He mined it for you. He worked waist-deep in icy water for days and days on end, long after the rest of us would quit, digging and washing and hunting, for gold—for you. He worked like one of your own slaves. He said he was going to get Wild-cliffe back for you—that he'd promised you. Well, you have your gold, Kitty. A lot of it. It's at the Linton cabin, sacks of it. Charlefour is guarding it for you. Take it, Kitty, and get out. Get out of Oregon. Go back to Wildcliffe, where you belong. I wish to God you'd never left the place."

The deadly monotone of his voice was low, not reaching beyond the room in which they stood, and each word jarred Kitty like a blow from his heavy fist. He spoke with only the slightest move-ment of his lips, slowly, deliberately, and meaning every word of it. Her face blanched, but her voice was as low and clear as his own.

"Where is Sunset?"

Curt let her have the truth in two short merciless words.

"He's dead."

Kitty recoiled. "No," she said, in the same even voice, "no. You're just saying that, to hurt me. He isn't."

"He's dead," Curt repeated, brutally. "Bull Le Seuer fired the shot. But it was we who killed him. You, Kitty. And I."

◈ 7 ◈

CHARLEFOUR sat with his great head drooping, his big, loose lips working; now and then he raised his handkerchief to wipe his one eye and his huge hand was shaking. His shoulders were humped as though he had carried too heavy a load too long.

He tried to face Kitty but he could not. She sat in Clara's rocker, her fingers laced tightly together, her eyes, enormous and stricken and tearless, on Charlefour. Charlie shot a quick look at her and then dropped his chin to his chest; he stared, unseeing, at the sacks of gold at his feet, and finally he began to talk, telling his story in his own way, miserably reliving it, sparing neither Kitty nor himself.

"We fix a shack, part tent, part wood. Bull Le Seuer, Lige Read, Lusty Weaver, Asa Hardin an' me, we play cards an' drink some." Charlie stopped, corrected himself honestly. "Drink much. We—we all pretty drunk.

"It near midnight. Someone ask if Curt and Sunset come to camp yet. They have tent near. Asa look out and say there light in tent. Read say Sunset sure work dam' hard. Read sit by Bull. All time they stay together."

Charlie swallowed and his big lips twisted. "I take jus' one more drink—"

He dropped his head in his hands and waited a minute before he could continue. Kitty neither moved nor spoke. Charlefour swabbed his face again and took a deep, noisy breath.

"It my fault, Kitty," he burst out. "I so drunk—" His great shoulders began to shake and he continued brokenly, "I sit against wall and Read and Bull at table. Bull laughs about Sunset works so hard. He say only fool kill himself for woman."

Kitty's eyes closed, her lashes sweeping her pale cheeks, and her hands tightened until the knuckles were white.

"They talk and get meaner and dirtier. Then Bull talk about Lisa and Curt. Bull's ver' proud of Lisa. He brag. He say—he say Sunset work for his beaut'ful wife—but you not pretty as his Lisa. Read say different. They argue and Bull say he prove it. He say Curt not give Lisa up for you. He say Lisa keep Curt away from you.

"Then—Read say he not sure. He laugh and he say Sunset better not take you walk by Witch's Face—"

Kitty's hands flew to the arms of the rocker and gripped them and she half rose. Charlie turned toward her at the motion, but he could not look at her. With his foot he shoved one of the sacks a few inches from him.

"I look up and I see Sunset stand in door."

Kitty sank back in the chair and covered her eyes with her hand. The Witch's Face at Wishram—Polly had told her about it a long time ago. Young Indians paraded their sweethearts and their wives before the Witch's Face, to test their faithfulness. The Eyes, Polly had said, would follow an unfaithful woman—

"I never see Sunset like that before. He look at Read and Bull like they rattlesnakes. They scared. Sunset walk into tent, slow. He awful tired, Kitty. Sometime he not sleep. He not move quick.

"He keep walking toward Read and Bull. They say nothin'. Sunset wear moccasins, he walk like panther. He not have gun, Kitty. He clench his hands like this—and he walk to Read—

"Oh, God, Kitty—"

Sobs shook Charlefour, long, gasping sobs. Kitty set her teeth till the cords on her neck hardened and stood out. Still she did not speak.

"If I not drunk—" Charlie said brokenly, sick with grief and self-condemnation—"I see Bull is scared. He push back from table, and his hands drop like he reach for his guns. Read stand up. Sunset do not watch Bull—but I, Charlie, watch him. Bull stand, and I shoot.

"I had time to shoot once. I aim at Bull's right arm. Crazy dam' drunk fool I am, Kitty! Same time he raise his gun—

"If I not drunk I remember. Ever'body know Bull shoot left-hand'. His right hand no good. He shoot almos' when I do. If he shoot right-hand', Kitty, I get him. I hit his right arm. But he shoot wit' his left hand ever since that—ever since Lisa knife him."

Sobs choked Charlie again and for a long time there was no other sound in the cabin.

"Sunset fall. He not suffer, Kitty. He jus' drop. I not move at first. Bull and Read run out door. Bull's arm bleed bad. Sunset look at me—surprise'. And then he sigh. Like he awful tired. Bullet hit him in heart, Kitty. He not struggle. Just sigh. And go to sleep.

"The shot wakes whole camp. Curt come in. He raise Sunset and try to make him talk. Curt ask me questions till he know whole story." Charlefour's hand went gingerly to his throat at the memory of Curt's questioning.

"We—we bury Sunset nex' day. Curt read over him. Nobody go near Curt. He awful mad. After buryin', men start form posse, go after Read and Bull. Curt tells them no. He tell them give him two days, and if he not come back then they send posse. He not let me go with him, Kitty. He tell me I drunk bum. He look at his guns and he leave.

"He come back second day. He not talk to me. He get his things and gold and we start for San Francisco. Ship *Janet* already sail and we jus' wait for ship.

"Asa Hardin come to town before we sail. He say after we leave camp they go follow Curt's trail. Curt got both Bull and Read and he leave them where he shoot them like rats. Asa say it mus' be hell of a battle. But Curt get them."

Charlefour, suffering, appealing, turned to look at Kitty. "It my fault, Kitty," he repeated. "I should save him. Curt hate me.

You hate me. I—I wish it was me, not Sunset. I no damned good, Kitty, and Sunset—Sunset, he good man—"

A little sigh came from Kitty's pale lips. Wearily she stood and smoothed down her bodice with slow hands. She came to Charlie and put her hand on his big shoulder.

"It's done, Charlie," she said heavily. "He's gone. . . . Blaming yourself won't bring him back. He wouldn't want you to blame yourself, Charlie. You tried. . . . It—it's hard to say who or what is to blame. I don't know. I don't know."

Charlie grasped the small white hand. "You—you not hate me, Kitty?" he pleaded. She shook her head and the candlelight seemed caught in her hair.

"No, I don't hate you, Charlie. It's—it's surprising, but—I don't hate anyone." She stared into space a moment, a puzzled look on her ashen face, her soft lips working slightly. "I feel—no hate," she repeated, wonderingly. "Only pity. Pity—for all of us, who are left without him."

There was the sound of many voices outside the door and Kitty moved back to the fireplace. She was standing there, dry-eyed, composed, when the group entered.

Clara, her face wet with tears, came to stand close beside her, and she held Kitty's hand tightly as the others filed by. One by one they came to Kitty, to speak a few words, or only to take her hand. Mary Mawson, unable to speak, bent to kiss her cheek.

Tommy Dundee's dark Irish face was twisted with grief. "Kitty," he said, "we'd never of made it into Oregon—the Lost Company—without Sunset. He was—he was—" He wiped his eyes with his hand, ducked his head, and moved on. A slim, blue-eyed girl slipped up to Kitty, and it was only after she had disappeared that Kitty recognized her, the little survivor of the Whitman massacre who had been her patient.

And still they came, old and young, to pay their respects to Sunset. Kitty did not know the time, she was not conscious of weariness. She was conscious only of the great number of friends that Sunset had made, and the true depth of their grief. To each one, Sunset's passing was a personal bereavement.

But when a man with snowy white hair, so tall he had to stoop to enter the doorway, came to her and took her hands, her self-control was shaken.

"Dr. McLoughlin," she said softly, "it was very kind of you to come." The sharp old eyes searched her face keenly, and then he stepped aside to make way for Joe Meek.

"I only wish I could have officiated at the hanging of Bull and Read," he said, tightly. "Sunset was one of the best friends I ever had—one of Oregon's best friends."

Thomas Manning put both his hands on Kitty's shoulders and looked into her face. Kitty met his eyes squarely, and now her own were swimming with tears, appealing and soft with terrible pain and deep gratitude to Sunset's friends who had come to pay tribute to him.

"He left his mark on everyone who was fortunate enough to know him, Kitty," Thomas said, "and on you—most of all."

◈ 8 ◈

Hours later, Kitty lay in the darkness alone. Her pillow was wet and she was spent and weak. From the larger room came the sound of lowered voices.

"I'll miss her so," Clara said, her voice husky with tears. "Mary, you know when Kitty came, it was the changing point for us. Jeff began to improve then. We owe her a lot. And she's so sweet—"

Kitty heard Jeff's low acquiescence. "She had vision and strength and she gave me hope again. She was such a lovely little thing. She made me feel like I could make something of myself after all. I'd never have got started in business without her. Clara'd still be carrying the whole load, and that was mighty unfair to Clara. I'll always be grateful to Kitty for helping me to get on my feet again."

"The way she helped the survivors from the massacre—there just wasn't anything she wouldn't do for them. And her teaching at the Seminary—she's been a wonderfully good influence in Oregon, I'll tell you. She's a real lady."

It was Mrs. Thornton's voice and Kitty turned her head and stared wonderingly at the closed door.

"She's never asked a mite of sympathy or help," Mary said. "I declare, I never saw anybody with as much courage. It don't seem fair, somehow, her having so many hard knocks. And never a whimper."

"They'll sure miss her at Newmarket. Martha'll grieve," Clara said, "and Lissa worships her. Wealthy and Reason—and Polly Careless—I don't know what they'll do without her. . . . She sure made Sunset happy the little time they had. I remember their wedding. You know, come to think of it, Sunset had an awful good life. He accomplished a lot, made friends—and everything he wanted, really, I think he had, though it was short. Lots of men live to be very old—and never have what Sunset did."

"She's the only woman in Oregon who was a fit mate for him," Mary said firmly.

In the darkness Kitty turned her face into her pillow and her tears were salt on her lips.

"All Sunset's friends here tonight," Clara said chokingly, "they are her friends, too. But I don't think she knows that. When Tommy Dundee came to find me at Rose Farm and told me Curt had been there, and about Sunset—I thought my heart would break, right then. Just a little while before I'd seen her and she never looked happier or more beautiful. She was singing "Oh, Susannah—don't you cry for me!" and dancing as she finished dressing. But when I went to look for her she was gone. The Indian caring for the horses said she'd come alone and taken her horse and ridden toward home. I couldn't believe—

"It took me a little while to find Jeff, and by that time the word had spread. She hadn't ought to of been alone. I can't understand why Curt let her go alone. . . . I'll never forgive myself I didn't find her quicker and come with her."

Clara's voice broke and she tried to muffle her sobs and Jeff's deeper voice comforted her. Kitty closed her eyes and gripped the sheets until her nails pierced them. There was a rap on the outer door and she heard it open again and another voice—Fortune's.

"I just heard," he said, and then, apparently at a sign from someone, his slow voice lowered cautiously. "I just got in. It's true, then? Is Kitty—"

Why, they are all thinking of me, Kitty thought, wonderingly. *They're my friends.* A little warmth began to steal over her and grateful tears came again. *I didn't know—I didn't know.*

After a while a name caught Kitty's ear and she raised her head, listening. "Where's Curt? I've hunted all over town for him."

"He's with Meek. The word come the Indians are ready to give up the Whitman murderers. Curt's gone to bring them in."

Kitty dropped to the pillow again. *I ought to hate him,* she thought. *I ought never to forgive him for the things he said to me.* The memory of his tortured face, the sound of each cruel word as it came from his stiff lips, came back to her. *But I don't hate him,* Sunset, she whispered. *There's not even bitterness in my heart. You took it from me, darling. You showed me the way. I pity him, Sunset—so deeply. He tried to ease his hurt by striking at me; by killing Le Seuer and Read. He wants to see those Indians hang. He thinks it will ease the pain in his own heart. And he is punishing himself, for he feels guilt. Once he really wished you were dead, Sunset; he wanted to kill you. You knew it—and you had no bitterness, only understanding. That weighs on his conscience now, and he blames himself, and me, because I was the cause of it. Poor Curt. Poor Curt. When will he find there is no peace to come from violence and hate and vengeance?*

I didn't tell you, Sunset, that I loved you. Why must we always wait until it is too late? But you knew. You always knew what was in my heart.

◈ 9 ◈

You did not have to attend the trial. You did not have to listen again to the bitter, sad stories of the survivors of the Whitman massacre, as they told them on the witness stand. The Indians themselves, Tomahas, The Murderer, Tiloukaikt, and their three accomplices, thought the trial unnecessary. They were ready to die. Their tribesmen had voted to sacrifice them to the whites— and they were ready.

They would have preferred, however, to die more honorably, by arrow or bullet in battle, rather than by hanging. But U.S. Marshal Meek, who held them in custody, was unmoved by their requests.

You didn't have to go to the three-day trial—but if you lived in Oregon City, some way you were drawn toward the State House, and the crowd of people gathered there. You knew when Elizabeth Segar, one of the orphaned immigrant children that Narcissa Whitman had mothered, had finished her testimony, and when Mrs. Eliza Hall took the stand. You knew all the stories of the killings, the atrocities, the destruction, the flight and rescue. All Oregon knew them, and was never to forget.

You did not have to attend the hanging, either, on that still June day in 1850; but most of the men of Oregon City did.

Kitty and Clara stayed indoors on the day of execution. They spent the time keeping Mathias quiet and occupied. And they did not discuss the hanging until the child was asleep.

Jeff told them of it. His face was still a little white from the memory. The five Indians had not pleaded nor protested. Meek had not hesitated when it came time to spring the trap.

"I wonder if that will be the end of it," Clara said finally. Kitty shook her head.

"Sunset said Indian trouble was like a forest fire. When you think it's out, it starts again, somewhere else. He said it would be many years before the Indians were completely subdued. They're building blockhouses at Newmarket now. We never felt we needed them before."

"The Rogue River Indians are giving trouble again," Jeff said, "and troops have gone to meet them. I don't think these hangings will stop it, either. It will take more than that. But—it's a lesson."

"Jeff, were there a lot of people there?"

"Yes. A big crowd."

Kitty stood with her back to the room, staring into the fire.

"Was—Curt—"

Jeff and Clara exchanged glances. "Yes, Curt was there."

"How—does he look?"

Jeff hesitated. "He—he looks bad, Kitty. He's very thin and tired. Haggard, I would say, and quiet. But then—today was a grim business."

Kitty sighed. Poor Curt, why must he go on torturing himself? Why must he have witnessed the hangings?

"Afterwards he went to the land office and paid his five-dollar fee. To hold his claim for two years. He said he was going to the States."

"To—get himself a wife," Kitty finished. She turned, half-smiling. "That's the law, isn't it? That a man may be gone for two years to the States, to bring back a wife?"

Jeff nodded uncomfortably.

"But Curt said the five-dollar fee was just incidental," he went on. "He said he'd made his money in the gold fields, all he was apt to need. He—he said he wasn't sure if he was ever coming back. He was thinking of going into the shipping business, probably sending ships out here to Oregon. He'd know the goods we need."

"When—does he leave?"

"He's gone, Kitty. We went to Dr. McLoughlin's house for a few minutes. The Doctor poured us each a drink. You know his custom—he pours the amount according to the age of the man. He gets a half-tumbler of rum, and Curt, being half his age, a quarter tumbler, me a little less, and so on. We drank Curt's health. Curt said he'd finished all he had to do in Oregon, with the hanging. He's on his way now. He figured to spend the night at Fort Vancouver—Columbia Barracks, I mean."

"He—he left no message?"

"No, Kitty."

She turned back to the fire and she caught her lip in her teeth. . . . Curt had said all he had to say to her at Rose Farm.

CALIFORNIA GOLD HAD CHANGED the face of Oregon Territory and the area to the north of The River was no exception. Settlements had sprung up along the Columbia's northern shore—Monticello, Cathlamet, Vancouver. There was a store and tavern at Cowlitz Landing, and mills; and northward, the whole length of Puget Sound were new settlements: Port Townsend, already a promising seaport; a new spot called New York-Alki, which meant, hopefully, "New York By-and-by"; and Seattle, which had sprung from the New York-Alki settlement. Cape Flattery and New Dungeness were sites selected for the erection of lighthouses for the benefit of Puget Sound, and Steilacoom, both the city and the fort, were prosperous and growing.

Edmund Sylvester returned from the gold fields with sufficient money to carry out the dreams of himself and his partner, Levi Smith, though Smith did not live to see it. On Smith's claim Sylvester laid out the town they had planned, and named it, first Smithfield, and then, in deference to the mountains which shadowed it, Olympia.

From Kitty's porch she could see the thin lines of smoke from the chimneys of Olympia. She could reach it by canoe or by the narrow trail just a mile through the thick woods, and soon that little trail would be widened to a sixty-foot wagon road. She had contributed to the fund for the road-building, and, thinking of it now, she smiled in anticipation. She would be living practically on the outskirts of Olympia when the road was completed and there would be considerable traffic by her place, to and from the mills of Newmarket, on to the settlements to the south, and to Cowlitz Landing.

A few years ago she would hardly have expected to be living on a busy thoroughfare, she reflected; but then she also had scoffed when Curt had prophesied that one day there would be stage coaches and mail and freight wagons running from Newmarket to Cowlitz Landing. She scoffed no longer. The express line of John G. Parker and Henry D. Colter had brought her parcels and papers from Oregon City this very morning.

She had waited many months for those packages, but now she was torn between her desire to open them and her eagerness to read the papers—the *Oregonian*, published at Portland, and the *Spectator*. The news they contained would be of greatest importance to her, to the future of all the Puget Sound country. She would glance at the papers, treating herself to a tiny taste of them, she decided, and then she would put them away until evening when she could savor them slowly.

For months there had been tense expectancy throughout northern Oregon. Oregon Territory was too big. There were so many new settlements north of The River, and the Puget Sound country was so far from the capital that the people had decided they needed a governor and capital of their own. The subject had been broached at a Fourth of July celebration, and had been greeted with rousing cheers. It was taken up formally at a convention at Clarke's new hotel at Cowlitz Landing, an occasion attended by every man who could possibly get there. The fact that they spent the night in celebration before getting down to the seriousness of the Cowlitz Convention had not weakened the memorial which resulted. Perhaps it strengthened it.

The memorial stated flatly that Oregon Territory should be cut in two, in an east-west line along The River and the 46th parallel from the Pacific to the summit of the Rocky Mountains. A new territory should be created from the northern half.

The petition had been promptly sent to Governor Lane, and he had immediately and without reservation approved it.

No one knew better than Joseph Lane that Oregon Territory was too big. He had known when he arrived that his tenure as Territorial Governor would be short. President Polk's term expired the day after Lane and Meek reached Oregon City, and

Zachary Taylor, Polk's successor, had been certain to appoint a Whig to the post. But it had not taken Lane long to decide that no matter who headed the Territorial Government, Oregon was too big for one administrator. There were too many Indian tribes to treat with, and they were increasingly hostile. Communications were too slow and distances too great. Protection of troops was needed at Puget Sound, a hundred and fifty miles from Oregon City, at Rogue River, two hundred and sixty miles to the south, and at Walla Walla, two hundred and fifty miles to the east. And there were a thousand and one additional pressing problems peculiar to Oregon by the very nature of its people.

There had been the problem of the "beaver money." It was illegal—and the settlers were well aware of that fact—for Oregon to mint its own money. But the Westerners had managed their own affairs so long that they had blandly disregarded the federal law for expediency. Governor Lane had called in the beaver money and sent it to the U.S. mint at San Francisco—and the Oregon people had grinned. The illegal beaver money was found to contain ten per cent more gold than the United States' coins. Legal or not, the people bragged, Oregon products—wheat or money, timber or fruit or cattle—were superior to government standards.

Lane recognized, too, that the Puget Sound men had to travel too far to the Oregon legislative assemblies, and even then, because the areas south of The River were more heavily populated, their votes carried little weight. When, after long debate, the capital was moved from Oregon City to Salem, almost forty miles farther south, the discontent of the people of Northern Oregon was intensified. The problem of roads, of navigation on Puget Sound, of the border between them and the British, and of finding a direct route from the east to the Sound through the Cascade Mountains, were questions of importance to Northern Oregon, and should be dealt with directly.

Lane had been succeeded as Governor by John P. Gaines, and Lane had become the delegate to Congress from Oregon. He had promptly introduced in Congress the resolution that Oregon Territory be divided.

And Congress had listened with a sympathetic ear. Kitty's eyes widened with delight as she read the triumphant news that all the area awaited. Oregon Territory had been cut in two, and the new Territory of Washington had been created out of the northern half!

She put the papers aside carefully, digesting the news as she turned to unwrap her parcels. Yes, it was a great step forward, but she felt a little regret, too, at being finally divorced from Oregon City. Oregon City was the mother town of all the West, and ties with her were still very strong. Kitty would always have a particularly warm spot in her heart for the old town. So would Californians, she reflected. For so many years Oregon City had been the seat of the only organized government in the West. It had been the place to which all settlers looked for help and supplies, the hub of the Oregon Country, of all the West Coast. The original plat of the city of San Francisco was registered there. Kitty remembered the excitement when Captain Irving of the bark *John W. Cater* had arrived with the map, drawn by William M. Eddy, with instructions to file it in the clerk's office of the U.S. District Court for the Territory of Oregon—and "hang the expense!"

The former Oregon City judge, Peter Burnett, had remained in California and had been elected that new state's first governor; and hadn't it been James Marshall, Oregon immigrant, who had discovered California gold in the first place? Travel north and south by land and sea was heavy. The Coast, now to be marked into three areas—Washington, Oregon and California—would always be closely knit with ties of blood and gold and tradition. The West Coast was a rapidly growing, lusty, noisy infant, and it was certainly making itself heard in the East. When Kitty recalled how many resolutions the Oregon Provisional Government had formed and sent to Congress in the old days, begging for recognition and action by the Congress, and the way in which that action had been delayed; when she contrasted it with the respect with which Congress listened to their messages now, and the speed with which it acted, she smiled with pleasure and pride.

She tore away the wrappings from her parcels and lifted carefully a large mantel-clock. She caressed the smooth surface of the wood, the glass face, beneath which the delicate hands lay. She was glad that Franklin Davis had been willing to send her this clock, from the library at Wildcliffe. It had been one of the few things she had requested from him. It had ticked away the hours at Wildcliffe for three generations—and now it would grace the mantel in her own home on Puget Sound.

There was a little tug at her heart as she carried the clock to her own living room and put it in its place. Once in a while came that sharp and cutting twinge of pain. But it was not only homesickness, a desire to see her old home again, after eight years, but loneliness. She was wise enough to know that deep loneliness would be with her wherever she was; she could not run away from it, she could not escape it, no matter how far she might travel or how fast.

Very gently she wound the clock, and she was delighted that it was uninjured and began, faithfully, familiarly, to tick, to begin again to measure the time in Kitty's life. She caressed it again, and then went back to her parcels on the porch.

Today was publication day of the *Columbian*, also, Kitty remembered, and Martha's day to come to visit. The year-old *Columbian* was published in Olympia, and it had become the voice of the people to the north of The River, seeking separate recognition. The *Columbian* would carry details of the formation of Washington Territory and perhaps would announce the President's choice of Governor.

She'd have few excuses now to make the trip to Oregon City each year, Kitty reflected. She had always enjoyed that trip, for she loved the Cowlitz and The River, and it brought back many memories. The Clarke Hotel at Cowlitz Landing was in almost the exact spot where Curt and Sunset had broken the horses furnished them by Dick Tom. . . . It was fun to ride The River on a steamboat—though not as thrilling as it had been in Curt's bateau.

Even her small shopping could be done in Olympia now, for new stocks arrived by ship regularly. Michael Simmons, who had sold his profitable mills, had built a business building in Olympia which housed his store, the Customs Office and Post Office. He advertised that he had a full supply of molasses, pork, sugar, broad axes, grindstones—and ale—for sale at his store. The town would grow still more rapidly now, and undoubtedly it would be named the Territorial capital. A new era was beginning.

There was one more package to open and Kitty hurried with it. It was her sidesaddle, and she lifted it from its packings, and stroked the soft leather of it. It was feather-light, after the heavy rawhide saddles to which she had become used. She put it aside as Martha came up the path.

"Land sakes, Kitty, I hurried so!" Martha panted. "Seemed like there was a hundred things to do, the last minute! Sparks 's feeling so good about us being a full-fledged Territory he told me to go ahead and buy my stove! The men are that excited. There's your saddle at last—it did come, then! I thought that parcel might be it. Did you hear from Clara? I had a letter from Mary."

Martha dropped into a chair, stroking the little saddle with rough, appreciative fingers. "Did you know Tommy Dundee is going to get married at last? And he wants us all to come to the weddin'. Pity he couldn't have found a girl to suit him three years ago when the Donation Land Law was passed. Wasn't there a rash of marriages though, so's every man could get that extra 320 acres! But I tell you I'm right glad I don't have to wonder all my life did Sparks marry me just to get twicet as much free land!"

Kitty laughed and touched Martha's shoulder affectionately as she passed. "I'll get my bonnet," she said. "Who's Tommy marrying?"

"New girl named Molly Calahan. Just arrived. Kitty," Martha followed her into the house and leaned toward her to speak in a loud whisper. "Mary says she seems nice, real high-spirited and she has Tommy in a daze. But—she wears bloomers!"

Martha straightened, her eyes dancing with excitement. Kitty glanced at Martha out of the corner of her eye.

"What do you think of it, Kitty? Bloomers, I mean?" Again Martha lowered her voice on the indelicate word.

"I think they're a rather hideous fashion," Kitty answered calmly, but the dimple twinkled in her cheek. "I suppose they might have some advantage; they'd be warm, likely and—"

"Well, riding astride, I thought they might—"

Kitty tried to keep her lips straight and she turned reproachfully to Martha.

"Martha Sparks, are you suggesting you'd like to have a bloomer costume?"

Martha's face reddened and she looked away sheepishly. Kitty's laughter rippled over the room.

"Well," Martha said defensively, "I just thought they might

be fun to try. But you now, Kitty, much as you believe in women's rights—you and Abigail Duniway!—I can see where bloomers wouldn't do for you. You aren't the type. Neither is Wealthy. Now she's fifteen and at fifteen you expect girls to do silly things. But I declare, Wealthy's more like you than she is like me. She's such a lady! She's a throw-back, I guess, to her grandmother. No, I guess neither you nor Wealthy'll ever try a bloomer costume. But Mary says a lot of the girls in the wagon trains this year were wearing them. Ain't been such a sensation since the soldiers hit Oregon City that time and turned the place upside down."

Kitty picked up her gloves. "I don't think," she said firmly, "that wearing bloomers is going to help women gain equal rights." She tucked a snowy handkerchief into her cuff. "I think it is a mistake to ape men."

"Maybe you're right," Martha said, reluctantly giving up the idea of adopting bloomers. She stopped to admire the clock on the mantelpiece. "Now, ain't that lovely, Kitty! I declare, you've made this place so pretty, ain't no wonder Wealthy likes to come to stay with you, rather'n stay home and help Reason with his chickens. You know that book you loaned her? She's cried her heart out over it, but she won't stop reading it. What is this Topsy and Eva, anyway?"

"I feared she'd cry," Kitty said. "But she wants to read everything, and I think it's a shame to deny her." She led Mowich from her stall and tossed the sidesaddle expertly into place. "I'm going to love having this saddle again! That book—I explained to Wealthy it was highly exaggerated. Actually, it's a dangerous book. It really could cause trouble. . . . But I do admire Harriet Beecher Stowe for writing it," she added thoughtfully. "Women should write what they believe—"

Her face grew serious and she mounted and turned her horse toward Olympia. Martha eyed her questioningly.

"Now, Kitty, what's on your mind? You're thinking up something again. What you going to do now?"

"I was thinking—about writing," Kitty answered absently. "People in Oregon should express themselves. People in *Washington* Territory, I mean!" she corrected herself. "About the railroad survey, for instance. How are government leaders to know how we feel if we don't tell them? The paper said that Jefferson Davis, the Secretary of War, recommends a railroad from the

Gulf States to San Francisco. Now that's because Mr. Davis wants to favor the Gulf States. It's very plain. He's no business to be making statements like that until he has all the facts. Until there is a survey from the Mississippi to Puget Sound, too. I think he should be reminded that he represents *all* the people of all the country, not just the Gulf States. I shall write to him."

Martha smiled. They rode single file down the little trail, Kitty in the lead, and Martha admired her straight little back, the grace with which she rode. Riding astride had never suited Kitty, Martha thought, and she shook her head, delighted, as always, with her loveliness and daintiness, and the big thoughts that went on in her beautiful golden head.

"Mary wrote that the reason that party worker from Illinois— Abraham Lincoln—turned down the governorship of Oregon Territory was because of his wife," Martha said. "Mrs. Lincoln refused to come to this 'wilderness'! Can you imagine that? I don't think that woman's going to be of much help to her husband in politics."

The two reined their horses in front of Simmons' store and Martha looked about her with pleased eyes.

"Wilderness!" she snorted again. "Why, Kitty, we have everything right here, almost. There's a dozen houses already, and two hotels, a livery stable, and docks— Think of it, and fourteen sawmills on the Sound and more a-building! Kitty, remember when we used to be scared in the woods because of the crazy sailors? And you found the man who nailed hisself to the wall in Deaf Wilson's cabin. I don't think about 'em any more, do you?"

"It's been a real help," Kitty said, knotting the reins, "to have the Army take them to Fort Steilacoom. The jail is finished at Steilacoom, too. I think that's real progress, to be a new Territory, and to have a jail for wrongdoers." Suddenly she grinned. "That is—if I can keep Charlie out of it." She turned to nod and smile at a venerable Indian. "Good old Chief Seattle," she murmured, as they entered the store. "Goodness, Martha—what a crowd!"

It was late afternoon when Kitty returned home and turned to her papers. She must keep these papers, she decided. The account of the formation of Washington Territory would be of interest some day, to Wealthy, perhaps, or Wealthy's children. She was very fond of sensitive, strong little Wealthy Sparks.

The clock tick was the only sound in the room as Kitty read. Actually, she should be very excited, she thought, at this great news, for all the settlers were jubilant. But, alone, she could only contemplate it with quiet satisfaction. President Fillmore had signed the bill creating the Territory of Washington just two days before his term expired; incoming President Pierce had nominated the officers for the newly formed Territory of Washington, and had named Major Isaac I. Stevens of Massachusetts for Governor.

But the biggest news of all, which the *Columbian* reported ecstatically, was that Congress had also voted the immense appropriation of $150,000 for a survey to determine if a railroad from the Mississippi to Puget Sound were possible or practicable. Governor Stevens was heading the survey party from the East; a young army officer by the name of George McClellan had started from the West, surveying routes on both sides of the Cascade Range, through the Cascades, down the Cowlitz and up the Columbia. Sometime in the fall the parties would meet, and Governor Stevens would arrive in Olympia.

The great question then, the question upon which the future of Washington Territory depended, would be answered: if slender iron rails could link Puget Sound with the States. Sunset and Curt had believed that it could be done. They had told the startled British so many years ago, away back in 1845—and this was 1853.

Kitty leaned against the mantelpiece beside the clock. Loneliness weighed heavily upon her. Tonight her memories were sharper than ever. She thought of her first trip to Newmarket, with Sunset and with Curt. It was odd, now, that she, the least likely of the three, was the only one remaining, when these great events the men had dreamed had actually come to pass. She had been the skeptic; yet she had stayed.

When the time had come for her to leave she found she could not go. Sunset had once told her that the roads to Oregon were made to come into it—not to go out, for the western slopes were steeper. She had found that she did not want to live where she could not sometimes see The Mountain. She did not want to live among people who had never known Sunset, people who had never ridden upon The River or known its great beauty and power. It had been, with her, as Sunset had said—"Seems like I just couldn't go *east* again!" She'd got the Oregon Fever bad, she decided; she'd come too far to go back.

But Curt had gone back. There were twenty thousand people on the Trail, headed west, the year that Curt had gone. And most of them, it was reported, were singing "God Damn The Overland!" and with good reason, for the wagons traveled, sometimes, three and five abreast; Asiatic cholera swept the trains—but neither death nor hunger nor suffering could stop the people headed for California gold. A great many of them had drifted on, into the valleys of Oregon, prospecting, or into the Puget Sound country to settle permanently, to help supply timber and produce to the ships in the harbor. But Curt, while thousands upon thousands were fighting, dying, slogging their way along the trail west, had gone the other way, a solitary figure, bucking the tide.

He had not returned at the end of the two-year period which was allowed a man to go to the States for a wife; he had not come back in 1851, when the Land Law granted every man an additional 320 acres if he married. Since the day of the hanging of the Whitman murderers, there had been no word of Curt. The pull of the land, his love of the Oregon Country, had not been enough to bring him back. His hate of her must go very deep, she thought, sickly, that he would give up all his dreams rather than to return to the place where she had lived.

She set her lips, knowing that loneliness and sadness were about to engulf her, and this on an evening when she should be glad and triumphant. Deliberately she forced herself to think of other things. She had found the only antidote for heartache was work —constructive activity.

If Sunset were here they could take a trip down the Sound, she thought, wistfully. There'd be music from the Catholic Mission at Priest Point on the late summer evenings. They could visit the new town of Seattle. The plat of the townsite had been filed at Olympia and she was curious to see it, perhaps even to invest in some lots there. It was said to be an excellent port, with great possibilities. And she had wanted to meet the women of the Denny party. The report was that they had thought the Sound the most God-forsaken, wind-and-rain-swept place in the world, when they first landed at Alki from the little schooner *Exact*. But very soon Mary Denny had loaned her clothesline to the men to use it in making soundings of the bay; and now the town was well established and growing. Mrs. Denny sounded like a woman worth knowing.

Kitty turned from the fire and went to her table. How many long evenings she had spent at this table, writing letters, adding columns of figures, figuring the amount of board-feet in her lumber, totalling her sales and her costs, poring over the plans Philip had drawn for the house and grounds. She looked at the well-worn plans now. Her orchard was thriving, but she would like a few more trees in the spring. Clara had written that the Lewellings had developed several new varieties of fruit which they felt would be particularly fitted for this climate. One was a wonderful cherry, which they had named for their Chinese handyman—Bing. She made a note to write the Lewellings about it.

Something constructive, that was it; she must not brood about the past. *No self-pity*, she said firmly, as was her custom—*don't you cry for me!*

There was no reason, she decided, tapping her chin with her quill, that she shouldn't visit Seattle by herself. She would ask Charlefour in the morning if he would take her, perhaps before the month was out. Autumn was a good time for trips on the Sound. They would camp one night between Newmarket and Seattle, probably on Vashon Island.

Meanwhile, she must keep busy. She pulled a blank piece of paper toward her and began to write in a firm, clear hand.

"Mr. Jefferson Davis," she wrote. "Dear Mr. Secretary—"

◆ 2 ◆

THERE were two hundred and forty men in Isaac Stevens' surveying party; they left St. Louis in May and by the time they had reached St. Paul, the head of steamboat navigation, the astute young Governor of Washington Territory had classified them well. By the time they had covered another hundred miles, to Little Falls, and before they started to the prairie of the Bois des Sioux, Stevens had weeded out a few incompetents; and he already knew which of the remainder would be of most value to him in the gruelling ordeal ahead.

He had selected his men carefully for this expedition, most of them from the army. Surprisingly, it was a volunteer, a man who had arrived unannounced at his St. Louis headquarters the night before their departure, who had become one of his most valued aides.

He interested Stevens from the first. He was a big man, possessed of remarkable strength and endurance—and reticence. His name was Fletcher—Curt Fletcher. He volunteered little more, except that he had lived in the Oregon Country, believed a railroad from the headwaters of the Mississippi to Puget Sound was practical, and was interested in the success of the expedition. The truth of that was demonstrated in every move he made thereafter; if anything, Stevens thought, Fletcher was even more anxious than he that the expedition be a success.

He was a keen observer, and, from the first, Stevens judged he was a resourceful man who could keep his head in a crisis and who could handle other men well. Before they reached the Cheyenne River, on the Fourth of July, Stevens was assigning Fletcher to head small parties sent out to either side of the main body to explore a wide belt of the country through which they passed.

Fletcher thrived on the grinding work. He seemed to enjoy the challenge to his strength and skill, and, as they moved westward, he began to relax slightly and his spirits lightened, and occasionally he revealed a flash of friendliness, even of warmth. Armed only with a barometer and a pocket compass, Fletcher brought in reports that were remarkably detailed and thorough, and sometimes, in camp, he volunteered quiet suggestions. Occasionally the name of his one-time partner, a mountain man, Sunset Lee, crept into the conversation. Fletcher prophesied that the route along the 47th parallel, following to a great extent the route of Lewis and Clark, would be the most favorable one; after they had explored seven passes through the Rockies, Stevens came to the same conclusion.

It was evident that the route to the Pacific must be determined by the course of the tributaries of the Missouri and the Columbia. Fletcher, Stevens noticed, always spoke of the Columbia, simply, as The River. But it was in September when they reached the summit of Cadotte's Pass, the eastern border of Washington Territory, that Curt's expression revealed him to Stevens completely.

It was there that Stevens issued his proclamation as Territorial

Governor—and then the descent, into Washington, began. Curt, standing quietly listening, had raised his head, his eyes narrowed, and there was an excitement and eagerness on his face that had not been there before. Major Stevens had seen that look, intense as hunger, on other men's faces; it was the homecoming look of men who had been long and far away.

The going was hardest of all from Sun River to the Spokane, a three-hundred and sixty-five mile stretch from the Rockies through the Bitter Root mountains. But Fletcher's efforts never lagged. It would be a major engineering feat to lay rails through that country, the men said. Fletcher had never before explored the Bitter Roots, but he knew there were four passes through them. Stevens found that two of them could be recommended.

They estimated the length of the tunnels that would be required, and the time it would take to blast through the solid rock. The engineers figured that progress might be made at the rate of ten and a half inches every twelve hours, where continuous blasting was required. The cost might be prohibitive, and they'd be unable to estimate it until they had McClellan's reports to add to their own.

There was much speculation among the men about Fletcher, but none ventured to question him. They had the highest respect for his judgment and his strength and his fairness, but they had learned early that he was not a man to give confidences. More than one had remarked at the scars across his back, and the faint marks still on his wrists, revealed when, stripped to the waist, he bathed in icy mountain streams. He made no attempt to hide them. And once, when he saw a boy staring at him and then quickly glancing away, he almost grinned, and as he pulled on his black shirt he spoke quietly.

"I'm no convict." The boy had mumbled a protest, which Curt ignored. "I was a sailor—an unwilling sailor. Those marks—" he indicated his wrists, "were from chains. And those on my back from a whip."

There was a heavy silence and finally an older man spoke jocularly, trying to lighten the tension. "If a man marked you up like that, Fletcher, I hate to think what happened to him."

Curt, fastening his shirt, looked at the speaker and his gray eyes were cool and sardonic. He walked away and no one spoke until he was out of earshot.

"My God, I bet he killed him," the man breathed, and no one offered an argument.

They carefully charted the places where timber would provide sufficient fuel and the plains, where coal must be transported. With every mile the men's hopes mounted. None of them wanted to report back to the capital that the railroad to the Northwest was impossible. Fletcher had unconsciously passed on to them his own deep desire to see those rails laid—pointing straight toward the Pacific, aimed toward the rich ports of the Orient. But this was a country more rugged than any of them had fought before. Fletcher matched it.

It was October when they came to Colville on the Columbia and were met there by McClellan's party, to learn that the exploration of the passes through the Cascades to Puget Sound had been completed. Fletcher was as engrossed in the reports as Stevens, but Stevens knew from his manner what was coming. He was not unprepared when Fletcher asked to be released from his duties, and he was not surprised when he disappeared the same night.

"He was talking to a couple of Indians in Chinook," one of his men reported, "and then they got out a canoe and headed down The River."

Now, Stevens thought, was as good a time as any to make discreet inquiries about Fletcher. His curiosity had been aroused, and Fletcher was a man he would like to have as a friend in Washington Territory. When he spoke to an old-time trapper the grizzled old fellow looked up sharply.

"Fletcher? You say Curt Fletcher come with you? Ee-yi! We wondered when he'd come back! There's some hopes for this railroad—begging your pardon, Governor, if Fletcher's into it! I'll tell you about him. Why, him and Sunset Lee—"

◈ 3 ◈

IT SEEMED odd to see steamboats on The River, both above and below the Cascades. It took Curt only four hours to travel from Portland to the mouth of the Cowlitz on the *Lot Whitcomb*, and, two days later, when he stretched out for a good sleep at the Clarke Hotel at Cowlitz Landing, he thought of his old camps at this spot. Jackson's house, The Highlands, had been enlarged to a story and a half, and it was not only his dwelling but the Jackson County Court House now, and still a stopping place for horsemen and stagecoach passengers. Curt did not wait for the coach. He rode alone, over the familiar old trail, remembering, too vividly, his trip over it with Sunset and Kitty.

What ship had taken her back to South Carolina, he wondered —and what was in her heart when she boarded it at last? Did she ever think of The Mountain—did she miss it, as he had missed it?

There was the bend in the trail where Kitty had flung her mittens. He had held her in his arms here. The memory was fresh and sharp.

The Sparks' cabin was just beyond. It was larger, more prosperous looking, with its garden and small orchard and a number of neat poultry houses. Curt smiled. Reason and Wealthy— they'd be sixteen and fifteen years old now—had done well with their chickens. He rode on. He was not quite ready to visit with the Sparks yet.

It was late afternoon when Curt came near to Kitty's old claim. His hand was steady on the bridle rein as he approached the clearing. He slowed his horse to a walk, and finally he halted and sat, his hand on the pommel, his gray eyes narrowed, surveying the place where Kitty once had lived. A thousand memories came back to haunt him. He remembered Kitty, stricken and shocked at Davis' death, clinging to him, as he took her away from the cabin. . . . Kitty's first Christmas at Newmarket. . . . He wondered if she had ever worn the little moccasins he had left on her hearth. Her tiny, beautiful little feet—

Kitty in her wedding dress. Kitty and Sunset standing in the door of the house, the light behind them. Curt rubbed his hand hard across his eyes and his creased forehead and urged his horse forward.

The house had been greatly enlarged. Great wings stretched out on either side of the original cabin and there was a hospitable porch along the front. The garden was already prepared for winter, rose-bushes carefully wrapped against the frost. To the rear was an extensive orchard, bare-limbed now, stark against the background of evergreens beyond. A stout fence surrounded it. Curt rode slowly to the gate.

There was a sign on the gate, as there were on so many Western homes. Curt's glance dropped to it and he froze in his saddle and he stared at it for a long time. Finally, slowly, he dismounted, pushed his hat to the back of his head, and then he ran his fingers, unbelievingly, across the one word carved into the wood. It said "Wildcliffe."

He opened the gate. It was stout and well hung. He left his horse and walked slowly, tensely, to the door. There was smoke coming from the chimney and from within he could hear the reedy notes of a melodeon. Before he knocked he turned and looked back at the road, glanced around the deserted garden; and then, abruptly, he rapped.

Immediately the music stopped and the door opened. Curt stood very still. The brown-haired girl looked up at him questioningly and then quickly a smile flashed across her face.

"I remember you! You're Mr. Fletcher!"

"You're Wealthy."

"Yes. Come in, won't you?"

Curt stepped across the threshold and Wealthy closed the door behind him. Ahead of him was the great stone fireplace, but it was in a hallway now, and rooms opened from it. Wealthy motioned to her right.

"Please come in, Mr. Fletcher. You've been away a long time."

"You've grown up, Wealthy," he said, slowly, regarding her. "Do you live here now?"

Wealthy shook her head. "No. I just come to stay sometimes. I love it here. Kitty has so many beautiful things, and she likes to have me here to care for them while she's away."

Curt turned his hat slowly in his hands. "I'd—supposed she'd gone back, to South Carolina, to Wildcliffe," he said, carefully.

Wealthy's laugh tinkled through the room. "But this *is* Wildcliffe, Mr. Fletcher! Haven't you heard? Everyone knows Wildcliffe. Everyone stops here, going and coming from Cowlitz Landing. Being so near to Olympia, Kitty keeps open house all the time. Won't you sit down? I'll have something for you to eat very soon. She always has things ready for guests. Or would you like to look around the place? You may, you know. Some of the furniture is Linton furniture—made in Oregon City from Kitty's designs."

"I'd—like to look around, Wealthy. It's greatly changed. Don't bother about food. I couldn't eat. . . . Where is she?"

"Kitty? Oh, how stupid I am! She left a week ago to take a trip around the Sound. She likes to watch the new settlements, and get acquainted with the newcomers, and all. She buys lots or timberland sometimes. She and Charlefour went to Seattle this time. That's the new town—it's two days by canoe. Mr. Fletcher, I'll bring you some coffee. Kitty should be home any day now, perhaps even tonight. She'll likely stop in Olympia for mail and for news. They expect the Governor any day, and they are preparing a big celebration for him. Ma's there helping, at Mr. Sylvester's Washington Hotel."

Wealthy hurried out. Curt stood in the middle of the room and looked about him. There was a little Chinese lacquered table against one wall; he remembered it well. A shipmaster had given it to Kitty. There was a handsome, polished highboy, which looked as if it might have come from the original Wildcliffe, and the melodeon, of rosewood. But the rugs on the floor were Indian-braided. There was a little workbasket on the hearth, with a bit of fine linen in it and a silver thimble. The basket was Indian-woven.

There was another basket on the small table and Curt picked it up. It was the one which Indian George had given to Kitty so long ago; in it were a handful of arrowheads, like small jewels, agate and carnelian and obsidian and pale chalcedony and yellow and red jasper. Curt fingered them. It was like Kitty to see beauty in these things, to save the bright, chipped bits of polished stone.

He moved back to the hallway, into the open door of the room beyond. It was a large bedchamber, a sparkling clean room with dainty curtains and a variety of flowering plants in the large window. A rocking chair stood there, with ruffled pillows in it, and a tiny footstool was before it. He looked at the footstool and then he started and went to it. Peeking from beneath it was a tiny moccasin. He picked it up, half-smiling. The toes had been worn through, and had been patched—more than once. He held it gently in his hand for a minute and then he put it back carefully.

There was a massive armoire against one wall and across the room a canopied bed, a well-polished, beautifully made bed, meticulously smooth. The cover on it was the familiar blue and white of the old Hudson's Bay Company. A washstand held a china bowl and pitcher and a multitude of dainty jars and bottles, and a delicate and familiar perfume came from them. The floor was fully carpeted with rag carpet, tacked tightly, and it was well-padded and warm; padded, Curt thought, with clean golden straw, laid thickly on the rough board floor beneath.

He stopped in the hall again, looking at the welcome open fire and the bench before it, and then he glanced back at the front door. Above it still were the deer horns on which Sunset's rifle had rested; a gun was there now, ready—and out of reach of small investigators.

He heard Wealthy humming and he went to find her. He passed a second bedroom, ready for guests, and found the kitchen.

"I'll be going on, Wealthy," he said. "Thanks just the same." Wealthy studied him searchingly. "I'll be seeing Martha and Fortune soon, and Reason, too. How's the chicken business?"

"It's fine," Wealthy smiled, but her eyes were troubled. Fletcher's face seemed white and tight. "I help some, but mostly Reason does the work. Mr. Fletcher," her face flushed with shyness but she wanted desperately to put him at his ease, "I still have the slate you brought me once from Oregon City."

Curt nodded and let himself out of the house. He picked up the reins and led his horse through the gate and he stood for a minute longer, looking back at the house, the gardens, the sign on the gate. He swung into the saddle then, and turned toward Olympia.

◈ 4 ◈

THE trip down the Sound had been pleasant and perhaps it would prove to be profitable. As Kitty stepped ashore in Olympia she was turning over in her mind the wisdom of buying lots at Seattle. She had almost made her decision; in fact she had left some money on deposit there, with Dexter Horton, the young clerk in Mr. Denny's store. Mr. Horton had a safety deposit made from a buried coffee barrel, and he had put Kitty's gold pieces in a sack and labeled it with her name, and placed it beside those of his other depositors. . . . If she decided to buy the lots she could send Charlefour with a note to Mr. Horton to that effect. Yes, she decided, after due reflection, Seattle was a coming town.

"Will you bring Mowich, Charlie, and leave her by Simmons' store for me? I'll stop for mail."

She turned into the little room used as a post office. Simmons was admittedly not book-learned, but he ran the office to the satisfaction of the settlers by the simple means of appointing a number of them his deputies, so they could get their own mail or help their neighbors. Kitty riffled through the pile of mail now, extracted a few letters bearing her name. There was one in Dr. Manning's handwriting and she was pleased. His letters were always like a pleasant visit. . . . He seemed to know her loneliness, she thought.

The post office was deserted, and Kitty went on into the store. It, too, was empty. Puzzled, she went back to the street. A few people were hurrying toward the Washington Hotel and she followed curiously. She found almost the entire population of the town gathered there.

The dining room was crowded and men were standing shoulder to shoulder about the entrance. They were silent, listening intently to a speaker from within.

Fortune turned and saw Kitty and made room for her. "It's Governor Stevens," he whispered and he tapped the shoulder of the man ahead of him to let Kitty through. Quietly the men made way for her until she stood where she could see the new Governor.

"Kitty," Martha whispered. Martha was greatly agitated, Kitty noticed, but Kitty shook her head at her to silence her. The Governor's voice was the only sound in the silent room, and Kitty held her breath as she studied him. He was a young-looking man, and bearded; he spoke with great sincerity.

". . . It is my pleasant duty to be able to report the complete success of the exploration and that a railroad *is* eminently practicable from the head of navigation of the Mississippi to your magnificent Sound—"

The voice of the crowd rose in a cheer that echoed from the ceiling and bounced off the walls. Kitty turned to Martha, clapping, and Martha tried again to speak but she could not make herself heard above the uproar. Kitty shook her head again, laughing, and the racket subsided enough so the smiling Governor could continue.

"I have now seen much of our Territory and am convinced that it is to play no secondary part in the future progress of our country. . . . Ours is the greatest roadstead where vessels engaged in the commerce and the protection of the commerce of the world can ride at anchor. This great roadstead is on the route of the Asiatic commerce—"

Oh, Kitty thought, if only Curt could hear that! If only I could share this with him! With a sharp pang she remembered the day on the bluff at Oregon City when the *Shark*'s officers had arrived. Curt had wanted to share that pleasure with her, and she had failed him. She understood now, how it had been with him; he had identified himself so closely with the country, its triumphs and failures had been his. . . . Happiness was the one thing which multiplied when it was shared, Kitty thought. Almost everyone in the crowd here had someone with whom to share it. Fortune and Martha, Kentuck and Lissa— But Kitty was alone.

Persistently Martha tugged at Kitty's sleeve and jerked her head meaningly toward the far side of the room. Kitty followed her glance. She heard no more of Stevens' speech.

Curt was leaning against the wall, his hands in his pockets, his eyes on Kitty. It was the same old easy, natural pose of his, but his face was not the same. The color drained from Kitty's face. Curt was not looking at her in the old bantering way, with half-closed eyes, and a self-assured grin. There was something very near a plea in his gray eyes now, and a yearning that even Curt could not conceal.

The cheers and the clapping began again, but Kitty did not move or speak, and Curt did not remove his hands from his pockets or take his eyes from her.

"I was that embarrassed!" Martha said, nervously twisting her fingers together. "We was gettin' things ready here in the dining room and this young man, this stranger, lookin' very tired and muddy, he came in and asked for a meal. Mr. Sylvester spoke right sharp to him; said, 'We're gettin' ready for a reception for the new Governor, due here any hour. We can't serve nobody. But you can go to the kitchen and ask the cook for something if you like.' Land alive—that young man *was* the Governor! He was tryin' to explain who he was when Curt—Kitty, you're not listenin'!—when Curt came and said this was Isaac Stevens. You coulda knocked me over with a feather—the new Governor—and Curt—"

The crowd was milling about now, but Kitty stood still. Curt was coming toward her, moving easily as always, straight and tall.

He was beside her, then, waiting, and, with a great effort, Kitty raised her face and met his eyes. He studied her for a long moment, hungrily; when he spoke his voice was as she remembered it, deep and low and steady—but he spoke more gently, more courteously, than he had ever addressed her before, as though he were uncertain if she would reply to him.

"Hello, Kitty. I—" The words caught in his throat. Kitty felt her eyes misting and she was afraid to trust her voice.

"Hello, Curt," she managed finally. "I—this is a surprise."

"Yes . . . Kitty—" Curt began again, and then, abruptly, "let's get out of here." He took her arm, his big body shielding her from jostling by the crowd. "That is—" he hesitated on the walk—"if you are going home?"

"Yes," she said quickly, "I'm going home."

"May I come with you?"

"Why—of course, Curt. Here's my horse."

Curt looked at the bay mare, at the sidesaddle, and a smile touched his lips. "Mowich?" he asked. She nodded.

"All my horses are named Mowich," she said. "This is the third. Charlefour hunted everywhere to find her for me."

"A bay with white stockings," Curt observed. He held his hand for her foot. "You don't ride astride any more."

She looked down at him, the same crisp black hair, the same gray eyes. She wanted to put her hands on his shoulders, to slide swiftly into his arms. She gripped the reins tightly.

"Our trails are less dangerous now," she said carefully. "I still ride astride where it seems sensible to do so. You were right about that, Curt."

He mounted his own horse and they turned toward the trail. She touched Mowich with the ends of the reins and the little mare leaped forward. She was glad for the narrowness of the trail, for they could not ride abreast. She needed the time to regain her composure.

"Charlefour and Polly are living on your old claim," she said, when they reached her gate. She dismounted quickly, before he could reach her. She could not risk his touch again. . . . "Charlie came on home just a little while ago," she added, "to take Wealthy home. He'll be heart-broken not to have been here to welcome you."

She opened the door, preceded him into the living room, and

began to tug at her gloves. He looked very big within these four walls, she thought. "Please make yourself at home," she said swiftly. "I—I've been away for a week. I've been to Seattle."

"Yes," he said. "Wealthy told me. There've been a lot of changes, Kitty, in three years. Only—some things haven't changed. Mount Rainier looks no different. I guess nothing will change that."

Kitty turned to him quickly, her brown eyes wide. "Mount—Rainier, did you say?" She smiled politely.

"Mount Rainier is the way we marked it on our charts."

"But of course that is not The Mountain's name at all," she corrected him sweetly. "That's the British name for it—Vancouver named it after a Rear Admiral of the British Navy. But of course we call it the Indian name—Mount Takhoma."

Suddenly Curt grinned and Kitty's face pinked. They shared the same thought—it had not taken them long to start an argument. And their roles had been reversed; Kitty had spoken as though Curt were the visitor.

Kitty laughed suddenly and Curt joined her. He was watching her face, the shining brown eyes, the lovely dimpled cheek. Kitty swept off her bonnet and pushed back her hair. She was not quite as elegantly dressed as in the old days, but she was much, much lovelier, Curt thought.

"Let's just call it The Mountain," he suggested, in compromise.

"All right," she agreed. "You mentioned your charts. You came with Stevens, then?"

Curt nodded. "Yes. I was on the East Coast, and I read of the Memorial to Congress, asking that this area be separated from the rest of Oregon and be made into a Territory."

"No doubt you heard of the creation of Washington Territory before we did."

"Yes. I staged a mild celebration all by myself. Then came the announcement of the authorization of the railroad survey. . . . I joined Stevens at St. Louis."

Kitty turned toward the fire. Darkness had fallen and the room had dimmed. Outside a light rain began to patter against the windows.

"I suppose you did not expect to find me here?" she asked finally. Perhaps, she thought, he wouldn't have come if he had known.

"No, Kitty." His low voice came to her from the shadows. "I supposed you'd gone back to South Carolina. Once I thought of trying to find you there. I wanted to tell you—" Kitty felt him move toward her, but he did not touch her. "I wanted to tell you, Kitty, that I'm sorry, for what I said at Rose Farm. And— here—on your wedding day." The words were not coming easily, Kitty knew. She was afraid to look at him, afraid to try to help him. "I—thought about it a lot, Kitty, and I wished I could—take it all back. I tried to forget it, Kitty, and you. I started for South Carolina once, and turned back. I thought maybe you'd not receive me, and I wouldn't have blamed you. I thought you might have married again, and would rather not be reminded of Oregon, or anything that happened here. It wouldn't have been a happy memory, if you'd gone back and started over again. So I decided it would be kinder if I didn't try to find you. But—I wanted to, Kitty."

In the silence the clock on the mantel ticked loudly. Kitty gripped the edge of the mantelpiece.

"That is what I wanted to say, Kitty. That's all, I guess. I've thought of it, night and day, since the night at Rose Farm. That was very cruel, Kitty—and unfair to you. I don't expect you to forgive me. That's asking too much. But I wanted to tell you I'm sorry."

He moved toward the door. Kitty turned then and he paused.

"I'll be going now, Kitty. Good luck to you."

"Curt—"

He looked up slowly, waited.

"You—you didn't ask me why I stayed," Kitty reminded him.

"Why did you stay, Kitty?"

"You and Sunset had a partnership agreement, Curt. Don't you remember? The surviving partner has a claim to the land. I've—tried to improve it, the way you and Sunset would have done. There's probably a lot of things I've failed to do, but I'm sure when you take it over again you can correct that."

"That partnership law, Kitty—" Curt was smiling now, "was under the old Provisional Government. Is it a Territorial law now? I doubt it."

"I don't know. But it doesn't matter," Kitty persisted. "It was the law when you and Sunset started out together. That was your agreement, between the two of you, and new laws don't change that. I've—kept it for you. I thought some day—you might come back. I'll be glad to give you an accounting, Curt, and a fair division—"

Still he stood in the doorway, but there was a new light in his eyes as he watched her go to the table that served as her desk. She pulled a ledger from it.

"The light's so dim—" she said, and glanced up at him.

For a long moment there was no sound in the room except the clock. Slowly Kitty put down the ledger. Her hands were shaking and her throat was tight. Curt would not cross the room to her. He would never demand or force her again.

But Curt was not the only one who had made demands, she thought suddenly. She, too, had been adamant. Loving, Sunset had taught her, was giving and forgiving. And she had never given—not forgiveness or understanding, to Curt. She'd made no effort to help him, to reach him. She had thought only of herself, putting her pride above all. Who was I to judge him? she thought. *Follow your heart, Kitty,* Sunset had said. She hesitated, her heart pounding wildly.

"That's very decent of you, Kitty," Curt said steadily, "but I've no share in your claim. There's still plenty of free land. I'll find a place, somewhere else. This country's mighty big. And there's a lot to be done. Why—we're just getting started!" He sounded more like the old Curt, she thought, and her throat ached with tears. He's come a long way, she thought, and he's paid so deeply. "I appreciate your offer, Kitty. It's good to know that we can—be friends—after all."

"Friends?" Kitty choked on the word, and she moved away from the table. Curt was watching her carefully. "Friends—Curt? Once you said we could never be friends. You were right. We can't. It's a weak word, you said, for what's—"

She was running toward him then, but Curt met her more than halfway.

THE END